Wake Up!

Miss Lori

Wake Up!

Trilogy Christian Publishers

A Wholly Owned Subsidiary of Trinity Broadcasting Network

2442 Michelle Drive, Tustin, CA 92780

Copyright © 2025 by Miss Lori

All Scripture quotations are taken from the New King James Version®. Copyright © 1982 by Thomas Nelson. Used by permission. All rights reserved.

All rights reserved, including the right to reproduce this book or portions thereof in any form whatsoever.

For information, address Trilogy Christian Publishing

Rights Department, 2442 Michelle Drive, Tustin, Ca 92780.

Trilogy Christian Publishing/ TBN and colophon are trademarks of Trinity Broadcasting Network.

For information about special discounts for bulk purchases, please contact Trilogy Christian Publishing.

Trilogy Disclaimer: The views and content expressed in this book are those of the author and may not necessarily reflect the views and doctrine of Trilogy Christian Publishing or the Trinity Broadcasting Network.

10 9 8 7 6 5 4 3 2 1

Library of Congress Cataloging-in-Publication Data is available.

ISBN 979-8-89597-222-9

ISBN 979-8-89597-223-6 (ebook)

To God Almighty

This book belongs to You.

You gave me the story.

You gave me the time and inspiration to write it down.

You gave me the path to publishing.

I pray You use it for Your purposes and

Your glory to produce much fruit.

Jesus said:

"I am the vine, you are the branches. He who abides in Me, and I in him, bears much fruit; for without Me you can do nothing."

(John 15:5)

Chapter 1

"Wake up, Maggie!"

Maggie pulled the covers over her head. Today of all days she did not want to get out of bed. She wanted to stay in bed with the covers over her head until it was over.

But Sandy was persistent. She knew Maggie didn't want to get up. She also knew that staying in bed all day was the worst way to handle this. She needed to get up, get out, and get over it. Not that that would be easy. She didn't think she could handle what Maggie was going through any better than Maggie was handling it. But as Maggie's best friend, she was going to help her through it no matter what it took.

"You might as well get up. You know I'm not going away."

Maggie knew that. She even knew that Sandy was right. She couldn't sleep. If she stayed in bed, she would spend the whole day thinking about…no, don't start thinking about it! Once she started thinking, she couldn't stop. Then she'd start crying and—

Then she heard Sandy say, "I'm getting the bucket." She knew what that meant. Maggie had spent many nights at Sandy's house while they were growing up. Whenever one of Sandy's brothers wouldn't get out of bed, her dad would say, "I'm getting the bucket!" If they didn't get up before he got the bucket full, they would be drenched in cold water right there in bed. After the first time, her brothers usually got up in time. Once Sandy's dad threatened Sandy with the bucket, but Sandy's mom stopped him. Sandy's mom didn't approve of this method, especially considering how long it took to dry out a mattress.

Sandy's mom wasn't there to stop the drenching now. "I'm up. I'm up!"

"Good, take a shower. We have a full day ahead of us."

Maggie didn't ask what they were going to do. It didn't really matter, did it? Wait, what was that smell? She took a deep breath—In-N-Out burger. Her favorite.

Sandy said, "Just a little reward for getting out of bed. But you can't have it until you are out of the shower."

As she stepped into the shower, she thought, In-N-Out burgers for breakfast. That was just like Sandy to find something to help her through this day. That was one thing about what happened—at least she still had Sandy. If she had…don't think about it. The first thought leads to the next thought, and pretty soon you were in a puddle of tears—again. Get out of the shower, get dressed, and eat your burger. Concentrate on the burger.

You know, she really needed to come up with a name for it. That way whenever she started to think about it, she could say, Don't think about the… What should she call it? The Disaster? No, that sounded like a tsunami. And although there were plenty of similarities to what happened and a wave of water washing across the land wreaking havoc and devastating lives, this wasn't that widespread—kind of like her own personal tsunami. How about the Devastation? No, she was going to get through this—wasn't she?—yes, she was. Devastation was too strong a word. How about Debacle? That had a word-of-the-day sound. A debacle was something bad, but you could come back from a debacle, right?

Whatever, she was dressed and ready for her burger.

Sandy said, "You can't wear that. Put on some tennis shoes."

"Why?"

"Because we are going to play tennis."

Right, when had they ever played tennis? Never that she could recall. Did they even own tennis rackets? Whatever.

She finished her burger, got her shoes, and they left to play tennis.

They played singles for a while. Then Sandy started flirting with the guys on the next court, of course. So they played doubles. The guys wanted to take them to lunch. Maggie begged Sandy with her eyes to say no. Sandy told the guys, "Only if we go to In-N-Out Burger."

Because of the Debacle, Maggie was broke. No, worse than broke, she was broke and in debt and unemployed. Stop thinking about it. Might as well get an In-N-Out burger now. Who knew when she would be able to afford one again?

Maggie was afraid that lunch would turn into an afternoon with these guys. The one who liked Sandy was clearly thinking along those lines. But the other one was getting discouraged. Probably because Maggie hadn't said two words to him the whole time. It was also pretty obvious that she wasn't doing much listening either. If Maggie wasn't so worn out from trying not to think about the Debacle, she would have felt bad for eating the burger he bought and then not paying the slightest bit of attention to him. But today she just didn't have the energy.

She needed to get Sandy's attention. This wasn't working. Sandy could just take her home and then go do whatever she wanted with both of the guys. Clearly that was what needed to happen. She doubted that Sandy agreed. Then, to her surprise, she heard Sandy telling the guys that they had other plans this afternoon.

Good, they were going home.

Bad, they were going home.

How was she going to not think about the Debacle if they went home? At least while they were playing tennis, she had to pay enough attention not to get hit in the head with a ball!

She was wrong again. It wasn't long after they got into the car that she realized they weren't going home. Now what?

"Should I ask where we are going?"

"Only if you want to know the answer."

They drove in silence until Sandy stopped at the beach.

"I don't have a swimsuit," Maggie stated drily.

"I brought you one," Sandy replied cheerfully. Sandy was a voluptuous brunette, and she wore clothes that didn't hide her figure. Maggie was afraid to see what suit Sandy had chosen for her. Maggie was a blonde stick next to Sandy. She always thought that they were living proof that the statement "Blondes have more fun" was absolutely false. Sandy was outgoing, fun, and flirtatious. She met guys wherever they went. Maggie wasn't jealous. Sandy was fun to be around. And Maggie didn't need to be the center of attention. She didn't want to be the center of attention, which was good because she never was.

Maggie and Sandy shared clothes so much that it was hard to remember who really owned any given piece of clothing. They were the same size. Things just looked better on Sandy. Maggie was pleasantly surprised to find a relatively modest swimsuit in the bag Sandy handed her. Sure, it was a two-piece, but at least it covered everything. Maggie raised her eyebrows at Sandy. "Would you have worn it if I had brought one of the less boring ones?" Ah, Sandy did know her well.

There was already a crowd of guys around Sandy by the time Maggie finished changing and found her on the beach. How did she find the energy to be so entertaining all the time? Even before the Debacle, Maggie had never understood why Sandy wanted all that attention. Of course, that probably had something to do with the Thing before the Debacle. He had been a nice guy, right? Then how could he have… Stop thinking. Look, there's an air mattress. Just grab the air mattress, go into the water, and get a tan.

She knew what she didn't want to think about. She needed to pick something that she could think about. OK, tennis was kind of fun this morning, she thought. Well, at least she didn't get hit in the head with the ball, right? That was some small accomplishment. It would have been embarrassing to get hit with the ball. She probably would have ended up with a concussion. Wait, don't you have memory loss when you have a concussion? That could have been nice. Maybe she missed an opportunity. She could have gotten hit in the head so hard that she forgot everything that happened. She could have gotten total amnesia. Sandy kept saying that this was a chance to start all over. It would be a lot easier to start over if she couldn't remember anything that had happened. She decided to put concussion on her to-do list, then drifted off to sleep.

Chapter 2

"Wake up, Maggie!"

Wait, was the day starting over again? No, no, she was on an air mattress in the ocean. Hey, she had finally gotten some sleep. She guessed it wasn't that surprising. She hadn't gotten much sleep since the Debacle. She hadn't slept that much before the Debacle because she was so busy pl... Wow, those thoughts like to sneak up on you. She was actually pretty proud of the fact that she hadn't cried at all today. Of course, the day wasn't over yet.

"Come on, these guys want to take us out to eat," said Sandy. Well, there is a surprise, thought Maggie sarcastically.

She wasn't very wet, so she pulled her clothes on over her suit. As she followed Sandy to the car, she decided her ocean nap hadn't helped much. In fact, she was feeling downright depressed. She closed her eyes as Sandy drove.

Sandy said, "Maybe this will cheer you up."

She opened her eyes to see—In-N-Out Burger. She wanted to smile at Sandy—she was trying so hard to help her—but even In-N-Out Burger wasn't going to work this time.

Sandy's voice softened, and she sounded a little choked up when she said, "Come on, it's almost over."

Maggie's eyes welled up. She thought they were both going to dissolve into tears. She was actually glad when the guys showed up, circling the car and knocking on the windows.

There were four guys this time, all vying for Sandy's attention. As Maggie ate her third In-N-Out burger of the day, she thought about what a great friend Sandy was. She knew Sandy hurt for her. After all, Sandy had been crying with her all week. She knew Sandy was putting out an enormous amount of effort to get her through this day. What would she do without her?

It was seven o'clock by the time they were done eating. That was close enough. They could go home now. Maybe tomorrow would be better. She doubted it, but what was she supposed to tell herself? Today was bad—tomorrow won't be any better—it will never get better. That was what she believed but it wouldn't be what she told herself.

When they got in the car, Maggie said, "Thanks, Sandy, I know I wasn't much fun today. But I never would have gotten through it without you."

Sandy looked hesitant and not nearly as sure of herself as usual. She said, "The day isn't over yet. I have tickets to a soccer game. You'll go, won't you?"

Tennis and now soccer. She didn't think she needed to point out to Sandy that neither of them knew the first thing about soccer.

"Where did you get soccer tickets?"

"This guy gave them to me."

"Of course."

"Come on. This is a professional soccer team, and this guy actually plays on the team. It'll be fun."

Maggie sighed.

"It won't be any better at home," Sandy said.

There was a silent game of tug-of-war in Maggie's head. One side was pulling her to go home; the other pulled her toward her best friend, who wanted to go to a soccer game. OK, how long could a soccer game take?

Chapter 3

Two hours. That's how long a soccer game takes. Now she knew. And now it was over. She could definitely go home. She made it. She made it through the whole day. It took tennis, the beach, a soccer game, and three In-N-Out burgers, but she did it. They just had to fight the traffic and make it home.

Wait, this was not the way home. She didn't know what Sandy wanted to do now, but this was where she drew the line. By the time they got home, it would be ten o'clock. A perfectly respectable time to go to bed even on a Saturday night.

"Take me home."

"But…"

"No, just take me home and then go wherever you have planned next. Look, I am ever so grateful for all you have done, but I am exhausted. I think I can sleep tonight. Just take me home."

"But I promised I would meet him at this bar."

"Fine, take me home and then meet him at the bar."

"But we are already here, and if I take you home, I'll miss him. The whole team will be there."

Why Sandy thought that would be an incentive for Maggie to go to a bar was a mystery. On a good day she didn't enjoy bars, and this wasn't a good day, and it was over as far as she was concerned.

Sandy parked the car in front of the bar and opened the door. "Come on. We won't stay long."

Right, thought Maggie. "I'm not going in."

"Fine, sit out here in the dark."

Maggie looked around. The street seemed especially dark. All she could see were guys going in and out of the bar. Maggie was afraid of the dark. She scowled at Sandy's back as she followed her into the bar.

There must have been more guys going into the bar than going out because it was full. Sandy grabbed the only available table and fixed her eyes on the door. Maybe she actually likes this guy, thought Maggie.

Sandy stood up and started waving at two guys who walked in the door. Maggie took a deep breath as they made their way over. Here we go again, she thought.

Sandy greeted the first guy (obviously the one she got the tickets from) and introduced Maggie. Maggie gave him a half smile while he introduced his friend. Maggie looked up into beautiful blue eyes. Mesmerizing was the word that kept bouncing around in her head. Just then the rest of the team walked in and crowded around the table. Sandy giggled as she learned the players' names and introduced Maggie. Sandy's guy's friend ended up behind Maggie as the players swarmed around the table. Maggie kept backing into him as each player approached her to introduce himself. Finally, the friend leaned over her shoulder and said, "Wanna dance?" He didn't wait for an answer—just grabbed her hand and led her to the dance floor.

"Sorry," he said. "The guys get excited when they see a pretty girl."

Maggie nodded and thought, Well, then, they will love Sandy. She glanced up at him. Wow, he had nice eyes, and he smelled good too.

When the song ended, Maggie walked back to the table. She leaned into Sandy and said, "Let's go." The next song had started playing loudly. She didn't think Nice Eyes could hear her. She didn't want to hurt his feelings, but she wanted to get out of there badly.

Sandy said, "We just got here."

"Just give him your phone number so we can go. Please."

This time the tug-of-war was in Sandy's head. She wanted to stay here with Brandon. He was a good-looking guy, and he was a professional soccer player. But this was a hard day for Maggie—not that going home would help—but Maggie wasn't a bar kind of girl.

Just then the friend came to the rescue again. "Hey, I'm ready to get out of here too. I live just down the street from here. Maggie, you could come with me. We could sit on the porch and talk. Sandy can pick you up when she's ready to go home."

Sandy looked hopefully at Maggie.

Maggie didn't like this plan. She looked up into his eyes to say no. Just then the swarm of soccer players was back. The no turned into a yes.

He grabbed her hand again and led her through the crowd and out the door. Once safely outside, he let go of her hand and put his hands in his pockets. As he walked down the street, he made small talk.

"Did you enjoy the game?"

She abruptly realized without Sandy she was going to have to actually talk to him. Maybe there was still time to dash back into the bar. Yikes, he was still waiting for an answer. Hmm, she could say that it was the best soccer game that she had ever seen. If you considered that she had never seen a soccer game before, it was technically the truth. If you considered that she couldn't remember a thing about the game, it was probably closer to a lie.

She settled for a noncommittal "Um-hum."

He chatted about soccer while they walked, then said, "This is it. This is my house. This is my porch. This is my porch swing."

She sat down on the porch swing and decided that she would stay right there until Sandy came to pick her up. She hoped Sandy was feeling really guilty about the whole situation. Maybe the guiltier she felt, the sooner she would get there.

Nice Eyes went inside but was back outside with a Coke in each hand before Maggie could get concerned. He leaned against the porch rail and asked Maggie about herself. Swinging slowly back and forth on the porch swing was soothing. As Maggie started to relax, her answers got longer.

"What do you do?" he asked.

"Well, I was a preschool teacher."

"What do you do now?"

"Nothing. I'm kind of unemployed."

"Why aren't you a preschool teacher now?"

This was getting too close for comfort. She certainly wasn't going to tell him about the Debacle. But he was being so nice, and whenever she looked into those blue eyes…

"I thought I was going to move, but then I…didn't."

After a pause, he started talking about soccer again. All she could think was Bless you, kind stranger.

She leaned her head back against the swing and listened to his voice. This wasn't such a bad ending to the day. They had been talking for what, maybe an hour or more, and she hadn't thought about the Debacle…

"Wow, do you look hot!"

That got her attention.

"I mean, your skin is turning red."

Come to think of it, it was pretty hot out here. She pressed her finger on her arm to check the color. Sunscreen. She had been out on the water all afternoon. She didn't remember putting sunscreen on. Well, that was stupid!

"That's quite a sunburn. You know, I have some aloe inside. Let me go get it."

He disappeared inside. Maggie thought about how stupid she was for forgetting sunscreen until she noticed how dark it was. Suddenly the swing wasn't up to the job of soothing her. She jumped up.

"Hey, can I use your bathroom?" she called out.

"Sure."

She congratulated herself on her quick thinking. She could hide in here until he was ready to go outside again. A quick look in the mirror ended the congratulations. She really did need that aloe.

She heard drawers slamming upstairs. She followed the noise to the doorway. He looked up and smiled. "Found it!"

The sunburn that she hadn't noticed outside was causing her considerable discomfort after she looked in the mirror.

"Great!" she said. She grabbed the tube, sat down on his bed, and started applying it gingerly to her arm. A blob landed on his bedspread.

He said, "Here, let me help you. Close your eyes." She closed her eyes and lifted her face to him. He slowly and gently applied the aloe to her face. Before she opened her eyes, he kissed her.

He moved away to the window and fumbled with the blinds. Maggie thought a moment, then did something completely out of character for her. She pulled off her top, laid down on his bed, and asked him to put aloe on her back.

Chapter 4

What had she done? That did not just happen. What had she done? Panic started to rise into her throat. OK, he was asleep. She needed to gather up her clothes and get out of there. Don't let him wake up. Don't let him wake up. What had she done? OK, quietly down the stairs, out the door. Lock it. There was no going back. What had she done?

Sandy drove up. Momentary relief. She ran to the car and dove into the seat.

"Where is he?" asked Sandy.

"Inside. Just go."

"Are you all right? You look kind of…disheveled."

"I'm fine. Just go."

Sandy started to get scared. "What happened? Did he hurt you?" Memories of another time flooded into Sandy's mind mixed with guilt. "It didn't happen again."

Maggie looked confused. "What? No, no. Please, just take me home."

"Did you sleep with him?"

The look of shame and remorse on Maggie's face was all the answer she got.

For what seemed like the billionth time that day, Maggie repeated, "Please just take me home." This time Sandy did.

Chapter 5

Maggie considered herself a Christian. As a matter of fact, she was a born-again Christian. She believed that Jesus died on the cross to forgive people's sin. She believed that if you believed in Jesus, you would go to heaven. She remembered the night that she accepted Jesus as her Savior.

Her parents were off on some exotic trip. Sandy was off with her family on a less exotic vacation. That left her home alone. She was bored, depressed, and desperately lonely. She decided to spend time with her only friend—the big-screen TV. She flipped through the channels until a kind man's face filled the screen. Before she had a chance to change the channel, he said, "You don't have to be alone." Well, this was news to her. She listened as he described a Friend that would never leave you, never forsake you. She wanted, no, needed, that kind of a Friend. When Billy Graham made the altar call, she was on her knees praying the sinner's prayer. It felt good to think that there was a God who cared about her.

She didn't go to church much, but she did pray. Not a lot but when she needed something. But she did feel less alone. She did feel like Jesus was her Friend, at least until the Debacle. She tried to do the right thing. She was a good person, right? How had she let last night happen? She actually believed that you didn't sleep with a guy until you were married. Married, you know, like virgin on your wedding night. That was the plan, and the plan was intact until last night. Sandy didn't think it was such a big deal. Of course, Sandy wasn't a Christian. Sure, she would go to church with Maggie once in a while. But she really saw it as a chance to dress up and meet new guys. But even Sandy never had a one-night stand. She would sleep with a guy but only if she really liked him.

What did this mean? Did it mean she wasn't really a Christian? Did it mean Jesus wouldn't be her Friend anymore? But for that matter, if Jesus was her Friend, how come her life was such a complete mess? She was a good girl before the Debacle—and it still happened.

How much would a concussion really hurt? Maybe if she fell off her bed and landed on her head, all this would go away.

Chapter 6

"Maggie?"

"Go away!"

"Come on. Let's go to In-N-Out Burger."

"No!" Today Maggie was actually going to stay in bed all day. She was trying not to be mad at Sandy. But the truth was if Sandy had only taken her home any one of the times that she had asked her, this never would have happened. OK, it really wasn't Sandy's fault. Nobody put a gun to her head last night. If somebody had, it would have been easier to explain. As it was, now when she did get married (if she ever got married), she would have a very difficult confession to make. Wow, the truth does hurt. It is painfully humiliating.

"Come on, Maggie. This isn't such a big deal."

"Go away."

Sandy decided to let her cool off. She was only trying to help yesterday. OK, maybe she shouldn't have let her go off with a stranger like that. But she asked Brandon. He said Mike was a good guy. Of course, they were teammates. Maybe they covered for each other. And who would have ever thought perfect little Maggie would succumb? Maggie could say no to any guy. She had an impenetrable force field around her. She never let her defenses down. Hmm, maybe that meant… That gave Sandy a brilliant idea.

"Maggie, you need to come out of there."

"What for?" She had spent the whole day in her room. It had been a miserable day. If anyone had told her that today would have been worse than yesterday, she wouldn't have believed them. She thought she had hit rock bottom yesterday. Somehow she had found a way to go lower. Where was that concussion?

"For supper."

"I don't want another In-N-Out burger." Even she had her limits.

"Good. I'm cooking grilled chicken."

"I'm not hungry," she said as her stomach growled. Sure, she hadn't eaten all day, but with all the calories in an In-N-Out burger, you'd think she shouldn't have had to eat for a week after having three yesterday. But she was hungry, and she loved grilled chicken. Sandy was a great cook.

Sandy knocked on the door again. "Hurry up! They will be here any minute!"

More guys. Well, she supposed she could tolerate two nameless, faceless guys for some chicken. She would eat and get back to her room. She looked in the mirror. Then immediately regretted looking in the mirror. She looked bad. Puffy, red eyes. Serious bedhead. Sunburned face. She could jump in the shower before the chicken. Her empty stomach urged her on. No need to dry her hair, just pull it into a ponytail. Just enough makeup to cover up the puffy eyes. She couldn't do anything about the sunburned skin. Good enough.

As she walked into the kitchen, Sandy yelled, "There she is! We're out back. Bring the lemonade." She picked up the tray with a pitcher of lemonade and four glasses. She took a deep breath and backed out the screen door to the porch.

"Hi, Maggie." She turned around to look into those blue eyes again. "Let me help you with that." He took the tray. She took a step back toward the door. Sandy was too fast for her, though.

She said, "We've been waiting for you." And pushed her into a chair.

OK, she knew she was new at this, but this couldn't be right. Someone needed to tell him after you have a one-night stand, you don't show up at the girl's house the next day. That has to be in every etiquette book.

Sandy took over the conversation, putting food on Maggie's plate and poking her to get her to eat. Maggie began a mantra. Eat some chicken, escape to your room. Eat some chicken, escape to your room. Eat, escape. Eat, escape. Occasionally she would interject a "yeah" or "uh-huh" when she thought (hoped) it was appropriate.

Where was that concussion? If a meteor fell from the sky right now and hit her in the head, that would do it, right? Of course, that might kill her. OK, if that was what it took to get out of this situation. Wait, when meteors entered the atmosphere, they burned up, right? They became... Sandy elbowed her hard.

"What?"

Blue Eyes said, "I said I know someone who needs a nanny."

Maggie gave him a blank look.

"You said you needed a job."

Sandy said, "She'll take it."

Maggie gave her a look. Sandy said, "The rent is due in two weeks."

Sandy took over, getting all the information. A single mom—nursing student—needed a nanny for her four-year-old little girl. Smart, sweet. She needed someone right away. He didn't seem to want to answer why she needed a nanny all of a sudden. But Maggie guessed that didn't matter. It sounded perfect, and Sandy said so. He said he'd talk to the mom.

Maggie figured she'd eaten enough chicken to make it through the night. She mumbled, "Excuse me." And went into the kitchen. Escape to her room, but on the way, she'd grab some chocolate. Yes, she definitely needed chocolate. Ahh, M&M's, that's the stuff. She popped a handful into her mouth. Then he walked into the kitchen. Why hadn't she waited to get to her room to eat the chocolate?

"I'm gonna take off," he said.

"OK."

"If you give me your number, I'll call you about the nanny job."

"I don't have a phone."

"Really? I thought everybody had a cell phone these days." He looked doubtful.

"Everybody but me."

He walked into the living room toward the front door. She felt bad. She didn't mean to be rude, but… He turned around and said, "Maggie, I'm sorry. I thought you knew I was coming."

She said, "No, I didn't." She was completely confused. He seemed like a nice guy, but then why…? Nothing made sense anymore.

He turned to leave. She turned to go to her room.

He stopped again. "Maggie?"

"What?"

"Maggie Lawson."

"What?"

"My name is— "

"I know your name!" Fresh humiliation.

"Do you?"

"Yes, it is either 'Good game, Mike' or 'Great goal, Mallone.' I'm not sure which. But I must have heard it twenty times at the bar last night."

He seemed satisfied with that answer. Then started, "About last night—"

She held up her hand. "Please, I don't want to talk about last night." This was excruciating. What could she say? How could she get him to understand without actually telling him about the Debacle? "If you knew the situation…"

"What situation?"

That didn't work. "Listen, if you had any brains, you would run away screaming. So that is my advice to you. Run away. Whether you scream or not is up to you."

He looked at her, considering what she said. He didn't scream. He just quietly said, "Good night, Maggie." And walked out.

"Goodbye, Mike."

That was brutal. Sandy and Brandon were still on the patio talking and laughing. She took her chocolate and went to bed. If anyone deserved a good cry, it was her. Last night was humiliating. Seeing him again today was humiliating. The fact that he thought that she slept with him without even knowing his name—beyond humiliating. She just couldn't take any more. She cried about last night. She cried about the Debacle. She cried about her crummy life. She wanted to pray. To talk to her Friend Jesus. But she couldn't. She cried because Jesus wasn't her Friend anymore. She didn't deserve to have Jesus as a Friend. She was completely alone.

Chapter 7

Monday morning. Sandy had already left for work. They had worked at the same preschool. She loved that job, but that was over for Maggie. Time to move on. Time to get over everything. She was going to take a shower, then start looking for a job. That nanny thing that Mike talked about would be perfect. Just one little girl to take care of. No looking for a job. No going on interviews. No talking to adults who would ask personal questions. No trying to explain things without really explaining things. But she'd blown it, just like everything else lately. She'd never see him again.

Shower done. Look for a job. OK, just because she couldn't have that nanny job didn't mean she couldn't have a nanny job. She would get on the internet and look for nanny jobs. She walked into the kitchen, looking for Sandy's computer. But first she would clean up the mess that Sandy left from the "dinner party" last night. Sandy was a great cook, but she was a messy cook. Maggie didn't mind. She liked cleaning. Cleaning made life feel organized and calm. The house wasn't really dirty because all last week, when she wasn't crying, she was cleaning. But there was always more dirt to tackle. She did the dishes, then cleaned the whole kitchen. As she scrubbed the floor, she noticed the dirt on the grout in between the tiles. An old toothbrush was just the thing to clean that.

Yep, this was helping. While she scrubbed the grout, she didn't have time to think about the Debacle, the Thing before the Debacle, or even her most recent mistake. Wow, the list of things not to think about was getting long. OK, so she had made a lot of mistakes (and the last one was a whopper), but the Debacle really wasn't her fault, was it? If it wasn't her fault, then why did it feel like God was punishing her? Her whole life was turned upside down. She had nothing. The only reason she even had a place to live was because the new roommate that Sandy had found backed out at the last minute. Maggie went over the events in her head again. She truly had not seen it coming. She was truly clueless. If there had only been some clue—

A knock at the door interrupted her thoughts. She opened the door to find an adorable little girl. She said, "Hi, my name is Sara Rose. We are going to see the Winnie the Pooh movie. Do you want to come?"

Why was there a little girl alone on her porch inviting her to a movie? Then he stepped into view. Him and his blue eyes. He just didn't know what was good for him. He said, "I thought you might want to meet Sara—she is the little girl I was telling you about last night."

She was surprised to see him and yet not really surprised. She didn't really know him, but yet it seemed like something he would do.

Sara was talking again. "Winnie the Pooh is my favorite."

Maggie loved talking to children. "Mine too."

"Will you come to the movie with me and Uncle Mike?"

Mike gave her a half smile and said, "Yeah, will you?"

Between Sara's adorable smile and Mike's blue eyes, she had no power to say no.

They all walked out to Mike's Jeep Wrangler. Sara jumped into the front seat. Mike said, "I think Miss Lawson might want to sit there."

Sara stumbled over the name. "Miss La-w-rson, do you want to sit in the front?"

Maggie kicked into preschool teacher mode and replied, "Well, I am sure you want to sit in the back in your car seat."

"I don't like my car seat."

"Oh, but it is much safer for little girls to sit in the back in their car seats. You might get hurt in the front seat."

"Why would I get hurt?"

"Because the airbag might come out. The airbag protects big people, but it can hurt little people."

"Oh, OK, you sit in the front seat, Miss Rawerson."

"The kids at school call me Miss Maggie. Can you buckle your car seat all by yourself?"

"Yes, I'll show you, Miss Maggie."

Mike was impressed. He could never get Sara to sit in the back seat.

Maggie actually enjoyed the movie. Winnie the Pooh really was her favorite. The kids at school were all talking about this movie. She'd felt a little left out that she hadn't seen it.

Sara sat between Maggie and Mike until she started to get sleepy. Maggie thought someone was missing her nap. Sara crawled into Mike's lap. Mike picked her up and moved into the seat next to Maggie.

Sara chatted about her favorite parts of the movie all the way to the car and into her car seat. "We are going to get ice cream now. 'Member, Uncle Mike, you promised."

"Yes, I did."

Sara continued, "I like chocolate ice cream. Uncle Mike likes vanilla. Do you like vanilla, too, Miss Maggie?"

"No, vanilla is too boring. I like chocolate ice cream with chocolate syrup and chocolate sprinkles."

Sara giggled, "That's a lot of chocolate! I want that too!"

Maggie leaned her head back against the seat. Sara was telling a story about a friend of hers. Maggie missed the kids in her class. She listened to Sara, asked questions about her friend, and answered questions that Sara asked. She could get used to hanging out with Sara.

At the ice cream shop, Maggie sat with Sara at the table while Mike ordered the ice cream—a scoop of chocolate with chocolate syrup and chocolate sprinkles for each of them. Maggie stifled a laugh. She didn't know how to tell him she was actually kidding about the ice cream. But it was good.

Mike was on the phone when Maggie and Sara got back from the bathroom. Maggie had helped her wash the chocolate syrup off her hands, face, and shirt! That's what happens when you give a four-year-old that much chocolate!

Maggie could only hear Mike's end of the conversation.

"Where are you now?"

"How long will it take you?"

"I can't. I have to go to that charity event."

"In an hour."

"OK, just meet us there."

Mike looked at Sara. "You have to stay with Uncle Mike a little longer."

Sara looked like she might cry. "Where is Mommy?"

"She's still at school. It's OK."

Sara crawled into his arms again. He picked her up and carried her to the car. Sara sure was comfortable with him. And she called him Uncle Mike. He and Sara's mom must be good friends.

Mike looked at Maggie. "I'm sorry. I was going to take Sara home and let you meet her mom, but Michelle is running late. I have a charity thing I have to go to. Can you stay with us?"

"Sure." She didn't see that she had much choice. Surely, he would take her home sometime, right?

Sara fell asleep in her car seat. Maggie leaned her head back on the seat. She was tempted to do the same thing.

As soon as Mike parked the car, he was on the phone again.

"Where are you now?"

"Just get here as soon as you can."

Mike looked apologetic. "She's stuck in traffic. I really have to go in here. Can you watch Sara until Michelle gets here?"

"Sure." She could definitely think of worse things than hanging out with Sara.

When Sara woke up, Maggie took her for a walk. They found a grasshopper jumping across the sidewalk and ladybugs in some bushes. Maggie kept an eye on the parking lot. When she saw a little red car speeding into the lot and parking next to Mike's Jeep, she asked Sara,

"What color is Mommy's car?" Sara answered, "Red." Maggie said, "I think she's here."

Maggie held Sara's hand so she wouldn't run into the street to get to her mom. Mike came out of the building, talked to the woman from the red car, and pointed toward Maggie and Sara. Maggie waved. Sara's mom met them halfway. Sara yelled, "Mommy!" and ran to greet her.

Michelle looked flustered until she was holding Sara. Then she managed to compose herself. She held her hand out to Maggie and said, "I'm Michelle Mallone."

Maggie shook her hand and said, "Maggie Lawson." Maggie was confused. "Mallone?" she asked.

"Yeah, I'm Mike's sister. Didn't he tell you?"

"No. So when Sara says Uncle Mike, she really means Uncle Mike."

"Yep, Mike says he's going to be a while in there, so I'll take you home. Do you mind if we go to my apartment first to get to know each other?"

"Sure." Again, what choice did she have? She really wasn't in control at all.

After Sara told her mom all about the movie and the ice cream, Michelle asked Maggie about herself. It sounded like small talk, but she guessed it was the interview for the nanny job.

The interview continued at Michelle's apartment while Michelle made chicken nuggets for Sara. Sara was hungry and cranky. Michelle grumbled, "Typical, always no nap and ice cream for supper when she is with Uncle Mike. But I shouldn't complain. She adores him."

Maggie could see that. Suddenly it dawned on her. If she became Sara's nanny, Mike might be around a lot. As much as she wanted this job, that didn't seem wise. Even worse, how could she take this job without telling Michelle about That Night?

Michelle asked, "So do you want the job?"

Maggie said, "Sara is a great kid. I would love to take care of her. But I mean…that is to say…I really shouldn't take this job."

"Why not?"

Maggie stuttered and sputtered. "You know, I just met Mike a couple of days ago."

"Yeah, I know all about it."

Maggie doubted that.

Sara finished her chicken nuggets. Michelle said, "Go get your jammies on. Then we will take Miss Maggie home."

As Sara scampered down the hall, Michelle looked Maggie in the eye. She repeated, "I know all about it. He tells me everything."

Maggie still didn't believe her. Surely, he wouldn't tell her that.

"You met after the game at that bar that the team likes to hang out at. He walked you to his house. You talked on the porch until you turned red. He rubbed aloe on you, which led to—"

The shocked expression on Maggie's face stopped her from finishing the sentence. She did know.

Michelle said, "I really need someone to watch Sara tomorrow. If you don't do it, I will have to skip school."

Maggie wanted to help her out. "Why would you want a nanny that behaved like that?" she asked as she stared at her hands in her lap, humiliation washing over her yet again.

"Look, I know Mike. He's not the kind of guy who picks up girls in bars."

Maggie thought, Oh, good, it's only me. Is that supposed to make me feel better or worse?

"It's just that it could get awkward." (Or more awkward.)

"OK, how about this? No commitment for either of us. If I find that your morals aren't good enough, I fire you. If it gets too awkward for you, you quit."

Maggie guessed she could live with that. "OK."

"Be here tomorrow at nine o'clock?"

"Oh, wait, I don't have a car."

"Then I will pick you up tomorrow."

Chapter 8

Things were looking up. She had a job. Better yet, she had a job that didn't feel like a job. She spent the whole morning having fun with Sara. Now Sara was just getting up from her nap.

Mike tried the door of Michelle's apartment, but it was locked. He had a key, of course. Should he unlock it? Maybe he should knock? He could hear voices through the open window. Maggie and Sara were discussing her afternoon snack. Sara said, "I want ice cream. I always have ice cream with Uncle Mike."

Mike flinched. He had to admit Sara had him wrapped around her little finger.

Maggie said, "It is OK to have ice cream sometimes, but not every day."

"Why not?" Sara whined.

"Because it is important to eat foods that have good vitamins."

"What are vitamins?"

"Vitamins are what make your body strong and healthy. Different foods have different vitamins. So you need to eat lots of different foods so you get all the different vitamins."

"Does ice cream have vitamins?"

"Not very many. So if you only eat ice cream, your body will get weak, and you might even get sick."

"What food has good vitamins?"

Maggie searched the cabinets. Not much in there. "These raisins have vitamins."

"I don't like raisins."

In the end they compromised. Sara ate Cheerios and two raisins.

Mike thought, Wow, she is good. Sara was a very picky eater. He walked over and knocked on the door.

He heard Maggie say, "Sara, you can't just open the door. Ask who it is."

"Who is it?"

"Uncle Mike."

Sara whispered loudly, "It's Uncle Mike. Can I open the door?"

For a minute, Mike wondered if Maggie would open the door for him. He wasn't at all sure she would be glad to see him. He probably should leave her alone. But he just couldn't seem to do it.

Sara opened the door and launched herself into his arms. He loved that little girl!

Maggie looked unsure. If he was here, then she didn't need to be. But she had no way to get home until Michelle got there. Maybe he and Sara would take her home.

But Mike sat down with Sara and asked her all about her day with Miss Maggie. Maggie opted to go into the kitchen and clean up the snack. She wiped down the table and the counters (even though the counters were clean). She swept the floor. Michelle's kitchen was small and spotless. Now how was she going to avoid him? See, this was awkward.

Sara called her in to ask what kind of bug they had seen in the park.

"Praying mantis."

"And Miss Maggie says tomorrow we can take a jar and catch it if we see it again. And maybe we can go to the library and get a book and learn all about praying mantises."

Sara loved her bugs!

Mike said, "That's a great idea!"

Sara said, "Wait, I need to show you something." She ran off to her room.

Awkward. As long as Sara was in the room doing all the talking, it wasn't as bad. But when she left—

"Sounds like you and Sara had a fun day," said Mike.

"Yeah, she's a fun kid."

Awkward silence while Mike looked at Maggie, and Maggie looked at anything in the room but Mike.

Michelle walked in. Sara ran into the room. "See, this is the picture that I drew of the—"

"praying mantis." Maggie finished her sentence.

Sara excitedly recounted the events of the day for her mom now.

Maggie fidgeted in her chair.

Mike said, "Chel, I'll take Maggie home."

"Thanks, Mike, I have a ton of homework."

Good, thought Maggie, more awkward silences.

"Sara, come say goodbye to Uncle Mike and Miss Maggie."

Sara ran back into the room and jumped into Mike's arms again. He swung her around and said, "Bye, my sweet Sara Rose."

"Bye, Uncle Mike."

He put her down.

"Are you coming back tomorrow, Miss Maggie?"

"Yep."

"Can we go to the library?"

"If I can find one that is close enough to walk to."

Mike said, "There's one just down the street. I'll show you."

"Cool. Bye, Miss Maggie."

"Bye, Sara." Maggie looked at Michelle. "Same time tomorrow?"

"Same time, same place."

Mike and Maggie walked out to the Jeep. He held the door open while she slid in. "Thanks," she mumbled.

He drove past the library and pointed it out to Maggie. Maggie was having trouble concentrating. She had no idea how he got to the library. She would have to google it later. Wow, he smelled good. Kind of manly, outdoorsy.

He was chatting about something, probably soccer. She really should start listening to what he was saying, not just the sound of his voice.

"What do you think?" Uh-oh, he was waiting for a response.

"The movie we were talking about at your house the other day. Do you want to see it?" he asked again.

"Oh, yeah," she had no idea what movie he was talking about. She really needed to tune into these conversations. She was spending too much time in her head.

"Do you mind? It will only take a minute." Oops, she did it again.

"Sure, that's fine."

He turned up the radio. She leaned her head back against the seat and closed her eyes. He stopped talking. That was probably good since she wasn't listening. And yet she missed the sound of his voice.

"Looks like Sara really wore you out."

"No, she's great. So smart. So curious. Especially about bugs!"

She looked at him and realized she hadn't thanked him. "Hey, thanks for getting me a job."

"Seems like it worked out for everyone."

He pulled into a parking lot. "I'll be right back." She guessed this was what was only going to take a minute. He started toward the door of the building, then turned back. He opened her door and pulled the window up and off and put it in the back seat. "Don't want you to get too hot out here."

As he left, she leaned her head against the seat again and closed her eyes. It sure was considerate of him to take his car apart for her. The thought made her smile just a little.

"Hey, there's Mallone's one-night stand!"

She looked out to see one of Mike's teammates pointing at her. Another one punched him in the arm and pulled him into the same door Mike had gone in.

She hung her head. Will the humiliation never end? That was what she would always be—Mallone's one-night stand. OK, God, she thought, I get it. I am being punished. I know it was wrong, but I didn't mean to sleep with him. It shouldn't have happened, but what can I do to change it now? Nothing, I blew it. There was no going back.

Mike returned. He opened the door and pulled the window off his side too. Then he got in. He turned to Maggie. "Everything all right?"

"Yeah." Sure, fine, peachy, never been better. She'd never be the same.

It was pretty loud in the Jeep without the windows. Loud and windy. Not conducive to conversation. Good.

Mike pulled into the In-N-Out Burger. She guessed he was hungry. "Everything on your burger?"

"No onions." When did she agree to go out to eat with him? Didn't he tell Michelle he was taking her home? At least he was going through the drive-through. Maybe he thought it would be rude to get a burger just for himself. Then he'd drop her off at home with a burger. Can't fault a guy for getting you an In-N-Out burger, can you?

Just a little while longer and she would be home. Then she could think this through. There had to be a way to handle this. She just needed to get her head straight.

He stopped at his house. Wait a minute.

"We can eat our burgers while we watch the movie."

Is this what he was asking before? She thought he meant do you want to see this movie some time—in a general sense. Not do you want to see the movie with me at my house right now. This was definitely not a good idea.

He bounded up the porch stairs. She followed, panicking. "I should really go home. Sandy might be worried," she said weakly.

"Just call her and tell her where you are."

"I don't have a phone."

Really? Mike thought. So she wasn't just making that up to get rid of him. Good to know.

"Come in. You can use mine."

She dialed the phone. Let her pick up. Let her pick up, she prayed. Just who was she praying to? It didn't matter. He wasn't listening. She got Sandy's voicemail.

Now what did she say? "I'm at Mike's. Come rescue me." That would never do. Number one, he could hear her. And number two, Sandy was the one who invited him over to their house the other day. Why did she do that? Why did he come? Sandy's message was over. She'd better say something. "I'm at Mike's." She wasn't known for her quick thinking.

OK, she still needed to get out of this. She was going to have to try to lie. She didn't usually lie. Lying was wrong, of course, but that wasn't the only reason she didn't do it. She wasn't any good at it. It was an established fact—she wasn't a quick thinker, so making up a story on the spot wasn't going to happen. But even worse, when she tried to tell a lie, one look at her face, and everyone knew she was lying. She had no poker face. She needed to put that on her to-do list. Get a poker face. Right after she got herself that concussion.

"Something wrong with your burger?"

"No, I like In-N-Out burgers."

"Doesn't everyone?"

Guess she would have to eat this burger and watch this movie. Then she could go home. What could go wrong?

He finished his burger and sat back on the couch next to her. He looked very comfortable with his arm draped across the back of the couch behind her. She ate her burger slowly, leaning over the coffee table. Concentrate on the movie. She was tired. She was always tired. She still wasn't sleeping much. That was it! When the movie was over, she would say she wanted to go home because she was tired. It wasn't even a lie. No problem. She could get through the movie, say, "I'm tired," and he would take her home. She leaned back and relaxed. Oops, she forgot his arm was there. Now he smelled like the outdoors and In-N-Out burger. Perfect combination. She could rest her head on his shoulder for just a minute. Her last thought before she drifted off to sleep was *Mmm, he smelled good.*

OK, so it was a juvenile move to leave his arm on the back of the couch, thought Mike. But it worked. She finally relaxed, and now her head was on his shoulder. She smelled like vanilla, just like he remembered. Sure, she was asleep, but that was OK. Now she would forgive him for his lack of self-control the first night they met. They could get to know each other and let the relationship develop naturally. He wasn't going to blow this again. Especially since Michelle kept telling him, "Don't blow this." Maggie was so good with Sara. Michelle needed the peace of mind that brought now that their grandma couldn't watch Sara anymore. He needed to tell Maggie what was going on—why he slipped that night. He wanted to tell her. But he needed to wait until she knew he wasn't the kind of guy she thought he was—the stereotypical jock that picked up girls in bars. Then maybe she would trust him enough to tell him what was bothering her.

Cars collided on the TV screen with a loud crash, waking Maggie up with a start. She was confused until she found herself lost in those mesmerizing blue eyes. As Mike kissed her, everything became incredibly clear. The solution was so simple. Why hadn't she thought of it before? All she needed to do was sleep with him again. Then she wouldn't be his one-night stand. She would show those evil soccer players.

Maggie clung to Mike. He knew he could take her upstairs. He wanted to, but he shouldn't, but he wanted to, but he shouldn't, but he wanted to…

"Maggie, are you sure?"

"Yes."

They both wanted to. They wouldn't be hurting anyone. He picked her up and took her upstairs.

Chapter 9

Maggie woke up and tried to figure out where she was. Deep remorse hit her as she realized she was in his bed again. What was wrong with her? How could she have done it again? Now here she was again, gathering up her clothes in the dark and sneaking out of the house, praying that he wouldn't wake up. Praying to who? She still knew there was a God, but she felt like dirty laundry. Clearly, God wanted nothing to do with her. She started to sob but stopped herself so she wouldn't wake Mike up.

Downstairs she looked out the window. It was the middle of the night. It was very dark. Bad things happened outside in the dark. Sandy wasn't going to come driving up to save her now. OK, she had two choices: she could stay here until it got light and face him if he woke up, or she could make a run for it in the dark. Her heartbeat wildly at the reality of either choice. She heard a noise from upstairs. He was waking up. She ran out the front door and locked it behind her. Her fate was sealed. She had to run for home now. She could walk all day long, but she wasn't used to running at all. But the memory of what had happened one night in the dark spurred her on until she was in the door of her house. Even inside the house, her hands shook, her breath came rapid and ragged, and her heart beat wildly in her chest. She was safe now, but she couldn't calm down. The terror lingered. She paced from window to window watching for a ghost from the past to appear. Quiet, she thought. Don't wake up Sandy. This time she wouldn't even tell her. It took almost an hour before her breath and heart resumed a normal rhythm. She wilted onto the couch and dissolved into deep sobs. Just before dawn she realized what she needed to do. She needed to never see him again. This just wasn't right. But that meant giving up the one thing that was going right in her life—Sara. She couldn't cancel on Michelle today, but she would definitely tell her—today. It wouldn't be that hard. All she had to say was, "It's too awkward." Surely Michelle would understand.

Michelle looked distracted, maybe even distraught, when she picked Maggie up a couple of hours later.

"Is everything all right?" Maggie asked.

Maggie thought Michelle had probably gotten as little sleep as she had.

Michelle responded with an unconvincing, "Yeah."

"Listen," said Michelle, "Mike can't pick you up today. And I need to go somewhere as soon as I get home from school. Any chance you could find a ride home today?"

"Let me borrow your phone. I'll call my roommate."

Class hadn't started for Sandy yet, so she picked up immediately. Maggie explained the situation and made the arrangements. Sandy said with a snicker, "Yeah, I'll pick you up. Then you can tell me all about last night!"

"No, I can't."

"Why not?"

"Gotta go."

She handed the phone back to Michelle. "All arranged."

She started to tell Michelle that today needed to be her last day, but Michelle looked weighed down by the world. Mike wasn't going to be around today—she could tell Michelle tonight. It could wait. It would be all right.

"I'm not going to tell you anything except I'm not going to see him anymore," yelled Maggie.

Sandy returned with just as much vigor, "Why not? He's a good-looking guy."

Wake Up!

All Maggie could think was nothing good ever started that way.

She refused to talk about it with Sandy anymore. Sandy left in a huff. "I'm going to Brandon's." She stormed out the door. But through the screen Maggie heard Sandy say quietly, "Call me if you need me."

OK, Maggie thought, I need to clean. She looked around. This place was spotless. Even the grout looked good as new. Looking at the grout made her think of Sara and Winnie the Pooh—and Mike. Wait, just because he didn't pick her up today didn't mean he wouldn't show up here tonight. That would be just like him, wouldn't it? So—she just wouldn't open the door. How would he even know she was here? Especially if she stayed in the back of the house and left all the lights off. Oh, great, so now she was going to cower in the dark because she was afraid he might come over. The shed—I will go out back and clean the shed. That was the place where they kept all the stuff that they would never use again (just like any good American). This was perfect. There was a mountain of mess back there. Hours and hours of cleaning. In addition, she could see the driveway. When he drove up, she could just wait in the shed until he got tired of banging on the door.

She spent two hours sweeping and dusting and organizing. He still hadn't shown up. Maybe he wasn't coming. She meant, Good, maybe he wasn't coming. Maybe he was finally taking her advice and giving up on her. You know, if he was avoiding her, then maybe she could keep her job. She really wanted to keep this job. It didn't pay much, but it would cover rent and food—mostly. What else did she need? Her parents could wait for her to pay them back. She wasn't really sure she needed to pay them back anyway under the circumstances. Hey, she hardly ever thought about the Debacle anymore! Maybe she was getting over it! It just took something worse to get it out of her mind.

She was tired. Maybe he really wasn't coming. Well, he could be mad at her for leaving in the middle of the night for all she cared. It was all his fault anyway. She was pretty sure he was hypnotizing her with those blue eyes and getting her to do things she would never do otherwise. That had to be the explanation, right? What else could it be?

Chapter 10

Today was a good day, finally. She hadn't seen Mike in two days now. Clearly, he was avoiding her, which meant she could continue to be Sara's nanny. Michelle had gotten home right after Sara's nap. Maggie was home even before Sandy was home from the preschool. She walked in the door, ignoring the mail in the mailbox. Couldn't be anything good anyway, right? Probably just bills. Inside, she changed her mind. She was on her way to recovery now. She wasn't going to be scared of anything, including the bills in the mailbox. Wrong move. It wasn't the bills that caught her attention. It was the postcard. He sent her a postcard from Aruba? Why? To remind her that that was where she would have been now if… She had to get out of there. She started walking and crying, crying and walking for hours. Finally, it started to sprinkle. It didn't matter. Nothing mattered. The rain came down harder and harder. She didn't care if she got wet. What difference could that make? Soon she was drenched. Water dripped from her hair, her face, her clothes. She began to shiver. OK, wet she didn't mind. Cold and wet she didn't care for. She looked around wondering where she was. There was a familiar porch. She shouldn't go up there. But she had to get out of the rain now. He probably wasn't even home. She wouldn't knock on the door. She would just wait on the porch until it stopped raining. Then she could go home.

The door opened. "What are you doing here? Come in out of the rain!" Mike pulled her in the door. This was bad. How did she get here again? Mike pulled her through the house and into the bathroom. He gave her a stack of towels and said, "Dry off."

She pulled off her socks and shoes. She hung the socks on the shower rod after squeezing out the excess water. She left the tennis shoes in the bathtub. Her shirt was 100 percent cotton and 100 percent soaked. She took it off and squeezed out the water. Her shorts were a synthetic running style, so she could just dry them with a towel. She dried her hair and wrapped a fluffy towel around her shoulders.

Mike knocked on the door. "Maggie, are you OK?"

"Yeah." She wasn't ready to come out, though. She washed the mascara off her face. What were the chances that she could convince him to take her home?

"Maggie?"

She took a deep breath and opened the door.

"What were you doing out in the rain?"

"I just went for a walk."

"Have you been crying?"

"No," she lied. He didn't believe her—she had no poker face.

"What's wrong?"

"Nothing." She stifled a sob. "Can you give me a ride home?"

"Is Sandy there?"

"I-I don't know." She sniffed.

"Let me call her." He called. She didn't answer.

Maggie was standing at the window, watching the rain and clutching the towel around her shoulders.

Mike stood behind her. "She didn't answer."

"She is probably with Brandon. She kinda likes your friend."

Mike didn't touch her. He said quietly, "Just tell me, Maggie."

He backed away, sat down on the couch, and waited.

"Um." Sniff. Deep breath.

"Well." Sob. Pause.

Where did she even start?

"He sent me a postcard. He went to Aruba—on our honeymoon—without me." Fresh tears rolled down her face.

"Maggie, are you married?" Mike asked, shocked.

"No, no. I was supposed to get married, but I—didn't."

"What happened?"

She was fighting to keep control, but she was losing the battle.

Mike took a guess. "He called off the wedding?"

"No, I did."

"Why?"

"Well, we were supposed to get married last Saturday." Pause, deep breath. Sob.

"The day we met?"

"That'd be the one. The week before that, he told me that"—deep breath—"he—he didn't—didn't want to have kids. And he had had a vasectomy to make sure we never did." Tears were streaming down her face now.

"Did you talk about having kids?"

"I did. I talked about it all the time." The words began pouring out now. "Shoot, last month we were in Phoenix looking at houses. At every house I'd say, 'This would be a good room for a nursery.' In fact, there was one house he really liked, but I said it was no good. The master bedroom was on the ground floor. The rest of the bedrooms were upstairs. The kids would be too far away. And, come to think of it, why were we looking at four-bedroom houses if we weren't going to have any kids? What were all those bedrooms for?"

She stopped to take a breath.

"The worst part is," she continued, "I didn't see it coming. I didn't have a clue. How could I not have known? I can't remember one thing he said about kids, positive or negative. Did he not say anything, or was I not listening?"

Mike walked over and put his arms around Maggie. She turned and put her head on his shoulder. He kissed her hair and said, "I'm sorry, Maggie."

She sniffed and said, "I'm pretty sure it's not your fault."

He smiled into her hair, trying to think of something to say that would be helpful. All he could think of was "that guy is a jerk." So he said it. "That guy is a jerk."

Maggie snuggled in and said, "Yes, he is."

All of a sudden, she pulled away, pulled the towel closer, and said, "You should take me home now."

"I don't think you should be alone."

"Fine, I can walk." She hurried to the front door and turned the door handle. Mike came up behind her and slammed the door closed with the palm of his hand.

"You can't go. It's still raining, and it's getting dark."

"So?"

"And you don't have your shoes—or your shirt."

She laid her forehead on the door. "You know, technically it's kidnapping if you don't let me leave."

How could she be so sad and so funny at the same time? He took her by the hand and led her to the couch. She looked absolutely despondent. He sat down next to her, put his arm around her, and said, "Do you want to talk about it?"

She said, "No."

So much for that plan. What was he supposed to say? What would make her feel better?

He heard scratching at the back door. "I'll be right back."

Maggie laid down on the couch and decided she would just die there. She felt a cold, wet tongue on her face. She sat up. "You have a dog?"

Maggie started petting the beautiful golden retriever. She slid to the floor to hug him and snuggle with him. Suddenly, Mike was jealous of his dog.

"What's his name?"

"Jackson."

"I always wanted a dog when I was growing up."

Maggie got back up on the couch and put her head on Mike's shoulder. She said, "You should talk."

"About what?"

"It doesn't matter."

He had suspected that she didn't really listen when he talked. That suspicion was confirmed now as he told her the same stories he had already told her. He guessed he should give her a break. This was a heartbreaking situation. What was wrong with that guy?

Maggie was exhausted physically and emotionally. She wanted to go to bed and sleep forever.

Finally, Maggie stood up. She knew she needed to leave. "This isn't your problem. I should go home," she said with a resolve she didn't feel.

Mike didn't want her to go. He held her tight, circling his arms around her and the towel.

She put her arms around his waist—her head on his shoulder. "I should go home," she said without moving. "I definitely should go home," she repeated as if she was trying to convince herself.

"I should take you home," he agreed, but he didn't move either.

Finally, she whispered, "Maybe it wouldn't be so bad if I stayed."

"You probably shouldn't be alone," he agreed. "I'll sleep on the couch."

"I can't kick you out of your bed."

"It's OK. I don't mind."

"That's all right," she said, holding on tighter. She wanted to stay right here in his arms until she felt better, and that could take a while.

"Maggie, I can't—I can't promise that nothing will happen if we stay in the same bed."

"That's OK. At this point what could it possibly matter?"

Clearly the right thing to do was take her home. But he thought if he did, he might never see her again. He couldn't take that chance.

"One condition: you let me make you breakfast in the morning."

"Uncle Mike's famous pancakes?"

"What?"

"Sara says you make great pancakes."

"Sure," he agreed.

"We'll see," she hedged.

"No. You have to promise you won't leave in the middle of the night."

"I don't sleep very well."

"Then you wake me up."

She looked doubtful.

"I don't like waking up in the morning and wondering if you got home all right," he said.

"Now I can't leave all night. You really need to look up the definition of kidnapping. You're really walking the line."

He took her by the hand and led her upstairs. "I haven't handcuffed you to the bed or anything," he joked.

"That definitely crosses the line."

"OK, good to know."

At the top of the stairs, she made a detour to the bathroom. She looked in the mirror. "God, I know this is wrong, but I am going to do it anyway. I just can't fight it. I don't have the strength." No response. He didn't care.

Chapter 11

Maggie woke up. The clock said twelve o'clock. Her stomach said, "Feed me." She couldn't wait for Uncle Mike's famous pancakes. She needed food now! She slid quietly out of bed and pulled on the shirt that Mike had been wearing. Down to the kitchen—there had to be something she could eat. She wouldn't leave. She didn't want to make another terrifying run in the dark. It was kinda nice that he worried about whether she got home all right. He really did seem to be a nice guy, but he didn't have any food. How could a soccer player not have any food in the house?

Upstairs, she heard Mike yell, "Maggie!" He sounded mad.

She ran to the stairs, "I didn't leave. I'm down here."

"What are you doing?"

"I was hungry. I was looking for some crackers or something. I kinda forgot to eat today."

He sighed from the top of the stairs. "What kind of pizza do you like?"

"Canadian bacon and mushroom. But I'll eat any kind. Where is it?" She searched the fridge.

He walked down the stairs, phone to his ear. "What kind of crust?"

"Thin. You don't have to order a pizza. Don't you have anything like a box of Cheerios?"

"Pizza will be here in twenty minutes."

"I don't know if I will make it."

"I have Gatorade."

"So the commercials are true. Athletes really do drink Gatorade?"

"Yeah, do you want one?"

"Not really—what, I'm not an athlete! I'll take a Coke."

They sat down on the couch to wait for the pizza.

Mike said, "Do you want to talk about it?"

"I will talk about anything but *it*. Politics, religion, sports. Oh yeah, sports. How long have you played soccer?"

"Professionally five years."

"Five years! How old are you?"

Mike smiled. "Twenty-two."

"Don't soccer players play in college like football players?"

"Some do, but I didn't."

She counted backward on her fingers—seventeen. "Did you graduate from high school?"

Mike groaned. "Yeah."

"Sorry."

"I went to a special high school. You study in the morning and play soccer in the afternoon. I was drafted straight from there."

"Hmm, you must be good."

Mike shrugged. "You've seen me play."

Maggie snorted. "I hate to break this to you, but I wasn't really paying attention. I don't remember anything from the game."

"Worse than that," she continued, "I don't know anything about soccer. I wouldn't know if you were good, even if I watched the game."

"In that case, I am good," Mike joked. "How did you manage to forget to eat today?" he asked.

"Well, you may have noticed that I haven't been sleeping well lately."

Yeah, he'd noticed.

"I couldn't sleep last night, so I got up to watch Nick at Nite. After four or five episodes of *I Love Lucy*, I must have fallen asleep. When I woke up, Michelle was banging on the door. Needless to say, I didn't have time for breakfast."

"Why didn't you eat lunch with Sara?"

"Sara wanted SpaghettiOs again. We really need to work on that kid's diet. I just couldn't choke those slimy noodles down again. But Michelle said she would be home early, so I figured I could wait. When I got home, I put some leftovers in the microwave…which I guess are probably still there, now that I think about it—good thing I didn't use the stove. Then I got the mail and found that postcard." She looked down at the floor. "Then I went crazy for a while. Fifteen minutes ago, I woke up with my stomach growling."

The doorbell rang. "Thank goodness!" Maggie cried out.

Maggie wolfed down the pizza in a very unladylike manner. Mike smiled as he ate a piece. He wasn't all that hungry. He didn't usually eat pizza in the middle of the night.

"What's his name?" he asked hesitantly.

She looked at Mike, then back at the pizza, and said, "Greg."

"What does he do?"

"He just finished school. He'll be a dentist when he gets to Phoenix."

"How does someone who just got out of school afford a four-bedroom house?"

This was getting uncomfortable.

"He's rich."

"Really? How rich?"

"Grew up in a mansion rich, corvette rich, trust fund rich."

"How long did you know him?"

"Three years."

"Wow, was he—"

Maggie interrupted, "So you have played soccer for five years?"

He looked at her, confused. Then he got it. Talk about anything but it.

"Guess what happened to Brandon at practice today."

Mike told the same old soccer stories again while Maggie polished off most of the pizza. She turned toward him and laid her head sideways on the back of the couch while he kept talking.

Maggie stifled a yawn.

"Finally," Mike said.

He got up, took her hand, and led her up the stairs. "I thought I'd tell you boring soccer stories until you were ready to go to sleep. It finally worked."

"Your soccer stories aren't boring. I could listen to them over and over again." She smiled just a little.

Oops, maybe she was listening. "Sorry, I thought you weren't listening."

"I tune in and out. Tell me about Brandon getting hit in the head with the ball again. That one is my favorite."

Chapter 12

"Maggie, wake up."

Every time she managed to fall asleep, someone woke her up.

Mike tried again. "Maggie, you need to get up. Sara will be here soon."

He wished he could let her sleep. He didn't need to get to training for an hour. He could watch Sara. But he didn't want to explain to Sara why Miss Maggie was sleeping upstairs. And Michelle would kill him.

"What? Sara is coming here? What time is it?" Maggie bolted upright.

"Here's your shirt."

"I can't wear the same shirt from yesterday! It has butterflies on it! Sara will remember it! She will ask me about it! What am I supposed to say?"

"OK, don't panic. Calm down. Here, wear this." He found one of his jerseys.

"Are you crazy? It says Mallone on the back. She can spell her own name. I can't wear your shirt."

"Don't worry—we'll tell her I gave it to you."

"I can't lie to her."

He handed the shirt to her. "There, I gave it to you. It's not a lie."

He went downstairs. She wondered if she would ever get control of her life again.

She got dressed and walked downstairs just as Michelle and Sara walked in. She took a deep breath and watched Sara run into the room and jump into Mike's arms.

Sara turned to Maggie. "That's Uncle Mike's shirt. Why are you wearing Uncle Mike's shirt?" she giggled.

Michelle glared at Mike and said, "Yeah, why is she wearing Uncle Mike's shirt?"

Maggie looked down. Mike said, "I gave it to her."

"Why did you give her your shirt, Uncle Mike?"

"Because she's my friend."

Sara was done talking about the shirt. "Are we making pancakes?"

Mike said, "Yep, right after you wash your hands."

Sara ran to the bathroom.

Michelle handed him a bag of groceries. "Here, everything you need to make pancakes."

"Thanks, Chel."

"I gotta go." She looked at Maggie, then at Mike. "You two behave yourselves."

Mike pushed her shoulder and said teasingly, "Get out of here."

Michelle yelled, "Bye, Sara."

Maggie finally entered the conversation. "Wait, how will we get to your house?"

"I'll take you on the way to training," said Mike.

Maggie guessed it had all been planned without her.

Mike went to the counter to take out the pancake fixings. He and Sara worked together to make the pancakes. Maggie sat at the table quietly watching them.

Mike decided his plan wasn't as great as he had thought earlier this morning. He had called Michelle to have her bring the stuff to make pancakes and bring Sara over to his house. That way Maggie could sleep a little longer. He had thought the idea of her wearing his jersey was brilliant. She could wear it to the game tonight! But now Maggie looked embarrassed and miserable. He hadn't thought she'd react that way. What was the big deal? Sara wasn't going to figure anything out, and Michelle already knew. He hated that she was so upset.

By the end of the pancake feast, Maggie was perking up. She and Sara were discussing what they wanted to do that day. Maggie got up and started cleaning up. Sara wandered into the living room.

Maggie asked Sara, "Are you finished?"

"Yeah," called Sara.

"Will you bring me your plate so I can wash it?"

"Uncle Mike can do it."

Mike looked apologetic. Usually, he did do it. He never made Sara clean up.

Maggie said, "Uncle Mike will bring me his plate. I think you should bring me yours. Besides Uncle Mike cooked the pancakes, so I think I will clean up. Doesn't that seem fair?"

Sara came into the kitchen. "I helped Uncle Mike cook."

"Yes, you did. The pancakes were very good," replied Maggie.

Mike took his cue and carried his plate to the sink.

Sara thought about it. "I can help clean up too."

"Thanks, Sara. That would be such a big help!"

Maggie and Sara cleaned up. Mike smiled in wonder.

At Michelle's apartment, Sara ran inside. Maggie looked at Mike. "Thanks for the ride," she said awkwardly.

"So, Maggie, do you want to come to the game tonight?"

"There is a game tonight? It's Friday. I thought the games were on Saturday," Maggie babbled.

"It varies. Sometimes they are on Saturday, sometimes Friday, sometimes Wednesday, or even Sunday."

Maggie felt bad again. "Why didn't you tell me?" she groaned softly.

As was so often the case when he was with Maggie, Mike was confused. What was she upset about now?

"Won't the coach be upset that some crazy chick kept you up half the night?"

"How is he going to know?" Mike joked.

Maggie didn't laugh.

MISS LORI   57

"Maggie, don't worry. I'm fine. Will you come?"

Maggie hesitated. "How much are the tickets?"

"Free."

"Then I think you better start looking for a job. Your team is going to go out of business."

"I reserved four tickets at the beginning of the year for each home game."

"Four?"

"Yeah, Sara, Michelle, you and Sandy."

"Sara and Michelle always go to the games?"

"Yeah."

"Who were the other two tickets for?"

"Tonight—you and Sandy."

Maggie looked at him, waiting for an answer.

He sighed, "I'd rather not get into it now. I promise I'll tell you tonight, OK?"

She considered, then relented. "OK."

"Michelle will pick you up at six o'clock."

Guess that was already planned too, thought Maggie.

The game was exciting. Way better than the myriad of baseball games she and Sandy sat through when Sandy's brothers played. There was constant action in a soccer game. In baseball, the action was sporadic at best.

They walked to the car chatting about the game. Michelle drove around to another parking lot and stopped next to Mike's Jeep. She said, "Mike wants you to wait here for him."

Sandy smirked. "What does Mike want me to do?"

Michelle said, "I'm taking you home."

Sandy looked at Maggie. "We'd better wait until he gets here." She knew Maggie wouldn't want to wait alone in the dark. Michelle didn't seem to mind.

Finally, Mike walked out toward the car. Maggie got out of the car to meet him. Mike stopped at Michelle's window to say goodbye to her and Sara and Sandy.

Maggie got into Mike's Jeep like this was the usual routine for her, never mind that they hadn't known each other for a week yet.

In the Jeep, Mike commented, "You changed shirts."

"Yeah, I didn't have time to wash your jersey yet. Then I will get it back to you."

"No, you keep it. I gave it to you. I thought you would wear it to the game." He seemed disappointed. Maggie was surprised. She had totally misunderstood. Was it really that important to him?

At Mike's house he walked into the kitchen and pulled a box of Cheerios out of the cupboard. Maggie laughed. "You went to the store."

"Yep."

"Did you remember to eat today?" he asked.

"I had a hot dog at the game. I don't like hot dogs all that much, but Michelle said it was a tradition. So I ate it."

He poured Cheerios and milk into two bowls.

Maggie yawned.

"Do you think you will be able to sleep tonight?" asked Mike.

"That would be nice. But just in case, do you get Nick at Nite?"

"I have no idea."

"Did you enjoy the game?" asked Mike.

"Yeah, it was exciting. I mean, most of the time, I didn't know what was going on. I know you are trying to get the ball into the goal, but the rest of the time, it kinda looks like a lot of guys just running around." She smiled.

"Why don't you ask Michelle? She could explain it to you."

"She's too busy yelling at the refs. You should have seen her when that guy kicked you. I thought she was going to jump out onto the field and beat him up! You really should warn the other team," she laughed.

He smiled—that sounded like Michelle all right.

"About the tickets." He paused.

Maggie had decided she didn't care who the tickets had been for. She knew he had had a girlfriend, Bianca. Sara said she was mean. She was sure they had been for her. It really didn't matter, did it?

"They were for my grandparents," said Mike, interrupting her thoughts.

"Oh, they couldn't go tonight?"

Mike looked away. He swallowed hard and said, "My grandpa… passed away."

"Oh, I'm sorry," said Maggie. "You mean Grandpa Willie?"

He looked surprised.

"Sara told me," she said. "She said he died a long time ago."

"No, not quite two weeks."

"I'm so sorry." She covered his hand with hers. "Were you close?"

"Yeah, our dad died in a car accident when Michelle and I were twelve. My grandpa was more like a dad to me after that."

"What? You were both twelve?" interrupted Maggie.

"Yeah, we're twins."

That explained a lot, thought Maggie.

"My grandpa came to all my soccer games. He paid for everything. Michelle lived with them. My grandma has watched Sara since she was born."

"I thought Gigi Rose watched her."

"Yeah, that's what Sara calls her."

"Why does she call her by her name?"

Mike looked confused.

"Gigi Rose."

"No, that's not her name. GG like in great-grandma."

"Oh. Is she OK? Sara said she was sick."

"Not really. She isn't doing well without Grandpa. She had a stroke last week."

Maggie didn't know what to say. This was too sad. Her eyes welled up. Finally, she asked, "Why didn't you tell me?"

He sighed. "I don't know. Everyone on the team knows, and they have been pretty good about it. But sometimes it's awkward. I guess it was kind of nice not talking about it. Like a vacation from it."

"I understand." She did. It was nice not talking about her recent problems too.

Actually, that wasn't the whole truth, thought Mike. He decided to confess. "Actually, I was feeling kind of guilty." Pause. "Grandpa Willie's funeral was Saturday."

"Last Saturday, the day of the game?" asked Maggie, surprised.

"Yeah."

"And you still played?"

That was why he didn't say anything. He shouldn't have played. "Yeah, I know I shouldn't have."

"Did the coach make you?"

"No. He asked if I wanted to. I said I wanted to, but I probably shouldn't have."

Maggie thought for a moment. "I don't think there are rules for grieving. I guess you just have to get through it as best you can."

"Playing a soccer game takes your total concentration. You get to forget for just a little while."

"Believe it or not, it's the same for being a preschool teacher. When the kids get there, you concentrate on them. That's why I like hanging out with Sara so much now."

"You don't know how much it helps to have you watching Sara. You are so good with her. I know it's a relief for Michelle to know she is with you." Pause. "Me too."

That sealed it. She couldn't flake on Michelle now. And Sara and Mike were a package deal. She might as well accept it.

"You look tired," she said.

He took their cereal bowls, put them in the sink, and took her hand to lead her upstairs. He said, "I am. This crazy chick kept me up half the night last night."

"It's your own fault. A good host feeds his guest before she goes to bed," joked Maggie.

"I know. I just did."

Mike woke up at five o'clock. Maggie wasn't next to him. Guess it didn't work to feed her before she went to bed. He went downstairs to look for her. The TV was on, and the box of Cheerios was on the coffee

MISS LORI 61

table. Maggie was asleep on the couch. She had one towel rolled up under her head; she was covered with another. Mike thought, I guess I need couch pillows. He'd call Michelle and have her pick some up. He had an afghan that his grandma made around there somewhere.

He watched her sleep. She was so beautiful. She almost always wore her hair in a ponytail, but now it was down around her shoulders. He liked it better that way. Her face was soft and relaxed. She was all curled up under the towel. All he could think of was what an idiot Greg was for letting her go. Greg knew her for what—three years? How could he not want to have kids with her? Maggie was meant to be a mother. Mike knew that before he knew her three days. Look how great she was with Sara. Greg didn't deserve her.

He should find the afghan and cover her up so she wouldn't get cold. Or…he could pick her up and take her upstairs and keep her warm himself. He liked plan B better.

He turned off the TV and closed the cereal box. He leaned down to pick her up. She startled when he touched her. But when he said, "It's OK. It's just me," she responded by wrapping her arms around his neck.

As he carried her upstairs, she said, "Good news."

"What?" he inquired softly.

"You do get Nick at Nite."

Chapter 13

"Wake up, Maggie."

He hated to wake her up again. Yesterday he had had to wake her up because he had all kinds of things to take care of for his grandma. Wednesday he and Michelle had moved his grandma out of the hospital and into a skilled nursing home. That was the only night this week he hadn't seen Maggie. It took forever for him to wade through the paperwork to get Grandma Rose released from the hospital. Then, when they finally got her to the skilled nursing home, he started wading through all that paperwork. By the time they got Grandma Rose settled in, it was too late to drop by Maggie's. Besides he hadn't been sure how he would have been received. The night before that, he had only brought her to his house to watch a movie. He would have been perfectly happy to snuggle on the couch. He certainly wasn't planning on talking her into anything. Problem was he wasn't prepared to talk her out of anything either. Then, the next morning, she was gone again, and he had absolutely no idea why. Was she mad at him? After all, it had been her idea. Did she wake up with regrets? Or was this some weird game she was playing?

He had actually been relieved when she showed up on his doorstep on Thursday looking like a drowned rat—until he realized she was crying.

He tried again, "Maggie?"

She blinked her eyes and said, "What?"

Then she sat bolt upright and said, "Is Sara here?"

"No, it's Sunday."

Maggie laid down again and murmured, "Don't soccer players ever sleep in?"

He smiled. "Sorry, I have to go pick up Michelle and Sara. We need to spend some time with my mom."

"Oh, OK," replied Maggie sheepishly.

After he dropped Maggie off, he picked up Michelle and Sara. Michelle looked like she was getting about as much sleep as Maggie was. She was constantly worrying about their grandma and missing their grandpa. Combine that with trying to catch up with her nursing school homework and taking care of Sara, and Michelle was about to break. Thank goodness Maggie was taking care of Sara during the day. At least Michelle didn't have to worry about that. Michelle leaned her seat back and closed her eyes. Sara was in the backseat—in her car seat—"reading a book." She was a great kid.

That left Mike to think his own thoughts. For as long as he could remember, Sunday mornings meant going to church. He had been raised Catholic. Catechism, altar boy, the whole nine yards. Grandma Rose had made sure of that. He believed in God, of course. That big bang theory that he learned in school just didn't make sense. There was nothing, and then it exploded. How did that explain how life began? There had to be a Creator—a God to get things started. He just wasn't sure how involved He was after that. Grandma Rose insisted that God loved His people and took care of them. But if that was true, then why did so many bad things happen? Why did his dad die in a car crash when he was only twelve? Why did Grandpa Willie have to die now? He was so strong, and he wasn't even seventy yet. How could he have died of a heart attack? He needed Grandpa Willie. How was he supposed to take care of Grandma Rose, his mom, Michelle, and Sara all by himself? It was just too much. And most of all, why did God let that thing happen to Michelle four years ago? How could Grandma Rose believe there was a loving God taking care of us after all that? And yet she did.

At his mom's, he looked at the list of things that needed to be done around the house—things that Grandpa Willie would have taken care of. Nail slat back on the fence—the white picket fence—his mother actually had a white picket fence. He guessed even white picket fences needed to be fixed sometimes. He got the hammer and nails.

Yesterday, he had taken care of his grandma's roses. They needed to be weeded, fertilized, and watered. Grandma Rose loved her roses. Her rose beds surrounded the house. Growing roses was something she and Grandpa Willie had always done together. Now he supposed it was one more thing that he would need to take care of. Not that he minded. After all she had done for him, he would do anything for Grandma Rose. She looked so small and fragile in her hospital bed yesterday when he had visited her. He had told her all about Maggie, of course. Well, he hadn't told her *all* about Maggie. Just about Maggie taking care of Sara—you know, so she wouldn't be worried about Sara. Grandma Rose would be very disappointed in him if she knew all about Maggie. Come on, it wasn't like what he and Maggie were doing was so wrong. They were two consenting adults, right? It wasn't like he was sleeping around. Everybody did it. It was no big deal, right?

"Ouch!" He missed the nail and hit his thumb.

If it was no big deal, why couldn't he tell his grandma?

His thumb was bleeding. He went inside for a Band-Aid. He could hear his mom, Michelle, and Sara in the kitchen.

Sara said, "Then Miss Maggie said that vanilla ice cream is boring, and we should get chocolate ice cream with chocolate syrup and chocolate sprinkles! Isn't Miss Maggie funny?"

Michelle said, "You are doing the potty dance. Do you want me to take you to the bathroom?"

Sara answered, "Miss Maggie says I am big enough to go to the bathroom all by myself," and walked off in a huff.

His mom said suspiciously, "So where did you find this Miss Maggie?"

"Mike met her after the game last Saturday."

"A week ago?! At that bar?!"

"Well, yeah."

"Let me get this straight. You are trusting your daughter to some soccer groupie that your brother met a week ago at a bar?"

Youch! That sounded bad, thought Mike. He took a step into the room to defend Maggie but stopped as he heard Michelle do it.

"She is not a soccer groupie. She is a preschool teacher, and she is great with Sara. Sara loves her. And I do trust her with Sara. And so does Mike!"

Mike pulled up in front of Michelle's apartment complex. He walked around to help Sara out of her car seat, but she had done it herself. Thank you, Maggie. He said, "Bye, silly Sara Rose."

"Bye, Uncle Mike."

He turned to Michelle. "Hey, Chel, thanks for standing up for Maggie."

"It's the truth. I don't know what I would have done if you hadn't"—she hesitated, glancing at Sara—"found Maggie. She is the only thing that's going right lately."

He had to agree with that.

He was tired. He really wanted to go home—veg out on the couch. But he needed to go see if Maggie was all right. Or did he just need to go see Maggie?

Sandy opened the front door, phone to her ear, and pointed him to Maggie's bedroom. Maggie sat on the floor, back to the door, surrounded by broken CDs. He watched as she picked up another case and opened it. She pulled out the CD, laughed the kind of fake, wicked laugh that you would hear on TV, and broke it in two.

Mike chuckled and asked playfully, "Whatcha doing, Maggie?"

Maggie looked up guiltily and responded, "Um, nothing."

"Let me guess, Greg's CDs?"

"It was an accident."

"Right." He smiled.

"Um—well, see, I was going to send them back to him, but then I realized I don't know where he is." She smiled and continued. "Then I decided I would just throw each one out of the window as hard as I could. Then I could say that I tried to get them back to him."

"Like guided missile CDs."

"Yeah! But then when I took the first one out of the case to throw it, it broke. I kinda liked that."

Wow, how crazy did she sound now?

Mike said, "I was thinking about going to In-N-Out Burger."

"OK."

"I mean, do you want to go with me to In-N-Out Burger?"

"Oh, OK." She smiled up at him. "I can finish this later."

As they walked to the Jeep, Maggie continued, "You know, they're not actually his. They're mine. He gave them to me because he likes jazz. He told me—and I quote, 'Listen to them. You will like them.'" She paused to look at Mike. "I listened to them. I didn't like them. I like them even less now."

Mike stopped at the Jeep and reached for the door. He gave her a quick kiss before he opened it to let her in and said, "You know, you could have sold them."

Maggie groaned, "Where were you thirty minutes ago with that suggestion?"

They were waiting in line at the In-N-Out Burger when a guy walked by and said, "Hi, Maggie."

Maggie looked toward the voice and said, "Hi."

After he passed by, Mike said, "Who is that?"

"Not a clue."

"Then how does he know your name?"

Maggie shrugged. "Don't know."

Mike ordered while Maggie went to collect napkins and straws. The guy approached Maggie.

"Don't you remember me?"

Maggie gave him a shrug.

"Diego—from last Saturday?"

Maggie took a guess. "From the beach?"

"No, we played tennis."

"Oh." She nodded. Tennis she remembered—him she did not.

"Maybe we could do it again sometime?"

Mike walked up and interrupted. "We have to go."

Maggie said, "I thought we were eating here."

"No, we are eating at my place." He stared the guy down and put extra emphasis on my place.

Maggie looked back at the guy, shrugged, and said, "Gotta go."

As Mike pulled her to the door, the guy shouted, "Say hi to Sandy for me."

In the Jeep, Maggie breathed in the smell of the burgers. She couldn't remember if she had eaten today or not.

Mike had thought it was a good idea to go to In-N-Out Burger, but now he wasn't so sure. He wasn't hungry. They'd had a big meal at his mom's this afternoon. And he didn't usually eat this much fast food. But he always wondered if Maggie remembered to eat. He knew she liked In-N-Out Burger and Canadian bacon and mushroom pizza. Pizza would take too long, so he decided on the burger. He didn't plan on some guy hitting on Maggie right in front of him!

Maggie said, "They're not really mine."

Confused, Mike asked, "Who?"

"Not who, what—the CDs."

Good, she wasn't even thinking about that guy, thought Mike.

Maggie continued, "Greg didn't want to move any of my stuff to Phoenix. He told me to sell everything. So I did—to Sandy—for one dollar."

"You sold everything you owned?"

"All but a few suitcases of clothes."

Mike was beginning to realize what a huge ordeal Maggie was dealing with. It wasn't just not getting married. Her whole life was completely altered by that one shocking announcement by Greg. "I'm sure she would give you your stuff back." After all they were best friends.

"Nah. For one, Sandy is much too smart to sell a whole apartment full of furniture for one dollar." She gave him a wry smile. "And two—I don't have a dollar."

Mike gave her a sympathetic look.

She smiled. "It doesn't matter. It's just stuff."

Before they got to the house, he asked, "Are you going to tell Sandy?"

"About the CDs? She doesn't care—she doesn't like jazz either."

"No, I meant—"

"About getting my stuff back? No, I don't want it. It isn't important."

He hadn't meant that either. "About the guy who said hi."

"The guy from the beach?" No, from playing tennis.

"I can't. He didn't tell me his name." Yes, he did—Diego.

"She wouldn't care—she has lots of guys hanging around her." He wasn't interested in Sandy. He was interested in you.

Let it go, Mallone. Why did you even bring it up? She wasn't thinking about that guy. He knew who she was thinking about—Greg.

Eating burgers, leaning over the coffee table, Maggie asked, "How is your mom doing?"

"OK, I guess."

"Did you go to see GG Rose today?"

He liked how she called his grandma GG Rose—just like Sara. "No, we had Sara with us."

"So?"

"We didn't have anyone to leave her with."

"How about her nanny?"

"You don't have to watch her on the weekend too."

"I wouldn't have minded." Pause. "You could take her with you. She misses GG Rose."

"I know. But I think it would be too hard on her."

Maggie thought it was hard on Mike.

Tentatively Mike asked, "Do you think we should take Sara to see Grandma Rose?"

Maggie gently shook her head yes.

"But she asks so many questions. What am I supposed to tell her?" continued Mike.

"The truth."

"How am I supposed to explain a stroke to a four-year-old?"

"It is not about explaining everything—it is telling her the simple truth so she can handle it. But believe me, she is wondering about GG Rose."

MISS LORI

"I don't know what to say."

"OK, tell me what happened."

"Grandma Rose had a stroke. It has mostly affected her motor skills. We moved her into a skilled nursing home, where she is going to physical therapy every day to relearn even the basics—from eating with a spoon all the way to walking. She may never be the same again." He was so sad it broke Maggie's heart.

"OK, tell Sara something like this, 'GG Rose is sick. Sometimes when people get old, they get sick. Sometimes their muscles don't work well anymore. GG Rose is staying at a place where there are people who are going to help her. They are helping her muscles get strong so she can walk again.'"

"What if she asks how long she will be there?"

"What's the answer?"

"I don't know."

"Then you say, 'I don't know.'"

"What if she asks if grandma will ever walk again?"

"You see, now you are thinking like an adult. If you don't bring it up, Sara probably won't either." Maggie continued, "You should probably end with something encouraging, like, 'We are going to go visit GG Rose because that will make her happy. Maybe we can make her a card that says, 'Get well.'"

"It sounds so easy when you say it." He smiled. "I'll talk to Michelle. Problem is Michelle still cries every time we go see Grandma Rose."

This is such a difficult time for their family, thought Maggie.

Mike asked, "Maggie, if I take Sara, will you go with me?"

"Of course. I'd love to meet GG Rose. Sara talks about her all the time. It's her second favorite subject."

"Oh yeah, what is her first, bugs?"

Maggie laughed. "No. You! All day long all I hear is Uncle Mike says this and Uncle Mike does that. Uncle Mike's favorite ice cream is vanilla. Uncle Mike's favorite color is green. Hey, and what is your problem with Candyland? It is the greatest kid's game ever invented. It teaches them colors and matching and taking turns."

Mike groaned. "It's so boring." He hated Candyland. Sara was always wanting him to play Candyland with her.

"I think it's fun!"

"Good! Then you two can play it together!"

"We will."

Chapter 14

It was always harder to get up for a midweek game, but he felt ready. As he jogged onto the field to warm up, he felt the urge to look into the stands. He usually didn't look into the stands before the game. But just one glance couldn't hurt, right? He found their seats. It wasn't hard. Michelle liked to sit in the first row in the middle of the field. That way the refs could hear her better! The seat near the aisle was empty, but then he saw Michelle walking down the steps carrying hot dogs. Sorry, Maggie. Four seats in, Sandy was standing with her back to the field talking to some guys behind her. Even from across the field, it was obvious she was flirting with them. In the middle, Sara sat on Maggie's lap. They must have been watching for him because Maggie was pointing in his direction. Sara saw him and jumped up, waving excitedly. He smiled and waved back.

He was glad he looked. Maggie was wearing his jersey.

"Where did you get that shirt?" asked the boy behind Maggie. He looked to be maybe ten or eleven.

"Um, Mike gave it to me."

"You mean he took it off and gave it to you after the game!" asked the boy, amazed. "You are so lucky."

"Actually, it was before a game," said Maggie hesitantly.

"You know Mike Mallone?" asked the boy's mother. "Any chance my son could get his autograph after the game? He's a big fan."

Maggie was embarrassed. She had no idea what Mike's policy on autographs was. She couldn't remember him ever signing autographs when she was around. Of course, she had only known him a week and a half. Well, all she could do was ask Michelle. She would know.

Michelle said, "Sure, we'll call him over after the game."

Maggie thought, I guess it's just that easy. Call him over after the game. She hoped Michelle knew how to get his attention. He hadn't come over after the last game.

It was a good game. Mike scored a goal. He looked so cute, all excited, running around and hugging the players after the goal. And Michelle was going absolutely crazy!

After the game, Michelle gave a loud, sharp whistle. Mike was still shaking hands with the other players. He waved his hand in her direction. Wow, secret twin signals, thought Maggie. After a couple of minutes, he jogged over. Michelle had picked up Sara and moved into the aisle to let the boy and his mother near the rail. Other people had realized what was happening. They crowded in on both sides of Maggie. Sandy had moved off with the guys she had been flirting with all game. Maggie watched as Mike worked his way down the row signing whatever they handed him and accepting their congratulations on the game and the goal with a good-natured smile. He stopped to talk to the boy, asking if he played soccer and what position. The boy's mom asked if Mike had any advice for her son. He said, "Eat right, train hard, and have fun."

Maggie was enjoying watching him. When he got to her, she smiled a huge smile and said playfully, "Hey, Mallone, can I have your autograph too?" Mike responded by reaching his hand around to the back of her neck and pulling her close, then kissing her soundly. He whispered, "See you later" in her ear; then he continued down the row, signing more autographs.

Chapter 15

"Wake up, Maggie."

Maggie opened her eyes and tried to get her bearings. Where was she?

Sandy said, "Wake up. What are you doing here? You have leaves in your hair!"

Maggie realized she was in the park. She had been sleeping in the park?!

Sandy handed her her phone. She said, "Mike wants you to call him. He has been calling all day."

Maggie looked at the phone. She was still groggy and confused.

"Aren't you going to call him?" Sandy demanded.

"Give me a minute."

As they walked to the car, Maggie tried to figure out what happened. Mike had left the day after the game. He was playing in Columbus this weekend. Maggie had felt she was doing all right. It was like she had two lives—her former life with Greg and her new one with Sara and Mike. She liked her new life. She spent her days with Sara and her nights with Mike. OK, she still felt guilty about spending her nights with Mike, but nothing was perfect, right? That left her no time to think about her former life. But he was across the country now. When Michelle had dropped her off at home on Friday afternoon, she had nothing to distract her. She obsessed about her former life all night. In the morning, she had been desperate to stop thinking about it. She decided to go for a walk. After hours of walking, she finally got tired and sat down. Then she laid down and fell asleep. This was pathetic. Now she was sleeping in the park like a hobo.

In the car, the phone in her hand rang. She jumped and dropped it between the seats. Sandy picked it up and looked at the caller ID. She answered it by saying, "Here she is." And handed the phone to Maggie.

"Hi," said Maggie.

"Where have you been all day?" asked Mike, clearly annoyed.

Maggie hesitated, "In the park."

"OK, whatever, listen, I don't have much time." He calmed down and tried to explain clearly but quickly what he wanted. "Remember after the last game when I was signing autographs and I kissed you?"

"Yeah."

"OK, well, I am being interviewed after the game tonight. I know they are going to ask me about it. Is it all right if I call you my girlfriend?"

Maggie wasn't quite sure what he was all upset about or why this was so urgent. But she decided to follow her policy of just letting him do whatever he wanted. It was a questionable policy, but it was easier that way. So she said, "Sure."

He said, "Great. I have to go. See you tomorrow."

"OK."

Sandy said, "What was that all about?"

"He is going to be interviewed after the game tonight."

"He bugged me all day just to tell you that?"

Maggie shrugged her shoulders.

Maggie and Sandy went to Michelle's apartment to watch the game. They had only basic cable—no sports channels—so it wasn't on at their house. The team was wearing their blue away uniforms. The game ended in a tie.

After the game, one of the sports reporters caught up with Mike. He asked what Mike thought about the game. After Mike answered, the reporter continued, "There's a video all over the internet of you signing autographs after the last home game. The question is, who is the lucky fan who got a big kiss instead of an autograph?"

Mike had seen the video. It looked like he was kissing some random fan during an autograph session. He had been avoiding the reporters, hoping they would get tired of asking. Maybe some other player would do something stupid and take the attention off that video. But his teammates had let him down again. Just like they had the day after he met Maggie. He hadn't told anyone but Michelle. But Sandy must have told Brandon that he and Maggie slept together because the next training session that was all they were talking about. Him, they were treating like a hero, but not Maggie. Sure, they all thought she was hot, but they also thought she was easy. The double standard is so unfair to girls. He got so mad about their comments, it almost came to blows. But Brandon, as the team captain, stepped in to break it up. He was mad at Brandon for telling them. He was mad at his teammates for their comments. But mostly he was mad at himself. After all, it was his fault. He was the one who ruined her reputation. They didn't know her. Maggie was beautiful and sweet and smart and funny. The one thing she was not was easy.

He pulled his attention back to the interview. Smiling for the camera, he answered, "That wasn't a fan. She's my girlfriend."

The reporter looked disappointed. "Hearts are breaking all over the country."

Michelle and Sandy exchanged a look of surprise when he said the word "girlfriend." Maggie didn't notice. She was thinking how the blue uniform was the exact same color as his eyes.

Sunday dragged by excruciatingly slowly. Maggie couldn't settle down to do anything—not that she had anything to do. So she spent her time walking by the window, looking for Mike's Jeep. She had no idea when his flight was. She just knew she wanted him to come back. She needed to get back to her new life because her old one sucked. Then she chided herself for thinking a bad word. Where was he? She could call Michelle. She would know when he was scheduled to get back, but she didn't want to seem…what was the word—crazy. That about summed up her behavior of the last couple of weeks.

Finally, he drove up. She tried to act calm and nonchalant. She couldn't pull it off. She ran unto the porch and jumped into his arms—

just like Sara always did. He caught her and kissed her as he walked through the door.

Sandy tactlessly interrupted the happy reunion by saying, "I have some steaks to grill. You want to stay for supper, Mike?"

He said, "Sure."

They sat down at the kitchen table, and Mike asked Maggie, "What did you do all weekend?"

She said, "Tortured myself with 'whys.'"

"Ys?" Mike asked, confused.

"Yeah, you know. Why did this happen to me? Why is Greg such a jerk? Why did I almost marry such a jerk? You know, same old, same old."

She decided to change the subject. "How was Columbus?"

"Cold and dreary." He almost added lonely, but he caught himself.

"You should have stayed here in California."

He wished he could have.

"I hear you and Sara went to visit Grandma Rose," he commented.

"Yeah, Michelle said it was all right," she said, wondering if he thought it was all right.

After their conversation last weekend, Mike had tried to take Sara to visit his grandma. But with the game on Wednesday and extra practices, he hadn't found time. Then he had had to leave town. But when he had called his grandma from Columbus, she had told him all about Maggie and Sara's visit. How they had stayed all morning and then ate lunch with her. Then Sara curled up on grandma's bed and took a nap right there. He hadn't heard Grandma Rose sound so happy for a long time—since, well, since Grandpa Willie died.

"You walked all the way over there?" asked Mike.

Maggie said, "Yeah, it was all right on the way there because Sara was so excited to see GG Rose. But the way back was tough. It's a long way for her to walk, and she's heavy. I can't carry her very far. Hey, you don't have a wagon for her anywhere, do you? We could go a lot more places if I could pull her in a wagon."

Sandy's phone rang. She answered and then handed the phone to Maggie. "It's your mom."

Maggie didn't look happy with that information.

"Hi, Mom."

"Have you called Greg?" her mom asked immediately.

"No."

"When are you going to call him?"

"I'm not."

"Margaret. He is not going to wait forever." Just what does she think he is waiting for? thought Maggie.

Maggie had one hand on the phone. With the other she rubbed her forehead. They had been over this before.

"I am not going to call him. I am not going to talk to him. I am not going to marry him."

Mike could only hear one side of the conversation, but he could guess the rest.

"Sandy says you are seeing some soccer player."

Maggie glared at Sandy.

"Yeah."

"Do soccer players make any money?"

"What? I don't know."

"Don't you think you should find out?"

"No."

"Why not?"

"Because I don't care." Maggie was getting exasperated.

"Your father has canceled your credit cards," announced her mother.

"I know." She had discovered that one day with a full cart at the grocery store. That was embarrassing.

"Well, what will you do for money without Greg then?"

"I have a job."

"How much can you be making babysitting for that soccer player's daughter?"

"It's not his daughter. It's his niece." This was getting them nowhere. "I gotta go, Mom."

"Margaret, relationships take compromise."

"What?"

"You and Greg can work this out if you are willing to compromise."

"Compromise?! He doesn't want to have kids, and I do. How do you compromise that—have half a baby?!" Maggie was talking quite loudly now.

"You can have a happy marriage without kids. Life may even be better without kids."

That statement was like an arrow to her heart. The pain felt so real that Maggie actually put her hand on her heart as if to stop the bleeding.

"I gotta go, Mom."

She closed the phone, threw it at Sandy, and said, "Don't ever do that again," through clenched teeth.

Maggie stalked to the bathroom and sat down on the closed lid of the toilet. What had her mom just said? Her marriage would have been better without kids. What kind of a mother tells her daughter that her life would have been better if she had never been born?

Maggie started sobbing. Sandy knocked on the door. "Are you all right?"

Maggie pleaded, "Just leave me alone. Please."

Maggie cried and cried. She had only had a few conversations with her mom since she called off the wedding. They had all been about her getting back together with Greg. Shouldn't her mom be on her side? Shouldn't her mom be mad at him for hurting her daughter? Shouldn't her dad be threatening to beat him up? But no, his only response was to cut her off financially. What a great family she had.

As the tears began to subside, Maggie stood up and looked into the mirror. She was tired of crying. She was tired of feeling miserable. She was tired of the whole stupid Debacle. She looked at her red, puffy eyes and her dirty hair in the ponytail. She decided this was the moment things changed. She couldn't change what happened, what other people did, or maybe even how she felt. But she could change her own behavior. From now on, no more dirty hair. She would take a shower now. And she would get up in time to take one every morning. So she got into the shower.

After her shower, she started to put her hair into a ponytail, then caught herself. No, she would dry her hair and even use her straightener so it looked nice. She could even put on a little makeup. If she wasn't going to cry anymore, she didn't have to be afraid to put mascara on.

In her room, she made another change. She had been wearing running shorts and T-shirts for a couple of weeks now. She always looked like she was on her way to the gym. Today, walking shorts and a shirt with a collar—and sandals instead of tennis shoes.

That felt better. OK, no more crying, no more talking to her mom for a while, no more thinking about Greg, no Daddy's credit cards, no more sleeping in the park, and no more hiding in the bathroom. She could do this…maybe. No, she could do this—probably. No, she was going to do this! She needed to get the book *The Little Engine That Could* and read it to Sara every day.

She was surprised to find Mike still there when she walked into the kitchen. He sure can take a lot of crazy, she thought. He was slicing cucumbers for the salad. Sandy was outside flipping the steaks. They smelled good!

"You're still here," she said.

Mike said, "I was offered a steak. I rarely turn down steak." He glanced at her and then did a double take. Wow, she looked good!

"Are you going somewhere?"

Maggie started slicing a tomato and answered, "No."

If he hadn't known better, he would never have guessed that she had been crying less than an hour ago. Well, her eyes were still a little puffy. He wondered what her mom said that had upset Maggie so much. He knew they were talking about Greg most of the time, but part of the time, it was about him. Was the thing that made Maggie cry about him or Greg?

"Are you all right?"

"Peachy."

"Do you want to talk about the phone call?"

"I don't remember any phone call." She smiled at him. "Weren't you telling me how horrible Columbus was?"

Supper was good. Good food. Good company. Good conversation. Mike talked about different places he had been to play soccer. Sandy talked about things she and Maggie had done in college. They were carefully avoiding subjects Maggie didn't want to talk about. So Maggie joined in talking mostly about stupid things Sandy had done. She had a million of those stories.

Finally, Mike asked Maggie, "I thought I would stop in to see my grandma. Want to go?"

Maggie smiled. "I would love to. GG Rose is such a sweetheart."

Mike said, "That's funny. That's exactly what she said about you!"

Grandma Rose was thrilled to see Mike. He leaned down to kiss her cheek and then said, "You remember Maggie."

Grandma Rose said, "Of course. Doesn't she look beautiful?"

Mike said, "Yes, she does."

Maggie ignored them both and told Grandma Rose, "You look nice. Did you get your hair cut?"

"Yes," answered Grandma Rose, "they have a sweet little girl who does it right here. She washed it, cut it, and curled it!"

"It looks great." Maggie smiled.

"How are you feeling?" asked Mike.

"Oh, I am exhausted! That physical therapist is like to kill me. Every day she makes me do more and more. She is never satisfied."

"She wants you to get better," said Maggie gently.

"Is it too much? Should I talk to her, Grandma?" asked Mike, concerned.

"Oh no, no. Don't mind me. I'm just grumpy. How was your trip, dear?"

Maggie sat in a chair and watched as Mike stood near his grandma's bed and told her about the game and the trip.

Finally, Mike said, "You look tired. We should go. Don't overdo it in therapy." He had already decided he would talk to the PT tomorrow. See how it was going.

Maggie said, "Bye, GG Rose."

Grandma Rose said to Maggie, "Will you please bring my baby Sara Rose to see me again soon?"

Maggie smiled. "Yes, I will."

Mike felt the need to jump in the shower before bed after his long day of traveling. When he came out, he found Maggie sitting on the floor, petting Jackson. She was talking to him, "I know. I missed you too. Did you have to stay here all by yourself? I should have come over and visited you."

She looked up. "Who feeds Jackson while you're gone?"

"My neighbor."

"He should come to my house next time. We could keep each other company until you get back."

"Your backyard isn't fenced in."

"He can stay in the house."

"I don't know. He's an outdoor dog." At least he used to be before Maggie started letting him in all the time.

Chapter 16

The next morning, Mike dropped Maggie off at Michelle's. He had a day off from training, so he planned to spend the morning working on Grandma Rose's roses. Then he could take Sara and Maggie with him to visit her. That way he could leave Sara with Maggie while he talked to the PT.

The roses needed a lot of work, so by the time he got to Michelle's, Maggie and Sara were already making lunch.

He asked, "What's on the menu?"

Sara said, "Blue eggs and ham."

"What?"

"Miss Maggie read me a book about green eggs and ham. She said we could have green eggs and ham for lunch, but I said I didn't want green eggs. I want blue!"

This should be interesting, thought Mike.

Maggie was standing at the counter cutting peppers. Mike thought, Maggie is going to try to get Sara to eat peppers. This I gotta see!

Sara said, "I want to help you cut the peppers, Miss Maggie."

Maggie said, "I'm sorry, but to cut peppers, you need to use a very sharp knife. It is not safe for kids. How about you get the eggs out?"

Mike jumped up. "I'll do it." He didn't want Sara to break eggs all over the place.

Maggie said, "Sara can do it."

Sara carefully got the eggs out of the refrigerator and placed them on the table.

Maggie said, "Can you find the ham cubes? We also need the milk and the salt and pepper."

Sara got everything Maggie asked for.

Maggie finished with the peppers. "OK, first we need to crack the eggs and put them in this bowl."

Maggie showed Sara how to crack the first egg, then Sara did the rest. Sara whisked the eggs while Maggie poured in the milk.

Maggie got the food coloring and asked Sara, "How many drops do you want?"

"Five."

They counted together, and Sara whisked some more.

Maggie asked, "How does it look?"

Sara said, "I want more blue."

"How many more drops?"

"Ten."

They counted together. Sara was satisfied with the color.

Maggie plugged in the electric frying pan. She carefully explained to Sara how it was going to get hot so she couldn't touch it.

Maggie poured the egg mixture into the pan and helped Sara carefully add the ham cubes. Maggie held the pan using an oven mitt and showed Sara how to gently stir the eggs. Sara was amazed and excited to see the egg mixture turn into scrambled eggs.

They all sat down to eat. Maggie had cut up a red pepper, an orange pepper, and a yellow pepper. Maggie said the orange peppers were her favorite and started to eat them. Mike was thinking he should get the ranch dressing—maybe then Sara would at least try the peppers. But before he could, he saw Sara take one of each. She tasted each one and decided she liked the red one the best. Then she asked, "Which one do you like best, Uncle Mike?"

Good job, Maggie!

As they finished eating, Mike said, "Let's go see GG Rose after lunch, OK?"

Maggie gave him a funny look.

Shoot, he forgot about nap time. "I mean after your nap."

He sat down on the couch while Maggie took Sara into the bedroom for her nap. He was tired from the morning of gardening. He could hear Maggie singing a little song to Sara. She must have made it up because he heard her sing the words "Sara Bug" in the middle of the song.

After Maggie got Sara down for her nap, she went into the living room. She started to say something to Mike but stopped when she realized he was asleep on the couch. He sure was cute—even with his eyes closed. He must be so tired with all the running around playing soccer. And the traveling. And taking care of Sara and Michelle and GG Rose. She certainly wasn't helping with all her emotional outbursts. Maybe it was time to stop feeling sorry for herself and start doing something to help him. She wasn't sure exactly what she could do, though. Well, at least she could let him sleep. The question was what she was going to do now. Sara usually slept for at least an hour—sometimes two. She wandered into Michelle's room. There was an ironing board set up in one corner and a basketful of very wrinkled clothes on the bed. She could do the ironing. It wasn't exactly helping Mike, but Michelle was pretty frazzled too. She finished a nurse's uniform and pulled out a shirt. What? thought Maggie, surprised. This is a man's shirt. Hmm, maybe Michelle had a friend. Sara's dad? Nobody ever talked about Sara's dad—even Sara—and Sara talked about everything! Maggie got the feeling the subject was off-limits, so she had never brought it up. But she had to wonder. Both Sara and Michelle's last name was Mallone. That probably meant that Michelle had never been married, right? But even if she never married Sara's dad, why didn't Sara have his last name? Maybe he didn't even know about Sara. That couldn't be it, could it? She also wondered who was really paying her. Michelle actually signed her checks, but she didn't have a job. Where was she getting the money? Child support from Sara's dad? But if he was paying child support, why didn't anyone mention him—good or bad? Was Mike really the one providing the money? She hoped that wasn't the case. That would be weird.

The ironing was finished. Maggie went into the laundry room. She put another load in the washer and took the clothes in the dryer into the bedroom. This was mostly Sara's stuff and some socks and underwear she didn't need to iron. She could fold it, though. She heard Sara getting up. She quietly called her in. Sara could put her own clothes away. She would leave Michelle's clothes on the bed. She felt like she had intruded enough. She didn't want to rifle through her drawers too!

"Shh, he is sleeping."

"No, he isn't," said Sara.

Mike woke up to Sara staring into his face.

"Snack time," announced Maggie.

"Come on, Uncle Mike. Let me show you what we are making," said Sara as she pulled on Mike.

At the table, she pointed to a picture in a kid's cookbook. "That one."

"Do you want bananas or strawberries?" asked Maggie.

Sara thought for a moment and said, "Both!"

Maggie gave her a butter knife, a banana, and several strawberries. Sara began cutting while Maggie got three juice glasses. Sara put bananas and strawberries in the bottom of each glass, then spooned in some yogurt.

"Maybe Uncle Mike wants more than that," commented Maggie.

"Do you want more than that, Uncle Mike?" asked Sara.

"Yes, please."

"Miss Maggie, what about the granola?"

"Oh no, I almost forgot!" exclaimed Maggie. She sprinkled granola on top.

"Do you like it, Uncle Mike?"

"Yes, it's delicious." Maggie sure had improved Sara's diet. She was eating all kinds of things he would have guessed she would never even try.

GG Rose was thrilled to see them. Mike went to find the PT. Sara jumped up into GG Rose's bed and started chatting about anything and everything. Maggie sat down and watched. Mike had such a nice, close family. She was so jealous.

Michelle was making supper when they got back—chicken nuggets and tater tots. Michelle went into her bedroom and came out with the man's shirt. She handed it to Mike.

"Thanks, Chel."

"Don't thank me. Apparently, the laundry fairy came this afternoon."

Maggie smiled as she got the leftover peppers out of the fridge.

Mike said to Sara, "Oh, I almost forgot. I got you a surprise!"

He took his shirt out to the car and came back in with a wagon.

"Yay, a wagon!!" exclaimed Sara.

"You found a wagon!" commented Maggie happily.

"You got her a wagon? You do realize this is a small apartment, right?" asked Michelle.

"I didn't mean for you to buy a wagon," said Maggie.

Mike told them both to relax and put Sara in the wagon and started pulling her around the apartment. Sara was giggling and giggling.

In the kitchen, Michelle said to Maggie, "Thanks for doing the ironing, but you didn't have to do that. You only need to watch Sara."

"It was nap time. Besides I have so much fun with Sara, I almost hate to take your money." Maggie left an opening for Michelle to tell her where the money came from.

Michelle didn't take it.

"Well, I don't know what I am going to do tonight. I thought I was going to spend all evening ironing."

"You should get some sleep. You look awful."

Michelle looked shocked. She said, "Thanks a lot!" sarcastically.

Maggie was undaunted. She said, "That's what friends are for. Sandy has been telling me the same thing for a couple of weeks now."

"Well, Sandy is right—you do look awful," Michelle retorted.

"Of course, I always tell Sandy to shut up!"

"No, you are the one who needs to shut up." Michelle smiled.

"You can't tell me to shut up. I just did all your ironing!"

On the way home, Mike said, "Thanks for ironing my shirt."

"Well, you're welcome, but I didn't think it was your shirt. I thought

MISS LORI

Michelle had a friend," Maggie said leaving an opening for him to tell her about Sara's dad.

"No, she doesn't." He didn't take the opening either. They really didn't want to talk about Sara's dad. She wasn't going to push. But someday it was going to come up.

Chapter 17

The next night Maggie and Mike sat on the couch in Maggie's house, kissing. Sandy was in the kitchen cooking supper. The doorbell rang. Sandy was expecting Brandon. She came running out of the kitchen, shouting, "I'll get it. I'll get it. Don't get up. Don't stop what you are doing!" She held her hand up, shielding her eyes as she passed the couch, laughing.

The smile left her face as she opened the door. She immediately locked the screen door so he couldn't get in.

"Margaret!" he shouted.

Maggie jumped up guiltily. She stood in the middle of the room, staring at the screen door and the man on the other side of it.

He yelled, "What are you doing?!"

Maggie couldn't seem to find her voice. She took a step backward.

"Who is he?!" demanded the man.

That made her mad. "None of your business," she answered gruffly. "What do you want, Greg?"

"I want to talk," he said, visibly trying to gain control.

"There's nothing to talk about."

"Margaret, come out here. I have something I want to say to you."

She wished he would go away, but she knew he wouldn't. She might as well get it over with.

She repeated, "What do you want?" as she opened the door and stepped out onto the porch.

She sat down on a chair, crossed her arms, and waited.

Sandy went over to the window to listen. Mike didn't know what to do. His first choice would be to go out onto the porch and punch Greg in the face. Why did she go out there with him? Why didn't she tell him to get out of there? Maybe she really wanted to see him. Maybe all this talk about never talking to him again was just an act. Maybe she had secretly been hoping that he would come back all along. Sandy shouldn't be listening at the window, but he got up to do the same. He regretted that decision when he saw Greg and Maggie kissing.

Maggie came in and found Sandy in the kitchen (where she had run when she saw Maggie getting ready to come in).

Maggie asked, "Where's Mike?"

"He left. Where's Greg?"

"He's gone."

"What happened?"

"He said he still wanted to get married. I said no. He left. Why did Mike leave?"

"Maybe he didn't like watching his girlfriend kissing her ex-fiancé."

Maggie furrowed her brow. "What are you talking about? I didn't kiss Greg. He kissed me. And it was just a good-bye kiss. Good-bye forever. Besides I'm not Mike's girlfriend."

"Well, he thinks you are."

"No, he doesn't."

"He told millions of people you were after the game in Columbus."

"That was just for the TV interview."

"What?"

"That's why he was calling all day Saturday. He knew they were going to ask about him kissing me when he was signing autographs. Did you know there was a video of that on the internet? He just wanted to call me his girlfriend. I guess it was the easiest explanation."

Sandy looked doubtful.

"I wonder why he left," thought Maggie out loud.

Sandy snuck into her room to call Mike.

"What? Are you calling to tell me she is back together with Greg?" grumbled Mike.

"No, Greg is gone. She's asking for you."

"So she can tell me she is getting back together with him?" He should have punched him when he had the chance.

"No, she sent him away."

"Right, then why was she kissing him?"

"She says it was a good-bye kiss and that it was Greg's idea."

Mike didn't answer.

"You know what else?" continued Sandy. "She doesn't think you meant it when you called her your girlfriend the other night on TV. Did you?"

"Of course, I did. That's why I called her to ask her to be my girlfriend."

"She thinks it was just for the TV interview."

Mike thought for a minute. "I'll be right over."

Mike had never considered himself a dumb jock until he met Maggie. He couldn't seem to figure her out. OK, the smart thing to do is to go back over there and let her tell him what happened with Greg. Maybe then he could figure out his next move.

Once he got back to Maggie's, she asked, "Where did you go?"

"Uh, I had to check on Jackson."

"Is he all right?"

"Yeah, so what happened with Greg?"

Maggie glanced toward the kitchen. Brandon was in there with Sandy. She didn't seem to want to talk in front of him.

"Let's go for a walk," suggested Mike.

As they walked down the sidewalk, Maggie started, "I really didn't think he would come back."

"What did he say?" Mike hoped he didn't regret asking that question.

"He said he was willing to get the vasectomy reversed and that he still wanted to get married."

Oh no, thought Mike. That was exactly what she wanted. Now she could marry Greg and have kids. This was bad.

MISS LORI

"He sounded like he was making a business deal," continued Maggie. "He said we could have one baby as long as I promised to leave the kid with a nanny when he wanted to travel."

"What did you tell him?"

"That I didn't think he should get the vasectomy reversed. That it was the right thing for him to do because he should never have children. Then I told him good-bye."

Mike hated to say this, but it was better to deal with this now. Get everything out in the open. "Are you sure, Maggie? It sounds like he was offering you everything you wanted."

Maggie was adamant. "No, he wasn't. I don't want to have kids with someone who doesn't want kids. He would be a terrible father." Pause. "You know what I can't figure out is why I ever wanted to marry him in the first place."

Mike had to admit he had blown this girlfriend thing. He had thought she understood that he really meant it—especially since she was obviously happy to see him when he got back. But when he thought about that quick phone conversation, he could see how she misunderstood. That was no way to ask a girl to be your girlfriend anyway. He would do it again, and this time he would get it right. He wondered if she would say yes.

Chapter 18

Mike was pretty nervous as he walked up to Maggie's front door. He was wearing dress pants and the shirt that Maggie had ironed. At first, he didn't think he could convince her to go out to a nice restaurant with him. She just kept asking why. He finally said there was a new place he wanted to try. Then he had had to find a new place.

Soccer was so much easier than this. Sure, there was a lot of running involved. It was physically exhausting. Sometimes you got kicked and bruised. There was sweat, pain, and sometimes even blood. And if you lost, it was frustrating. But at least there were rules to the game. Where Maggie was involved, if there were rules, he had no idea what they were!

Maggie came to the door looking simply beautiful. Simply was the key word. Just a sundress and sandals. Her hair was down and straightened. She was a natural beauty without even trying.

He said, "You look beautiful."

She ignored the compliment and said, "Who are you? I was expecting this guy in soccer shorts." She looked around him. "Oh well, you're kinda cute. I guess you'll do!"

Mike laughed.

At the restaurant, Maggie was in a good and very chatty mood. She was telling him all about the last two days with Sara. They had used the wagon to go to a different park, one that was farther away from Michelle's apartment. They found a bush that was swarming with ladybugs. That prompted a trip to the library, of course. She was telling him how wonderful it was to have the wagon. Sara could ride in it when she got tired, but Maggie could also put the books in it so she didn't have to carry them home from the library. Today they had used the wagon to go visit GG Rose. Sara had drawn all kinds of pictures of ladybugs to decorate GG Rose's room. On the way home, they stopped at the grocery store to get ingredients for the recipes that Sara wanted to try from the kid's cookbook—one of which was ladybug cupcakes. She didn't even have to worry about how many groceries she got because she could just put them in the wagon!

After dinner, he decided to broach the subject that prompted him to bring her there. She was so happy tonight. He hoped he wasn't about to ruin it.

"Maggie, I wanted to ask you something."

"What?" she asked, taking a spoonful of the crème brûlée they had gotten to share. "This is good. You should taste it."

He wasn't sure quite what to say—or how to get her attention now that she was so intent on eating the dessert.

He grabbed her hand before she could get the next spoonful to her mouth. She looked at him. "I wanted to ask. Will you be my girlfriend?"

"You mean for real?"

"Yeah." He waited holding his breath.

She put the spoonful of crème brûlée into her mouth as she looked thoughtfully into his eyes. She smiled and said, "OK."

"Really, you really want to be my girlfriend?" he asked hopefully.

Her smile grew bigger as she said, "Yes, I do."

He exhaled, picked up a spoon, and started eating crème brûlée.

After a couple more bites, Maggie asked, "So what exactly is involved in being Mike Mallone's girlfriend? I mean, I'm sure it means cheering for you at all your games."

"Naturally."

"What else?"

"Well, no more kissing Greg."

Hmm, thought Maggie, maybe that did bother him. "Agreed."

"And you have to wear this." He gave her a small jewelry box. She opened it to find a heart necklace with M & M engraved on it.

"M & M," she whispered.

"Mike and Maggie."

She put it on and asked, "How does it look?"

The sunburn she had gotten the day they met had turned into a deep California tan. The gold necklace accented it nicely. "Perfect," he said.

"Thanks," she said softly.

"How about me—what do I need to do to deserve you as a girlfriend?"

"Ummm, you're doing all right. Just keep doing what you're doing." Pause. "Well, that kissing thing should apply to you too."

"Right, I promise not to kiss Greg."

"Good, because that would definitely be a deal breaker!" she laughed.

"I have one more thing for you." He pulled out another box and laid it in the middle of the table.

She stared at it.

He said, "You can open it."

She didn't make a move. "I don't want you to buy me presents."

Here we go again, thought Mike. Would someone please explain the rules of Maggie to him? "Why not?"

"You know I don't have any money. I can't reciprocate."

"I don't care."

"I do. Please don't buy me things."

What girl doesn't want her boyfriend to buy her presents? He started to say, "I just gave you a necklace. Isn't that a present?" But he was afraid she would give it back, so he decided on a different approach.

He opened the package and pulled out a cell phone. Maybe if she saw it, she would want it.

"You know I can't afford a monthly cell phone bill." She looked miffed.

"You don't have to pay a monthly bill. I put you on my plan."

"Oh, well, then, definitely no."

This was getting frustrating. But he wasn't about to give up.

Miss Lori

"Michelle is already on my plan, so it cost virtually nothing to add you. Plus, I just got a new phone, and it was buy one get one free."

"So you are saying this present cost you nothing."

"Basically yes." OK, that was a lie, but what could he say?

"Then I don't want it because you are cheap."

And you are a pain!

"Look, what if you are out somewhere with Sara and there's an emergency and you need to call for help?"

"I live in LA. Everybody has a phone."

Everybody but you.

"You know, sometimes Michelle needs to talk to you."

"She can call you. I'm always with you."

"Not during the day when you are with Sara."

Maggie looked away. Good, thought Mike, this is working.

"And, you know, I'd like to be able to call my girlfriend when I'm out of town."

"So you are saying this is not a present for me. It is for you and Sara and Michelle."

"Right."

She picked up the phone. "OK, but only if you promise not to buy me anything else."

"Maggie."

She started to give him back the phone.

"OK, all right. Look, I already programmed in your favorites, me, Michelle, and Sandy. Do you want me to put anyone else in—your mom, maybe?"

"No. I'm not going to call her. And I don't want her to call me. Besides it's only for incoming calls."

"No, it isn't. You have unlimited minutes."

"Really unlimited minutes for free? That's quite a deal you got there."

He knew he wasn't fooling her. He just wanted her to have a phone because he was going out of town again.

On the way home, Mike asked, "Can you drive a stick?"

"Yep, my car was a standard."

"Car? You have a car?"

"I don't have a car. I had a car."

"What happened to it?"

Why does everything always have to lead back to my former life? thought Maggie. "Greg sold it."

"Why?"

Big exhale. "Well, he said he didn't want me to drive all the way to Phoenix all by myself. So he wanted to sell it here, and then he would buy me a new one when we got to Phoenix. But I think there were other reasons in play."

"Like?"

"Well, Greg is pretty snooty. He probably didn't think it was dignified enough."

"What kind was it?"

"A Mustang—I loved that car. It was so fun to drive. But also, Greg couldn't drive it. He can't drive a stick—which I did not think was funny before, but now I find it hilarious! What kind of a man can't drive a stick?!"

Mike smiled. "I guess you could have taught him."

"I didn't see him that much. Only on weekends. He lived two hours away. Besides I don't think it bothered him that he couldn't drive a stick. It bothered him that I had a car he couldn't drive."

"What happened to the money?"

"I spent it on the wedding that never was."

"All of it?"

"It was a very expensive wedding. I owe my mom and dad a bundle of money for calling it off. My mom likes to remind me of that when she calls."

"Did you used to have a phone too?"

"Yep."

"Did Greg sell that too?"

"Nooo."

"Let me guess—you threw it into the ocean."

"Now why would I do that? Do you think I'm crazy?"

Mike gave her a look that said he was sure she was.

"Actually," said Maggie, "I gave it away. One of the kids in my class had a single mom. Her phone broke. She couldn't afford to get a new one. So I gave her mine. My contract had already run out at the beginning of February. Greg was going to get me a new phone and add me to his plan when we got to Phoenix."

"He left you without a phone for over a month. Why didn't he do it right away?"

"I don't know. I guess he was busy."

"Wait, he lived two hours away. He only saw you on weekends. And you didn't have a phone for over a month. Didn't that bother him?"

"He could always call Sandy's phone. Besides he didn't call that much. Only to make plans if we were getting together on the weekend."

"If?"

Maggie was starting to get uncomfortable.

"Doesn't it strike you as strange that your fiancé didn't want to be able to call you?"

"It didn't at the time," mumbled Maggie.

Mike couldn't believe this guy. Why did he make her get rid of all her stuff? And why didn't he make sure she had a phone? Mike had only been away from Maggie for a couple of days last weekend, and it almost drove him crazy not to be able to talk to her.

Anyway, back to the reason he had asked her about driving a stick in the first place.

"I was thinking. I'm going out of town tomorrow," began Mike.

"Again?" Not again. She hated it when he went out of town. Wait, she couldn't let him know that. She hardly knew him. Wait, she hardly knew her own boyfriend? Something was wrong here.

"Yeah, if you want, you can use my Jeep while I'm gone."

"What? You would let me drive your Jeep?"

"Sure, it would be easier on you and Michelle."

"I don't think this is a good idea."

"Why not? Don't you like my Jeep?"

"Your Jeep is very cool."

"Do you remember how to drive a standard?"

"It was only a month ago. I think I can remember." Wait, it was only a month ago. Warning bells were going off in her head.

"I don't understand. What's the problem?"

What was the problem? "I'm doing all right without a car. It's only a few days that you'll be gone, right?"

"Ten."

"What?"

"Ten days. I will be gone ten days."

"That's a long time! Where are you going?" asked Maggie, shocked and dismayed.

"We are playing three road games: DC, Toronto, and Kansas City."

No, no, no. This was not good. Ten days without him meant ten days of obsessing about her old life. She couldn't do this. Wait, she couldn't go ten days without him? She had only known him for a couple of weeks. Wait, she had only known him for a couple of weeks, and now she was his girlfriend. She touched the necklace around her neck. She was getting too dependent on him. This was bad.

Mike could feel it coming. She was definitely going to go crazy on him again. What would it be this time?

They got to Mike's house and went inside. See, thought Maggie, I am spending every night here. I shouldn't be doing that. But I can't stop. I tried that before. It didn't work. It was too early to be his girlfriend. Maybe that was what was bothering her. It was only a couple of weeks ago that she was going to get married to some other guy.

"I was thinking," started Maggie.

No, Maggie, thought Mike, don't start thinking. "That could be dangerous," he joked.

She didn't laugh. She was still fingering the necklace. "I should give you this necklace back."

"Why?" he asked.

"I just should."

"You don't want to be my girlfriend?" His frustration was starting to show.

"No, it's not that. It…it…it isn't fair—to you."

"How so?" He wasn't going to panic just yet.

"You know I haven't figured this Greg thing out yet."

"I know."

"Well, I probably should figure it out first, don't you think?"

"No. Maggie, all I am asking is that you don't see anyone but me while you figure it out. Can you do that?"

"Well, yeah, but I think—"

"Maggie," interrupted Mike, "don't think."

Chapter 19

Maggie went with Mike to the stadium so he could catch the team bus. He got out of the Jeep and grabbed his bag. She walked around the back as well. He handed her keys to his Jeep and to his house. She was going to use the Jeep and be in charge of Jackson.

"Are you sure you want to do this?" she asked.

"Why? Are you a bad driver?"

"No, I am an excellent driver. But you do have insurance, right?"

"Should I be worried you are going to wreck my Jeep?"

"This cool Jeep? No way. You should be worried that I will run off in it!"

"I'm not too worried. You don't have any gas money."

"How far could I get on one tank of gas?"

"You can go as far as you want as long as you are back here to pick me up a week from Sunday!"

That put an end to the kidding around. He kissed her and then walked off toward the bus. She missed him already.

They lost the game on Saturday in DC. Mike was in a crummy mood. At least he could call Maggie.

"Hi, Maggie."

"Hi."

"Did you see the game?"

"Yeah." Maggie was worried. This was the first time they had lost since she met him. She had no idea how he reacted to losing or what she was supposed to say.

"So what are you doing?" he asked changing the subject.
"Just thinking."
"I thought I told you not to do that!"
"Come here and stop me!"
"Where are you?"
"I'm at your house. Is that all right?"
"Sure."
"You know, Maggie, we have a saying, 'It is what it is.' Sometimes you have a bad game. But once the whistle blows, it's over. There is nothing you can do to change it."

OK, so he gets philosophical when he loses. Good to know.

Mike continued, "It isn't always easy to stop thinking about it. But you have to believe me when I tell you it doesn't help to obsess about it."

Wait, maybe he wasn't talking about the game.

Maggie said, "OK, but don't you have to think about it? You know, figure out what went wrong so you don't make the same mistakes again."

"True, but that's just one training session. You look at the tape. Acknowledge your mistakes from the last game. Then you start looking forward to the next game."

"What if you don't know what you did wrong? How do you keep from doing it again?"

"Maybe you didn't do anything wrong. Maybe it just wasn't meant to be."

OK, soccer wisdom. Let's try it on for size, thought Maggie after the phone call. It is what it is. She was not going to marry Greg. She could accept that. She was not going to move to Phoenix. She could accept that. She would not have a four-bedroom house. She could accept that. It was never about the money. She was poor now. OK, that one was harder. But she was doing all right. She could accept that. She would never get her car back. She gritted her teeth. She didn't like that one. She missed that car. But, OK, she could accept that. She owed her mom and dad a bunch of money. Wait, why did she have to accept that? It wasn't her idea to have a big fancy wedding. Four hundred people were supposed to go to that wedding. She didn't even know most of them. Her mom and dad wanted that big wedding. Still did. Why did they still want her to marry him? Why did they like him so much? All of a sudden, she understood. It was so clear. Why didn't she realize this before?

The Wednesday game went better. They won. Mike called Maggie. "Did you see the game?"

"Of course! Congratulations!"

"Sometimes after a bad game, you come back even stronger."

More soccer wisdom. Maggie liked that.

"Where are you?" asked Mike.

"I watched the game at your house."

"Why didn't you watch at Michelle's?"

"Well, Sandy watched at Brandon's house. She's been spending most of her time with him." (Brandon was hurt, so he hadn't traveled with the team.) "I didn't want to have to go home alone in the dark, so I just watched here."

"All by yourself."

"No. I am here with my good friend Mr. Jackson." What? thought Mike. Who is this guy, and why is he at my house?

"We have been hanging out all week. Had some great conversations. He's a really good listener. I don't think he likes soccer much, though. He fell asleep on the floor during the game."

"Maggie!"

"Don't worry. I don't let him anywhere near the bed."

"What?!"

Maggie laughed. "Mike, you do know I'm talking about your dog, right?"

"Of course." No, he didn't, but he was never going to admit it.

Maggie laughed and laughed. "You thought I brought some guy over here to your house to watch you play soccer!!"

"I did not," he said weakly.

"OK, just for the record. I wouldn't do that." She laughed again. "And if I did, I wouldn't be stupid enough to tell you!"

He did not enjoy that conversation. The only way to describe his reaction was crazy jealous—of his dog. He needed to get himself together.

OK, he had time to pay some bills online.

Maggie seemed to be in an especially good mood—making fun of him and all. She usually wasn't that happy when she spent so much time alone—no, Jackson didn't count. Maybe something happened. Maybe she wasn't as alone as she wanted him to think. Maggie wouldn't lie to him, would she? Wasn't she missing him? He was certainly missing her. If she was lonely, what would she do? Call Greg? It was certainly within the realm of possibility that she was using the phone he bought her to call Greg. Maybe they had been talking all week, remembering all the good times. Would he get home from this long road trip to find that she had run off to Phoenix in his Jeep? OK, now he was just being crazy.

He found the phone bill online. Would it be spying on her to see who she was calling? He was paying the bill—he certainly could look at it! Now he just felt stupid. She hadn't called anyone—not even Michelle or Sandy. There was only one person calling her over and over again. Him. Wow, he called her a lot. Was it considered stalking if it was your own girlfriend?

Chapter 20

The game in Kansas City was good. The weather was bad. It was even worse the next day when the team was trying to fly home. Thunderstorms with lightning. The flight had already been delayed several times. He wasn't going to get home until late. He called Maggie to tell her to leave the Jeep at the stadium. Sandy could go with her and give her a ride home. He knew Maggie wouldn't want to pick him up in the dark.

They had already been waiting in this airport for hours. Looked like he had even more time to just sit and think. His thoughts turned to Maggie, of course. He tried to imagine what it was like for her. She had thought she was going to marry a rich guy. He was going to give her a big house, a car, pretty much anything she wanted. She was expecting to live on easy street. She voluntarily gave it all up. Now she had no car, no money, nothing. She certainly wasn't living on easy street. How tempting would it be for her to give in and call Greg? He would probably get her on the next flight to Phoenix. Add to that the pressure that her parents were putting on her to marry Greg. No wonder she acted a little crazy now and then. He wished he could get home to her and see how she was. She sounded pretty happy every time he called. He wondered if she thought he was calling too much, but she always picked up right away, except once yesterday. But then she called right back and explained that she had been driving. She actually pulled over, called him back, and sat in a parking lot talking to him for almost an hour. He would be happy to play some home games for a while.

It was the middle of the night, but he was finally back in town. He wondered where Maggie was. Wherever she was, she was asleep. He wasn't going to call and wake her up. She probably went back to her house with Sandy after dropping off the Jeep. That would make sense. Still, as he drove up to his house, he looked for signs. The porch light was on. Maybe she was here! Wait, she could have just left it on knowing that he would be home late. Inside, the afghan was strewn across the couch as if someone had been sleeping there recently. Had she been waiting up for him? That could have happened before she took the Jeep too. Then he heard a tapping noise coming down the stairs. Jackson was in the house! That had to mean she was here! He bounded up the stairs, Jackson in tow. There she was sleeping in his bed! He quietly slipped in next to her. She woke up and said, "Good, you're home," put her head on his chest, and went back to sleep. He could get used to this—coming home to Maggie.

Mike woke up to the smell of bacon. He looked at the clock: 10:00 a.m. Maggie walked in with breakfast on a tray.

"That smells great. I'm starving!"

"I know—your stomach was growling so loud this morning, it woke me up!"

"Sorry."

"Well, it wasn't only that. Jackson wanted to go outside too."

"Jackson is supposed to sleep outside."

"He told me he didn't want to be an outside dog anymore. He gets lonely out there."

"He told you this?"

"Yes, he also said he wants to cuddle with me on the couch when I can't sleep."

"Oh yeah?"

"And he wants to sleep on the bed with me, but only when you're not here."

"Maggie, did you let him sleep in the bed?"

"No."

"Maggie."

"I didn't! I didn't let him sleep on the bed." Maggie paused and then finished quickly, "I did let him sit on the couch. But I vacuumed the dog hair off so you wouldn't know."

Then she laughed and said, "I guess if I didn't want you to know, I shouldn't have told you."

He smiled. "Inside, OK. On the couch occasionally, but only if you brush him. Bed, no."

"OK."

"Where's Sara?"

"Michelle has been fighting a cold all week. She decided to stay home from school today."

"Sara is with her?"

"Yeah, I told her I would still watch Sara so she could sleep, but she wanted to keep her."

Good, he had Maggie all to himself.

His phone rang at about three o'clock in the afternoon.

Sandy said, "Hey, you two out of bed yet?"

Well, no. Mike said, "What's up, Sandy?"

"I was just wondering if you and Maggie wanted to come over for supper tonight."

"What did Maggie say?"

"I didn't ask her. You know she is going to do whatever you tell her to. I decided to skip the middleman."

What did that mean? "Yeah, sure, about six o'clock?"

"See you then."

What was that all about? Maybe Sandy didn't want to drive all the way out to the stadium last night so Maggie could drop off the Jeep.

Maggie came back from the bathroom and crawled into bed. She snuggled in and asked, "Who was that?"

"Sandy, she asked us over for supper."

"Are we going?"

"Yeah, I mean, if you want to."

"Whatever you want to do."

"Is Sandy mad at me for some reason?"

"I don't know. I hardly talked to her this week."

"Why not?"

"She spent all her time taking care of Brandon."

Supper was good. Maggie ate a couple of helpings of everything. He wondered if she hadn't been eating while he was gone. Brandon looked healthy and rested. He said he was ready to go for the next game. Mike guessed that Sandy had taken good care of him. Sandy was her same old, happy, flirty, entertaining self. Maybe he was just paranoid.

Dessert was huge fudge brownies with ice cream and hot fudge. Delicious.

After supper, Mike and Maggie stopped by GG Rose's house. He felt guilty about spending all day in bed with Maggie. He should have been here working on the roses. He dreaded seeing what condition the roses were in. He wanted to take care of them himself, but that probably wasn't realistic. He was going to have to hire someone.

Maggie ran out in front of him and turned around at the first rose bed. She flung her arms wide and shouted, "Surprise!"

He stared at the perfectly tended roses. Not a weed in sight. He smiled at her. "You did all this?"

"Me and Sara."

"So you are also an expert gardener?"

"Nope, don't know a thing about roses. I was carefully supervised at every step."

"By?"

"GG Rose, of course."

"How did she do that?"

"Well, one day Sara and I went to visit GG Rose. But we stopped by her house on the way to water the roses. Sara picked the prettiest ones so we could bring them to her."

"That was nice."

"Well, I thought so, but then GG Rose was kind of sad. She said, 'I wish I could see my roses.' Well, one of the nurses heard her. She told me I could sign her out if I wanted to and take her to her house. I asked

Michelle, and she said it was OK. So the next day, Sara, GG Rose, and I went to her house, and we worked on the roses all day."

"Well, haven't you been busy?"

"Some nice guy lent me his Jeep. You can get so much more done when you have transportation."

"Thanks, Maggie."

"It was a team effort. Should we pick some now and bring them to her?"

"Yeah."

Maggie went to the shed and found the shears. She walked over to a huge rose bush covered with pink rose buds. She said, "This one is my favorite."

"That's the one that Grandpa Willie and Grandma Rose planted the day Michelle and I were born," said Mike.

Maggie smiled at him. "I know."

Chapter 21

The next evening, Mike walked in his front door. He had stayed at practice later than usual. Maggie was already there. Michelle had come home early and brought Maggie over.

"There you are," she said brightly.

She sure was happy lately.

"What are you doing?" asked Mike.

"I'm making supper. You eat too much fast food. I read that you should be eating fish."

"Where did you read that?"

"On the internet. Did you know your team has a website?"

"Yeah." He didn't know that she knew.

"Anyway, the trainer said you should eat fish and vegetables. So I got fish and vegetables. Problem is I don't know how to cook fish. Sandy always does the cooking at our house. And she doesn't cook fish. And I don't know how to cook anything unless it's in a kid's cookbook. Do you know how to cook fish?"

"Yeah, I'll put it on the grill."

"Great!"

She had bought a lot of groceries. "Let me pay you for the food."

"That's all right."

He knew she didn't have much money. "You don't have to buy food for me to eat. Let me pay you back."

"I eat your food all the time."

"And I eat at your house all the time."

"Then we're even."

She was frustrating.

He came back in from lighting the grill. "I was thinking. I was going to hire someone to take care of Grandma's roses."

"You don't have to do that. I'll take care of them."

"That would be great. I'll pay you."

"Michelle already pays me."

"That's for watching Sara. This would be for the roses."

"But I do that while I watch Sara."

"I want to pay you."

"No."

"I am going to pay someone—either you or somebody else."

"Then get somebody else."

Silence.

He took the fish out to the grill.

The fish and vegetables were very good and very healthy. Halfway through the meal, Maggie finally broke the silence. "I figured out why I was going to marry Greg."

"You did?" he asked uneasily.

"It's kind of a long story. Do you want to hear it?"

"Does it end, 'And that is why I am going back to him'?"

Maggie snorted, "Of course not."

"Then I want to hear it."

She took a deep breath and started, "My parents never wanted to have kids." She paused.

Wow, she is starting before she was born, thought Mike. This really was going to be a long story—and a painful one from the look on Maggie's face.

She continued, "My dad owns his own business. He works about eighty hours a week. My mom works for a big company as kind of an events planner. They have conferences all over the world. She makes all the arrangements. All these fancy resorts want their business, so she gets complimentary trips to all sorts of places.

"My mom and dad love to travel. That's pretty much all they do—work and travel.

"So they weren't all that happy when I came along. But as far as I can tell, I didn't really slow them down much. They still worked. I stayed with a babysitter. They still traveled. I stayed with a babysitter.

"I met Sandy on the first day of kindergarten. We became best friends right away.

"Pretty soon my mom decided I didn't need a babysitter because I was always at Sandy's house. I was a latch key kid by the time I was seven."

Mike could see the loneliness in her face and hear it in her voice.

"By the time I was twelve, they didn't bother with a babysitter even when they went out of town. They just left me some money until I was old enough to use a credit card. Once I got the credit card, I could buy anything I wanted. My dad never even asked me about what I bought; he just paid the bill.

"The day I turned sixteen, I came home, and there was a brand-new car in the driveway. I went into the house, and my dad handed me the keys. I was so happy until I tried to drive it. I went back inside and said, 'Dad, I don't know how to drive a standard.' He said, 'You don't?' like he was really surprised. I asked, 'Will you teach me?' He said, 'Oh, I don't have time for that. Just find yourself a class. I'll pay for it.'"

She paused, thinking.

"Anyway, Sandy has four brothers—two older and two younger. Sandy's oldest brother, the nice one, had taught us both to drive in the first place in their family car. Sandy is older than me, so she got her license first. Then she drove me to get my license.

"There weren't any classes to learn to drive a standard. So the car sat in the driveway for over a month. Sandy's oldest brother was back at college by then, so Sandy had to bribe her next oldest brother. He isn't as nice. He wanted to go out with this girl, but she wouldn't go out with him because he didn't have a car. Sandy made a deal with him. He could tell her my car was his, if he taught us to drive it."

Maggie paused, lost in thought again. Mike waited. He wanted to let her tell the story her way—at her own pace.

"Anyway, I survived. Sandy and I went to college. When I was a sophomore, I met Greg at a reception for this professor that we could go to to get extra credit for a class. He must have called me for a month before I agreed to go out with him."

Mike asked, "Why didn't you want to go out with him?"

Maggie thought about the real reason but then just said, "Uh, I guess he didn't ask me to do anything I wanted to do. We dated for a while. I didn't even know he was rich until he took me home to meet his parents at the mansion. Then he asked to meet my parents. They loved him from the minute he walked in the door. Things got way better with my parents after that. All of a sudden, my mom was calling me and asking how everything was going. She was constantly asking about Greg and inviting us to the house."

Maggie smirked. "I thought that it was because I had grown up. They didn't have any use for me as a kid, but now that I was an adult, it was all good."

Maggie stared off into space. They had finished eating but were still sitting at the table. Mike put his hand on Maggie's. Maggie jumped like she had forgotten that he was there.

"Greg asked me to marry him on Thanksgiving at my parents' house. Turns out he had told my parents and his before he even asked me. Our moms had already been planning the wedding for a month.

"But when I agreed, I really meant it. It wasn't because he was rich or because my parents liked him. I wanted to marry him."

Maggie looked at Mike. She was back in the present again. She continued, "Then the other day, I was talking to Jackson about it."

"Jackson?" he asked.

"Yeah, he really helped me work this out. I was talking to Jackson, and I realized. Greg is just like my dad. My dad had always bought me anything and everything. But he never spent time with me or talked to me. Shoot, for my sixteenth birthday, he bought me a car I couldn't drive! Greg was the same way. He never called me just to talk. He didn't want to hear about my day. He hated it when I tried to tell him things that happened at the preschool. He didn't care that it was important to me to have kids. He probably didn't even know."

"So basically, you were going to marry your dad," said Mike summing it all up.

"Yeah, I guess I could have just told you that. Sorry I rambled on for so long."

"That's OK. I didn't know all that stuff about you growing up. It doesn't seem like I know much about you at all."

"That's funny. I know a lot about you."

"Oh, you think you do, huh?"

"I have heard stories."

"From who? Sara?"

"And GG Rose. According to her, you were quite the little rascal growing up."

Mike looked embarrassed.

"Yep, all the while I was working on the roses, GG Rose told me 'my little Mikey' stories. Like how you rode your bike off the front porch and needed stitches. And how you broke the window playing baseball and tried to blame it on the neighbor kid."

Mike smiled, remembering. "I didn't break it."

"So it really was the neighbor kid?" asked Maggie, surprised.

"No, Michelle did it."

Maggie looked doubtful. "How come GG Rose thinks it was you, then?"

"That's what we told her. Michelle was scared that Grandpa Willie was going to spank her. So we tried to blame it on the kid next door. But Grandma Rose didn't believe us. So I said it was me."

Maggie thought, Oh, how sweet. "Did he spank you?"

"No, I wish. He didn't let me play in the baseball game that night. Even worse—he made me go watch but not play."

"Ohh," Maggie sympathized.

"But the next day he showed me how to replace a window." He used to love working with Grandpa Willie. "Which came in handy. I have broken several windows playing baseball."

MISS LORI 117

"I guess baseball is not your sport. Why didn't Michelle confess so that you could play in the game?"

"She wanted to, but I talked her out of it. They wouldn't have believed us anyway. They would have thought she was covering for me. It was much more believable that I did it."

"Poor little Mikey," said Maggie.

"Please don't call me that," he groaned.

"Why not? I think it's cute how GG Rose calls you my little Mikey!" teased Maggie.

Mike gave her a warning look.

"All right, all right. I'll make you a deal. I won't call you Mikey if you never call me Margaret."

"Why not?"

"I hate being called Margaret. That's what my mom always calls me—and Greg. It sounds so snooty."

If that's what Greg called her, then he never would. "You don't look like a Margaret. You look like a Maggie."

"That's funny—you look like a Mikey," Maggie teased. He didn't look amused, so she said, "OK, OK, never again!"

"Did GG Rose tell you any other stories?"

"Yeah, tons! But I get the feeling that Michelle has the best stories."

"Why do you think that?"

"Because every time she starts to tell one, she looks at Sara and stops. It must be good if she can't tell it in front of Sara. One of these days, she and I are going to have to hang out without Sara."

Mike thought that would be a good idea. Not so Michelle could tell stories about him—it seemed like Maggie was hearing enough of those, but Michelle could use a friend like Maggie.

They cleared the table and did the dishes together. Maggie was quiet until she said, "The one thing that Jackson and I didn't figure out was why Greg wanted to marry me."

Mike looked surprised. She really didn't know, did she? Should he tell her?

118 Wake Up!

Chapter 22

Maggie was busy with Jackson. First, she fed him. Then she sat down on the floor in front of the couch to brush him. As she did, she talked to him. She explained that if she brushed all the extra hair off of him, then he could sit on the couch and watch TV with her. She apologized that he wouldn't be able to sleep on the bed with her. It sounded a lot like a conversation. He was starting to believe that Jackson actually did tell her things.

He was surprised by the story of her childhood. He never would have guessed that she was a rich kid. He assumed that she had always lived like she did now paycheck to paycheck. She sure didn't act like a spoiled rich kid. She actually was kind of weird about money. She wouldn't let him buy her presents. She wouldn't let him pay for groceries. She wouldn't let him pay her to work on the roses. What was all that about?

He stopped to watch her brushing Jackson. How could she not know why Greg wanted to marry her? She was so beautiful. Any guy would be thrilled to walk into a restaurant with her on his arm. Clearly that was what Greg liked to do. Take her out and show her off. The night that Mike had taken her to the new, fancy restaurant, Maggie had said that it wasn't all that new. She had already been there with Greg. She listed off dozens of fancy (or snooty, as she called them) restaurants that he had taken her to.

The question was if he should tell her. He saw the looks that she got everywhere they went. There was always some guy opening the door for her or trying to get her attention somehow. He was constantly pulling her close so that the other guys would know that she was with him. He hated to let her out of his sight. But, as he thought about it, he realized, she never noticed any of them. Even if they had met before, like the guy at the In-N-Out Burger, she never remembered them. Come to think of it, she pretty much ignored him whenever he complimented her too. That was kind of rude. At least she could say thank you. Maybe she had just heard it so many times before. But if that was the case, then why did she think the guy from In-N-Out Burger was interested in Sandy? Was it possible that she didn't know how beautiful she was?

Now he was really in a quandary. This could really work to his advantage. He went out of town a lot. He liked that she spent her time with Jackson while he was playing away games. If he didn't tell her that she was beautiful, maybe she would just stay home waiting for him. That way there was much less chance of her meeting someone else. But how could he not tell her? He wanted to tell her. He wanted to tell her every day. Plus, he knew how obsessive she was. She would drive herself crazy trying to figure out why Greg wanted to marry her. He could tell her and save her the pain.

She finished brushing Jackson, and she sat down on the couch. Jackson jumped up on the couch and snuggled up beside her. Mike sat down on the other side. Maggie took the remote and pointed it at the TV. Mike took the remote out of her hand and said, "I know why Greg wanted to marry you."

Maggie looked at him skeptically. "How would you know that?"

"Because I'm a guy."

Maggie gave him a look of utter disbelief. She said, "Please," and took the remote back.

Mike took the remote and threw it behind the couch. "It's because you're beautiful."

Maggie rolled her eyes at him and tried to reach over the back of the couch for the remote.

Mike grabbed her and pulled her into his lap. "You are beautiful. That's why he wanted to marry you. That's why he took you to fancy restaurants to show you off. Didn't he ever tell you you were beautiful?"

Maggie struggled to get up. He wouldn't let her. "Yeah, right before he told me to go change clothes because what I was wearing wasn't snooty enough." She smirked.

Mike could tell she didn't like this subject, but he didn't know why.

"We didn't only go to fancy restaurants, you know."

"What else did you do?"

"Mostly we went to these big charity events with his parents."

"That you had to get all dressed up for?"

Maggie regretted bringing that subject up. "You don't know how long it took Greg's mom to get me to look good enough to go to those things."

Mike let her up. She sat next to him on the couch. She continued, "It was an all-day ordeal. She would take me to this spa. You know, at first, I thought, Cool, I get to go to the spa. But that got old quick." Maggie stared off into space, remembering the comments she had overheard at that spa. "She's awfully skinny, isn't she?" and "Maybe we can cover that with makeup" and "What will we do with that hair?" It had been humiliating.

She continued, "She always wanted to dye my hair."

"Why?"

"I don't know. Maybe she didn't like blondes. I know she didn't like me."

Why wouldn't Greg's mom like Maggie?

"Didn't anyone else ever tell you you were beautiful?"

"My dad used to write it on a card every time he gave me a present. To my beautiful daughter. I always wondered if it was because he couldn't remember my name."

Maggie looked at Mike and said, "You're wrong. Let's just drop it."

"No." He caught her gaze and kept it. "You are beautiful. You are beautiful when you wake up in the morning. You are beautiful when you go to sleep at night. You are beautiful with your hair up in that silly ponytail and you are beautiful when it is down around your shoulders. You are beautiful when you are reading a story to Sara and teaching her something new. And you are especially beautiful when you smile at me."

Maggie's eyes welled up.

Mike pulled her close and whispered, "You are always beautiful to me."

Chapter 23

Maggie liked going to church. She felt a sense of reverence as they walked down the aisle between the pews of the old Catholic Church. It felt like something important happened here. That's why you wear your Sunday best—because this is where God is. Michelle walked in first and chose their seat. Maggie followed her. Mike slid in next to Maggie after he got GG Rose settled in her wheelchair at the end of the row. Maggie drank in the atmosphere. The stained-glass windows, the paintings of the saints, the cross with Jesus hanging on it. She felt peaceful.

The atmosphere was wonderful, but halfway through Maggie felt the chill of the air conditioning. She was wearing a white sundress—no sleeves—and a pair of sandals, which was perfect outside in the California sun, but not inside in the air-conditioned sanctuary. She rubbed her arms to generate a little heat. Mike noticed she was getting cold, so he put his arm around her shoulders. That was nice. But then Maggie's mind started to wander back to last night. Mike had played a big game against New York, their biggest rival. He had scored two goals. His adrenaline was still pumping long after the game ended. They barely made it in the house before he was kissing her and pulling at her clothes. They didn't make it upstairs. Maggie was ashamed. Here she was sitting in church in her little white sundress pretending to be all innocent when last night she was, well, sinning. She was such a hypocrite! She didn't belong here. It wasn't just last night. She spent every night with Mike. She knew it was wrong, but what was she supposed to do? It was funny how she felt so guilty sitting here in church. Outside of church it didn't seem so bad. Mike didn't seem to feel guilty. Sandy definitely thought Mike was good-looking enough for Maggie to sleep with. Michelle teased them once in a while, but she certainly didn't act like she thought it was wrong unless Sara was around. Funny how they could tell other adults that they were sleeping together without being married, but they couldn't let a four-year-old know. Well, not all adults—they didn't tell GG Rose. How many times did she have to change what she was about to say so that GG Rose didn't know she was sleeping with Mike? She couldn't say Jackson woke her up in the morning. Or that she and Mike ate Cheerios for breakfast. Or she was cold last night until she cuddled up next to him in bed.

So, the question was, was it wrong or not? The commandment said, "Thou shall not commit adultery." That was clearly wrong. Once you were married, that was it. Of course, cheating on your husband was wrong. But that didn't apply here, right? Of course, if she asked the priest, he would definitely say premarital sex—wrong. But she had to admit when Mike held her in his arms, that didn't feel wrong. She felt warm and safe and taken care of. Maybe God had sent Mike to help her get over Greg. She decided to pray. She was in church after all. "Lord, I want to do what is right. But I'm not sure what that is. Help me to do what is right. Amen."

Maybe there was a loophole that she didn't know about. Maybe there was some way that she could keep sleeping with Mike and not feel guilty. That was what she was really praying for.

The church service ended. Michelle went to pick Sara up from Sunday school. Mike went to get Michelle's car. Maggie wheeled GG Rose toward the parking lot. Along the way, GG Rose stopped to chat with some friends. She introduced Maggie to each one, saying, "This is my grandson's girlfriend. Isn't she beautiful?"

Mike walked up to try to help Maggie disentangle GG Rose from the crowd of people. GG Rose said, "There's my handsome grandson."

Mike shook hands with a couple of fans, who congratulated him on the game last night, then ushered Maggie and GG Rose to the waiting car. Once Michelle and Sara joined them, they were off to Sunday dinner at GG Rose's favorite restaurant.

Sara and GG Rose both needed a nap. So Mike dropped them off at their respective places. On the way back to Mike's, Maggie joked, "I think GG Rose has forgotten my name. She thinks it's 'my grandson's girlfriend.'"

Mike joked back, "That's not your name. That's your title. Your name is 'isn't she beautiful?'"

"Yeah, she was working pretty hard to sell that one."

"Everyone agreed, didn't they?"

"They were in church. They had to be nice."

Mike looked at her intently. She still didn't believe it, did she?

"Maggie, I thought we had settled this. You are beautiful."

"Well, it's nice of you to say that, but I know the truth."

Mike looked at her in disbelief.

Maggie continued, "I know beautiful. I have lived my whole life with Sandy. She is beautiful."

Mike couldn't believe what he was hearing. He was speechless.

Maggie continued again, "You know that Peanuts comic strip with Charlie Brown and Snoopy? Remember Pig Pen. How he always had a cloud of dirt surrounding him—following him wherever he went. Well, that's how Sandy is, except it's a cloud of guys following her around. They don't even notice me."

Mike still didn't respond.

Maggie said, "Don't get me wrong. I'm not jealous. I wouldn't have it any other way."

Mike said, "Sandy has to try to be beautiful." He had never seen Sandy without full makeup and hair perfectly done and clothes that were meant to get a guy's attention. "You are beautiful without even trying."

Maggie laughed, "Just give it up. Guys have literally stepped over me to get to Sandy." That was actually the truth. A guy had stepped over her at the beach to go talk to Sandy—gotten sand all over her!

Mike stopped the Jeep so he could look at her while he said this. He again doubted the wisdom of saying it. But he couldn't stand the thought that she thought guys preferred Sandy to her.

"Maggie, Sandy is a big flirt. She is easy to talk to. A guy doesn't need to work to get her attention. But believe me, guys are looking at you. You are just harder to get to."

"So your theory is that they are all after me, but I play hard to get."

"You don't play hard to get. You are hard to get. It's not that they are not noticing you. It's that you are not noticing them! They can't get your attention, so they go on to an easier target."

Maggie stared back at him. "If this is true, why would you tell me? Wouldn't it be better for you if I didn't pay any attention to other guys?"

She had him there. "I'd like to be able to tell my girlfriend that she is beautiful and have her believe me. Maybe even get a 'thank you.'"

She laughed, "You're crazy."

He replied, "You're beautiful."

She smiled. "Thank you."

Two days later, Mike and Maggie took Sara to the grocery store. Mike stopped to tie Sara's shoe. Maggie went ahead to get a cart. A guy beat her to it, pulled out the cart for her, and looked her up and down. Maggie glanced at Mike. He gave her an "I told you so" look. She mumbled thank you to the guy before Mike and Sara caught up with her. Mike and the guy sized each other up like two dogs in the dog park. The guy skulked away with his tail between his legs when Mike asserted his dominance.

Maggie turned away from Sara and asked Mike, "Am I supposed to flirt with him now?"

"No way, you are supposed to ignore him."

"Ignore who?"

"The guy who gave you the cart."

"What guy?"

Mike smiled at Maggie. "Good girl."

They walked down the aisle for a while. Then Maggie said, "He wasn't as cute as you are anyway."

"Who?"

"That guy who gave me the cart."

Mike looked at her hard. "What guy?"

"Oh, right. There was no guy." Pause. "But if there had been, he wouldn't be as cute as you."

Chapter 24

"No, I can't," stated Maggie firmly.

"Come on," said Sandy.

"Please," pleaded Michelle.

"It's too much money," said Maggie. "I can't pay my share."

"You don't have to pay anything," said Michelle. "Just come with us."

"Oh yeah, and where are you two going to get all that money?" asked Maggie.

Sandy and Michelle exchanged a guilty look.

"Oh no. You are not going to ask him!" shouted Maggie.

"Come on," said Sandy. "He'll do it."

Maggie looked at Michelle. Michelle said, "He won't mind."

"Look, maybe he would pay for you." Maggie pointed at Michelle. "But why would he pay for you?" She looked directly at Sandy.

Sandy shrugged. "We're a package deal."

Maggie looked from one to the other. "You already asked him," she accused.

Sandy said, "No."

Michelle said, "It was his idea."

"Three against one—that's not fair," Maggie murmured as she walked out to the patio.

Maggie sat down on a patio chair and kicked off her sandals. She felt the sun warm her feet and legs. She had thought she was doing pretty well with this being poor thing. She couldn't go shopping, but she had so many clothes that she really didn't need to. It really wasn't so hard being poor. You didn't have money, so you didn't spend money. But this would be really fun. If she still had her dad's credit card, she would go in a heartbeat. But she didn't want her dad's money. And she didn't want Mike paying for things either. She wanted to take care of herself. If you weren't depending on anybody, nobody could let you down.

Mike knocked on the door to Sandy and Maggie's house. Sandy let him in. He looked from Michelle to Sandy and back. He could tell it didn't go well.

"She said no?" he asked.

"She said no," Michelle confirmed.

"Why?" he asked.

"She won't let you pay," said Michelle.

"I thought we weren't going to tell her that part," he said.

Sandy chimed in, "She figured it out. She's not stupid, you know."

"I know," said Mike looking rather defeated.

"Well, don't give up," said Sandy. "Go out there and convince her."

"How am I supposed to do that?" asked Mike.

Sandy rolled her eyes and pushed him to the door. "Just go out there and flash those baby blues. You know she'll do anything you tell her to."

Mike gave her a look of doubt. He didn't know why Sandy was always saying that. She didn't do whatever he wanted, especially when it came to money.

Out on the patio, Mike sat down in a chair next to Maggie's and said, "Hi."

"It's too much money," she said immediately.

"It's not that much."

She looked at him with raised eyebrows. "Gas money to San Jose and back, hotel room, and tickets to the game—that's several hundred dollars."

"Don't you want to go watch me play?" He looked a little hurt.

"Of course, it's just too much," she repeated.

"Why don't you let me decide how much is too much?"

Maggie looked away. How fun would it be to go on a road trip with Sandy and Michelle? And, of course, she wanted to go cheer for him. But she didn't want him to start paying for stuff for her.

Mike tried again. "I would really like for you to go. I like to know you're in the stands cheering for me."

"We cheer when we watch you on TV too," countered Maggie.

"But I also think this would be good for Michelle," continued Mike. "She never does anything fun anymore. All she does is go to school, do homework, and take care of Sara. I think this would be good for her. Don't you think it would be fun?"

"Of course, it would be fun!" But Maggie was worried. She had depended on her dad's credit card. She had depended on marrying Greg. She didn't want to make that same mistake again.

"Someone has to stay with Sara," she said weakly.

"My mom is coming to spend the weekend with her."

That wasn't good. What if they went without her? A weekend without Mike, Sandy, Michelle, and Sara. Alone with her thoughts all weekend. That was scary. You know going on a trip didn't make her dependent on him, right? It wasn't like he was paying her rent or anything.

So, of course, she gave in. "I don't have the right color jersey for an away game."

He smiled. "I'll get you one!"

He kissed her and said, "Thanks, Maggie."

"Yeah, like I'm doing you a favor."

They walked back into the house. Sandy and Michelle looked expectantly at Maggie.

"Well, I guess I have to go. You wouldn't have any fun without me!"

Sandy shot Mike an "I told you so" look.

Mike said, "I'll go get the tickets."

Michelle said, "I'll go get the hotel room."

Sandy said, "I'll go get the snacks."

Maggie thought, I'll just stay here and compromise my principles.

They were on the road by 5 a.m. so they could be there before lunch. They were in Sandy's car because she wanted to do the driving, but

Michelle had Mike's credit card because, as Mike pointed out, Maggie wouldn't spend enough and Sandy would spend too much!

In San Jose, Mike and Brandon were waiting for them in the hotel lobby. Mike checked them in. He carried Maggie and Michelle's luggage. Sandy carried her own. The guys had had a light practice in the morning. Now they were free until the game. They took the girls to lunch and then walked down the street, window shopping.

Michelle felt like a fifth wheel. In the car, Sandy was in the front seat, driving. Brandon was in the front passenger seat. Maggie sat in the middle of the back seat with Mike and Michelle on either side. The car was pretty small, but there was plenty of room for Michelle since Maggie sat so close to Mike. As they got out of the car at the restaurant, Michelle was painfully aware of how everyone paired up except for her. After they finished eating, they took a walk. Sandy and Brandon led the way teasing and laughing. Mike held Maggie's hand. It wasn't that Mike and Maggie were ignoring her. They talked to her and included her, but there were also intimate whispered conversations and stolen kisses. Michelle told herself she wasn't jealous. But truth be told she was. She wanted Mike to be happy, and Maggie was great—way better than his last girlfriend, Bianca. But for so long it had been her and Mike against the world. Now it wasn't Mike and Michelle like when they were growing up—it was Mike and Maggie. For a split second, she wished there was someone for her to pair up with, but that was never going to happen. She would never trust a man—never ever. Not after what happened. She could never trust anyone.

Back at the hotel, Sandy and Brandon went to his room. Mike, Maggie, and Michelle went to the girl's hotel room and ordered a movie. Mike and Maggie sat on one bed, leaning against the headboard. Michelle took the other. When Michelle needed to go to the bathroom, they paused the movie. Michelle thought, Well, now I'm not the fifth wheel, but I'm still the third wheel. As she opened the door, she caught Mike leaning over to kiss Maggie. She ducked back in, thinking they would rather be alone, but where was she supposed to go? She guessed she could stay here in the bathroom. What a fun trip, she thought sarcastically. Actually, it had been a fun trip on the way up. Maggie and Sandy liked to turn the radio way up and sing to their favorite songs. They had been singing and laughing and eating all the way. She hadn't had that much fun in a long, long time. She needed to stop feeling sorry for herself. She needed to find a way to thank Mike.

Mike called out, "Hey, are you coming out of there, Chel? We're trying to watch a movie!"

The game was fun. Very different to be at an away game. But the girls cheered their hearts out.

After the game, the girls met Mike and Brandon at the bar in the hotel lobby, where they hung out until the guys needed to go upstairs—they had a curfew. Mike walked the girls up to their room to say good night.

Sandy was complaining that it was too early on a Saturday to be in for the night. After all she didn't have a curfew. She wanted to go out and have fun. She decided she would try to convince Michelle. Maggie would come along if Michelle wanted to go somewhere.

"Let's go," said Sandy.

"Where?" asked Michelle.

"Just out to have fun!"

"I don't know. It's kind of late."

"Come on, how often do you get a night out? Let's go find some guys."

That was definitely where she lost Michelle. "We better just stay here. We have a long drive tomorrow."

Sandy grumbled, "You guys are no fun." Then she brightened. "Let's play Truth or Dare."

Maggie said, "How old are you?"

Sandy said, "You are still such a stick in the mud. I thought you would loosen up after you had a one-night stand."

Maggie glared at Sandy. "I am not doing any of your stupid dares."

Sandy said, "Then tell the truth."

"How will that be fun? You already know everything."

Sandy countered, "Then I guess Michelle gets to ask you questions."

Miss Lori   133

Michelle thought that could be interesting. Plus, she was feeling kind of bad about refusing Sandy's last idea. She said, "OK, I'll play." She could always lie if they asked a question she didn't want to answer.

Sandy said, "Maggie goes first. Truth or dare?"

"Truth, of course," said Maggie.

Michelle thought for a moment. "Do you miss Greg?"

Maggie sighed.

Sandy jumped up. "She isn't going to answer. Here is your dare. Go sneak into Mike's room."

"I'm not going to sneak into his room."

"Why not? You know you want to," teased Sandy.

"Number one, he would get into trouble, and number two, I'm not twelve."

Michelle laughed.

"Then you have to answer the question," said Sandy.

Michelle had to admit their bickering was pretty funny. It was like they had been friends so long that they could say anything to each other.

"I will answer—if you shut up and let me think for a minute," scowled Maggie.

She looked at Michelle. "No, I don't. You know, he really wasn't around all that much. He lived two hours away, so I only saw him on the weekends, and then only if he wasn't busy with school. It's not like with Mike. He's always around. Even when he is halfway across the country, I keep expecting him to walk through the door!" Suddenly Maggie wondered if this trip was about Michelle spying on her.

Michelle read her thoughts. "I'm not spying on you for Mike. I was just wondering."

Sandy said, "OK, Michelle, your turn. Truth or dare?"

Michelle said, "Truth."

Sandy considered, then asked, "Was Sara's dad hot?"

Michelle gulped. Sandy had hit on the one subject that she would not talk about. "No," she answered.

"Come on, Sara is adorable. He must have been a hottie," teased Sandy.

Michelle gritted her teeth.

Maggie said, "Leave her alone. She answered your question."

Sandy sighed, "OK, my turn. I take dare."

Maggie said, "Naturally." She considered. "OK, I dare you to go downstairs to the lobby, find five good-looking guys, look them in the eye, but not talk to them."

"What kind of a stupid dare is that?"

"A dare that you can't do," laughed Maggie.

"Come on, let me do something better. Let me bring some guys up here."

Maggie smiled. "I told you the dare. Either you do it, or we quit playing."

"Oh, all right, but you guys are no fun!" Sandy stormed out of the room.

Maggie felt the need to apologize to Michelle for Sandy's behavior. "Sorry about Sandy. She has been boy crazy since kindergarten. I mean, it was fun for a while. But now I wish that she would just pick one. She has hundreds to pick from. I don't know what she thinks she is looking for."

Michelle said, "That's all right. Sandy is fun."

Maggie realized they had never spent any time together without Sara. She asked, "How's Sara? Have you called your mom?"

"Yeah, she's fine. But I miss her like crazy."

"Me too." Maggie smiled. "She is so fun and smart and cute."

"I liked that French braid you put in her hair the other day. Some day you have to teach me how to do that."

"How about today?"

Michelle had straight, shiny black hair. Maggie got a brush and then started working it into a French braid. As she worked, she asked, "So what was it like growing up with a twin brother?"

"Mostly good. Mike's always been my best friend. We did everything together." She laughed, remembering. "When we were in grade school, all the soccer coaches in the league wanted Mike to play on their team."

"Naturally," said Maggie.

"But he wouldn't play unless they let me play too!"

"You played on a boys' team?"

"Yeah, it was great!"

"Didn't the boys pick on you?"

"Mike wouldn't let the boys on our team say anything. The boys on the other team didn't usually figure it out. I was kind of a tomboy. I wore my hair real short. That only worked for a while. Then I had to play with the girls."

"Did you go to the soccer high school like Mike did?"

"No, that's only for boys. But I did get a scholarship to play in college."

"Wow! Which college?"

"It doesn't matter. I didn't go."

"How come?"

"Sara came along." There was definitely a tinge of sadness in her voice.

Maggie waited, but Michelle didn't continue. Maggie finished her hair. She said, "You look gorgeous. If I had a camera, I would take a picture."

Michelle said, "Your phone has a camera."

"No, it doesn't."

"Sure it does. Mike paid extra so you would have a camera."

"Mike paid extra on this phone he got for free!?"

Michelle thought, Oops, I shouldn't have said that.

Maggie started to get mad but decided to just let it go. She hadn't really believed he got the phone for free anyway.

She asked, "How do you use it?"

Michelle showed her, and then Maggie took a picture of Michelle. She said, "I guess I'll wait until tomorrow to send it to Mike. I don't want to wake him up."

Michelle said, "He isn't asleep yet."

"Yes, he is."

Michelle grabbed the phone and pushed send.

Maggie said, "If he gets mad, I am going to tell on you."

Michelle said, "Why would he get mad?"

Maggie got a text back almost immediately. "Nice! :)"

It kind of irked Maggie that Michelle knew him so much better than she did.

Michelle said, "Your turn."

They switched places. Now Maggie sat on the floor, and Michelle sat on the bed and started brushing Maggie's hair. Then she got Sandy's curling iron and made long, vertical curls in Maggie's hair. Michelle guessed that it was her turn to ask the questions.

"What's it like to be rich?"

"I'm not rich."

"You grew up rich, and you almost married a rich guy. I wish I had a credit card from Daddy so I could buy anything I wanted."

Maggie smirked. "Until you do something he doesn't like."

"Still, it must have been hard to walk away from Greg knowing he would give you anything money can buy."

"Sometimes money can't buy what you want. I hate to break this to you, but money doesn't make you happy. It might make life a little easier, but it definitely does not make you happy," stated Maggie firmly.

"Well, that I wouldn't know," offered Michelle.

Again, Maggie wondered where Michelle got the money to pay her. But she knew Michelle wouldn't want her to ask. So instead, she teased, "I guess I could introduce you to one of Greg's friends. I mean, you can't have Greg, but I know some other rich guys. What do you say?"

"Pass."

Maggie laughed, "I guess that's good because I'm sure none of them would talk to me!"

Michelle considered. "Why not Greg? Aren't you over him?" You know, she really did sound like she was spying for Mike. But it wasn't that. She just wondered how Maggie was dealing with this whole difficult situation.

Maggie returned, "Sandy and I have a rule once one of us dates a guy, the other never can." Maggie laughed as she continued, "Which means Sandy can't go out with Greg or Mike, and I can't go out with—well, pretty much any other guy I have ever met!"

Michelle laughed with Maggie.

"I guess technically that rule doesn't apply to you. But if you started seeing Greg, I would definitely have to stop being Sara's nanny."

"Why would I want to see him? He sounds like a jerk!"

"That's what I've been saying!"

Michelle put down the curling iron and said, "Finished!" She took Maggie's cell phone and took a picture to send to Mike. She thought, Mike is going to love this.

Mike texted back. "Beautiful—now I have photographic evidence!"

Michelle decided that was how she could thank him. She got out her real camera and called, "Maggie?" When Maggie looked, she snapped a picture. She had been taking pictures all weekend. She would print up the best ones for Mike. He would like that.

Mike stared at the picture on his phone. He was dying to call Maggie. It had already become his normal routine to talk to Maggie after away games. But he really had wanted this trip for Michelle. OK, not only for Michelle but also for him. But he wanted Michelle to have the opportunity to get out and do girl stuff. And now she and Maggie were doing each other's hair. That was definitely girl stuff. But he was feeling about as left out as he knew Michelle was feeling before. He wanted to give them time together, but this was hard. He never broke curfew. He didn't feel the need to go gallivanting around at night after a game. But this time it was tempting. He could go down to their room. See the new hairdos in person. He could even bring Maggie up here. It wasn't like Brandon was around. He was probably somewhere with Sandy. But that would leave Michelle alone in the hotel room. And who knew if Maggie would even come up here with him? He really never knew how she was going to react in any given situation. He needed to just go to sleep.

Michelle woke up when she heard Maggie talking on the phone in the bathroom.

"Where are you?" She must be talking to Mike.

"Please just come to the room." She wants him to sneak into our room?

"She's asleep." Thanks for thinking of me.

"Come on, I can't go to sleep until you get here." That was kind of pushy.

"Whatever you do, don't leave the hotel." Wait, why would she tell Mike not to leave the hotel?

"I don't want to come down to the bar. Please just come here!" Michelle thought Maggie sounded like she was going to cry. Who was she talking to?

"What if something happens to you?"

"Yes, it could happen to you. Please come up here."

"OK. I'm coming down. Just stay there." Who was she going to meet?

"Good. Thank you."

Maggie hung up, quietly left the bathroom, and got back into bed.

Several minutes later, the door to the room opened. Michelle saw Sandy sneaking in—but not very quietly. Michelle had thought she had come back long ago. Maggie didn't get up or say anything except, "Lock the door."

Chapter 25

"Wake up, Maggie," Mike whispered as he fingered one of her curls.

Maggie opened her eyes and smiled. "Hi."

"Good morning. Your hair looks nice."

"Yeah, I'll bet." Mike wondered if she would ever learn to take a compliment.

"How'd you sleep?" he asked.

"I was cold. I forgot what a blanket hog Sandy is." She smiled. "How about you?"

"Not too good."

Maggie sat up. "Why? Are you hurt?"

He just said, "No."

Sandy was in the shower. Michelle had returned to the mirror after she let Mike in. She was trying to recreate her French braid from last night.

Mike said, "I have to go catch the team bus."

Maggie walked him to the door. Michelle finished her braid and grabbed her camera. She snapped a picture of the two of them together.

Maggie gave her an exasperated look. "Would you stop taking pictures of me? What are you, the paparazzi?"

Michelle looked undeterred. She said, "Just want to remember the trip."

"Well, could you at least wait until I get dressed!?"

Maggie had slept in Mike's jersey and a little pair of shorts. Just then, Maggie heard the bathroom door opening. She pushed Mike out the door. She didn't want him to see Sandy in case she came out in only a towel. She leaned halfway out into the hall using the door to block his view. He kissed her goodbye, but not before a couple of his teammates came walking down the hall.

"Go, Mallone!" they said.

This time it was Mike pushing Maggie through the door. They didn't need to see her fresh from bed, all cute and curly.

On the bus, Mike took a seat wishing he could drive home with the girls. He plugged his earphones into his phone and turned on his playlist. He looked at the picture of Maggie that Michelle had sent him last night.

One of the guys from the hallway sat down next to him. He grinned as he said, "You were up early this morning."

Mike decided if he ignored him, he might just go away.

"Why so grumpy, Mallone? I would think you would be good and happy this morning!" he leered.

Mike glared at him.

"What? I'm just saying I'd sneak into that hottie's room too!"

"That's my girlfriend you're talking about," said Mike through gritted teeth.

"I know. I'm just saying she's hot, and apparently she's also…"

Mike pushed him out of the seat into the aisle. He said, "Get out of here."

"Touchy," groused his teammate.

Mike had thought once he announced Maggie was his girlfriend on national TV, the guys would stop talking about her behind his back, but no such luck. They still thought of her as the girl he picked up in the bar—his one-night stand. Sorry, Maggie.

The ride home for the girls was quieter than the ride there had been. For one thing they all had raspy throats from singing so loudly on the way up and then cheering at the game.

Michelle sat in the backseat looking at the pictures she had taken. She smiled when she thought of Maggie calling her the paparazzi. Once Michelle had the idea to take pictures for Mike, she had taken a lot of pictures. She even had pictures of Maggie sleeping! It was all right. She knew Maggie wasn't really mad. Maggie was pretty easy to get along with. Not like Bianca. Michelle couldn't imagine taking a road trip with Bianca. That would definitely not have been fun. She never hung out just with Bianca. Or with Bianca and Mike for that matter. Bianca had demanded all of Mike's attention. She didn't want Michelle or Sara or anyone else around ever. Maggie was so different. How many times had she seen Maggie watching and smiling as Mike played with Sara? Or Maggie waiting quietly while Mike talked to GG Rose or discussed something with Michelle? Of course, Mike was usually holding Maggie's hand or had his arm around her. If she did wander away for a moment, he always watched to see where she was going. And it wouldn't be long until he was by her side again. It was funny. Bianca demanded his attention but never really had it. Maggie never demanded his attention but always had it.

Maggie texted back and forth with Mike until he got on the plane.

"Look," shouted Maggie, "a roadside stand. Let's stop and get fresh strawberries!"

"I don't like strawberries," groused Sandy.

"Mike does," said Maggie.

"Who cares if Mike likes strawberries?" jeered Sandy.

"What's your problem? You could be nicer to him, you know."

"That's your job."

"He paid for you to go on this road trip, too, you know."

"So?"

"I didn't see your boyfriend chipping in." That was true. Mike had paid for all the gas, the hotel room, and the tickets. When they went out to eat, he paid for himself, Maggie, Michelle, and Sandy. Brandon had only paid for himself.

"He's not my boyfriend," Sandy said angrily.

Maggie's attitude softened. "What happened?"

"Nothing," said Sandy defiantly.

"Weren't you at the bar with him last night?"

"No, he was with some other ugly chick."

Maggie was surprised. After all the time Sandy and Brandon had spent together a couple of weeks ago when he was hurt, she had thought they were getting pretty close. Looked like Sandy had thought so too.

But Sandy was defiant. "It's no big deal. We weren't exclusive."

"Do you want me to drive?" asked Maggie.

"No, you drive like a grandma. We'd never get home."

But after they stopped for lunch, Sandy crawled into the back seat and laid down. She wouldn't admit that she was upset about Brandon—even to herself. She knew they weren't exclusive, but she at least thought he would have preferred her to some random girl. Forget him. There were plenty more where he came from. Yeah, there were plenty more like him, but wouldn't it be nice to meet a nice guy for a change? Where were all the nice guys? OK, she had to admit it—a nice guy like Mike. Sandy sighed. Only Maggie could have a one-night stand and end up with a nice guy. And a good-looking one at that! She wasn't jealous. She didn't want Mike. Mike was Maggie's. And the way he fawned all over her was a little sickening, right? He sure was smitten. OK, it would be nice to have a guy that would do anything for you—like pay for a road trip for your best friend. But Maggie's behavior was kind of sickening too. She acted like a doormat when Mike was around. She would do anything he wanted her to. That was all right for Maggie, but not for her. She didn't need any guy telling her what to do.

The first thing Mike did when he got off the plane was text Maggie. Maggie was driving, so when her phone buzzed, she handed it to Michelle. Michelle thought it was interesting that Maggie didn't even look at the caller ID. She just assumed it was Mike. So Michelle got to text back and forth with Mike. OK, most of the time he was texting something that she was supposed to tell Maggie, but it was something.

Mike went directly to Michelle's apartment to see Sara and his mom. Sara jumped into his arms.

He said, "Hey, Miss Sara Rose. How was your weekend?"

She said, "Where is Mommy? Where is Miss Maggie?"

His mom was in the kitchen making chicken nuggets for Sara's lunch. She called out, "Sara, I told you Uncle Mike was getting home first."

Mike could see that Sara didn't understand. He sat down with her and tried to explain it like Maggie would. "Uncle Mike was with the team. The team flew home on an airplane. Mommy, Miss Maggie, and Miss Sandy are driving in Miss Sandy's car. Airplanes go faster, so Uncle Mike got home first."

Sara said, "Oh, when will Mommy be home?"

Mike's mom walked into the room. She said impatiently, "A couple of hours. Now go wash your hands for lunch."

Before Sara got up from his lap, he said to Sara, "They will be home after nap time."

While they ate, Mike asked Sara what she and Grandma had done all weekend. Sara didn't seem to have much to say. Mike was surprised. Sara was usually brimming with stories. After a day with Maggie, she was always excited to recount every detail of their day. Oh, well, it wasn't Mom's fault, thought Mike. Maggie is just really good with kids.

After lunch, Mike's mom cleaned up the kitchen and started to gather up her stuff. Mike asked, "Aren't you going to stay until they get here?"

"I need to get home. You can watch Sara, can't you?" she answered.

"Yeah, but why don't you stay? Then you could meet Maggie."

"Ah, the famous Miss Maggie. All weekend that's all I have heard. Miss Maggie this and Miss Maggie that."

"Isn't it a good thing that Sara likes her nanny?"

His mom's only answer was, "Tell Michelle I will call her later."

"I think you would like her too if you met her," said Mike.

"Who?"

"Maggie."

MISS LORI

His mom gave him a look of doubt and went over to Sara to say goodbye.

He thanked her, and she left.

"Hey, Sara, let's call Mommy and Miss Maggie."

He called Michelle's phone and pushed the speaker button so they both could talk. Michelle answered and did the same with her phone. They talked about San Jose and the game until the call was dropped. They were out of service.

Mike thought about his mom's reaction to Maggie. Why didn't she want to meet Maggie? Sara adored Maggie. She wouldn't have said anything bad about her. OK, let's look at it from his mom's perspective. She knew that he had met Maggie in a bar and three days later she was Sara's nanny. But she didn't know he had slept with her. She had seen the video on the internet of him kissing Maggie while he was signing autographs. She was watching TV when Mike proclaimed Maggie was his girlfriend after he had only known her for two weeks. He knew GG Rose only had good things to say about Maggie, but he also knew his mom wasn't happy that Maggie sometimes checked her out of the nursing home to work on the roses. Michelle always stood up for Maggie. She had even told their mom about Maggie's situation with Greg. Mike hadn't been happy when Michelle did that, but she said she was only trying to help. Problem was it didn't help. He got out his phone and looked at the picture of Maggie with curly hair again. Well, there was a simple solution to this. He would take Maggie to see his mom. Once his mom met Maggie, she couldn't help but like her, right?

The phone buzzed. It was Michelle texting, "What are you doing?"

"Waiting."

"That sounds boring. What is Sara doing?"

"That's a silly question."

"Why?"

"You know what she is doing."

"No, I don't."

"It's nap time. She's sleeping."

Michelle stared at her phone. Mike put Sara down for a nap?! That was a first!!

Mike was bored. What did Maggie do while Sara slept every afternoon? He wished they were home.

Maggie wished they were home. She was tired of driving. The traffic was getting worse the closer they got. And her hair was bugging her. She wore it in a ponytail so much now that it bothered her when it was down. She should have put it up this morning. But Michelle had insisted on curling it again. They would have been home by now if Michelle hadn't taken so much time on Maggie's hair. But Michelle just kept saying, "He likes it down."

She thought Michelle's reaction to Mike putting Sara down for a nap was so funny! She just couldn't stop saying, "I can't believe he put her down for a nap!" Actually, he was getting a lot better with Sara. He always made her sit in her car seat. He didn't carry her everywhere they went—just some of the time. Maggie smiled. But he still wouldn't play Candyland with her. She guessed every man had his limits!

Maggie drove into the parking lot at Michelle's apartment complex. She thought, Finally we are back!

The door opened to Michelle's apartment. Mike thought, Finally they are back!

He and Sara stopped cutting bananas for her snack and went to meet the weary travelers at the door. Sara ran straight to her mom. Mike went straight to Maggie. Sandy went straight to the bathroom.

Mike was anxious to get home, so after a little small talk, he was escorting Maggie to the door.

He said, "I like your hair."

Maggie said, "Your sister should be a hairdresser. She wouldn't let us leave this morning until she did my hair again."

Mike wondered if she would ever say thank you when he gave her a compliment.

Mike opened the door of the Jeep, but before he let her in, he kissed her like he hadn't seen her in a month. He buried his hand deep in her hair at the base of her neck. Maggie thought, Hmm, this is nice. Note to self—wear your hair down more.

Michelle and Sandy were watching from the window of Michelle's apartment.

Sandy asked, "Have you ever been kissed like that?"

Michelle said, "No." She turned to Sandy and said, "I need ice cream."

Sandy responded, "Good call."

Chapter 26

This is the life, thought Maggie, sitting in the California sun on a Sunday afternoon watching her man play soccer. All the games should be on Sunday afternoon with a barbeque at her house afterward just like they were going to do today. That wouldn't work for away games, but hey, why did he need to go to away games? Even the other teams should want to play here, where the weather was always perfect. In Seattle they played in the rain. In Salt Lake they played in the snow. The stadium in Dallas was so hot that they called it the Oven. So it was decided—all the games would be played here on Sunday afternoons. She wondered who she should call to make that happen.

Suddenly all her attention was focused on the field. Mike was down. He wasn't moving. The replay on the big screen TV showed the opposing player committing the foul—a high kick, his foot connecting with the side of Mike's head. But Maggie wasn't watching the TV. Why wasn't he getting up? The trainers ran onto the field with the stretcher. After a few moments, Mike managed to get up and walk off the field between two of the trainers. Michelle sighed, "He's all right."

Maggie thought, He doesn't look all right.

The game resumed, but Maggie watched the bench where the trainers continued to work on Mike. Finally, they sent another player onto the field in his place.

Michelle looked at Maggie—she had seen Mike go down before. He was always all right. "He's all right," she repeated.

Maggie said, "Then why are they taking him to the locker room?"

Michelle had no reply for that.

Maggie took out her phone and stared at it. Maybe he would call.

He didn't, but he did send a security guard to escort Maggie into the locker room.

Mike was sitting on an examining table. When he saw Maggie, he said, "I'm all right."

She nodded her head. She was scared and unsure of what was happening. She tried to calm herself down. OK, he was breathing—that was good. He was sitting up. He was talking. This couldn't be that bad, could it? But in her mind, she could still see him lying motionless on the field.

The trainer said, "Your boyfriend here took quite a shot to the head."

Maggie's eyes opened in fear. Mike wondered if he should have had Michelle come to the locker room. She could have handled this better. But his head hurt—he wasn't thinking straight at the moment.

He told Maggie, "I'm fine."

The trainer continued, "He's going to have quite a headache for a while. You need to watch him for signs of concussion." He handed her an instruction sheet. He added, "You drive home," as he left the room.

Maggie went to him. He repeated, "I'm fine."

She finally found her voice. "You are not fine. You have a concussion."

"I might have a concussion."

"Does it hurt?"

Mike thought, Yeah, it hurts! But he said, "A little bit."

She knew nothing about concussions. What was she supposed to do? She wasn't a doctor. But she knew a nurse. She called Michelle.

"He has a concussion."

Mike closed his eyes against the pain and said, "Might have."

He could hear them discussing what to do and where to take him. He said, "I'm going to your house for a barbeque."

Maggie looked doubtful. She and Michelle kept talking. Maggie thought it would be better to take him to his house.

Mike said firmly, "Maggie, I am going to your house."

Michelle heard him. Maggie listened and then said, "Michelle wants to know if you can walk."

He growled, "I can walk."

"Michelle wants to know if you remember where you parked your car."

Mike was clearly annoyed. "Yes!"

Maggie said into the phone, "Is grumpiness a sign of concussion?"

Michelle answered, "Probably."

Then Maggie smiled a little and said, "Then that's what he has."

Maggie felt better after talking to Michelle. She would take Mike to her house. Michelle would meet them there, and then she would fill her in about what to do about a concussion.

Maggie picked up Mike's bag and said, "Let's go."

She helped him off the table and put her arm around him to steady him.

He said, "Maggie, I'm fine."

She smiled and said, "Yep, you look fine."

At the Jeep, their roles were reversed. This time she was the one to open the door and help him in. Then she went around to drive.

Mike laid his head back against the seat. As soon as the medicine the trainer had given him kicked in, he would be just fine. Then he wouldn't have this splitting headache. Not a split, just a spare. Oh man, bowling jokes—maybe he did have a concussion.

Maggie thought about how many times she had wished for a concussion after she broke up with Greg. Now it didn't seem like such a good idea. God, I said I wanted to get hit in the head and have a concussion—not him! Well, as long as she was talking to God—dear God, please let him be all right and let me know what to do. Amen.

Sandy had invited a couple of guys from the team to the barbeque. She was done with Brandon. Now she had her eye on Owen.

They were sitting in the living room talking about the game and such. Mike looked all right. Nobody would have guessed that he was out cold on the field just a couple of hours ago. But Maggie noticed a difference. Usually he was up and around, helping with the food, playing with Sara. He never sat still for long—except today.

After they ate, Michelle and Maggie cleaned the kitchen. They went over the concussion instruction sheet. Wake him up every four hours and ask him questions like what year it was and who the president was.

When they came into the living room, Sandy and Owen were sitting on the couch talking, but Mike had left his spot. Maggie looked around and finally found him in her bed. She sat down on the bed and asked, "Are you all right?"

"Yeah."

She started rubbing his back and stroking his hair. Her heart melted. After a while he fell asleep. She decided that was probably what he needed most. She quietly got up. He said, "Don't leave."

She said, "I'll be right outside if you need me."

"No. Stay here with me."

Her bed was a twin size. "It's a very small bed."

"That's OK."

"And you are kind of in the middle of it."

He moved over. She laid down next to him. He said, "Stay all night, not just until I go to sleep."

That had been her plan. "OK, I'll be right back." She got ready for bed and set the alarm on her cell phone for four hours. Then settled in next to him.

Beep, beep.

Maggie turned the cell phone alarm off.

She touched Mike's shoulder to wake him up.

She asked, "Are you all right?"

"I'm fine."

Maggie tried to remember what she was supposed to ask him.

He said, "The year is 1776, and the president is George Washington."

Maggie was confused.

He said, "I don't have a concussion. Now let's go back to sleep."

Chapter 27

Maggie tried to grab the keys from Mike. "You can't drive."

"I don't have a concussion. I can drive," said Mike.

Maggie looked at Michelle. Michelle backed Maggie up. "You can't drive until you see the doctor. If he says it's all right, you can drive home."

"Chel, I know I don't have a concussion. I can drive."

Michelle said firmly, "My daughter will be in the car."

Mike gave in. He gave the keys to Maggie.

From the backseat of the Jeep, Sara asked, "Are you sick, Uncle Mike?"

He responded, "No, I'm not sick."

"Then why are you going to the doctor?"

Mike didn't want to scare Sara. He looked at Maggie for help.

As always, Maggie told Sara the truth, "Remember at the game yesterday? How Uncle Mike got hurt?"

"Yeah."

"That's why he needs to go to the doctor."

"You said you weren't hurt, Uncle Mike," accused Sara.

Now what was he supposed to say?

Maggie said, "We are going to the doctor to make sure he is all right, OK?"

"Mommy says Uncle Mike is tough. He will be OK."

Maggie smiled. "I'm sure that's true."

The doctor confirmed that Uncle Mike was tough and he was OK. He had some memory loss, but really the only thing he couldn't remember was actually getting kicked in the head. He could do without that. Everything else checked out fine. He just had a headache. He could go back to training the next day. He could also drive. He took the keys from Maggie and gave her an "I told you so" look. She didn't seem to mind. Mostly she just seemed relieved.

Mike was late. Practice had gone pretty well. He still had a headache, but otherwise he felt good. But after practice he needed to convince the trainers of that. That was why he was late. He called Michelle. She was pretty annoyed. Maggie and Sara were at his house. They wanted to visit GG Rose today, and his house was closer. So the plan had been for him to pick them up after training. That way Michelle could go straight home and start cooking. They were all going to eat at her apartment. By the time he called, she was already in the middle of cooking. She couldn't go get them. She made it clear she wasn't happy with him. He hung up. He didn't want to talk to another angry female, so he just texted Maggie, "I'm on the way."

He wondered how mad Maggie would be. He should have called before he talked to the trainers, but he had no idea that it would take so long. She was probably mad. Bianca would have been. Of course, Bianca was always mad at him. He could never seem to do right by her. She wasn't mean like Sara said, but she was demanding.

He looked at his phone before he got out of the Jeep at his house. She hadn't texted him back. That couldn't be good, right? He walked in and looked around. Where were they? Then he heard the squeak of the hammock in the backyard. Maggie was leaning back on the hammock with her feet on the ground swinging slowly back and forth. She was facing away from the door. Sara was cuddled up next to her, looking at the book Maggie was reading to her. He reached out for the handle of the screen door but stopped when he heard the question that he and Michelle always dreaded.

"Miss Maggie, where is my daddy?"

This was bad. What would Maggie say? He should interrupt, but he didn't know how to answer that question.

Maggie said calmly, "I don't know, honey. You will have to ask your mommy."

"Mommy says I don't have a daddy. Everybody else has a daddy. Why don't I have a daddy?" said Sara.

That broke his heart. How would they ever explain this to a little girl?

Maggie said, "Sometimes it's better to think about what you do have and not so much about what you don't have. You have a great mommy who loves you and takes care of you. You have a grandma and GG Rose who love you. And you have Uncle Mike."

Sara pouted. "Uncle Mike is late."

"Oh, Sara, that's OK. Everybody is late sometimes. That doesn't mean he doesn't love you. You have lots of people who love you."

"Miss Maggie, you forgot someone!" exclaimed Sara.

"Who?" asked Maggie.

"You love me and take care of me!"

"Yes, I do. I love my Sara Bug!"

Mike smiled as he opened the door and said, "Sorry I'm late."

Sara jumped up and said, "That's OK. Everybody is late sometimes."

Mike looked at Maggie and tried to gauge if she really meant it or if it was just what she told Sara. She just smiled and said, "Let's go. I'm hungry!"

As they walked to the Jeep, Mike said, "I had to talk to the trainers after practice."

"Are you all right?" asked Maggie.

"Yeah, I'm just saying that's why I'm late."

Maggie was quiet on the way to Michelle's.

When they got there, Sara ran ahead. Mike tried again. "I would have called, but I didn't think it would take so long."

"What did they say?"

"Who?"

"The trainers."

"Nothing—I'm just trying to explain why I was late."

"I know why you were late. What I don't know is if you are all right."

"I'm all right."

"Did the trainers tell you that, or did you tell the trainers?"

"Maggie, stop worrying. I'm fine."

"Would you tell me if you weren't?"

"Well, yeah."

She obviously didn't believe him. "So you are telling me that you got kicked in the head hard enough to knock you out and it only hurt a little bit? I guess you are tough," she said sarcastically.

OK, so she wanted the truth. "OK, it did hurt. When I woke up, I was woozy, and I couldn't see straight. And my head hurt a lot. But by the time we got to your house, the medicine had kicked in, and it wasn't too bad. I was just tired. That's why I went into your bedroom. The next morning it was just a regular headache. I still have one, but it's not bad."

"What about the actual kick?"

"I don't remember that."

"I do," said Maggie softly.

He pulled her close. "Sorry."

"Don't get kicked in the head anymore."

"I'll try to avoid it."

She kissed his cheek. Then she pulled away and smiled a big smile. "Don't worry. I still think you're tough!"

After supper, Michelle tried to put Sara to bed, but Sara insisted she had to ask Miss Maggie one last question. While Maggie was tucking Sara in, Mike said to Michelle, "Sara asked Maggie about her dad."

Michelle looked panicked. "What did Maggie say?"

"It's OK. She did good. She told Sara to be happy about all the people who love her and not to worry about not having a dad."

Michelle didn't respond.

Mike said, "Chel, we need to tell her."

"No! You can't tell her! Don't tell Maggie what happened!"

His heart hurt for his sister. "Chel, Sara is going to keep asking. We can't avoid this forever."

"What exactly am I supposed to tell Sara?"
That was the problem. He didn't know.

Chapter 28

On the drive to Mike's, Maggie was thinking about Sara. Sara wanted to make a butterfly garden like they had read about in one of the library books. Then Maggie's mind jumped back to the question Sara had asked in the hammock. She knew that Mike and Michelle didn't want to talk about Sara's dad. But she also knew Sara would ask again.

She got out of the Jeep and walked up the stairs to Mike's porch. She didn't want to pry. She guessed the best way to handle it was to tell Mike that Sara had asked. Maybe he would tell her something about Sara's dad. She turned to tell him, but he wasn't behind her.

Where was he? She looked back at the Jeep—he wasn't there. It was dark. Where was he? It was really dark. She said, "Mike?" Her hands started to shake. Where was he? OK, she had a key. She started fumbling in her purse. Where was the key? She could feel the panic rising. She said, "Mike?" a little louder. Her heart was beating faster. Where was the key? Where was he? "Mike!" she shouted. "Just a minute," he called back. Her breath was coming faster and faster. "Where are you?!"

Finally, he came around the corner and bounded up the stairs. "I was just—"

"I don't care—just open the door." She looked around wildly.

He took forever to unlock the door. Once he did, she jumped inside and immediately locked it behind them. She went straight to the back door and checked to make sure it was locked. Then she walked from window to window staring out into the dark.

Mike asked, "Did you let Jackson in?"

"No. He's an outside dog."

Mike watched her pace from window to window. He asked, "What's wrong?"

"Nothing—nothing." She checked the front door again, touching the lock just to make sure.

Mike went to the back door.

Maggie cried out, "Where are you going?!"

"I need to check the gate. I think Jackson may have broken it."

"You can't go out there!"

"Why not?" She sure was acting strange.

"Because it's dark."

"So?" He knew she was afraid of the dark, but he wasn't.

"You won't be able to see anything anyway. You can do it tomorrow."

"What if he gets out?"

"He won't." She looked absolutely panicked.

"OK, OK. I'll just let him in."

Maggie stared at him wild-eyed. "Lock the door."

Maggie watched him as he let Jackson in and locked the back door. Then she went to the door to make sure it was locked.

Mike watched her pace to each window again. This was weird—even for Maggie. He knew she had a thing about the doors being locked. Whenever she walked into the house, she immediately locked the door—whether she was at his house, her house, or Michelle's apartment. Whenever he got home, the door was locked. Whenever he went to Michelle's, the door was locked. If Maggie was inside, the door was always locked. He believed in safety first, too, but this was a bit much.

He tried again, "Is something wrong?"

"No, we just don't want to forget to lock the doors. This is a big city. A lot of crime. It's safer. You know, better safe than sorry."

She was talking really fast. She knew she sounded crazy. She even sounded crazy to herself. She needed to calm down. But she couldn't calm down. And telling herself to calm down was making it worse.

She went upstairs to the bathroom and locked the door. She sat down on the closed lid of the toilet and put her hands over her face. She rocked back and forth, tears streaming down her face. She flashed back to that night. She could see him. She could feel the terror in the darkness.

Mike knocked on the door.

She squeaked out, "Just leave me alone."

He said, "No, let me in!" She could tell he meant it.

She pleaded, "Not yet."

"I'm coming in!" he stated in no uncertain terms.

She wondered if he would break the door down. But he just used a screwdriver to unlock it from the outside.

"Don't tell me nothing is wrong!" The minute the words were out of his mouth, he regretted how harsh they sounded. He pulled her to her feet and into his arms. He could feel her shaking and her heart beating a mile a minute. He kissed her temple and said, "It's OK; it's OK. I'm here. You are safe." He held her until she started to calm down. Then he said, "How about some hot chocolate?"

He led her downstairs to the kitchen table. It wasn't cold, but she was shivering. So he got the afghan his grandma had made and wrapped it around her shoulders. No one said anything while he made the hot chocolate. He even put the little marshmallows in, just like she liked it.

He put the mugs on the table and looked at her. "What happened?"

She stared into her hot chocolate. She glanced up at him—he was waiting for an answer. What could she say? She could say nothing, but he probably wasn't going to let it go at that. At the other end of the spectrum, she could tell him the truth. But she had never told anyone—never actually put it into words.

"Maggie."

He was still waiting for an answer. Why did she have to go so crazy? It happened a long time ago. Why couldn't she just pretend it didn't happen? Just forget all about it?

"So you have played soccer for five whole years?" she tried weakly.

Since the first night she had told him about Greg, that was the line she used whenever she didn't want to talk about something. Usually, he just let it go then, but not this time. This had to be connected to her fear of the dark. He had never seen her go crazy about it, but she carefully arranged every situation so she wouldn't be alone in the dark.

"Why are you afraid of the dark?"

"Bad things happen in the dark."

"What kind of bad things?"

"Lots of bad things can happen in the dark—you could fall in a hole; you could trip over something and get hurt; you could get lost."

"What happened to you in the dark?"

"I can't tell you."

"Why not?"

Her eyes welled up. "I can't say it out loud."

"Come on, Maggie." He needed to know. Already his imagination was starting to take off.

She walked over to the same window that she had stared out of the night she told him about Greg. Mike had a strong sense of déjà vu as he sat down on the couch. The two situations seemed strikingly similar, only this time she was clutching an afghan around her shoulders instead of a towel. He waited, wondering if he would need to prompt her again.

"When I was a freshman, I went to a frat party," Maggie began.

Fear gripped Mike—not a frat party.

"There was this guy. It was loud. He said it was too loud. He said, 'Let's go outside' because it was too loud." Her story came in spurts—was disjointed.

"I am an idiot, so I went outside with him."

No, no, no, not Maggie too!

"It was dark. We walked for a while. Then I got scared. We were too far away from the party." She paused thinking how utterly stupid she was. "I said I wanted to go back. It was so dark." Sob. "He pushed me down behind a bush and landed on top of me. That's probably what broke my rib." She rubbed the rib as if it was still sore. "I tried to scream, but I couldn't get any air. He was holding my hands above my head." She rested her head against the glass and sobbed, remembering the pure terror that she felt.

Mike was sorry he asked. He wanted her to stop talking. He knew how these stories ended.

She continued, "Finally I caught my breath. I started to scream. He hit me. That's how I got a black eye." The shame was overwhelming. "I stopped struggling after that. He let go of my hands to… Anyway, suddenly I realized there was a rock in my hand. I don't know where it came from. I took it and slammed it into his knee as hard as I could. He started screaming and cussing, but he rolled off of me. I got up to run away, but he grabbed my ankle. I fell down face first. He wouldn't let go. So I turned over and kicked him in the same knee that I hit before. Then I got up and ran away."

Mike asked, "You mean he didn't…"

She turned to look at him. "No, he just beat the crap out of me."

As horrible as that story was, Mike was relieved. It could have been so much worse. "Did you call the police?"

"No, I ran to Sandy's car and hid in the back seat until she came to find me. We went home and locked the doors. I was so scared he was going to find me. I sat on the couch staring at the front door for three days. I don't know why—I could barely move. It hurt just to breathe. I wouldn't have been able to do anything if he had found me." She walked over to the couch and sat down next to him. Now that the story was over, she was ready for some comfort. He put his arm around her. She put her head on his shoulder.

"Didn't you go to a doctor?"

"The next day—but only because Sandy made me. We made up a story about falling off a horse. I don't think he believed it. He kept asking me if I had a boyfriend." She sniffed. "So either he didn't believe me, or he was hitting on me." Pause. "And one side of my face was completely swollen, so I doubt he was hitting on me."

"What did the doctor say?"

"He said, 'You have a broken rib.' I said, 'I know that.'"

"Didn't he give you painkillers?"

"Yes, I didn't take them."

"Why not?"

"We already established this; I am stupid. I thought he was going to find me. I didn't want to be knocked out when he came to finish me off. After a couple of days, Sandy crushed up the pain pills and put them in my food. Yes, my best friend drugged me. I don't remember anything for about three days after that."

They sat in silence for a moment. Then Maggie said, "I have never told that story to anybody before."

"Nobody?" asked Mike. "Nobody knows about it?"

"Just Sandy because she was there."

Mike didn't believe it. "You didn't tell your parents?"

"No. They were out of the country. But I wouldn't have told them anyway."

"How about Greg—you never told him either?"

"No."

"Why not?"

"It's not my favorite subject."

"When were you going to tell him?"

"I wasn't. I wasn't going to tell anyone—ever. I was just going to pretend that it never happened. I shouldn't have told you."

She stood up and faced him. "Look, I know it's stupid to be afraid of the dark. But that was really scary"—she teared up again—"and it hurt a lot. I just don't want to do it again."

She sat down again, but not too close. She looked at him, waiting nervously for his reaction. Would he tell her how stupid she was for going off alone with a stranger? She knew that. Would he tell her it didn't make sense to be afraid of the dark? She knew that too. Would he say it happened a long time ago and never mention it again? Of those choices she would take option three. Please give me door number three, Monty.

He wasn't sure what to say. He took a deep breath and started, "First of all, stop calling yourself stupid. You are not stupid. Second, I am so sorry that that happened to you. I can't believe a person could be that…evil." Pause. "But you know what? I'm proud of you."

She looked at him, surprised. "Proud? Of what? My ability to take a beating?"

He winced. "No. Can't you see? You won."

"Won?! What are you talking about? Weren't you listening? He beat the crap out of me!"

"But he wanted to do much worse. You stopped him."

She stared at him, considering what he said. She had never looked at it that way before. She would have to think about that. Finally, she said, "I don't know if I won or not, but I certainly don't want to play that game again."

Chapter 29

After that emotional roller coaster, it wasn't long before Maggie was asleep on the couch curled up with Jackson. Mike watched her sleep. He was so angry he wanted to put his fist through the wall. How could anyone be so evil? How could anyone want to hurt her like that? What was wrong with this world? See, this is why he couldn't believe there was a God that cared. Why would God let that happen? Why didn't He punish evil? Maggie didn't deserve this. She had had a rough childhood, a stranger attacked her, and then Greg stomped on her heart. Why wouldn't God give her a break?

He knew he needed to get his anger under control. How scared would Maggie be if she woke up to him in a fit of rage? He knew that wouldn't help her. He remembered the last time he lost control. Gotten himself kicked out of a soccer game—straight red card—for a wild tackle. The kind of tackle that can cause major injury. The other guy wasn't badly hurt, and Mike had since apologized. But it hadn't changed the situation that made him angry one bit. But what was he supposed to do? Turn the other cheek? God, why do you let men hurt women like this? It isn't right—it isn't fair.

He got down on the floor and did sit-ups. Then he turned over and did push-ups. Sit-ups, then push-ups. Sit-ups, then push-ups. Hundreds of them until he couldn't do one more—until he was too physically exhausted to do something stupid.

He looked at Maggie sleeping peacefully. He should pick her up and take her to bed like he had done a dozen times before. But what if it scared her? What if it reminded her of being attacked? What if she went crazy again? Maybe he should leave her there. Let her sleep.

Lick. Lick. Wet tongue on her cheek. That was Jackson's way of saying, "Maggie, wake up."

She got up and let him out. Why was she on the couch? She rolled her neck and blinked her eyes. Her eyes hurt from crying. Her neck was stiff from sleeping on the couch all night.

Mike came downstairs.

"Hey, how are you this morning?" he asked.

Maggie didn't look at him. Her only response was, "I have a crick in my neck." She wished she hadn't told him. She didn't know what he thought or what he might say. This was awkward.

He didn't know what to say. "I talked to Michelle."

Maggie spun around. "You didn't tell her, did you?"

He shook his head no.

"Please don't tell anyone—not even Michelle. I know you tell her everything—but not this, please. You can tell her anything else—you can even make up stories about me. Just don't tell her this!"

"It's OK. I didn't tell her. It's your story. I won't tell her. I won't say a word until you tell her."

"I'm not going to tell her. I am never going to tell anyone else. I wish I hadn't told you!" Maggie stormed upstairs.

Mike thought Maggie and Michelle needed to talk.

On the way to Michelle's, Maggie accused, "I know what you are thinking."

He was thinking it would be good to get to the field and kick some soccer balls and leave all this behind for a while.

She continued, "You think that I am as bad as Greg. That I was keeping a secret from him, just like he was keeping one from me."

He actually hadn't thought about that at all.

"But it isn't the same." She didn't explain how it wasn't the same—wasn't sure if she could.

He decided to let the secret part go, but he still didn't understand how she could have been about to marry the guy and this had never come up. She had known him for three years.

"How could he not know you were afraid of the dark?"

"He knew that—everybody knows that."

"But he didn't know why?"

"No."

"Why didn't you tell him?"

"He never asked."

The reason he had called Michelle that morning was to tell her he had a charity dinner to go to with the team that evening. He thought it would be better for Maggie to stay with Michelle until he was done with it. He didn't want Michelle taking Maggie to his house and leaving her there alone until he could get there. In general, it wasn't good to leave Maggie alone too much, but who knows what would happen if she was alone after last night. Better she stay with Michelle and Sara.

When Michelle got home from school, Maggie and Sara were in the kitchen cooking yet another recipe from the kid's cookbook that Sara liked so much. Then they played Candyland. Sara, of course, won. She had quite a knack for the game.

Once Sara was tucked in bed, Maggie and Michelle sat on the couch, flipping through the channels. They couldn't find anything they wanted to watch.

Maggie said, "I wonder when Mike will be back." She was exhausted. She just wanted to go to bed.

Michelle felt that twinge of jealousy again. She felt like she and Maggie were friends now. They were comfortable together, so before she could stop herself, she said, "I am so jealous."

Maggie was surprised. "Of what?"

"You and Mike."

Maggie said, "What? Why?" Pause. "Am I taking up too much of his time?"

"No, it's not that. I just wish…"

"That you had someone?" finished Maggie.

"Yeah, but that won't happen."

"Why not? You are gorgeous. You can't be having trouble finding a guy."

Michelle didn't respond.

Maggie teased, "OK, here's the plan. You and Sandy go out together. She is great at finding guys. She'll find you one."

"Me and Sandy? What about you?"

"I already have a guy." Maggie smiled. She hoped that was still true even after last night. "I'll stay here with Sara."

"I think I am going to pass on that."

"Come on. Why not?" Maggie looked at Michelle. "You already found one. Come on, who is he? What's his name?"

"There's nobody."

Maggie knew that wasn't true. "Why don't you go out with him? I'll babysit."

"Mike would love that," Michelle said sarcastically.

"He goes out of town all the time. New plan. Next time Mike goes out of town, Sara stays with me. You go out with whoever this guy is."

Michelle said, "Not going to happen."

Maggie hesitated, then asked, "Because of Sara's dad?"

For a moment Michelle wondered if Mike had told her. He wouldn't have, would he?

Maggie said, "Sara asked me about him."

Michelle said, "I know."

"You do?"

"Yeah, Mike overheard."

"She's going to ask again."

"I don't know what to tell her."

"What about the truth?"

"You can't tell a four-year-old that."

"What happened?" At first Maggie thought Michelle wasn't going to answer. It was clearly a painful subject.

Then Michelle opened up. "When I was a senior in high school, we won the state championship in soccer. All the girls wanted to go out and celebrate. One of them had a brother in college. So we went to a party at his frat house."

Maggie didn't like this. Bad things happened in frat houses.

Michelle continued, "I wasn't even drinking alcohol. I was drinking a Coke. That's the last thing I remember."

Michelle was crying. So was Maggie.

"The next morning, I woke up in a bedroom in an empty frat house. I told my mom I had spent the night at a girlfriend's house. I didn't tell anyone what happened."

"Not even Mike?" asked Maggie.

"He was out of the country playing in a big soccer tournament." Pause. "I didn't really know if anything had happened. I decided I would pretend nothing did. I wasn't going to tell anyone."

That is exactly how I reacted, thought Maggie.

"It was a while before Mike got home. He knew something was wrong. He just wouldn't let it go." I hear that, thought Maggie.

"I finally gave in and told him. He made me take a pregnancy test."

"Sara," whispered Maggie.

"I thought I was going to give her up for adoption, but I just couldn't do it. In the end, I moved in with Grandpa Willie and Grandma Rose. I don't know what I would have done without them."

They sat in silence, blowing their noses and drying their tears when Michelle finished her story.

Finally, Maggie said, "I understand." Then, for the second time in two days, she told the story that she had never planned to tell anyone.

Mike walked into Michelle's apartment to find two girls with red, puffy eyes and a mountain of wadded up Kleenex. Since he knew both their secrets, he was pretty sure he knew what had happened.

Chapter 30

Maggie was exhausted. Secrets were exhausting. Who would have thought that telling your secret would be even more exhausting than keeping it? And she didn't even have the energy to think about Michelle's secret. She wanted to sleep for days. Once they got to Mike's house, she went straight upstairs. Neither of them had said much on the way home. What was there to say?

Mike decided to go check on the gate. All the secrets were out in the open now. The question was, would that help or not?

Maggie woke up early the next morning. She tried to open her eyes. She felt like she was looking through slits. That was the problem with crying so much in the last two days. Her eyes were sore and puffy. At least now that she had told her story, she wouldn't have to talk about it anymore.

She was surprised to find that Mike was up even earlier than she was. Good, now she could go put cold water on her eyes. Get herself together before she had to face him.

Nothing really helped her appearance. Time to go downstairs. Face the awkwardness.

He wasn't in the kitchen. Where could he have gone this early in the morning?

Wait, there he was sleeping on the couch. Why was he sleeping on the couch? Did he fall asleep watching TV? No, the TV wasn't on. His head was on a pillow—the pillow that was usually on his bed. The pillow that had been on his bed when she went to sleep. He had to have gone upstairs to get the pillow and then gone back downstairs to sleep on the couch. Slowly it was dawning on her. She remembered how Michelle had described herself last night. "Damaged goods." Maggie had never thought of herself that way. Then it became clear. That was what Mike thought. Why else would he be sleeping on the couch?

The tears started again. This was too much. She didn't need this. She was out of here. She would make this real easy for him. Before she left, she put her phone on the coffee table. She didn't need anything from him.

Mike woke up when he heard the front door close. "Maggie?"

She didn't answer.

He wasn't sure what was happening. Did Maggie just leave? Why was her phone on the coffee table? Oh no, she was going crazy again!

He pulled on his jeans and shoes and ran out the door. It didn't take long to catch her. She was walking down the street crying.

He reached out his hand to catch her arm but stopped. He was afraid to touch her. He didn't want to scare her. So instead, he ran out in front of her and asked, "Where are you going?"

She seemed surprised to see him. "Home."

"Why?"

She walked past him. "I'm just going home."

He reached out to touch her again. Then stopped himself again. She saw it—that hurt.

She walked away faster.

"If you need something at your house, I can drive you," tried Mike.

"I don't need anything—nothing at all—especially from you!"

He stopped and watched her walk away. Why did he always have to guess what upset her? Why wouldn't she just tell him? Even yell at him. That would be better than constantly having to ask her what's wrong again and again. Maybe he should give up. Enough was enough. No—he wasn't going to let her walk away without telling him the problem. If he did, he might never see her again. They were going to talk about this. But not here—at his house.

He ran after her, caught her, picked her up, and threw over his shoulder.

"Put me down," she yelled.

"No," he said calmly but firmly.

"Let me go," she yelled.

He ignored her and walked off toward his house.

Soon she stopped struggling and said, "This isn't very comfortable."

He put her down but immediately grabbed her hand, held on tight, and pulled her to his house.

Inside, he said, "OK, now, tell me what happened."

She looked him straight in the eye. "Why did you sleep on the couch last night?" she asked tersely.

He hesitated.

"And why did you leave me on the couch the night before last?"

He took a deep breath.

"And here is the biggest mystery of all," she continued. "Why did you come after me?" Pause. "Look, I get it. You don't want anything to do with me now that you know. That's fine. I was just making it easy on you." It didn't look like it was fine with her. "Just let me go."

His response was exactly the opposite of what she expected. He pulled her close. He said, "I don't want you to go."

"Then why?"

"I just…I don't want…I'm afraid that I will do something that reminds you of that night."

She looked at him, considering what he said, but didn't respond.

He looked at the floor, then said, "The first night, the night we met, I would have stopped if you had said stop."

She said, "I know." Pause. Finally, she gave a little smile. "You're an idiot. Nothing you do reminds me of that night. That night I was scared—terrified." Pause. "I'm not scared of you."

Chapter 31

Maggie wished she could always be with Sara. Of course, she had spent the day with her. Now they were all spending the evening together. It was so much better when Sara was around. Nobody talked about things that should never be talked about. Nobody told their deep, dark secrets. But now it was time for Sara to go to bed. Maggie quickly volunteered to read the bedtime stories. She read so many that Sara was deep asleep before she left her room.

She cautiously walked out into the living room. Maybe tonight there would be no gut-wrenching confessions. Maybe tonight she wouldn't have to cry again. Maybe.

Michelle looked at Maggie and said, "I was telling Mike that I got the number for a counselor—one that specializes in—" It was hard to say the word "rape."

Maggie said, "Oh."

Michelle continued, "I made an appointment."

Maggie said, "Oh."

"We have to talk to someone about what to tell Sara."

Maggie nodded. She said, "I guess that's a good idea." She hurt for her friend.

"So you will go?" asked Michelle.

"Me? No, I thought the 'we' was you and Mike. I'll watch Sara. I'll go along with whatever you decide."

"I can't do it alone."

"That's why you are going with him." She pointed to Mike.

"But if you go," pleaded Michelle, "then we could both tell our stories. It would be so much easier." She bit her lip, trying to hold back the tears.

"What happened to me has nothing to do with Sara." Maggie's eyes were welling up. So much for a night without crying. Maggie looked out the window. She wanted to get out of there badly. But it was a really long walk home from here.

"Look," Maggie continued, "I know that you need to talk to someone for Sara's sake. And I will help you with that however I can, but I don't need to talk to anyone. I'm fine."

Mike and Michelle both looked at Maggie like she was crazy.

"OK, I have this little, bitty fear of the dark. But it's no big deal."

Mike finally entered the conversation. "Maggie, what I saw the other night was not an itty-bitty fear of the dark. It was an all-out panic attack."

"Well, you shouldn't have left me alone in the dark," she accused.

"I didn't. I was just around the corner of the house."

Maggie looked out the window again. She fingered her phone. She could start walking and then call Sandy to come and pick her up. But that was risky—she didn't always answer her phone.

Mike said, "What if Sara had been with us?"

Maggie said, "Look, I know your game plan. You always do this. You use Sara and Michelle to talk me into things I don't want to do." Why did she let Greg sell her car? If she had her car, she could get out of here. Stupid Greg.

"It's not going to work this time," she continued. She looked at Michelle. "You know I would do almost anything for you. And I would walk through fire for Sara. But not this, I can't do this."

Michelle gave in. "OK, I'll cancel the appointment."

"No, you should go. You have to go for Sara."

"If you can't do it, then I know I can't. You are much stronger than I am."

That elicited a laugh through the tears from Maggie. "Me, strong!? Where on earth did you get that idea? You are much stronger than I am. You are raising a daughter all by yourself. I can't even go outside in the dark." Well, thought Maggie. If that wasn't an admission that she needed counseling, she didn't know what was.

They all three knew that Michelle and Maggie were going to counseling together.

So Maggie started grousing, "Stupid Greg. You know, if he hadn't sold my car, I could get away from you guys. Then you wouldn't be able to talk me into doing things that I really don't want to do."

Michelle took a deep breath. "Thanks, Maggie. The appointment is tomorrow afternoon."

Maggie was back to panicking. "Tomorrow? No, that's too soon." She looked at Mike. "Do I have to?"

He said, "You don't have to, but you need to."

Sometimes you say, "I can't wait for tomorrow." Those tomorrows are slow in coming. Other times you can wait for tomorrow, but it comes really fast. This was the fastest tomorrow Maggie had ever experienced. Why did she agree to do this?

Mike and Michelle decided on the plan. Mike would drop Maggie and Michelle off at the counselor's. He would take Sara to the park and then pick them up when they were done.

Maggie had a plan too. She decided she would steer the conversation to Sara and what to do about her every chance she got. She would say, "Yes, I got attacked in the dark, but what should Michelle tell Sara about her dad?" Foolproof. She glanced at Michelle in the backseat. She looked about as scared as Maggie felt. OK, that was plan B. Plan A—convince Michelle to sneak out the back door as soon as Mike dropped them off.

Michelle looked at Sara. She had to do this for Sara. Sooner or later, she was going to have to tell Sara something about her dad. But sooner had come too soon. Maybe she should wait until later. Maybe they should just sneak out the back door when Mike dropped them off.

Mike could feel the fear in the air. Some from Maggie, some from Michelle—but a good measure of it came from him. He didn't know if either one of them could handle this. He wouldn't be surprised if they snuck out the back door after he dropped them off.

After the longest hour of his life, he was back to pick them up. One look at the two pair of red, puffy eyes, and he knew they hadn't snuck out the back door.

He left Sara in the car and walked up the sidewalk to meet them. He put an arm around each one and asked, "You guys all right?"

Michelle said, "Yeah."

Maggie said, "Let's go."

Maggie got into the backseat with Sara—which was different. Usually, Michelle sat in the back with Sara.

Sara said, "Hi, Miss Maggie!"

Maggie said, "Did you have fun at the park with Uncle Mike?"

Sara was excited. "Yeah, we played on the teeter-totter and the monkey bars and the slide. I even went down the big slide with Uncle Mike! Then Uncle Mike pushed me on the swing!"

"Did you show Uncle Mike how you can pump?"

"No, Uncle Mike likes to push me. He pushed me really, really high!"

"Really, how high?" This was much better therapy for Maggie.

"Up to the sky!"

"Well, if you were going really, really high, I hope you were holding on really, really tight!"

"I was. We got you a surprise."

"Really, what is it?" Maggie felt better and better talking to Sara.

"I can't tell you 'til your 'ppointment is over. Uncle Mike, is the 'ppointment over?"

Mike said, "Yes."

"Can I tell the surprise?"

Mike repeated, "Yes."

"We got ice cream! Guess what flavor."

Maggie guessed, "Strawberry?" "No." "Bubble gum?" "Nooo." "Umm, ladybug?" Sara giggled, "Ladybug—there is no ladybug ice cream, is there?" Maggie smiled. "No. I give up. What kind is it?" "Chocolate, you silly!" "Chocolate, I never would have guessed chocolate!"

At Michelle's, Sara and Maggie went ahead to dish up the ice cream. Mike and Michelle stayed in the hall.

"What did he say?" asked Mike.

"He said we can't tell Sara anything until I work through it myself. We have another appointment for next week."

He gave her a hug and said, "You're doing the right thing."

Later, at Mike's house, Mike asked Maggie, "How did it go?" She really looked pretty happy after eating ice cream with Sara.

She said, "He said Maggie is all right. Maggie doesn't need to talk about this anymore, ever. Maggie is just fine."

"That's funny. He told Michelle you needed another appointment."

"So she ratted me out again. You know that sister of yours ratted me out several times today. I would say, 'I'm all right.' She would say, 'No, she isn't.' I would say, 'I have my fear of the dark under control.' She would say, 'No, she doesn't.' What she wouldn't say is what happened to her. All she would say is she couldn't remember anything."

"She can't."

"I know—she is so lucky. I wish I couldn't remember."

Time for the next "ppointment" as Sara called it. Maggie decided this one couldn't be that bad. She had already told her whole story—there was no more for her to tell. This time Michelle would have to do the talking.

Pastor Dave wasn't only a counselor. This wasn't a counseling center—it was his church. From the front it looked like a regular store front—which is what it used to be. Inside was a small sanctuary with a set up for a band including a drum set. Outside was a beautifully manicured lawn with a picnic table, a playground, and even a picturesque waterfall.

Pastor Dave started with, "How was your week?"

Neither one answered. They were each waiting for the other to talk first.

Pastor Dave thought this was why he usually didn't do therapy with two people at the same time.

"I'm glad you decided to come back."

"Well, Mike said I had to," joked Maggie.

"Mike is right. We both need to," said Michelle.

There was that name again. Last time he didn't ask because he wanted to keep them on track. But this time he asked, "Who is Mike?"

"My brother." "My boyfriend." They answered at the same time.

"Sounds like he is important to both of you."

Now this was a subject Michelle liked. She talked about her childhood with her twin brother until Pastor Dave asked, "What did Mike say when you told him you had been raped?"

Michelle shut down at that.

After an awkward silence, she blurted out, "Maggie slept with Mike the day they met!"

Maggie looked at Michelle in shock with eyes and mouth wide open.

Michelle looked away in shame. She was sorry she said that.

Pastor Dave ignored the comment. One of the things he knew was that he needed to be unshockable. He wasn't here to judge people. That was Jesus' job—not his.

He said to Michelle, "I understand that it's difficult talk about the rape. Typically, women try to ignore it, pretend it didn't happen. Was that your experience?"

Michelle said, "I don't remember anything. I didn't know I was… until I found out I was pregnant."

She was obviously done talking.

Pastor Dave looked at Maggie. "Was that your experience after you were attacked?"

"Yeah, I didn't tell anyone for a long time."

"What changed that?"

She just said, "Mike."

"Why did you tell him?"

"I kind of had to. I got scared in the dark. I went a little crazy. Mike called it a panic attack. I had to tell him. He doesn't let that kind of thing go."

"He seems important to you," Pastor Dave repeated.

"I didn't mean to sleep with him the day I met him." Maggie looked at her hands.

"What happened?" Pastor Dave asked calmly.

"I was having…it was a really bad day. Sandy, my best friend, was trying to keep me busy. Keep my mind off of, uh, things. She wanted to go to a bar after a soccer game to meet this guy who had given her tickets to the game. That's where I met him. I didn't want to stay there, and neither did he, so we walked to his house. I wasn't even going to go in. But then he went inside. He said he would be right back, but I was scared to stay out there by myself in the dark. So I went inside."

Pastor Dave waited.

"I don't know what happened after that. I can't explain my behavior. That isn't like me."

"Sometimes we tell ourselves lies. And that changes our behavior, especially at a weak moment."

Maggie thought for a moment. "I was supposed to marry another guy that day. I told myself that it was OK. That it was my wedding night. I had waited until my wedding night, and then the wedding never happened. It wasn't my fault. At that point it seemed like…like I deserved it."

"How did you feel afterward?"

"Ashamed, embarrassed. I thought I had just had a one-night stand."

"But it wasn't a one-night stand?"

"He just kept showing up at my house. And then he got me a job as Sara's nanny, which I really needed. I wasn't going to sleep with him again. But I told myself another lie. I overheard one of his teammates calling me his one-night stand. I decided if I slept with him again, I wouldn't be his one-night stand. But that didn't make me feel any better. After that, I tried to stay away from him. But I just couldn't. I just can't. I know it's wrong, but I just can't stay away from him." She looked at him hopefully. Maybe he would tell her it was all right. Maybe he would say it wasn't so bad. She didn't have to feel guilty.

No such luck. Pastor Dave said, "I am sure you know the commandment, 'You shall not commit adultery.' God didn't say that because He is mean and wants to keep you from having fun. He wants to protect you. God wants us to save sex for marriage. Here is your homework—imagine a world where God's commandment about adultery is honored. What would that world be like?"

Maggie wouldn't talk to Michelle on the way home. Michelle drove them to her apartment. As they got out, Michelle said again, "Maggie, I'm sorry."

"Yeah, whatever," replied Maggie.

Maggie didn't want to even go in. She wanted to wait out there for Mike to come out and take her home. But she was still afraid of the dark. She really needed to get over that.

Inside, Mike asked, "How did it go?"

Maggie said, "Let's just go."

Michelle looked like she was going to cry. "I am so sorry. I shouldn't have said that."

Maggie said, "No, you shouldn't have. You need to talk about your own stuff. You are never going to get over this if all you do is rat me out so you don't have to talk."

Mike asked, "What happened?"

They both ignored him.

Michelle apologized again, "I'm sorry. I'm sorry. I promise next time I will talk. I won't do it again."

"Next time—you are crazy if you think there will be a next time!" shouted Maggie. Mike said, "Shh. Sara is asleep."

Maggie calmed down. She looked at Michelle. She really did look sorry. Maggie softened. "It's OK. It's not like it wasn't true. But you owe me. Next time you talk the whole time."

"Deal."

Mike asked again, "What happened?"

Maggie said, "Nothing—your sister is just mean."

"Maggie!"

Michelle said, "And your girlfriend is awfully sensitive and a little lacking—you know, in a moral sense."

"Michelle!"

But Maggie was laughing. "Oh, no, she didn't! I will get you for that one!"

She grabbed Mike's hand and pulled him to the door. "Come on, tonight you are going to tell me all your sister's deep, dark secrets. Then I will have some ammunition for next time!"

Mike didn't know what that was about, but they seemed happy enough now, so he let it go.

Chapter 32

At the next appointment, Maggie sat on the couch with her arms crossed. She was determined to make Michelle keep her promise to talk. And Michelle did talk. She told them about finding out she was pregnant. She told them about feeling ashamed and hiding at Grandma Rose's house. She told them she was afraid that the baby would be a boy and that he would grow up to be a rapist. She told them that she wanted to give the baby up for adoption. She told them that she still worried because half of Sara's genes were from a rapist. She told them that she didn't know how she would ever explain this to Sara.

Michelle was crying. Maggie was crying right along with her. Listening to Michelle's story wasn't any easier than telling hers. Finally, Michelle exhausted the subject and exhausted herself.

Pastor Dave knew she needed a break. So he asked Maggie, "I was wondering. The night you met Mike, was it dark when you walked home with him?"

"Well, yeah, but it was all right. I am not scared of the dark when I am with someone I trust."

"But you just met him, right?"

Maggie couldn't believe it. She had done the exact same thing that she had done with the guy at the frat party. Why had she done that? She could have been attacked again or even raped. She looked at him for answers.

He said, "You avoid being in the dark because you think that will keep you safe. Who do you feel safe with in the dark?"

"Sandy, Michelle, but mostly Mike."

"From the first time?"

"Yeah."

"But he was a stranger then, right?"

"Yeah."

"So you walked home with a stranger, and you were safe?"

"Only because it was Mike."

"But you didn't know that then."

"OK, so I was stupid again. I just lucked out that time."

"Are you with Mike every night?"

"When he is in town. He goes out of town a lot."

"What do you do then?"

"Stay home."

"Do you ever read the Bible?"

"No, I don't even have a Bible."

He found a Bible and put a marker in the middle. "Try reading this."

Michelle dropped Maggie off at Mike's. Maggie went outside and sat on the patio. It would be hours before Mike was home.

Maggie sat on the patio, getting some sun and thinking. She realized she had never done her homework from last time. What would the world be like if everyone obeyed God's rules about sex? Well, her first thought was if everyone had just one partner for life, there would be no sexually transmitted disease—no AIDS. There would be no unwed mothers. No pregnancy scares. There would probably be a whole lot less divorce since no one would be cheating on their spouse. There would definitely be less pain and betrayal. She imagined a world where every child was raised in a family with two parents. And if everyone obeyed, there would be no rape. That in itself would be worth it. And just think of all the shame and embarrassment she could have saved herself if she hadn't slept with Mike. If she had stayed out on the porch and they had just talked. Then they could have just started dating. They could have gotten to know each other—so much less awkwardness. That would have been so much better. She was so sorry for what she had done. She wished she could go back in time and change it somehow. She wished she could still be a virgin on her wedding night. She still thought that was the right thing to do.

Then she remembered her other homework. She found the Bible Pastor Dave had given her. She opened it to the bookmarked page. Psalm 91. It was verses 4–6 that caught her attention:

> He shall cover you with His feathers,
>
> And under His wings you shall take refuge;
>
> His truth shall be your shield and buckler.
>
> You shall not be afraid of the terror by night,
>
> Nor of the arrow that flies by day,
>
> Nor of the pestilence that walks in darkness,
>
> Nor of the destruction that lays waste at noonday.

She reread the part that said, "You shall not be afraid of the terror by night." It felt like Jesus was speaking directly to her. What was the verse saying? That He—Jesus—would protect her?

She kept reading until it got too dark to see. Then she sat there thinking—and praying. Asking Jesus to protect her. She felt calm.

"Maggie? Where are you?" asked Mike.

"Out here."

"You're sitting out here alone in the dark? Are you OK?"

She smiled. "Yeah." OK, she was sitting in a fenced-in backyard with Jackson. She knew Mike would be home any minute. It wasn't a particularly dangerous situation, but yesterday she couldn't have done it. Maybe Jesus was with her. Maybe that was the secret to staying calm. Talking to Jesus.

Chapter 33

Michelle said, "His name is Scott."

"Who?" asked Maggie. When she looked at Michelle, she knew. "The guy you like?"

Michelle nodded.

"Well get him over here! Let's take a look!"

"No."

"Mike is out of town this weekend. You make a date with him. I'll watch Sara."

"No, that won't work. You have to go with me."

"You want me to go with you on a date! That wouldn't be awkward at all!" said Maggie sarcastically.

"Not just you, you and Mike. Like a double date. OK?"

"What about Sara?"

"Would Sandy babysit?"

"She probably wouldn't give up a weekend, but I guess she would if it was a weeknight."

Maggie and Michelle sat in a booth with a round table at the In-N-Out Burger. They were meeting both Scott and Mike there. They ordered and then sat down together leaving room on either side for the guys. Michelle was pretty nervous. Maggie thought it didn't seem like much of a date.

Scott walked in just as the waiter called Michelle's name to pick up her food. He waved and stopped by the counter to pick up the food. He took the food to the table, taking their cups, and asked, "What do you want to drink?" He ordered his food and then filled their cups with Coke like they asked.

Maggie said to Michelle, "He is quite the gentleman!"

Michelle looked white as a sheet.

Scott worked at the hospital. He was a first-year resident. Michelle saw him often because her nursing school had her at the hospital often doing practical work.

Scott sat next to Michelle but talked mostly to Maggie. Mike walked in. He shook Scott's hand and then sat down next to Maggie. The three of them chatted. Michelle mostly stared at her Coke. Suddenly it dawned on Maggie. It was the Coke that was throwing her. Michelle was afraid to drink the Coke. It didn't make sense; he hadn't had the opportunity to drug her Coke. But it made sense to Maggie—it was just like her fear of the dark. Avoid the situation. Maybe she could help Michelle. Maggie took a drink of Michelle's Coke. At first, Michelle looked petrified. But Maggie gave her a steady look as if to say, "Nothing is going to happen to me."

Michelle swallowed hard. What if the Coke was drugged? What if Maggie was knocked out? Then she realized. Nothing would happen to Maggie. Mike was here. He would never let anything happen to Maggie. Of course, he wouldn't let anything happen to her either. She took some calming breaths. Maggie didn't pass out from drinking Michelle's Coke, so Michelle relaxed. She started eating and even joined the conversation a little.

It was definitely a short date. Mike had to leave early in the morning for Houston. Maggie wanted to go home with him. Michelle had no intention of staying with Scott alone. So they split up not long after they finished eating.

At home, Michelle answered Sandy's questions. "Was Scott hot?" "Not exactly hot, but he was nice-looking." "What does he do?" "He is a doctor." Sandy was impressed. "When do I get to meet him?" "I don't know."

Michelle confessed her inability to drink her Coke. Sandy knew about Sara's dad now. Sometimes she watched Sara so Maggie and Michelle could go to therapy together.

She teased Michelle, "Maggie is afraid of the dark, and you're afraid of Coke. You two are quite a pair! No wonder you are in therapy together!"

Michelle said, "Shut up!" But she wasn't really mad. She didn't mind Sandy's teasing. It was nice to have her as a friend.

Chapter 34

Sandy tried as hard as she could, but Michelle wouldn't budge. She would not invite Scott over to watch the game with them. Sandy liked having guys around. Mike and Owen were both in Houston. The only guy left to invite was Scott. Besides, she still hadn't met him. Michelle talked to him every day at the hospital and apparently every night on the phone after Sara went to bed. She talked about him all the time. But she wouldn't invite him over.

Maggie looked wistfully at the TV screen. She missed Mike. It seemed like lately the only time they were alone together was when they were asleep. Michelle had Maggie going to counseling all the time. Mike was worried about Michelle, so they usually ate supper at Michelle's and stayed at least until Sara's bedtime. That was when he was home. It was the middle of the season, so he was pretty busy with training, team meetings, and traveling. She was anxious to get a glimpse of him on the TV.

The therapy sessions were going well. At first it had been awkward seeing Pastor Dave after Michelle had confessed Maggie's secret sin. She had expected him to tell her she was going to go straight to hell. He didn't. He made it absolutely, unequivocally clear that he thought it was wrong. And he had the Bible verses to back it up. Yet somehow, she was still comfortable with him. More than once she wondered if he had truth serum pumped into the room. She was always spilling her guts there. But he never made her feel guilty about it. She still felt guilty but not because he thought it was wrong—because she did.

Maggie settled down on the floor with Jackson to enjoy the game. And she did enjoy it—eating hot dogs with Michelle, Sara, and Sandy, cheering for the team, and yes, yelling at the refs.

After the game, Maggie drove home in Mike's Jeep—by herself—in the dark. That was why she brought Jackson to Michelle's. She figured she could make it home if she recited her Bible verse and prayed. But just in case she brought Jackson. She made it without a problem. Maybe she could get over this fear of the dark thing. After all, it didn't happen because it was dark. It didn't even happen because she was with a stranger. It happened because that one guy was evil. She would still avoid dangerous situations—she would still be cautious. But Jesus would protect her. That brought peace to her heart.

The next day, Mike called and said she didn't need to pick him up. He would catch a ride with Owen. Owen was going to see Sandy anyway. Maggie was disappointed. She wanted to pick him up.

She put on his jersey because he liked that, took her hair out of the ponytail because he liked that, and went upstairs to wait in the bedroom. She figured they would end up there anyway. She got out the laptop. Maybe she could take care of all the emails before he got home.

"Maggie?"

"I'm upstairs."

One email left.

Mike came into the bedroom.

"Hi." He sat down on the bed and started kissing her.

"Are you done with that?" he asked.

"Mmhmm," she murmured without opening her eyes.

He continued kissing her. "Can we put it away?"

"Um. Sure. OK." But she didn't.

Finally, he pulled back, took the computer, and shut it down.

Maggie had forgotten all about the computer on her lap. Wow, she got stupid when he kissed her.

"I didn't know you had a computer," said Mike.

"I don't. Well, I do, but it doesn't work," Maggie answered.

"Whose is that then? Sandy's?" He pointed to the laptop he had put on the nightstand.

"No, Scott's."

Mike was surprised. "Why do you have Scott's computer?"

"Well, Michelle and I were at therapy on Friday. When we came out, there was Scott. Apparently, he goes to Pastor Dave's church. Did you know he was the one who gave Michelle Pastor Dave's number in the first place? Anyway, he started telling us about the charity he is working with. It's called Operation Christmas Child. They pack Christmas presents for poor children and send them all over the world."

"Christmas presents? It's June!"

"Yeah, I guess usually they do this in October and November. But Scott is working with these Trailmen on a summer service project. Did you know Scott has a Trail Life USA troop?"

"No, I didn't."

"Scott was a Boy Scout when he was growing up. In fact, he is an Eagle Scout. He always thought he'd become a troop leader someday, but one day a friend from church told him about Trail Life USA. He looked into it and liked its Christian values. So he started a troop.

"A couple of years ago, he started doing Operation Christmas Child with his troop. Last year more troops joined the effort. This year there are Trail Life troops all over the city collecting items to put into shoe boxes. Then they are going to have a big packing party."

"So you need his computer for…?"

"Oh, see, it's growing so big that Scott was having trouble keeping track of everything that each troop is doing. So Pastor Dave suggested he get somebody to help him. I volunteered."

"And he gave you his computer as a reward?"

"No," Maggie laughed. "All the troop leaders are emailing Scott to let him know what they are doing. Some are collecting toys outside of stores. Some are getting donations from businesses. Some are raising money. I am checking the emails and keeping track of what has been donated. Then he can decide what to use the money for. For example, we have a big donation of pencils but no pencil sharpeners."

"I told you before you can use my computer."

"I didn't need a computer until now. Besides this one is all set up for everything I need."

"I'm hungry," said Mike.

"I'll you get you something. What do you want?"

"I don't know. You stay here. I'll go get us a snack."

"OK." She smiled.

She could look at that one last email really quickly. Another donation of pencils—that's good. She clicked to enter it on the spreadsheet. That was strange. She picked up her phone and dialed.

Mike came back with a tray loaded with food. He heard Maggie talking on the phone.

"Hey, I have a question for you. Didn't we already have a donation of pencils?"

"Oh."

Mike showed her the tray. She held up one finger.

"Oh. OK."

She smiled into the phone. "That makes sense. OK, see you later."

Mike asked, "Was that Scott?"

"Yep, wow, you are hungry. It's the middle of the afternoon, you know."

"What can I say? The game yesterday…"

Her phone rang. He grabbed it out of her hand and answered it, "Hello?"

"I was looking for Maggie," said Scott on the other end.

"She's busy," said Mike. Maggie was laughing. "Give me the phone!"

Scott said, "Is this Mike?"

"Yeah."

"This is Scott. I didn't know you were back."

"I'm back. Maggie can't talk right now, Scott."

Scott could hear Maggie in the background. "Give me the phone!"

Scott said, "Not a problem. It isn't important."

Mike hung up.

"I'm not that busy," Maggie giggled.

"Yes, you are," replied Mike.

A couple of days later, Mike had a break during training. It was almost time for Sara's nap. Maybe he could talk to Maggie for a while.

She answered, "Hello?"

There was a lot of background noise—kids screaming, music playing.

"Maggie? Where are you?" asked Mike.

"Chuck E. Cheese," Maggie giggled. Then she started laughing right out loud.

"What's going on?"

She was still laughing. "Scott is in the ball pit, pretending to be a monster. All the kids are screaming!"

Mike had a million questions. "Why are you at Chuck E. Cheese? Why is Scott there? Where is Sara?"

Maggie laughed, "She's in the ball pit, screaming! He's so funny. All the kids love him."

"Maggie, why are you at Chuck E. Cheese?"

"This morning Scott needed help sorting through the donations. So he picked up me and Sara."

"Does Michelle know this?" Mike demanded.

"Yeah, anyway he said Sara was such a good helper, he would take her to Chuck E. Cheese. Then Sara lost her shoe in the ball pit. Scott volunteered to go in and find it. Now, neither one of them wants to come out!"

Mike didn't like this situation at all.

Wednesday night Scott invited them to go to church with him. Mike didn't want to go. He thought it was enough to go on Sundays with GG Rose. But Maggie looked so disappointed, he gave in. After the service, the grownups sat outside at the picnic table drinking Cokes from the snack bar while Sara played on the playground. Mike was tired. His ankle hurt. Brandon had kicked him hard at practice. It was an accident, but it still hurt. Scott and Maggie were talking about the packing party and such. Mike was wishing they could go home. Michelle was staring at her Coke. Maggie finally noticed, so she picked up Michelle's Coke and took a drink.

"Hey, that one is Michelle's," laughed Scott.

"Oops." Maggie smiled.

Maggie and Scott were having a great time. Mike and Michelle—not so much. Mike finally brought up that it was past Sara's bedtime. They had to go. They walked out to the cars. Scott offered to take Michelle and Sara home. But Michelle said, "That's OK. Mike will do it."

Sara was settled in her car seat. Michelle settled in the back seat with her. Maggie was still talking to Scott.

Mike said, "Let's go."

Maggie said, "Just a minute," and kept talking.

Mike said, "Come on, Maggie."

"I'll be right there."

Mike was tired and grumpy. He walked over to Scott's car, grabbed Maggie around the waist, and carried her to the car. Maggie giggled and said, "Guess I gotta go. See you tomorrow."

In the car, Mike asked, "Why will you see him tomorrow?"

"Someone donated bags and bags of socks. They need to be rolled into pairs and organized by size before the packing party. I said I would do it."

True to her word, Maggie was rolling socks when Mike got to Michelle's the next day. The problem was—she wasn't doing it alone. Scott was there with her. Sara was asleep.

Mike didn't like this situation, but he didn't want to look like a jerk, so he sat down and helped them. When they finished, he helped Scott carry the socks to his SUV. He expected him to leave, but he didn't. Apparently, Michelle had invited him to dinner.

Michelle was determined to handle this better tonight. She was fine until they started eating. She didn't even have a Coke. They were drinking lemonade; it didn't help. She just couldn't get past this.

The oven timer dinged. Michelle and Maggie went into the kitchen to get the bread.

"Come on, Michelle, you made the lemonade yourself. He hasn't even touched your glass. You can drink it."

"I just can't. I know it's stupid, but I just can't."

"Mike is here. Nothing is going to happen. Just relax."

"I'll try. But don't leave before he does."

"Well, you better tell Mike because you know if he decides it's time to go, he will just pick me up and carry me out."

"Well, you could stand up to your boyfriend!"

"Well, you could—"

"Are you two coming back?" yelled Mike.

As they walked back into the dining room, Maggie whispered, "Put your glass close to me. I'll take a drink."

"Thanks," said Michelle.

It was a good evening. At least Maggie and Scott thought so. Maggie asked Scott about being Boy Scout as a kid. He told them about camping trips and earning badges. He talked about all the service projects they did. Maggie peppered him with questions. She was amazed that he had time to lead his Trail Life troop, work with Operation Christmas Child, and be a doctor.

Mike started talking about leaving. Maggie looked at Michelle—she stalled until Scott thanked Michelle for the meal and left.

The next day Mike got home, and there was Scott's car in his driveway. OK—enough was enough.

"Maggie!"

She didn't answer.

"Maggie!" he yelled louder.

She walked out of the bedroom. "You're home early."

He said, "Yeah, where is he?"

"Who?"

"Scott!"

"At the hospital."

"Maggie, his car is in the driveway. Where is he?"

He walked past her into the bedroom, looking for him.

Maggie just stared after him. What? Did he think Scott was hiding in the closet?

He came back into the hallway. "Where is he?"

Maggie spoke very slowly, "At…the…hospital."

"Then why is his car here?"

Maggie had never seen Mike mad before—grumpy, maybe annoyed. But this was all out mad.

Maggie said, "OK, calm down. Scott had to go to a bunch of places to pick up donations today. He asked if I wanted to go with him."

"With Sara?"

"No, Sara had to take a nap. Michelle had a half day of school. So she stayed with Sara."

"And you went with Scott?"

"Look, I tried to get Michelle to go. It's not my fault she can't be alone with her own boyfriend."

Mike didn't say anything. His jaw was still tightly clenched.

Maggie tried to lighten the mood. "I am beginning to question her friendship. She is scared to be alone with him, but she is fine with me being alone with him."

Mike didn't laugh. He growled, "That doesn't explain why his car is here."

"Oh, he got called into the hospital. He asked if I would drop him at the hospital and then finish picking up the donations. So I did."

Mike wasn't convinced. He looked like he expected Scott to appear at any moment.

Maggie's phone rang. She looked at the caller ID—Scott. She answered it, looking at Mike. "Hi."

"This isn't a good time."

"I'll call you back."

She hung up.

They went down to the living room. Maggie sat down on the couch and waited.

Mike paced back and forth. "Maggie, I don't like this. You are spending an awful lot of time with him. You're using his computer, going to Chuck E. Cheese with him, and now you're driving his car!"

"It's just for this packing party," Maggie said quietly.

"I don't care about the packing party!"

"Come on, Mike, it's just Scott. I can't think of a safer guy than Scott."

"Safe. What does that mean?"

"You know what I mean."

"No, I don't."

She got up and walked up to him. She stood close and looked up at him and smiled just a little. "I have to admit I really like it that you're jealous. But there's no reason to be."

"Are you sure? No reason at all?"

"None."

"It seems like you like him."

"Well, sure, I like him, but not like I like you."

"Really?"

"Really," she assured him.

"You aren't attracted to him? He is a doctor."

"He's a little nerdy."

"You don't like smart guys?"

"No, no, I like smart guys, but he isn't very strong."

"No?"

"I think I can lift heavier boxes than he can."

He chuckled and put his arms around her. "So you like smart and strong. Anything else?"

"Well, he has to have soft brown hair and beautiful blue eyes," she giggled, "and drive a Jeep Wrangler—oh, and have a dog named Jackson."

"Really, his dog has to be named Jackson?"

"Yep, that's a deal breaker!" She pulled away so she could see him. "Look, I'm not attracted to him, but even if I was, I wouldn't do anything about."

"Really?"

"Of course not. I promised you I wouldn't. Plus, he belongs to Michelle—he is off limits."

"So you and Scott are just friends."

"He feels more like a brother. Like one of Sandy's brothers—the nice one." Pause. "Mike, I really like working on this charity thing. But if it bothers you, I won't do it."

"Really?"

"Of course not."

Chapter 35

The next morning over breakfast, Maggie said, "Look, you are going to have to explain to Michelle that I can't hang around with Scott anymore. You know she's scared to be alone with him."

"What about Scott?"

"I will just say no when he asks me to help."

"It's just that easy?"

"Sure, I am good at saying no to guys." She looked sheepish. "Well, except to you."

"Maggie, you can work on the packing party with Scott."

"Really, you don't mind?"

"I may have overreacted a little bit last night."

"You mean when you were looking for Scott in all the closets?"

Now it was his turn to look sheepish.

She smiled and held her hands out like she was weighing something on a balance scale. "Overreacted a little bit—went crazy jealous," she said moving her hands up and down.

She was still smiling. "You set the rules—where you draw the line. If you don't want me to use his computer, then I won't. If you don't want me to drive his car, then I won't. If you don't want me to go to Chuck E. Cheese with him, then I won't."

"It's OK, Maggie. I trust you."

"Good, 'cuz I really like Chuck E. Cheese!"

They had a good weekend—without Scott. Now Mike was on a plane to Costa Rica playing in an international tournament. The game was on Thursday. As he got off the plane, his phone rang. He talked to Maggie on the team bus on the way to the hotel.

"How's Costa Rica?"

"Pretty nice. Where are you?"

"I'm at Michelle's with Michelle and Sara and Scott. I wanted to ask you something."

"What?"

"Can I go to church with them tomorrow night?"

He felt bad. Now she felt like she needed to ask his permission? "Maggie, you don't have to ask me for permission. You can go if you want to."

Maggie looked at Michelle and Scott. She walked into Michelle's room for some privacy. "Here's the thing. I will be alone with him."

"Why?"

"He is going to pick me up first, then Michelle and Sara, and take us to church. Then afterward take Michelle and Sara home first and then take me home last."

"That doesn't make sense. His house is closer to Michelle's. My house is on the way to the church from there."

"I know, but Michelle can't be alone with him."

"Why doesn't Michelle drive and you guys can meet him there?"

"That's what I said, but she thinks this is a date and he has to pick her up."

"That's crazy."

"I know. If you don't like this, I won't go."

"Do you want to go?"

"Yeah, I like going to Pastor Dave's church. Last time I learned so much. I really want to go and hear the teaching again. But I don't have to."

"I think if you want to go, you should go."

"Even if it's on Michelle's crazy date with Scott."

"Yeah, I trust you."

"I hope she gets over this soon. You know, if they ever get married, I'll have to go on their honeymoon with them! And be her drink taster!"

Mike laughed.

"I know this is hard on her," Maggie continued. "But come on, this is Scott. He is the safest guy I know."

"What about me? Aren't I safe?"

"Nooo. You are not safe!"

"What does that mean?" He sounded annoyed.

"You know what I mean."

"No, I don't!"

"You know. He's safe." Why couldn't she explain this? "No one is safer than Greg—I mean, Scott."

Mike didn't like the sound of that. Maggie didn't feel safe with him? She felt safe with Scott and Greg, but not with him? What was that about?

Maggie enjoyed church. She felt hungry for the biblical lessons that Pastor Dave was teaching. She wanted to come every week so she didn't miss anything.

Scott was almost done with his taxi service duties as he drove up to Mike's house. Maggie and Scott had been discussing the teaching. When he stopped in the driveway, she realized she had forgotten to leave the porch light on. It was dark. She was getting better about the dark, but she wasn't prepared tonight. She was feeling a little panicky. She looked at Scott. "Can I make a confession?"

"OK," he answered.

"The reason I go to therapy is that I was attacked several years ago. Now I am kind of afraid of the dark."

"I'd be happy to walk you to the door."

She breathed a sigh of relief. "Thanks."

They walked to the door, and she unlocked it.

"Are you all right now?" he asked.

"Yeah—well, could you come in just until I let Jackson in?"

"Sure."

After Jackson was safely in and the back door was locked, Maggie joked, "I keep telling Michelle that you are quite the gentleman."

Scott smiled. "Can I ask you a question?"

"Sure."

"Why do you have to ask Mike if you can go to church?"

"Well, I don't have to."

"But you did."

"Well, last week he thought I was spending a little too much time with you. He gets a little jealous."

"Just a little?"

"OK, more than a little." She smiled.

"So he didn't want you to go tonight?"

"No. We had talk. He's OK with it now."

Scott had an uneasy feeling about this, but he let it go. "You have my phone number. You can call me if you get scared while Mike is gone. Or even when he's here."

Maggie laughed, "Why would I be afraid if he's here? But thanks."

On the way home, Scott called Pastor Dave. "Hi, I'm sorry to bother you at home, but I have an uneasy feeling about something I wanted to share with you."

"No bother. What's the problem?"

"Well, I don't know if there is a problem. I just dropped Maggie off at Mike's house. I'm a little worried about her."

"Why?"

"Well, some things she has said. Some things I've seen."

"Like what?"

"Well, she asked Mike's permission to go to church. She told me he gets jealous. He wouldn't let me talk to her on the phone once, even though I could hear her in the background. Once when he wanted to leave, he picked her up and carried her to the car. Things like that."

"Do you think he's hurting her?"

"Not that I know of. I am probably way off base here. I know she's in therapy with you. I'm not asking you to tell me anything. I just wanted you to know in case you had the same concerns."

"Thanks for letting me know."

Chapter 36

There were Trailmen all over the church. Maggie was used to three-year-olds. But these were grade schoolboys—they were bigger and louder. And it was chaotic!

When it was time to start, Scott gathered all the boys and had them sit on the floor. He thanked them for all their hard work. He explained that these boxes would go all over the world and be given to children who may have never received a present in their lives. But even more important they would receive a booklet that would tell them all about Jesus. Then Maggie read the booklet to them. All the moms in the room were tearing up. They knew how important this was.

Then the boys got to work. They packed boxes. They wrote letters to the kids. They labeled them boy or girl. Then they stacked them in the middle of the room. Before they dug into the pizza that Scott had provided, they stood in a circle holding hands and prayed a blessing over the boxes.

Michelle took a load of pictures before the party broke up. Then the boys went home.

Michelle, Maggie, and Sara sat down at the picnic table to take a break and eat a piece of pizza. Scott brought over three Cokes. He opened one and poured some in a cup for Sara and gave another to Maggie. The last one he opened, took a drink, and handed it to Michelle. Maggie put her hand on her heart—how sweet was that? Michelle looked into his eyes as she took the Coke and took a sip.

Scott and Michelle were cleaning up the pizza plates and cups left by the Trailmen. They just weren't working very fast. Michelle had finally relaxed around Scott. Scott wasn't about to waste this time cleaning.

Maggie wanted to give them their space, so she was transferring the boxes that the Trailmen had packed into the storage room. Sara was supposed to be helping her, but she was busy playing with some Barbie dolls that were too big to fit in the box. Maggie had been taking four boxes at a time until she decided that was going to take forever. So this time she was trying for six. Maybe that wasn't such a good idea. She was having trouble keeping them balanced. That was when Mike walked in. He jogged over to take the boxes from her. She said, "Hey, I thought you weren't coming!"

"I just got back. How was the packing party?"

"Loud, chaotic, and so much fun! Look at all the boxes we packed!"

"That's great." He smiled.

"Now I'm trying to get all these boxes into the storeroom."

"All by yourself?"

"Well, my partner got distracted by the Barbies."

"Where's Scott?"

"Outside alone with Michelle," Maggie said, raising her eyebrows.

Mike was concerned. "Is she all right?"

"Yeah, major breakthrough on the Coke front," explained Maggie. "Don't worry. She is with Scott—he is—"

"Safe, yeah, I know."

"You have to be tired."

"I'm fine. I slept on the plane."

She didn't believe him. "Why don't you go home?"

"Not without you. I'll help you."

"You don't have to do that. Why don't you go play with Sara?"

"Barbies? I'll pass."

He added the boxes he had taken from her to the stack in the storeroom and then leaned in to kiss her.

Suddenly they were interrupted by Michelle clearing her throat loudly and saying, "Child in the room."

Sara said, "Uncle Mike likes to kiss Miss Maggie."

They all laughed.

It didn't take long to move all the boxes once they started working together.

Mike was ready to go. He looked at Michelle. "You ready?"

Michelle said, "That's OK. Scott can take me and Sara."

"Are you sure, Chel?"

She nodded and smiled.

Before Maggie finished getting ready for bed, she got a text from Michelle. Mike asked her why she was smiling. Maggie said, "He kissed her."

"What happened tonight? Did she tell him?"

"Not that I know of—he just shared a Coke with her."

Maggie seemed so happy for Michelle. He had really misread this whole Scott thing.

Chapter 37

Pastor Dave hadn't been worried about Maggie's relationship with Mike until Scott called him. The issues Scott brought up could be red flags. He felt like he should check into it a little further, which shouldn't be a problem. She and Michelle loved to talk about Mike.

"How's Mike?" asked Pastor Dave.

"Great." Maggie smiled.

"He's outside with Sara," added Michelle.

Pastor Dave thought this might be a good chance to talk to him today.

"How are you two doing?" He looked at Maggie.

Maggie thought it was time to be done with therapy. He was just making small talk now.

"Great," she repeated.

Pastor Dave just waited.

"Well, we had a little miscommunication for a while there. But everything is fine now."

"What kind of a miscommunication?"

Does he have to know every detail of my life? thought Maggie. "He thought I was spending too much time with Scott."

"He did?" asked Michelle.

"Yeah, he got a little jealous. I think it's hard for him because he is out of town so much. He likes to know what I'm doing."

"Did you have an argument?" asked Pastor Dave.

"Well, not an argument—he just said he didn't like it."

"You do spend a lot of time with Scott," said Michelle, like she had just realized that.

"Then what happened?" asked Pastor Dave.

"I told him there was no reason for him to be jealous."

Michelle voiced her thoughts again, "You do spend a lot of time with Scott. And he talks to you more than he does to me when we're all together."

Maggie couldn't believe her ears. "That's because you spend all your time staring at your Coke. It's not my fault you can't be alone with your own boyfriend."

"He's not my boyfriend."

"Well, he could be."

"Why are you spending so much time with Scott?" Pastor Dave tried to get them back on track.

"It was just for the packing party. It was all perfectly innocent."

Michelle glared at her.

"Come on, Michelle. You know I wouldn't do anything. Scott is off-limits. He's yours."

Michelle didn't look absolutely convinced.

"Besides you may have noticed I kinda like your brother."

"What did Mike do about his jealousy?" asked Pastor Dave.

"Well, he didn't do anything. He said he didn't like me hanging around with Scott so much. I told him if it bothered him, I would stop."

"Then what happened?"

"He said he trusted me and that I could keep helping Scott with the packing party." Pause. "He's still a little mad at me, though."

"Why?"

"I told him Scott was safe. Then I misspoke and said that Greg was safe. When he asked if he was safe, I said no. He didn't like that."

"So you think Scott and Greg are safe, but Mike is not?"

"Well, you know what I mean."

Michelle said, "No, what do you mean?"

"You know, Scott is safe." Why couldn't she explain this? She looked to Pastor Dave for help.

"You feel safe when you are with Scott and Greg."

"Sure."

"But not when you're with Mike?"

"No, no, no, of course I feel safe with Mike. I feel safest when I'm with Mike."

She looked at Michelle. She was still miffed at the idea of Maggie spending so much time with Scott now that she knew Mike had concerns—she wasn't going to be any help.

Pastor Dave asked the question directly, "Has Mike ever hurt you?"

Maggie was shocked to even hear him ask that. "No! Of course not! That's not what I mean. I mean," she closed her eyes and continued, "haven't you ever been around a person who, you know, you just can't think straight when you are around him? And then he kisses you, and your brain turns to mush, and all of a sudden, you are doing things that you never meant to do."

"So you feel out of control when Mike is around?"

"Yes, yes, that's it." Maggie felt relieved.

"And you're afraid that he will make you do things you don't want to do?"

"No, not things I don't want to do, things I shouldn't do."

"You said he always wants to know where you are."

"Yeah, when he's out of town, that's always the first thing he asks when he calls." Maggie smiled.

"He calls a lot when he's out of town?"

"Yeah." She looked at Pastor Dave. This didn't feel like small talk anymore. "I like that."

"Does he need to know where you are all the time when he is in town?"

"I don't have a car, so I am always wherever he left me last—except when I was with Scott."

"What about phone calls? Does he need to know who you call?"

"He gave me the phone! Look, you are on the wrong track. He doesn't control me. He just doesn't want me hanging out with other guys. That seems to be reasonable behavior for a boyfriend, right?"

"You tell me."

"Look, I like it that he calls me when he's out of town. I like it that he asks about what I'm doing. I like it that he's interested in my day. Greg never was."

"So he's different than Greg?"

"Like night and day! They are complete polar opposites."

"How so?"

"In every way.

"Mike has blue eyes.

"Greg has brown eyes.

"Mike wears jeans and T-shirts.

"Greg wears dockers and polos.

"Mike likes sports.

"Greg likes politics.

"Mike works out all the time.

"Greg has never seen the inside of a gym.

"Mike is always around.

"Greg was never around.

"Mike calls me several times a day every day—even when he is across the country.

"Greg rarely called me. Sometimes I didn't even talk to him for a week.

"Mike is always telling me what to do.

"Greg never did." Maggie paused. She had never really thought about how different they were.

"Why does Mike tell you what to do?"

"Well, there are so many schedules to consider every day—Michelle's classes, his training, what Sara wants to do. So every morning he comes up with a plan."

"Why does he get to decide?"

"He's my transportation. You don't need to look at me like that. He considers Michelle and Sara and me in the equation. As a matter of fact, he considers us first, long before he thinks of himself."

Pastor Dave looked at Michelle for confirmation.

Michelle said, "That's true, except he thinks of Maggie first, then Sara, and then me." She was smiling. She wasn't worried about Maggie spending time with Scott anymore. Maggie was pretty hung up on Mike. Besides she didn't need Maggie to be there when Scott was around anymore. She wasn't worried about being alone with him. But she did know what Maggie meant, except for her, it was Scott who wasn't safe. She had mushy brain syndrome as well.

Michelle needed to get to class. Pastor Dave asked if he could talk to Mike. Maggie volunteered to go get him.

"Pastor Dave wants to talk to you," said Maggie.

"Me? Why?" asked Mike. He didn't need therapy. He was much more comfortable sending Maggie and Michelle. Why would Pastor Dave need to talk to him?

"I guess he wants to meet the guy he has heard so much about."

Mike looked surprised. "You talk about me?"

Maggie smiled. "Come on, he is talking to me and Michelle. Your name comes up—a lot!"

Mike shook hands with Pastor Dave.

"Thanks for agreeing to talk to me."

"Is something wrong?" asked Mike.

"No, I just wanted to see how you are dealing with this situation."

"I'm fine."

Pause. Usually if Pastor Dave stopped talking, the other person would fill in. It always worked with Maggie. It didn't work that well with Mike.

"How did you feel when Michelle told you she had been raped?" asked Pastor Dave.

"Angry." Mike clenched his jaw. "How was I supposed to feel?"

"That's a typical reaction. What did you do with that anger?"

"Got myself kicked out of a soccer game. Look, I was only seventeen."

"What about when Maggie told you?"

"I was mad then, too, but I didn't do anything. When you play soccer, you learn to control your emotions on the field."

"Are you still angry?"

"Well, yeah. It's not right that these guys got away with it. Why does God let that happen? Where's the justice?"

"How do you know they got away with it?"

"Neither one of them called the police. At least Maggie got to fight back. I hope she broke his kneecap. I hope he still walks with a limp."

"So you are in control of all your emotions?"

"Why? What did Maggie say?"

"I can't answer that."

"OK, I get jealous. I don't have any practice at controlling jealousy. I have never been jealous before. But she's mine. I don't want her hanging around with other guys."

"Do you trust her?"

"Well, yeah, I trust her, but I don't trust other guys with her. She is so beautiful and smart and funny. I don't want someone to steal her away from me," he said, revealing much more than he had intended. Maybe Maggie was right. Maybe he did pump truth serum in here.

"How long have you known Maggie?"

"Since March 10th."

"So—three months."

"Yeah. So we are still getting to know each other, but Maggie and I are fine. And before you say anything, I know you think we shouldn't be sleeping together, but that just kind of happened. I made it right as soon as I could."

"How did you make it right?"

"I asked her to be my girlfriend. We are in a monogamous, exclusive relationship."

"And that makes it right?"

"Well, it's better. Just for argument's sake, what do you think would make it right?"

"That's not up to me."

"Then what does God think is right?"

"God thinks sex is reserved for marriage."

"So I am just supposed to stop sleeping with her?"

"Yes." Pause. "By the way, God also says, 'Vengeance is Mine.' That's in Deuteronomy chapter 32, verse 35, in case you want to look it up. Just because the police didn't catch those guys doesn't mean God didn't punish them."

Pastor Dave was glad he talked to Mike. He wasn't concerned about Maggie's safety. He now knew that the trouble they were having was because they had jumped into a relationship so quickly. He wished they would try it God's way. So often God's way didn't seem to make sense, but he knew from experience it was always the best way. He stopped and prayed for Mike and Maggie.

When Mike left Pastor Dave's office, he watched Maggie playing with Sara for a minute. Sara fell down and started to cry. Maggie picked her up and took her to the picnic table. She carefully looked at Sara's scraped knee. She dipped a napkin in the waterfall and gently cleaned the dirt from her knee. Then she sat down with her, wrapped her arms around her and rocked slowly back and forth, kissing her on the forehead. Sara snuggled right in.

Pastor Dave was wrong. What he was doing with Maggie was the adult version of what he had just seen. He needed to keep Maggie close to him so he could take care of her. He was doing for Maggie what Maggie had just done for Sara.

Chapter 38

Every time Maggie left therapy, she felt guilty about sleeping with Mike. She knew she should stop. But she always talked herself out of it by the time she got home.

When she was talking to Pastor Dave, she was convinced it was wrong. But as soon as she left the church, she had doubts. She still thought it was wrong the first time, but now what would it matter if they stopped? You can't unring a bell. It may not be exactly right, but stopping wouldn't change anything.

That evening Mike and Maggie were watching a sitcom. The woman in the show had a rule. She had to go on sixteen dates before she could sleep with a guy. Maggie harrumphed. She said, "That's ridiculous."

Mike said, "Why? What's your rule?"

She looked at him. "Well, apparently it's one date—wait, you didn't take me out on a date. I guess it's zero."

"How about with Greg? How many dates did it take?"

She looked at him. He looked like she was about to hit him with a sledgehammer. He didn't know, did he? She had to admit she liked it when he got jealous.

She said, "Let me get the calculator."

"The calculator? You don't need a calculator—just a ballpark figure."

"No, no. You asked." She found a calculator. "Let's see, I knew Greg for three years. Multiply that by fifty-two weeks equals 156. I probably saw him an average of once every two weeks, so I will divide by two. That's seventy-eight dates. So the answer is at least seventy-nine. Seventy-nine dates."

Mike raised his eyebrows. "You never slept with Greg?" He smiled big. He felt like jumping in the air like he did when he scored a goal. This was awesome!

"So the day I met you?" he asked.

"My first time."

He felt a bubble of joy filling his chest.

"Me too," he confessed.

"I know."

"How do you know that?"

"Michelle told me."

He kept smiling until it hit him. She was one week away from marrying Greg, and she hadn't slept with him.

"Why didn't you sleep with him?"

"Because it's wrong. You are supposed to wait until your wedding night."

The bubble burst. The joy evaporated. It wasn't only Pastor Dave who thought what they were doing was wrong. Maggie thought so too.

The next morning Mike was watching Maggie sleep. She looked so beautiful when she slept. He tried to examine his feelings. On the one hand, he was happy that she hadn't slept with Greg. The thought of her with him had always made him crazy. On the other hand, he was mad at himself for what he had done. She had wanted to be a virgin on her wedding night. He had taken that away from her. He sighed as he rolled over onto his back and looked at the ceiling. He thought, What a wonderful gift to give to your husband on your wedding night. He wished he hadn't messed that up.

Mike was still thinking about it when Maggie came down for breakfast.

She said, "Good morning." And got herself a bowl and a spoon.

As she poured Cheerios into her bowl, Mike said, "I'm sorry."

Maggie looked at him. "For what?"

"For sleeping with you the day I met you."

She got up to get some orange juice and said, "Water under the bridge," without looking at him again.

"I didn't know you were…saving yourself for marriage."

Maggie didn't like this subject. She mumbled into her Cheerios, "It's not your fault."

"What do you mean?"

"A girl crawls into your bed. What are you supposed to do?" She picked up her bowl and took it into the living room to eat.

Mike sat in the kitchen thinking about double standards. In this culture, the girl was supposed to say no. The guy got to do whatever he could get away with. Even Maggie believed that. It didn't make sense. Either it was right, or it was wrong for both of them. It was both their faults. Actually, it was more his fault than hers. He knew something was bothering her. There was no two ways about it. He took advantage of her. He liked to think that it wouldn't have happened if it hadn't been the day of his grandpa's funeral, but he couldn't be sure of that. After he had put aloe on her face, he couldn't resist the urge to kiss her. He went over to close the blinds to try to get himself under control. But he lost that battle. He knew he shouldn't have done it, but he did it anyway. Now Maggie was giving him a free pass. This wasn't right.

Mike had been traveling with soccer teams since he was a kid. At first it had been exciting. As he grew up, he still enjoyed playing away games—he'd play soccer anywhere, but the travel was boring. At this point, he accepted that it was part of the job. He never minded it that much until he met Maggie. Now it wasn't going to an away game. It was leaving Maggie.

Maggie was bored. Mike was on the road again. The packing party was over, so she didn't have any volunteer work to do. Michelle wasn't afraid to be alone with Scott, so they didn't ask her to tag along on dates anymore. They tended to go to kid-friendly places and take Sara with them, so they didn't ask her to babysit. Sandy was always out at places where she could meet guys, which didn't appeal to Maggie. So she stayed home and cleaned Mike's house. The only upside was that she rarely thought about Greg anymore. She was surprised to realize it had only been a few months since the big Debacle. So much had happened, it seemed like ages ago. Ancient history.

They all met at Michelle's house to watch the game, eating hot dogs and cheering for the team. It was a new team in Canada, so the guys didn't have much trouble putting it away. Maggie watched the post-game show to see if they would interview Mike. She liked watching him on TV. He was always so good-natured, saying it was a team effort. He never bad-mouthed the opposing team no matter what happened on the field.

Sandy and Maggie had a running joke. The players almost always said obviously before they started their comments. It was so common, they always laughed when they heard it. Tonight, Brandon was being interviewed right after the game. Sandy was pretty much over what happened with him, so she only booed a little when he came on. He said obviously five times through the course of the two-minute interview. Sandy and Maggie were rolling on the floor before the interview was over. Michelle and Scott didn't know what happened.

After Brandon's interview, the TV cut back to the commentators in the studio. They announced there had been a little incident before the game as the guys got off the bus. They cut to a tape of some girl running up to Mike and kissing him. Then the tape ended. Maggie stared at the screen. She didn't even hear what the commentators were saying about it.

She found her purse and left without saying a word.

Chapter 39

Maggie got into the Jeep and drove. It didn't matter where. She couldn't wrap her mind around what she had seen on the television. Who was that girl? Was it Bianca? Then she realized she didn't even know what Bianca looked like. He never talked about her. Who broke up with who? Did Mike break it off with Bianca and she wanted to get back together with him?

Of course, it might not even be Bianca. Every time they went to a game, Maggie wore Mike's jersey. Every time someone asked her about it. Most of the time it was a fan wanting to know where she got it. But once it was this aggressive female fan. When she started making a fuss about the jersey, Sandy said, "Back off—she's his girlfriend." You know what the response was? "That's only because he hasn't met me yet." It bothered her when it happened, so she stopped talking to that kind of fan. But maybe she was right. Maybe now he had met her. Or another girl like her. Or girls. What if soccer players were like sailors, but instead of a girl in every port, it was a girl in every stadium? Remember Brandon in San Jose? Was Mike like that too?

Michelle was on the phone to Mike before Maggie was out the door. She had to leave a message; he was probably still in the shower.

He finally called her back. "Hi, Chel."

"What happened?" she fired back immediately.

"What? When?"

"When you got off the bus before the game."

"I know that was wild. How do you know about it?"

"It was on TV."

He felt his heart sink. "Did Maggie see it?"

"Yeah!"

"Let me talk to her."

"She left."

"I gotta call her. I'll call you back."

Maggie was sitting at a red light when her phone rang. She looked at the caller ID. It was Mike. He always called after the game. Did he know he had been caught red-handed? On TV? Was he going to pretend nothing happened? Or was he calling to tell her who the girl was?

She stared at the phone until the light turned green and the car behind her honked his horn.

She hit the gas without answering it.

It rang again. Mike again, and again she didn't answer it. She didn't want to know who the girl was. She was stupid and ugly. And he could have her for all she cared!

The next call was from Michelle. She didn't answer that one either.

Another phone call, this one from Sandy. So Mike was calling Sandy now. She wasn't going to talk to anyone. She turned the phone off.

What was she supposed to do now? Where was she supposed to go? She always went to Mike's house. She practically lived there. Well, she couldn't do that now. Now that it was over. She was crying. She could hardly see. She better stop or she would wreck Mike's Jeep. Although that would serve him right.

She needed to walk. She thought better when she walked. She stopped at the beach. It was actually a place where Mike had taken her to watch the sunset not too long ago. How could he have done this? They had been talking this afternoon. He said he missed her. This didn't make sense.

She hadn't seen it coming—just like Greg. Why was she so stupid? Mike seemed like such a nice guy, but she had thought that about Greg too.

It was starting to get dark. She needed to go—but where? She wanted to be alone. She didn't want to talk to anyone, even Sandy. Especially since if Mike did want to talk to her, he would be calling Sandy. But how could she go to Mike's house? That seemed wrong—and painful. But at least she would be alone. Mike was still in Canada, so there was no chance he would come home. And she would need to get her stuff before he got back. She could go there now and start gathering her stuff. She would take everything to her house in the morning. Then tonight she could be alone—except for Jackson. Oh, Jackson—she needed to go feed Jackson! Poor thing—it wasn't his fault his owner was a jerk.

As she drove back to the place she used to call home, she thought it was her own fault. What did she expect to happen when she slept with a guy the day she met him and then basically moved in with him—"living in sin" as the old saying goes? This was always headed for disaster. She teared up again. He had been so nice to her. Now it was over. She knew it was wrong to sleep with him. Now God was punishing her.

She hadn't left the beach in time. It was already dark. This was too hard, Lord.

There was an SUV parked on the street. A man got out. Maggie was beginning to panic until she realized it was Scott.

"What are you doing here?" asked Maggie.

"I wanted to be sure you were all right."

"So you can report to Mike?"

"I think he would like to know you are safe."

"You can walk me in, and then you can leave, OK?"

"OK."

They walked to the door. Maggie unlocked it and went in. "Are you going to call him?"

"Yes."

"What are you going to tell him?"

"What do you want me to tell him?"

"Nothing." She took his phone out of his hand. She texted Mike, "She is home safe." She waited until it was sent, then turned off the phone. "That should do it. You are a good Boy Scout. Your job is over."

"Do you want to let Jackson in before I go?"

"OK."

She let Jackson in. She felt guilty about making him wait so long for his supper. She got his food while Scott waited.

Scott asked, "Anything else I can do for you?"

"Can you erase memories?"

"No." He smiled. "I may be able to explain it for you if you want."

She stared at him for a long time. "I don't want to know."

"Are you sure?"

"I don't care who the stupid girl is."

"It's dangerous to make decisions without all the facts."

"When did you two become such good buddies that you are going to stick up for him?"

"I may have information that would make you feel better."

"Nothing is going to make me feel better." She thought about how jealous Mike got about her being with Scott. How dare he?!

In the end, Scott left without explaining anything. He called Mike.

"Did you explain what happened?" asked Mike.

"She didn't want to hear it."

"You should have told her anyway!"

"She probably needs to hear it from you."

"She won't talk to me."

"Patience."

"Yeah, right."

Mike wanted to get on a plane and fly home and make her listen to him. She was so frustrating! He took a deep breath. She was home now. She wouldn't leave in the dark. He would have to find a way to talk to her tomorrow. He hadn't done anything wrong. As soon as he explained it, everything would be fine.

Maggie was tired. There wasn't any hurry to pack her stuff. He wouldn't be back until Thursday. He was flying to Portland tomorrow. The team would play there on Wednesday before returning home. She could pack tomorrow. She got into bed. Jackson rested his head on the bed, begging for attention. Maggie said, "Come on, Jackson. Get up." She cuddled up with him and went to sleep.

The next morning, she knew she needed to get out of there. It was Sunday. Scott, Michelle, and Sara were supposed to pick her up. Then they would pick up GG Rose and take her to church. Maggie wanted to go to church, but she didn't want to talk to anyone—especially Michelle. She would definitely want to talk about what happened last night. Maggie wasn't going to talk to anybody but Mike about it. And she wasn't ready to talk to him yet.

But she really wanted to go to church. Maybe she could leave here early, wait until she saw them go in, and then sneak in the back without them seeing her. That was risky. Wait, she could go to Pastor Dave's church. She loved to hear the teaching Wednesday nights. This would be her chance to go on a Sunday morning.

The teaching was good. Pastor Dave always reminded her that, just like Billy Graham had said on TV long ago, Jesus was her Friend—no matter how many mistakes she made.

Pastor Dave was surprised to see her. They chatted for a while after the service. Maggie told him how much she missed working on the packing party for Operation Christmas Child. He wanted to give her some information about how to volunteer for OCC in October. They went to the storage room to get a brochure. "This place is a mess," teased Maggie.

"Organization is not my strong suit," replied Pastor Dave simply.

"I could clean it up for you," volunteered Maggie.

"That would be great. I'll have to take you up on that some time."

"I'm free now."

"You are? Where's Mike?"

"Out of town."

Maggie was in heaven—there was so much to do in this storeroom, she wouldn't have time to think at all!

Hours later, Pastor Dave came back from visiting some church members at the hospital. Maggie proudly showed him all her work. "Look," she raved, "all the paper clips are in one box marked paper clips!"

He laughed. He could never find anything in there. Every time he needed a paperclip, he went out and bought a new box—there had to be a dozen boxes of paperclips in there!

"Thanks, Maggie. This is really going to help me out. But I feel guilty for making you work all afternoon."

"It was my pleasure." Especially considering the alternative—dodging people and phone calls.

"I'm hungry. Do you want to get something to eat?" asked Pastor Dave. He was in his late twenties and unmarried. He had no family to hurry home to.

Maggie was starving but penniless as usual.

She said, "I better not."

"Come on—my treat."

She was wavering.

"I owe you," stated Pastor Dave.

Maggie gave in. They went to Pastor Dave's favorite Italian restaurant, where he ate spaghetti and got spaghetti sauce on his shirt.

Maggie teased him again, "You are just a mess, aren't you?"

Mike called Sandy again. "Where is she?"

"I don't know," answered Sandy for the hundredth time.

"You are her best friend. You should know where she would go in a situation like this."

"There haven't been any situations like this before," said Sandy drily.

"It isn't like it looked on TV. I didn't do anything wrong."

"I know," said Sandy.

"Does she?"

"I don't know."

"Haven't you talked to her at all?"

"Nope, she is avoiding me too."

"Why would she be avoiding you?"

"Because she knows you will be calling me. She's not stupid, you know."

"I know that. Can't you go find her?"

"I told you I don't know where she is."

"You found her last time I needed to talk to her. Before she had a phone."

"That was easier."

"Why?"

"She didn't have a car. She could be anywhere now."

Mike growled.

"Don't get mad at me," exclaimed Sandy. "You're the one who gave her wheels!"

Monday morning, Michelle called Mike the minute she saw Maggie driving into the parking lot at her apartment.

Maggie came in and greeted Sara. Michelle, she ignored. "Hey, Bug!" Maggie had been calling Sara, Sara Bug practically since she met her because Sara loved bugs so much. The nickname now was shortened to simply Bug.

"What do you want to do today?" asked Maggie.

"Can we go see GG Rose?"

"That's a great idea! We need to take those books back to the library too. Can you go find them?"

Sara ran off to her room.

Michelle tried to hand Maggie her phone. "Mike wants to talk to you."

Maggie stared at the phone in Michelle's hand. "Not now."

"He didn't do anything wrong."

Sara ran back into the room and showed Maggie the books.

Maggie said, "There's one more. Remember the one with the ladybugs. Do you know where it is?"

"Oh yeah, I remember," answered Sara. She ran back to her room again.

Michelle said, "Come on, Maggie. At least you can talk to me about it."

Maggie didn't say a word.

Michelle tried again, "I thought we were friends."

Maggie looked at the phone that Michelle hadn't closed. Mike was probably on speaker. She said, "Right now you don't seem like my friend. You seem like his sister."

"I can still explain what happened."

She looked Michelle straight in the eye. "We both know you would lie for him."

Maggie was right, but if anything, that just annoyed Michelle all the more. "The least you can do is talk to him!"

Maggie replied, "Said his sister."

Sara ran back into the room with all the library books.

"Good job, Bug, let's go. Say goodbye to Mommy."

When Michelle came home from school, she tried again. But Maggie wasn't going to listen. She wanted to hear the explanation from Mike, yet she wouldn't answer his calls or call him. She knew Mike was frustrated, but she couldn't see any way to help him. Maggie was being pretty stubborn.

Instead of staying at Mike's, Maggie went to her own house. She found Sandy and asked, "You want to hang out?"

"It's been forever since we hung out just the two of us," replied Sandy.

"No phone calls, OK?" asked Maggie.

"Are you ever going to talk to him?"

"Not yet."

They settled down to watch their favorite chick flicks and eat popcorn, ice cream, and chocolate. After a while, Maggie paused the movie. "Am I making the same mistake again?" she asked Sandy.

"What do you mean?"

"You know, like with Greg, I put all my eggs in one basket."

"Then the bottom fell out of the basket."

"Now I'm doing the same thing, right? All my eggs are together—just in a different basket."

"You know I'm a fan of going out with as many guys as possible!" joked Sandy.

Maggie continued, "I practically live with him."

"What do you mean practically? You do live with him."

"I pay rent here."

"But you sleep there." Maggie didn't respond. "Every night." Still no response. "Even when he's out of town."

"I have to take care of Jackson," tried Maggie. "So I am making a mistake, and I should move back in here. Is that what you're saying?"

"Mike and Greg are not the same. Mike's a nice guy."

"We thought Greg was a nice guy too, didn't we?"

Sandy had to admit she had her there.

Tuesday morning Michelle didn't try to explain anything. She was happy Maggie was still watching Sara. Even if she wasn't being fair to Mike.

Nap time—Maggie didn't have anything to do. Michelle's apartment was clean; the laundry was done. She couldn't resist. She turned on her phone. It clamored with text messages and missed calls. She didn't listen to any messages or read any texts. She just texted, "Hi."

Mike was surprised and excited and not a little scared. How should he respond? He finally decided on, "Wanna talk?"

Her response: "No."

He decided to take the bull by the horns. "I didn't do anything wrong."

"So I hear."

"Will you let me explain?"

"Not now."

"When?"

"When you get back."

"It wouldn't take long."

She didn't respond. He thought he blew it. But he tried one more time. "I miss you."

"Have a good game."

"Will you watch?"

"Sure, I'm a soccer fan from way back."

"Way back? I thought it was March."

"Seems like a long time."

"Yeah, it does."

"Bye."

"See you Thursday."

Mike felt marginally better after that short conversation. Maggie didn't seem mad—at least now. She was still watching Sara, still driving his Jeep, still taking care of Jackson, still staying at his house. He had called his neighbor, Mrs. Anderson—the one who used to take care of

MISS LORI 233

Jackson for him. She told him Maggie was there and Jackson was in the house at night. He couldn't figure out exactly what was going on in that crazy, beautiful head of hers. He wondered what would happen Thursday when he got home.

Michelle was there to pick him up on Thursday. Disappointment—he was hoping it would be Maggie.

"Hi, Chel. Thanks for picking me up."

"Somebody had to do it."

"Where is she?"

"Your house."

"That seems good. Got any idea where she is on this?"

"Not a clue." He seemed so sad and unsure. He was just as hung up on Maggie as she was on him. She decided to give him some hope. "There is one thing I noticed. She hasn't taken off the necklace you gave her."

Since the day he formally asked her to be his girlfriend in the fancy restaurant, Maggie had worn that necklace with the M & M on it. She never took it off. She couldn't be too mad if she still had it on.

Maggie sat on the porch swing at Mike's house and waited for him to get home. She still hadn't heard the explanation. It didn't matter. She knew exactly what was going to happen. He was going to explain. She would believe him—no matter what he said. Things would go on exactly as before with her basically living with him.

She wasn't worried about the explanation. Even when she was walking on the beach after the game, she couldn't believe he had actually kissed someone else. It just didn't seem like something he would do. Then she got home and could tell that Scott thought there was a reasonable explanation. Michelle insisted that Mike had done nothing wrong. And Sandy had called him a nice guy. She knew for sure that if there was any doubt about what happened, Sandy would not have called him a nice guy.

The problem wasn't that kiss. The problem was she was in too deep. So that when this did fall apart—it was going to be bad. If she had any brains at all, she would get her stuff and move out for good. But it wouldn't matter if she moved her stuff back to her house. He would just find her and sooner or later, she would be right back here living with him. She wished there was a middle ground where they were just dating or something. But it felt like all or nothing. Either she lived with him, or she moved to another city or to a cave somewhere where he couldn't find her.

She decided to try a prayer before he got there. "God, I know this is wrong, but I can't help it. I want to do what is right. Please help me. Amen."

Mike walked up the steps to the porch slowly, hesitantly. He started with, "Hi."

Maggie took a deep breath and said, "OK, tell me."

Mike leaned on the porch rail and looked at Maggie sitting on the porch swing just like the first day they met and braced for the storm.

"It's really very simple. There was a breach in security. That girl ran past the guards. She ran up to me when I was getting off the bus. I never saw her coming. I don't know who she is. The guards caught her and arrested her for trespassing."

Maggie was staring intently at him, trying to figure out if she would know if he was lying.

Mike continued, "There is video of it on the team's website. It explains the whole thing. Did you watch it?"

"Why would I want to see that again?"

Good point, he thought. As bad as this was, it was good to know that she cared that much.

"I'm sorry," he said.

Maggie jerked her head back to look at him again. "Why? I thought you didn't do anything wrong."

"I didn't. I just meant I'm sorry that you saw it."

"So, if it wasn't on TV, you wouldn't have told me about it."

Of course not! he thought, but he said, "I know how it feels."

So Bianca cheated on him? "What did she do?"

"Who?"

"Bianca. Did she cheat on you?"

"No—it wasn't Bianca."

"Then who?"

"You!"

"Me?" said Maggie exasperatedly. "I never did anything with Scott. It was all perfectly innocent."

"Not Scott."

"Then what are you talking about?"

"Greg. I saw you kiss Greg."

"That's completely different."

"How so?"

"I saw my boyfriend kiss some random girl on TV."

"I saw my girlfriend kiss her ex-fiancé on the porch. Just minutes after she was sitting on the couch kissing me!"

Maggie felt like she was supposed to apologize for that, but she hadn't done anything wrong that night. "I wasn't your girlfriend then."

"I thought you were."

"You asked me after that."

"I asked you before that—I just didn't do it very well."

She thought for a moment and then asked, "Are you waiting for an apology? 'Cuz good luck with that!"

"No, Maggie, that's not it."

"Oh, I get it. Now we're even. You saw Greg kiss me, so now you get a free pass to kiss some depraved fan."

"I didn't kiss her. I pushed her away." The tape hadn't shown that.

"Then why did you bring up Greg? To distract me?"

"No. All I am saying is that I know it hurts to see someone you care about kiss someone else no matter how completely innocent that person is."

Mike could tell Maggie was done arguing. He went over and sat down on the porch swing next to her. "So we good?"

"Yes, Mr. Innocent. Mr. I can't help it if random girls are stalking me."

He smiled but needed reassurance just one more time. "So you believe I didn't do anything wrong."

"I always believed that."

"Really." It wasn't a question. It was a statement of disbelief.

She confirmed. "Really. It doesn't seem like something you would do."

"I wouldn't." Pause. "Wait—then why wouldn't you talk to me?"

"Just because I believe you didn't do anything wrong doesn't mean you didn't do anything wrong."

"What?"

"As I see it, there are still two possibilities. Either you are as innocent as you proclaim, or I am real easy to lie to."

He knew which one she thought was true.

"You know, it could be both." Pause. "Even if you were easy to lie to, it wouldn't mean I would lie to you."

As they made supper together, Mike wanted to know all about what Maggie had been doing when she wouldn't talk to him.

"So what did you do after the game on Saturday?"

Maggie looked at him, then said, "I went for a drive." Pause. "Did you ever want to get into the car and just keep going? Not think about where you are headed. Not care where you ended up. Just keep going?" she said looking off into space.

"How far did you go?"

She came back to reality. "Just to the beach. I didn't want to run out of gas. I might be crazy, but I'm not stupid. But if I still had my dad's credit card…"

"Did you do that before when you did have his credit card?"

"Nope. Never felt the need." Pause. "Just think. When I had that card, I could have been gone for weeks. I would have had money for gas, hotel rooms, food. Being poor stinks."

That was the first time he had heard her complain about being poor.

"So you went to the beach," he prompted. "Then what?"

"I walked around, and then it started to get dark."

"I'm surprised you came back here to my house. I thought you would be mad and go to your house."

"I had to feed Jackson."

He was relieved to hear that she was still sensible enough to worry about running out of gas and remember to feed Jackson. That was good to know. His imagination had run wild that night worrying about what she would do until he got the text from Scott.

"What did you do on Sunday?"

"I went to church."

"No, you didn't."

"How do you know?"

"Michelle told me you were gone when they came here to pick you up on Sunday."

"I went to Pastor Dave's church."

"Oh, then what?"

"What did your spies tell you?"

"I don't have spies." Maggie looked at him. "OK, nobody knows where you were until you got back here at about eight o'clock."

"How do you know it was eight o'clock? Scott wasn't here Sunday night."

He was caught. "I called Mrs. Anderson and asked her to call me when you got home."

"So another spy."

"You could have called me. Then I wouldn't have needed any spies."

She didn't respond.

"What did you do on Sunday?" he repeated.

"I said I went to church."

"After that."

"I stayed at church all afternoon organizing Pastor Dave's storage room. You know, you don't have to know everything I do."

"But I want to. OK, that was the afternoon. What about after that?"

"Are you sure you want to know?"

"Why? What did you do?"

"Sandy is always saying, 'Don't ask the question if you don't want to hear the answer.'"

"I want to hear the answer. What did you do?" He didn't look like he wanted to hear the answer.

"I went out to eat with Pastor Dave."

He clenched his teeth.

Maggie raised her eyebrows. "Jealous?"

"A little bit."

"Good."

"Why did you go out to eat with Pastor Dave?"

She waited a little while. Just to make him suffer a little bit. Then she shrugged her shoulders. "He said he wanted to thank me for organizing his storage room—and I was hungry."

He considered. She continued, "He is funny. He has ADD, which probably explains the mess in his storage room. He was telling me about all the crazy stuff he did as a kid. He grew up in New Mexico. He lived in an adobe house with a flat roof. Once he convinced his three-year-old brother to play hide and seek on the roof!"

Maggie was smiling, but Mike didn't seem to be enjoying the story as much as she was.

He asked, "Didn't he try to convince you to call me?"

"Why would he do that?"

"Wouldn't that be the Christian thing to do? To call me and give me a chance to explain?"

"He didn't know there was anything to explain."

"You didn't tell him?"

"Nope."

"Why not? He is your therapist."

"Because it's embarrassing. Even if you didn't do anything wrong, it's not something I'm going to go around telling people about."

Now he looked embarrassed. "I thought you told him everything."

"Apparently they don't pump truth serum into Italian restaurants. Besides he is not my therapist anymore. Didn't you hear? I am cured. I'm not crazy anymore."

"Yeah, you're not crazy," he said sarcastically and then smiled at her.

"OK, church all day Sunday, then dinner with your pastor. Sara told me about going to the library and to visit GG on Monday. How about Monday night?"

"You don't know what I did Monday night?"

"All I know is that you came back here sometime because Mrs. Anderson said Jackson was in the house."

"Ha! You need new spies—I did not stay here Monday night!" At least she knew Sandy wasn't reporting back to him—that was good.

"Then where was Jackson?"

"I took him to my house and had a girls' night with Sandy."

"What happens during a girls' night?"

"We watch chick flicks, eat junk food until we feel sick, and talk about boys." She smiled. How many girls' nights had she and Sandy had doing just that?

"What did you say about boys?"

"I'm sorry. You are not a girl, so that is strictly confidential."

"What about Tuesday?"

She shrugged. "I just hung out here." *And packed up all my stuff and almost moved back to my house.*

"And Wednesday night? Did you watch the game?"

"Yeah, how come you didn't play? Are you hurt?"

"No. The coach wanted to give another player some experience. It's no big deal."

"Oh." Pause. "OK, now you are all up to date. What did you do all that time?"

"Waited for my phone to ring."

"That sounds boring."

"It was—and frustrating."

"Oh."

"Next time this happens—"

Maggie jerked her head to look at him. "Next time?"

"Yeah, next time you are mad at me for something I didn't do."

"Oh, that next time." She smiled.

"Next time, you need to call me. Even if it's to yell at me. You can't just ignore me. It isn't fair."

"We'll see."

"No, you have to promise."

"Well, I can promise. But promises go out the window when people get mad," she said with a little smirk.

"What did you do?" he asked suspiciously.

She bit her lip and then giggled, "I let Jackson sleep with me all week! There is dog hair all over your bed!"

"Maggie!" He feigned anger, but he was actually relieved if that was the worst thing she did.

After supper, he took his bag upstairs. When he came down, he asked Maggie, "What's that box in the bedroom?"

"Oh, that's just my stuff."

"Why is your stuff in a box?"

She hesitated. "Um, I just gathered it all up—you know, trying to keep organized."

Mike didn't believe her. "Were you going to take it to your house?"

"Kind of."

He studied her for a moment and then asked, "What changed your mind?"

Again, she hesitated, then admitted, "I couldn't get the box in the Jeep."

He pulled her into his arms and said, "I'm glad you changed your mind."

He started kissing her but needed to know one last thing. In between kisses he asked, "Can I ask you something?"

Maggie replied, "Umhmm," without opening her eyes. She was lost in the moment.

"Was your dinner with Pastor Dave a date?" More kisses.

"Um, sure, OK."

Mike pulled back suddenly. "What!?"

Maggie looked like she just woke up. "What?"

"It was a date!?"

Maggie had no idea what he was talking about. She was totally confused. "What? What?"

"Your dinner with Pastor Dave was a date?"

"No, it wasn't a date. Of course not."

"You just said it was."

"When?"

"Two seconds ago."

She chuckled. "I can't believe you haven't figured this out yet."

"That you are cheating on me with Pastor Dave?!"

"No. You are such an idiot!" But she was smiling. "That I say yes to everything you ask me when you kiss me."

"What?"

"I can't think straight when you kiss me. So anything you say I just agree with. I don't even know what you're asking."

"What are you talking about? Why in the world would you do that?"

"Because if I say no, you might stop." Pause. "OK, I know that this is a stupid thing to do, and it is probably even stupider to tell you, but when you start kissing me, I am just going to say yes to anything you ask."

Mike couldn't believe what he was hearing.

She continued, "That's why you're not safe." Pause. "Scott and Greg are safe—and Pastor Dave for that matter—because I am in no danger of losing control. But with you—it all flies out the window."

Mike was having a hard time wrapping his mind around this, but he could remember several times this seemed to be the case. "So I shouldn't ask you things while we are kissing?"

"Not if you want a coherent answer."

Chapter 40

Mike got to the field early before the game. It was a beautiful, sunny California day. He looked over the field and thought, Life is good. They had weathered the storm. It wasn't that long ago that he had sat on this same bench before the first game of the season, missing his grandpa. So much had happened in that short period of time. He had been sitting on this bench sad and angry about his grandpa's death—worried and scared about his grandma's stroke. Then beautiful, crazy Maggie had come into his life like a whirlwind. He smiled thinking about how much better things were now. He still missed his grandpa—always would. But GG Rose was doing so much better. She was still in the skilled nursing home, but she made progress daily. He knew that Maggie took Sara to see her as often as she could—every day when she had his Jeep. GG Rose often said that was the best therapy. And Sara was so happy with Miss Maggie. She was always a great kid, but she was even better now. She was so reasonable. She was eating well, cleaning up, and learning new things every day. And Michelle—the difference in Michelle was the most astounding. He had thought that Michelle would never get over being raped. She was always adamantly against therapy. She never would have done it without Maggie. But now Michelle had come out of her shell and was seriously dating Scott. If he believed in miracles, that would definitely be one!

He smiled as he thought about Maggie—the whirlwind—again. She was like a whirlwind. She came into their lives like a big wind stirring everything up, but that was where the metaphor ended because Maggie didn't leave chaos in her wake like a whirlwind. Things were better because of Maggie. And things were better for Maggie too, right? He wondered if she was over Greg. She never talked about him. One thing was better for sure—her fear of the dark. He couldn't say that she was completely over it, but the therapy had helped her put things into perspective about the time she was attacked. He didn't know what had happened to those guys. But it did help to think that maybe God had punished them—you know, with lightning bolts or something. The important thing was that both Maggie and Michelle were OK now and on the right track.

There had been a lot of storms—his grandpa dying, his grandma's stroke, Maggie breaking up with Greg, Maggie's panic attack and fear of the dark, and then, of course, his jealousy and that demented fan incident. But all those storms were over. He and Maggie were closer than ever. It looked like smooth sailing from now on.

Maggie looked in the mirror as she put the finishing touches on her hair. It struck her as kind of silly to put so much effort into her hair when she was wearing Mike's jersey, which was clearly too big for her. But that was her game-day uniform!

She liked soccer. The game was fast-paced and exciting. She liked watching Mike play soccer. She smiled—she liked Mike. She still had her concerns, but at least for today, she was going to embrace Mike's soccer philosophy—it is what it is. And it was good.

Sara had the flu. Maggie's little angel was decidedly crabby—and whiney—and clingy. Unfortunately, it didn't seem to be the twenty-four-hour kind. It had been lingering, and Maggie was exhausted.

On the drive home from Michelle's, Mike commented, "You look tired."

"Thanks, you look good too," returned Maggie sarcastically.

Whoa, he wasn't trying to insult her. Maybe this wasn't the best time to do what he had planned, but he had to. He was leaving town again tomorrow.

As he drove into his driveway, he said, "Let me see your keys."

"Why?" she asked suspiciously.

"Just give them to me."

Oh, great, he was taking her keys—he didn't want her using his Jeep anymore. That was going to make this flu thing with Sara so much easier, she thought sarcastically.

She handed him her keys—what could she do? It was his Jeep.

He took a small key and put it on the key chain. He said, "This is for the console." He showed her how to open the compartment between the seats. Then he took out his wallet. "This is a gas card." He put it into the console and handed her back her keys.

She considered for a moment. "You're giving me a gas card?"

"I don't want you to run out of gas."

"Do you not remember our little conversation last time you came home? How the only reason I didn't drive off and disappear for weeks was because I didn't have gas money?"

"I remember."

She laughed. "Well, then you are either very trusting or a little bit stupid!"

He smiled. "The one thing I know I can trust you with is money."

"So you're not afraid I will go crazy and run off with your Jeep?"

"Nope. And if you did, I would find you."

She smiled. There was no doubt about that. "I promise to only use it in an emergency."

"Actually, I want you to use it. Every time I come home the tank is empty. I don't even have enough gas to get to training. You can fill it up whenever you need to, but fill it up before you pick me up, OK?"

"OK."

That went pretty well, he thought. He was going to take it one more step. "Can you do me another favor?"

"Probably."

"Jackson will run out of food before I get home. Will you go to Wal-Mart and pick some up?" He handed her a Wal-Mart card.

"OK."

"And get some food too. I also always come home to an empty refrigerator."

"Sorry."

"Don't be sorry. Just use this card to buy what we need—like food and toothpaste and stuff. OK?"

She was starting to get uncomfortable. He knew it, so he got out of the Jeep and acted as if she had already said OK. If that didn't work, he could always kiss her. Like she said, then she would agree to anything.

Mike was rubbing Maggie's back. She knew what he wanted. He had to leave early this morning, catch a plane to Dallas. She opened her eyes. It wasn't even light out. For the very first time, she wanted to say no. She wanted to go back to sleep. But she couldn't say no to him right before he went out of town. She better make sure he was fully satisfied so that he wouldn't go looking for it somewhere else.

Mike was on the other side of the stadium—she could see him, but she couldn't get to him. And she couldn't find her shirt. He was handing out shirts to everyone on the other side of the stadium. People were chasing her, trying to take her shirt.

Maggie was only half awake still processing the dream. Her heart beating as if she had actually been chased.

Mike came in to kiss her good-bye. He was catching a ride with Owen.

He kissed her and then left.

Maggie was awake but still tired from yesterday, still upset from the dream. But mostly upset because he was leaving again. Doubts tortured her. What if he was lying? What if he really did know that girl from Canada? What if there was a girl he knew in Dallas? Or just a girl who wanted to know him? There was no what if to that—there definitely were girls who wanted to know him. Why wouldn't they? He was gorgeous and charming and athletic. Every girl at the games wanted to meet him. What if some other girl crawled into his bed? What if he found someone he liked better than her? Someone prettier?

She was sobbing into her hands now. This was going to be bad. This was going to be worse than the last time. He was so much better than Greg. So much nicer to her. This had disaster written all over it.

Mike had forgotten his favorite picture. There had been a big fireworks display after the home game on the Fourth of July. He had gone into the stands to watch the fireworks with Maggie, Sara, Michelle, and Sandy. He sat in Sara's seat. She sat on his lap. The team photographer had taken a picture of him with Maggie and Sara. Sara was leaning back against his chest looking up at the fireworks. There was a look of innocent wonder on the face of his sweet Sara Rose. He had his arm around Maggie. She had her head on his shoulder, smiling down on Sara. He was resting his cheek on the top of her head with a look that could only be called contentment. That picture symbolized everything he wanted. He always took it with him when he traveled.

He ran upstairs to get it.

"Maggie, what's wrong?"

She tried to cover up, sniffing and wiping away the tears. "Nothing."

"Maggie, I don't have time for this. Owen will be here any minute. Just tell me what's wrong right now."

She spilled. "This is just too hard. You think everything is going along all right, and then it hits you. You don't even see it coming. And it knocks you down, and you can't get up. Can't catch your breath. It's too hard. I don't want to do it again."

He thought she was talking about being attacked until she looked at the box full of her stuff. It had bothered him that she was still living out of that box. Now he knew why she had never unpacked it. She wanted to be ready. She was going to bolt.

"It's not going to happen again. I am not Greg."

She wasn't convinced.

He continued, "I'm not going to cheat on you."

"Then it will be something else."

"There's not going to be anything else. Everything is all right."

She looked him straight in the eye. "Yeah, because all lasting relationships start as a one-night stand."

Mike thought about that exchange all the way to the stadium and then all the way to the airport. Before he got on the plane, he sent Maggie a text, "Are you OK?"

She tried to blow it off. "I'm fine. Just tired. Had a bad dream. It's OK. I am sane again."

He doubted every word of that text. "What was your dream?"

"You were giving away my shirt. It was dumb."

That certainly wasn't enough to cause what he had seen. "Got to get on the plane. Call you when I get there."

"Have a good flight."

He doubted that the flight to Dallas would be long enough to figure out this puzzle. OK, when you do a puzzle, you start by laying out all the pieces. Here were the pieces:

Maggie had all her stuff packed so she could move out at a moment's notice.

Maggie was crying when he left.

Maggie thought it was wrong for them to sleep together.

Maggie's relationship with Greg had ended suddenly and badly.

Maggie thought the same thing was going to happen to them.

Maggie thought she was his one-night stand.

Maggie thought he was going to cheat on her.

Maggie thought if he didn't cheat on her, he would do something worse.

Now what did he do with all these pieces? He could be mad at Greg for causing all this trouble. Well, he was mad at him, but that didn't change anything. He could try to convince Maggie that he had never intended for her to be a one-night stand. But why would she believe that given the circumstances? He could promise her again that he wouldn't cheat on her. How would that help? He needed to do something to prove it to her. But how do you prove that you're not going to do something? If you promise to do something, then you do it—there is the proof. But if you promise not to do something, at best all you can prove is that you didn't do it yet. There was always the chance you would do it in the future. This would be so much easier if she trusted him. Why didn't she?

He had never done anything to lead her to believe that she couldn't trust him. Then her words from before hit him. "A girl crawls into your bed. What are you supposed to do?" Why should she trust him? She crawled into his bed. He slept with her. She had every right to think that it could happen again. He knew it wouldn't. He didn't want anyone but Maggie. But he could understand how she thought that it could. What in the world could he do about that?

It took him several days to figure out what he needed to do. Now he knew for sure. He didn't want to do it. He knew deep down that it was the right thing. But he did not want to do it. Wasn't completely sure that he could. He needed to stop sleeping with Maggie. He needed to prove he had self-control. He needed to prove to her that this was not about sex. He needed to find someone to talk to about this. He couldn't talk to any of his teammates. They would all think he was crazy. They'd say, "If you don't want her, I'll take her." Brandon was his best friend, but he wouldn't be any help. In Portland, Brandon kept telling Mike to go out, have some fun, and meet some girls. His take on it was if Maggie was going to punish him for cheating on her, he might as well go out and do it! Mike hadn't, of course. Maggie was way too important to him to play it that way.

Scott—he needed to call Scott. Scott was a Christian. He probably believed in waiting until marriage. He was dating his sister—so he better be behaving himself! Wow, what a hypocrite he was. It wasn't all right for Scott to do with Michelle what he was doing with Maggie. You know, he had thought he was a good person until now.

Chapter 41

Scott called Pastor Dave.

"You know that thing we have been praying about for Mike and Maggie? It's about to happen."

"No way."

"Yep, they are going to have a talk as soon as he gets home."

"So Maggie is going to tell Mike she wants to be celibate!?"

"No! Mike is going to tell Maggie! All I can say is we better pray for him!"

Pastor Dave was surprised. He shouldn't be. He knew God had His ways, but, still, he hadn't expected this. He knew God was working on Maggie's heart, but he had no idea He was working on Mike's. He'd better start praying.

Maggie was bright and cheerful when she picked Mike up. His gas tank was full, his dog was fed, and his refrigerator was stocked. As soon as she saw him, all her doubts disappeared. She was being silly the day he left. It was just being tired and having that weird dream. Now he was home—everything was fine.

Maggie chatted about things while Mike drove, but he didn't drive home. He had thought long and hard about this. Scott had advised him that if this was going to work, Mike needed to avoid temptation. He definitely could not take Maggie to his house. He knew what would happen there—what always happened there. He didn't want Sandy listening in, so he didn't want to talk to her at her house either. He had decided on the beach. Private enough that they could talk. Public enough that he couldn't change his mind and do exactly what he was proposing they stop doing.

Maggie finally noticed. "Where are we going?"

"To the beach."

That was confusing. "Why?"

"I need to talk to you about something."

Fear crept into her heart. She looked at him closely. He wasn't smiling. He looked kind of—what? Subdued—maybe scared, determined. This was going to be bad. She felt the tears coming already.

She swallowed. "About what?"

"Wait until we get there."

She had this crazy urge to jump out of the Jeep. Whatever he wanted to say, she was sure she didn't want to hear it.

By the time they got to the beach, Maggie knew it was over. She was heartbroken. He had been so nice to her. Now it was over. She had known it was coming, but that didn't help. She was holding her phone thinking she would call Sandy for a ride home and then give it back to him. She could barely hold back the tears.

Mike got out of the Jeep. He started walking, thinking. This was the hardest thing he ever had to do. OK, he had practiced this.

"Maggie, you are important to me. I'm sorry for the way I have treated you."

She wanted to run. She didn't want to hear any more. She decided to end the agony. "It's all right. I understand." She turned to walk away and dialed the phone with shaky fingers.

He was confused. "What are you doing?"

"Calling Sandy for a ride. As soon as I get ahold of her, you can go."

"What? No, I haven't told you anything yet."

"I don't need to know. It doesn't matter. I knew this wouldn't last. I'm surprised you lasted this long with all the crazy. You should have run away screaming like I told you in the first place." She was still facing away from him, looking at the sand, longing for Sandy to answer the phone.

He grabbed her arm and turned her to him. He took the phone. "I'm not breaking up with you."

She was still looking down, trying hard not to cry. All he wanted to do was pull her into his arms, tell her everything was all right. Forget this whole thing—let things continue on like before.

She looked up at him—tears still in her eyes. This was even worse. He did something that would make her want to break up with him.

He tried to pull her close. She broke away. "Let me go."

"No."

"Look, I don't want to know what you did or who she was. You can have all the crazy, demented fans you want." Pause. "Just let me go," she pleaded.

He pulled her close. "I'm not letting you go. I'm not breaking up with you. I didn't cheat on you. It's not like that at all. I just need to tell you something. Please, just listen to me."

She sobbed into his chest in spite of herself. He thought, What have I done to her? The guilt was overwhelming. He was more resolved than ever to do right by her.

She tried to calm herself. She had no more guesses about what this could be. There was no way to prepare for the blow. She was just going to have to take it—whatever it was—without knowing. Just like with Greg.

He walked her over to a rock and made her sit down. She clinched her hands in her lap and looked at his shoes.

He started again, "Maggie, you are important to me." He paced back and forth in front of the rock. "I'm sorry for the way I have treated you. I shouldn't have slept with you the first night we met. I shouldn't have taken advantage of you when I knew you were so upset."

Maggie looked up from his shoes to his face—he looked tortured. Where was this going?

He continued, "It was all my fault. I'm sorry. I want to make it right."

Maggie started, "It wasn't your—"

He interrupted her. "Yes, it was," he said, a little too vehemently.

He calmed himself. "I know what you think. You think it was your fault. You asked me, 'Some girl crawls into my bed. What was I supposed

MISS LORI

to do?' I was supposed to have some self-control. I was supposed to treat you better—with some respect. I was supposed to not take advantage of you—that night or the nights that followed."

She had had no idea he felt that way. "I started it every time. It was my fault," she claimed.

"I knew it was wrong, but I still did it every time. It was my fault," he countered.

She smiled just a little. "Well, it is true—you weren't all that hard to convince." Pause. "Don't worry about it. It's in the past. Let's just move on." She was actually feeling pretty relieved if that was all that was bothering him.

"It is not all in the past. It's still affecting you—us. You think that because when you crawled into my bed and I slept with you, I would do the same with any other girl if the opportunity arose."

She wanted to deny it, but he was right. That was exactly what she thought. And she thought that the likelihood of there being another opportunity was high. "So I should trust you."

"No."

She jerked her head up in surprise.

"It's not that you can't trust me," he explained. "It's that I have no right to expect you to."

"So what do we do about this?" she asked.

"I want to do right by you. I want to earn your trust." Deep breath. "I think we should stop sleeping together."

"What? You want to stop sleeping together? Mr. Morning, Noon, and Night?" she blurted out without thinking.

He winced. "I think it's the right thing to do."

Chapter 42

Maggie walked in her front door.
Sandy asked, "What are you doing here?"
"I live here."
"Where's Mike?"
"I guess he went home."
"What? Did you break up?"
"I'm not sure."
Maggie went to get some ice cream. As she was scooping it into a bowl, her phone rang. It was Mike.
"Hi, Maggie."
"Hi."
"I was wondering if you needed any of your stuff. I could bring it over."
"No, I'm good."
"OK, I'll bring it over tomorrow."
Long pause.
"Mike?"
"Yeah."
She hesitated, then asked quietly, "Am I still your girlfriend?"
"Yes! Of course! And I want you to tell that to everyone you talk to!"
"Oh." It helped to know that—but she was still confused.
"Do you?"
"Do I what?"

"Tell everyone you talk to."

She smiled. "Well, not your fanatical female fans."

"Why not?"

"I am afraid of them," she joked. "I try to avoid talking to them."

"Me too." Pause. "How about the guys?"

"Well, not exactly. I usually work in the two magic words as soon as possible."

"What magic words—get lost?"

"No, that would be rude," she giggled. "My boyfriend. It doesn't even matter what you say after that. I could say, 'My boyfriend is a flying monkey.'" She laughed at her own joke. "I should do an experiment. I should say that and see what happens!"

He laughed, "As long as it works."

"It works pretty well. Not as well as that honking big engagement ring I used to have—" Oops, she shouldn't have said that.

"What did you do with it?" Mike asked quietly.

"I gave it back. I'm pretty sure you're supposed to."

Mike didn't respond.

"I wish I hadn't."

His heart fell. "You do?"

"Yeah, I could have sold it. I probably could have lived off that thing for a year!"

That was better. He smiled. "What would you do if you got a whole lot of money? You know, like won the lottery or something?"

"Well, I wouldn't quit my job like the people you see on TV. I would still be Sara's nanny. I would probably do it for free!"

"Michelle would be happy to hear that!"

"How about you? What would you do if you got a bunch of money all of a sudden?"

"I would buy—a bunch of stuff." He caught himself before he said he would buy her a car.

"Like what?"

"I don't know. A big house on the beach. A big truck—a really big TV."

"Just anything big?"

"Yeah, I guess," he laughed.

"Would you still play soccer?"

"Of course! But not for free. I like money. I'm not weird about it like you are."

"I'm not weird about money."

"Yes, you are."

"Maybe I just know that money isn't all that important."

As per Scott's advice, Mike made rules for himself. He didn't take Maggie to his house anymore. He left her house no later than 10:00 p.m. He tried not to be alone with her any place that had a bedroom. And the biggest and hardest rule—he didn't kiss her like he used to. He kissed her on the forehead or on the cheek. He would allow himself one hello kiss and one goodbye kiss. That was about all he could handle. Scott called him often to check up on him. He called it accountability. He said it would be easier for Mike to stay on the straight and narrow if he knew he had someone to answer to.

It still wasn't easy, but he was learning a lot more about Maggie. Like the house she lived in actually belonged to Sandy's parents. They had bought it before their oldest son started college. He lived there until he graduated from college. The second oldest son was two years younger. He started going to college but dropped out just before Sandy started. Sandy didn't want to live in the house alone so she convinced her parents that Maggie should live there with her. That was where the deception started.

Maggie had gotten a full scholarship. But Sandy didn't. Sandy's parents were going to pay about half her tuition, but Sandy had to find a way to make up the difference. Mike wasn't surprised in the least when Maggie confessed that she would have given her scholarship to Sandy if she could have.

Maggie had proudly told her dad about the scholarship when she got it. But not surprisingly he had forgotten. He asked her how much her tuition was just before she started school. She reminded him that she had a scholarship. He just said OK. Then he asked how much she needed for rent. Sandy's parents had already agreed to let Maggie live at their house rent free. But Maggie was mad at her dad for forgetting that she got a scholarship, so she lied and said rent was exactly the amount that Sandy needed for tuition. When he didn't seem to mind that, she said, "Plus utilities." He said fine. He'd set up an account for her to make sure she had plenty to cover her expenses. So, every month, Maggie wrote a check to Sandy for rent. Sandy used it for tuition money. When Sandy's tuition went up—so did Maggie's rent.

When Mike commented that that was quite a little scam they had going, Maggie said he was right and that she would confess the very next time her dad called her. Of course, that would also be the very first time he called her.

While Sandy and Maggie were still in college, Sandy's parents moved out of the state. They wanted to sell the house after Sandy graduated since Sandy's younger brothers wouldn't be going to college in California. Sandy wanted to keep living there, so they compromised. They wouldn't sell the house, but she had to cover the mortgage payments herself. That was why Maggie had to pay rent now. That was also why whenever anything broke, they had to pay to get it fixed themselves—which wasn't easy considering neither of them were making much of a paycheck.

One night they were sitting on the couch watching TV. Maggie was sitting close enough to Mike that he could smell her shampoo. Sandy and Owen were there, sitting together in the big La-Z-Boy chair. He knew it wouldn't be long before they wandered off into her bedroom. That wouldn't help at all. He knew this situation spelled trouble. He saw a commercial for a new movie. He jumped up and said, "Let's go see that." Owen and Sandy agreed. Maggie said, "Movies are too expensive. We should just stay here."

Mike decided he had had enough of her not letting him pay for anything. He said, "Go put your shoes on. We're going to go to the movie."

"I don't have to go to the movie if I don't want to," answered Maggie. He said, "Fine—you can go without your shoes." He picked her up. She laughed, "All right, all right, all right—let me get my shoes!"

She and Sandy went back into their bedrooms to get ready to go out.

Mike thought about something Maggie had told him the other day. She said that after she and Greg got engaged, he sent her a big bouquet of flowers every week. He said, "That was nice." She said, "Yeah, but it was weird." One day he came over to see her, and the flowers were delivered while he was there. She asked him why he didn't bring them himself. Why did he have them delivered when he was coming to see her anyway? He said he had forgotten they were coming. And that it was easier to have them delivered. That was when she figured it out. He had set it up for her to get flowers once a week. Had probably made one phone call, set it up, and then forgotten all about it. She wasn't nearly as impressed after that.

Maggie came out of her room looking beautiful but with a little grin on her face. She stood in front of him and said, "I decided I'm not going to go."

"Oh yeah?" he said.

"Yeah, what are you going to do about it?" she challenged.

He picked her up and threw her over his shoulder.

"Hey," she exclaimed. "Not that way. I don't like it when you carry me that way!"

He said, "I know."

They took Owen's car because it was bigger. In the backseat, Mike told Maggie, "It's not the same, you know."

"What's not the same?"

"It's not the same as with Greg. I'm not going to throw money at you and then ignore you."

She was still in a silly mood, so she said, "I can't imagine you ignoring me!"

"That's right—so I can take you to a movie."

She wrinkled her brow and responded, "We are going to a movie."

"And I'm going to pay for the movie." Pause. "And we could go out to eat. I could even buy you a present now and then."

She crossed her arms and considered. Was that why she didn't like the idea of him paying for things? Greg—and her dad, for that matter—

paid for everything and then ignored her. Mike wouldn't ignore her—whether there was money involved or not.

She looked at him and said, "Hmm—you're pretty smart for a soccer player."

He smiled and said, "I have my moments."

Chapter 43

Maggie hadn't been to Mike's house for almost a month. She felt a little naughty being there now without him knowing. But she had a mission. Today was his birthday. Yes, just his—Michelle's was tomorrow. Even though they were twins, they didn't share a birthday because he was born three minutes before midnight, and she was born two minutes after. She and Sandy had a plan for tomorrow for Michelle, but tonight they were celebrating Mike's birthday.

The plan was GG Rose's idea. She knew Mike had all kinds of memorabilia from past soccer games—the ball from the tournament where he had scored the winning goal autographed by each member of the team, jerseys he had exchanged with famous players, and a bunch of trophies and medals. Michelle gathered up all that stuff, and then GG Rose and Maggie planned how they could display it—a shelf for the trophies, frames for the shirts, a glass box for the ball, etc. GG Rose provided the money; Maggie did all the leg work. Now she was here at his house in the room that he used as an office. She decorated the room according to plan. It looked great. She thought Mike was going to love this.

She finished with plenty of time to spare before she was scheduled to pick up Mike from his road trip to Philadelphia.

She wandered around his house. She missed living here—she didn't want to go home yet. So she let Jackson in. She missed Jackson—hadn't seen him in a month either. After she played with Jackson—and brushed him and cuddled with him—she started cleaning. It wasn't that it was all that dirty—that was what she always did. As she cleaned and tidied, she thought about their new arrangement. It was definitely the right thing to do. It was what she had been praying for all along, right? Then why did it feel so bad? She was shocked when he suggested it and had wondered if it was his way of breaking up with her—just trying to do it slowly. You know, spend less and less time together, and all of a sudden, they were no longer a couple. But that hadn't happened. He called her just as much as he ever did—probably more since they weren't always together. They would spend every evening together when he was in town. Then he would go home. But he always called her once she was ready for bed, and they would talk until they were too sleepy to make sense anymore.

Then she thought maybe he just wanted to be friends. Maybe he didn't want her to get mad and stop being Sara's nanny, so he would keep things friendly but create some distance. He didn't kiss her nearly as much as he used to, but he took her out on dates all the time now. They went to movies, out to eat, and dancing at the bar where they met. He didn't act like they were friends. He still got jealous when any other guy even looked at her, and he never let her dance with anyone else at the bar.

She couldn't figure out why he suggested this. The only explanation he ever gave was that it was the right thing to do. But she didn't really believe that he thought it was the right thing to do. Sure, she thought that—but did he? Maybe it was the right thing to do, but it wasn't an easy thing to do. If anything, things were more awkward. Sure, they talked a lot more (they had lots of time to fill). She learned a lot about him. She loved to listen to him talk about growing up, especially stories about his dad and grandpa. Like how every year they scrimped and saved so they could go to a baseball game. The four of them—his dad, his grandpa, he, and Michelle—would go to one game a year. At the game they always ate hot dogs. It was part of the tradition—which explained Michelle's hot dog obsession at the soccer games.

She loved hearing those stories, and it felt like they were closer because of them. But still, it was awkward now. She never knew if she was supposed to sit next to him or keep her distance. Sometimes they would be laughing and joking and having fun, and all of a sudden, he would find some reason to get up and move away from her. It was confusing at best and frustrating at worst.

She knew she had asked God for some kind of middle ground. She remembered asking Him to help her do the right thing. In fact, she remembered thinking that it would be better if they hadn't been sleeping together and were just dating. Well, she changed her mind. She didn't like this. She felt like she was waiting for the other shoe to drop. If he didn't like her anymore, she wanted it to just be over. Nice and quick—like ripping off a Band-Aid. No middle ground. She either wanted it to be over or wanted to live here with him. OK, that wasn't true. She didn't want it to be over. Truth be told, she wanted things back the way they were—right or wrong.

Everybody was already gathered at Mike's house for the party before she left to pick him up—Michelle, Sara, Scott, Sandy, and GG Rose. A few of the guys from the team were coming, too, after they got into town. It was all going to be a surprise to Mike. The only part she hadn't worked out was how she was going to get him to take her to his house now that she wasn't allowed to be there anymore. If she couldn't make it happen, she was going to secretly text Michelle. She would call with some excuse.

It became immediately apparent to Maggie that they wouldn't need plan B when Mike came limping up to the Jeep and walked to the passenger side. Last night he had told her again and again that he was fine, even though she saw the trainers wrap a big bag of ice on his leg after he came out of the game. Now, of course, he still claimed he was fine. His leg had just stiffened up on the plane ride home. Nothing to worry about. Maggie decided to let it go since, for once, she was in control of where they were going, and she was taking him to his house—no matter what he said!

He hadn't said much for a while (his leg must really hurt, Maggie thought) until he realized where they were going.

When he asked, "Where are we going?"

Maggie replied, "I'm taking you home," matter-of-factly.

Mike tried to take over and told Maggie that that was a good idea. She could drop him off at his house. Then she could take his Jeep to her house. She could bring it over tomorrow. Maggie didn't argue as she drove up to his house. She didn't argue as she got his bag out of the back of the Jeep. Mike kept going on and on about how he wanted to sit on the couch and veg out. Maggie didn't argue as she put her arm around his waist to help him up the porch steps. Mike told her he was fine—she could go home. She stopped in front of his door and said, "You really don't want to do anything tonight?"

"I really don't," he replied.

Maggie exhaled slowly and said, "Well, then, I'm sorry for this."

She opened the door. All the guests (including his teammates who had parked down the street and snuck in the back door) yelled, "Surprise!" Sara, as usual, launched herself into Mike's arms and shouted, "Happy birthday!" Maggie caught Mike's arm before Sara threw him off balance and knocked him over.

Mike looked surprised but not unhappy. Maggie gave a little apology shrug when he glanced at her. Then he made the rounds shaking his teammates' hands, hugging his grandma and his sister, and thanking people for coming.

Sara grabbed his hand and said, "We have a birthday surprise for you!"

He said, "I know—this is a great surprise party."

"No, another surprise!" she said.

Maggie smiled from across the room.

GG Rose carefully got up from her chair and said, "Follow me."

Mike followed behind GG Rose walking slowly with her walker. He teased her that she was going so fast that he could hardly keep up. She swatted at his arm good-naturedly. Maggie thought today he might be telling the truth.

She led him to his office and then, with a sweep of her hand, said, "Ta-da!"

Mike stepped into the office and looked around—soccer memories flooding through his mind. The party guests took turns stepping into the office and admiring Maggie's handiwork. Mike kissed GG Rose's cheek and said, "Thanks, Grandma. This is great!"

"I didn't do it alone." GG Rose smiled, glancing at Maggie.

Sandy announced, "Time for cake!" The guests paraded into the kitchen, leaving Mike and Maggie alone in the office.

Mike smiled. "So you did all this?"

"A little bit." She shrugged.

"I thought you forgot it was my birthday."

She laughed, "I hang out with your whole family—didn't you think someone would remind me?"

"I guess I didn't think of that."

"We've been working on this for months."

He looked around the room and said, "Clearly. Thanks, Maggie. I love it."

"You know, if you had told me you hurt your leg—I could have toned it down or something."

"Who? Me? I'm not hurt. My leg is fine."

"Well, maybe the one you're standing on. But the other one…"

"is fine too."

She stepped close to him and said, "So if I gave you a little push, you wouldn't fall over?"

He sat down on the edge of the desk and said, "Nope."

She was standing so close, and she smelled like vanilla. He thought surely it would be all right if he kissed her just this once—after all it was his birthday. So he did. He kissed her. He kissed her like he used to kiss her. Maggie closed her eyes and savored the moment. She leaned into him. Suddenly Mike realized what he was doing. He grabbed her shoulders and gently pushed her away.

Maggie was surprised and disappointed. She turned away and said, "I guess we should get some cake."

They sang "Happy Birthday" and ate cake, and Mike opened a few more presents. Soon the party started breaking up. Scott volunteered to take GG Rose home and then return for Michelle, Sara, and Maggie. Sandy and Owen left for her house. Brandon and the other players were tired from traveling, so they called it a night too. Maggie and Michelle worked together cleaning up. Sara sat on the couch chatting with Uncle Mike until she couldn't stay awake any longer.

Finally, Scott returned. Michelle picked up the sleepy Sara and wished her brother a happy birthday one last time. Scott helped her take Sara out to the car.

Maggie brought Mike some ice and wrapped it around his leg with a towel. Her birthday wishes turned to birthday kisses. Scott walked back in to find Mike and Maggie locked in a passionate embrace.

He breathed a silent prayer and said, "Maggie, are you ready to go?"

Maggie looked at Scott, trying to hide her annoyance. She said, "I think I'll stay for a while."

Scott said, "I don't think that's a good idea."

"It's OK. I can go home in Mike's Jeep later."

"It's dark out."

"That's OK. I can go home in the dark," she lied.

"Maggie, I think you should come with us," stated Scott firmly.

She was getting miffed, so she said, "Well, now that's not your decision, is it?"

Scott looked at Mike. There was a mighty battle waging inside Mike. He did not want Maggie to leave. Of course, he didn't. But he knew what would happen if she stayed. They all knew what would happen.

Maggie broke the silence. "Look, Scott, he's hurt. I'm just going to take care of him for a little while. You can go."

Mike finally spoke up, "Scott is right. You should go. I can take care of myself."

Maggie was hurt and embarrassed. But she had no choice. She got up to leave. This was all Scott's fault. If she could have gotten him to leave, Mike would have let her stay. She was mad at him, so as she walked by, she said, "Don't you ever get tired of being a Boy Scout?"

Michelle chatted about what a nice party it had been all the way to Maggie's house. Maggie didn't agree. She didn't say anything, but she didn't agree.

As soon as Scott stopped at Maggie's, she jumped out of the car. Scott called out, "Do you want me to walk you to the door?"

Maggie said, "No," and sprinted to the house.

Mike sat on the couch thinking that was a close one. Scott had warned him that temptation would come. It was hard to resist temptation on your birthday, when you were tired, and your leg hurt, and she smelled so good! If Scott hadn't been here, he would have blown it for sure. Then what would Maggie think of him? He tried calling her. No answer. She should be home by now. Maybe she was brushing her teeth or something. He limped up the stairs and got ready for bed. He would call her from there. But once he got there, he was so tired, he forgot.

Maggie was up and out early. It was Sunday. She had heard Mike tell Scott he was going to stay off his leg and skip church today. But she knew Scott would still be over to pick her up. Well, she wasn't going anywhere with that Boy Scout. They would go to GG Rose's church. She would walk to Pastor Dave's church. It was a long walk—it would take over two hours—but that was OK. She didn't have anywhere else to be.

Scott knocked on Maggie's door. No answer. He knocked again. Sandy opened the door in her bathrobe. Scott asked, "Is Maggie ready?"

Sandy said, "I didn't think she was here." She walked back to Maggie's room and looked in. She came back with a smile. "I don't think she came home last night. You should try Mike's house."

Scott wasn't smiling. "She did come home last night. I brought her here."

Sandy shrugged. "I would still try Mike's house."

Owen came out of the kitchen in his boxers. "According to this note, she is at church—but she will be back in plenty of time. What does that mean?"

Sandy and Scott understood. Maggie would be back in time for Michelle's birthday surprise. But Scott wondered if Maggie was really at church or at Mike's. He decided all he could do was pray for them. He had helped them avoid temptation last night—and Maggie was plenty mad at him for that—but he couldn't stop them from sleeping together if they really wanted to. He would leave it in Jesus' hands.

Pastor Dave spotted Maggie at the very beginning of the church service. She didn't usually come to church on Sunday morning, but that wasn't why she caught his eye. She looked miserable. He made up his mind to catch her before she left and find out what was bothering her.

Pastor Dave's congregation was small—no more than thirty people a week. So, during his sermon, he could look them each in the eye. Usually (on Wednesday nights) Maggie was one of the people he preached most to. She was always actively listening and making eye contact. Not today. She barely looked up, and he was sure she didn't hear a word he said.

As the last song played, he hightailed it to the back of the room. Maggie was sitting way in the back, but he caught her before she left and said, "Would you hang around? I need to talk to you."

After she muttered OK, he said, "Why don't you wait in my office?"

In Pastor Dave's office, Maggie turned on her cell phone. There was a message from Mike—"Call me after church." Why? she thought. So you can push me away again?

She sat in the chair that she had sat (and cried) in so many times before when she and Michelle had been there pouring their guts out. She looked up on the wall behind Pastor Dave's desk and read the Bible verse posted there. "Trust in the Lord with all your heart, and lean not on your own understanding; In all your ways acknowledge Him and He shall direct your paths" (Proverbs 3:5–6).

She had read it so many times in this office that she had it memorized.

Pastor Dave walked in and said, "I was surprised to see you here this morning."

"Oh," said Maggie. She wasn't in a particularly chatty mood, so she just waited for him to tell her why she was in his office.

Pastor Dave's heart broke for her. She looked so sad, so lost. He had to admit of all the people in his congregation, she was one of his favorites.

Finally, he asked her, "What's wrong?"

She just looked down and muttered, "Nothing." But her tone of voice and her attitude let him know that what she really meant was everything.

"If you tell me, maybe I could help."

She sighed. He was such a nice man. He would be thrilled to hear that she and Mike weren't sleeping together anymore. She could tell him that—he knew everything else about her—at least this would be something good to tell him. But she didn't want to get into it. She was ashamed of her behavior again last night.

Her phone buzzed. She looked at the text. "Is church over?"

"Was that Mike?" asked Pastor Dave. She nodded. "Feel free to answer him," he offered.

"Maybe later," she said.

Pastor Dave waited her out.

Finally, Maggie said, "I really try to be a good person." Pause. "But I just can't." Pause. "I don't understand."

"What don't you understand?" asked Pastor Dave gently.

Here we go again, thought Maggie.

"Mike said we shouldn't sleep together anymore—which is the right thing to do. I know it's the right thing to do."

"So what's the problem?"

"Me. I'm a bad person. I don't know what's wrong with me. He says, "Let's do the right thing," and I, well, I throw myself at him."

"Did you sleep with him?"

"No, but only because Scott was there. What's wrong with me?"

Pastor Dave responded, "You are a sinner."

Maggie sobbed.

Pastor Dave handed her a tissue and repeated, "You are a sinner, just like me and every person who has ever walked on this earth, except for one. Only one person who walked this earth was perfect. You know who that is, right?"

"Scott?" she sniffed.

He smiled. "No, Maggie, Scott isn't perfect. Only Jesus is perfect."

"Good, 'cuz I kinda hate Scott right now."

Maggie laid her head on the back of the chair and considered. "So you are saying that I am a bad person. I can't do the right thing—so what? I might as well just go to Mike's house right now and sleep with him. There's no use in even trying to be good?"

"No, Maggie. We all face temptation. We need to fight it."

"But that's what I am trying to tell you. I can't. The first night that I met him, I crawled into his bed. It was all me—all my fault. The next time I was at his house. Again—my idea. I started it. And the next time, I was upset about Greg. He said he'd sleep on the couch. But I said no—he didn't need to sleep on the couch. All along I knew it was wrong. Every time I would leave here, I knew it was wrong. But I did it anyway. I just can't help it. And last night, I did it again. I was the one who wanted to stay at his house last night."

"Maggie, what you're doing is what we call 'white-knuckling it.' You know, like when you're on a roller coaster and you hold on so tight that your knuckles turn white. You are holding on and trying to be a good person. But you can't do it. None of us can. It's not in our nature. You can't do it in your own strength. You need Jesus to help you. You need to use His strength."

What does that mean? thought Maggie. This wasn't helping.

Pastor Dave could see she didn't understand. He said, "Trust in the Lord with all—"

Maggie joined in, "Your heart, and lean not on your own understanding."

Pastor was surprised. "You know that verse?"

"Yeah, it's written above your head."

He looked behind him. "So it is. Do you know what it means?"

"Not a clue."

He smiled. "It means it's OK if you don't completely understand how it works—trust in Jesus, and He will help you through it." He continued, "Are you still afraid of the dark?"

"Not as much as I was. I can go outside in the dark by myself now sometimes."

"How do you calm yourself in those situations?"

She smiled because she knew that he knew. He was the one who taught her to do it. "I pray, and Jesus protects me."

"How?"

"I don't know. He just does."

Pastor Dave continued the verse, "In all your ways acknowledge Him and He shall direct your paths."

"So I acknowledge Him by praying."

"And leaving it in His hands. He will help you through it."

"Oh." Pause. "Are you absolutely sure it's wrong to sleep with Mike? I mean, I know it was wrong the first time. But does it really matter that much now?"

"Yes. It matters to God. He wants you to do things His way and put Him before everything else."

"Even Mike?"

"Yes."

There was one more thing that was bothering her. "Is God going to take Mike away from me because I slept with him?"

"God is going to do what is right for you."

"He took Greg away from me."

"God is always right, and His way is always right. He wants you to acknowledge Him. To do things His way—then you will be happy."

"So, if I don't sleep with Mike, we can stay together?"

"I don't know if you and Mike will stay together. Remember how you used to tell me about how jealous Mike would get?"

"Yeah, he still does."

"Why does he get jealous?"

"Because he wants me all to himself."

"Well, God is like that. You are important to Him. He loves you so much. He is jealous for you. He wants you all to Himself. He wants you to love Him more than anyone or anything else in this world. He's not in the business of taking good things away from you. But He wants to be the most important thing in your life."

She wasn't convinced she was all that important to God. Especially the way she had been behaving lately. But she was convinced of one thing. She needed to spend more time praying.

Chapter 44

She had plenty of time to pray on the long walk home and she did pray. She confessed that she was wrong to sleep with Mike. She confessed that she couldn't stop. She begged Jesus to help her. She poured her whole heart out to Jesus. By the time she got home, she felt much better. Now she was ready to concentrate on Michelle's birthday surprise.

Michelle (and Mike) thought that they were having a birthday dinner for Michelle at Maggie's house. But even Sara knew that wasn't really what was going to happen. Scott was going to take Michelle out on a real fancy date—not In-N-Out Burger, not Chuck E. Cheese. A real adult date without Sara. Maggie had carefully explained it to Sara. Sara was supposed to pack a backpack with her pajamas and her toothbrush without her mom knowing. Then Sara would get to have a sleepover with Miss Maggie and Miss Sandy so Michelle and Scott could stay out as long as they wanted to.

Scott had made reservations at a fancy dinner theater—that was his part of the present. Maggie and Sandy were going to get Michelle all dolled up and then babysit Sara—that was their present.

Michelle showed up as instructed after Sara's nap.

Sara said, "Look, Miss Maggie. I brought my backpack."

Maggie smiled and said, "Good job, Bug!"

Michelle asked, "Where is everybody? Where's Scott?"

Maggie and Sandy exchanged grins. "He isn't here yet," said Sandy. "Come on, we have to get you ready!" said Maggie.

Michelle looked down at her clothes. "I am ready," she said, confused.

"Not for what we have planned!"

Michelle was a couple of months away from graduating from nursing school. She spent more and more time at the hospital practicing being a nurse. The more she worked as a nurse, the more she dressed like a nurse. She had beautiful, long, dark hair. But at the hospital she always wore it in a bun. It was easier to keep it up and out of her way.

She had thought tonight was going to be casual. Just a dinner with friends. So she dressed casually. She looked very nice but not ready to go out on the town.

Maggie, Sandy, and Sara took Michelle back into the bathroom and started to work on her. Sandy worked on her hair. Maggie worked on her makeup. Then they gave her a slinky red dress and matching sandals to change into.

The doorbell rang, and Maggie went to let Scott in. He was dressed in a coat and tie. He was carrying a dozen red roses. He looked good, but there was something different. Hmm, thought Maggie, is Mr. Calm, Cool Doctor a little nervous?

He said, "Hi, is Michelle ready?"

Maggie said, "Nope. You will have to wait." She was still a little mad at him. She knew she shouldn't be, but she still was.

He said, "Oh, OK." He stood near the door, fidgeting just a little.

Maggie was enjoying this—way more than she should be.

"How much longer will she be, do you think?" he asked.

"Sit down—relax. It'll be worth the wait." Pause. Maggie decided to take a little jab at him. "She's way too good for you, you know."

He looked her straight in the eye and said, "I know."

Maggie smiled. "Good answer—there may be hope for you yet."

"Oh yeah?"

"Yeah." She held her finger and a thumb about an inch apart. She squinted through them and said, "Just a little."

Maggie left Scott in the living room—sitting uncomfortably on the couch. She walked into the bedroom where Michelle was ready to go. She looked gorgeous. In the end, Sandy and Maggie hadn't done much but provide her clothes. They did convince her to take her hair out of the bun. Sandy had been ready to curl it and style it, but at last they all decided she should leave it long and straight. Maggie applied mascara to her eyelashes and red lip gloss to her lips to match the dress. But that was all the makeup Michelle needed. She was a natural beauty. As good as she looked, she looked even more nervous.

Maggie announced, "Scott's here."

Sandy asked, "How does he look?"

Maggie said, "He looks good, but he's sweating bullets!"

Michelle asked, "Are you sure I look all right?"

Sara said, "You look beautiful, Mommy!"

Michelle started to tear up. Maggie cried, "Don't cry—you'll mess up your makeup! OK, don't come out yet. You need to make an entrance."

Maggie went back to the living room. She wondered where Mike was. He should be here by now. She'd hate for him to miss this.

Maggie told Scott that Michelle was ready.

He said, "How do I look?"

She said, "I guess you'll do." Then she walked over to him to straighten his tie. She was starting to feel bad about her behavior.

"I'm sorry I got a little snarky last night," she said quietly.

"That's all right."

"No, it's not all right. That Boy Scout comment was over the line."

"It's OK. I understand. Maggie, if you need to talk…"

She held up her hand and said, "I talked to Pastor Dave today. I am full up on advice!"

The doorbell rang. Sara ran past them to see who it was.

Maggie stood back from Scott. She brushed a stray piece of lint from his coat and said, "There, now you are perfect."

Sara ran back to Maggie and said, "Uncle Mike is here."

Maggie said, "Did you let him in?"

"No. I'm not supposed to let anyone in."

Maggie and Sara walked to the door. "I meant strangers. Uncle Mike is not a stranger. You can always let Uncle Mike in." Just before they got to the door, Maggie leaned down to say, "But only Uncle Mike, OK?"

Mike had been standing at the door for a while. He watched while Maggie fussed with Scott's tie. He knew he was late. This morning his leg was still stiff. But as he walked around the house, it loosened up, and he was feeling better. The swelling had gone down. He hadn't talked to Maggie at all yet today. He had waited for her to call after church but finally had turned on the baseball game and fell asleep on the couch. He woke up twenty minutes ago. Now he was listening to her tell Scott he was perfect.

Maggie opened the door for him and apologized. She looked down at Sara and commented, "I guess I have her too well trained."

Mike asked, "What's going on?"

Sara said, "We are making Mommy pretty."

Mike looked at Maggie confused. Maggie explained, "Because Mommy is going out on a big date with Dr. Scott."

"And I am staying here all night!" chimed in Sara.

Maggie called out, "OK, we're ready."

Sandy spritzed Michelle with cherry blossom fragrance just before she walked out of the bedroom and into view.

Maggie whispered to Mike, "Isn't your sister gorgeous?"

Mike agreed. "Wow, Chel!"

Maggie watched as Scott walked over to Michelle, handed her the flowers, and told her she looked lovely. Michelle looked embarrassed to have all the attention on her. She accepted the flowers with a small thank you. Scott extended his arm and said, "Shall we?" Michelle handed the flowers to Sandy and smiled at Scott as they walked out the door.

Mike watched Maggie smiling at the beautiful couple, her eyes dancing. "Have fun!" she called after them.

Maggie turned to Mike and sighed.

He said, "Michelle didn't tell me they were going out tonight."

"She didn't know." Maggie smiled.

"You are just full of birthday surprises, aren't you?"

"Nope, that's it. The last one."

"So, Maggie, when is your birthday?"

Maggie and Sandy exchanged a guilty look.

Maggie said, "How's your leg today?"

"Better," he replied hesitantly.

"You should probably sit down."

They sat on the couch. Mike tried again, "Maggie, when is your birthday?"

"Not for a long time. Do you need some ice? I'll go get it."

She tried to get up. He grabbed her arm and pulled her back down.

"Maggie, when is your birthday?"

Sandy said, "Hey, Sara, I have Candyland in my room. Do you want to go play?"

Sara exclaimed, "Yeah, I love Candyland!"

Mike waited a beat and then said, "Do I have to ask again?"

Maggie stated, "March."

"March? Before or after we met?"

Maggie hesitated before she conceded, "After."

"Why didn't you tell me?"

"I don't really like birthdays."

Mike looked at her and shook his head. Maggie decided that argument probably wasn't going to hold water after the last two days. "OK, I like other people's birthdays, just not my birthday."

Mike thought she grew up rich. How bad could your birthday be if you were rich?

"Was I out of town?"

"Nooo."

"Did we do anything together?"

"We spent the whole day together."

"When was it?"

"Remember that long road trip you went on at the end of March?"

"Three away games? Yeah, I remember."

"It was the day you came back."

Mike thought back. "Hey, you made me breakfast in bed that day!"

"Yes, I did—I guess you owe me."

He remembered that day. They had spent most of it in bed. But then they came over here for supper. He commented, "Then we came over here, and you ate a lot of food!"

"You remember how much I ate?"

"Yeah, you ate so much, I was worried that you hadn't remembered to eat while I was gone."

"You were worried that I didn't eat?"

"I always worry that you don't eat when I'm gone."

Aww, how sweet is that? thought Maggie.

"Sandy made all my favorite food—that's why I ate so much," she informed him.

"And the big chocolate brownie—that was like the birthday cake, huh?"

"Yeah."

"I feel bad. I didn't give you anything for your birthday."

"Actually, you did."

He didn't remember.

Maggie continued, "Remember after we ate, we went to GG Rose's house."

"Right and you showed me how you had taken care of the roses."

"Yep, and then we cut some roses to bring to GG."

"Yeah—"

"And you took one of the roses and gave it to me—and you said, 'A pretty rose for a pretty lady.'" She smiled at him. It felt like a moment to snuggle into his arms, but she resisted the urge. "Actually, it was a pretty good birthday."

Mike didn't believe her. He said, "Come on. One year you got a car for your birthday. I bet you got all kinds of presents when you were growing up."

"Yeah, I got presents."

"You can't tell me that wasn't great."

Actually, she could tell him that. "OK, here was my birthday when I was growing up. I would wake up in the morning and go downstairs and find a mountain of presents, which I would open—all by myself. My mom and dad were always either at work or on a trip. Then one of two things would happen. Either Sandy would convince me to do some crazy thing, her parents would find out, and she would be grounded for a month, or I would spend the whole day listening to Sandy tell me I am boring because I wouldn't do whatever crazy thing she wanted to do."

"Still, you did get a mountain of presents."

"Yep, every year my dad got me a new TV. When I was a kid, I thought TVs only lasted a year. So each year he got me a bigger TV, maybe a new phone or a new tablet. My mom would buy new clothes. Lots and lots of clothes. Then one year he got me a TV that was actually smaller than the one he got me the year before. And I remember thinking why did I want a smaller TV—especially since the one I had still worked. Once I thought about it, I realized. I didn't need a new TV every year. I didn't need any more new tech or clothes. That was when I stopped opening the presents. It wasn't ever anything I wanted. It was just more stuff. I almost never wore the clothes my mom bought me—she has horrible taste." She paused to look at him. "Come on, I'll show you."

She grabbed his hand and led him through her bedroom into another room. She said, "This used to be a third bedroom, but we made it into a closet."

Mike looked around. It looked more like a store than a closet. There were racks of clothes and shelves of shoes—all organized—mostly by color.

Maggie said, "That red dress that Michelle was wearing tonight—that came from here." She pointed to the red section. "I rarely wear red. I don't look good in red. I wear pastels like pink and baby blue. My mom has never figured that out, so I have a whole section of red clothes that have never been worn." She continued, "Sandy is an autumn. So she wears these—browns, oranges and greens. Nobody wears the red. I should give them all to Michelle." She smiled. "She looks good in red."

It was hard for Mike to wrap his mind around this. Most people would be thrilled to have all these clothes. He thought about birthdays when he was growing up. He and Michelle would get one, maybe two presents. He would have loved to wake up to a mountain of gifts. But it seemed like, for Maggie, it had all come at too great a cost.

She wandered back out of the "closet" into her bedroom. He followed her and asked, "What about when you were with Greg? Didn't you have nice birthdays with him?"

"No. I never spent a birthday with Greg. It never landed on a weekend."

"He couldn't make time to see you on your birthday because it was a weekday?"

"I told him he didn't have to. It was just a birthday. It wasn't important."

"He probably sent you a nice present, though."

She shrugged. "I don't remember. It probably got mixed in with whatever my mom and dad sent."

All of a sudden, they both realized they were standing in her bedroom. They looked at the bed. She had been in a hurry this morning, so she hadn't bothered to make it. The rumpled sheets and blankets looked warm and inviting.

Maggie said, "Ice! I was going to get you some ice." She hurried out of the room.

Sandy and Sara had finished playing Candyland and were out in the living room when Mike and Maggie came out of the bedroom. Sandy smiled and raised her eyebrows at Maggie. Maggie ignored her.

Sandy announced that she and Sara were going to get a pizza. Maggie said, "Why don't we all go?"

Sandy said, "That's all right. We got this." And rushed Sara out the door.

Maggie and Mike were alone in the living room. He sat down on the couch and propped his leg on the coffee table. Maggie decided she better not sit next to him, so she sat down in the La-Z-Boy. Uncomfortable silence surrounded them. Maggie searched her mind for an acceptable topic of conversation.

"When is GG Rose's birthday?" Maybe they could start planning a party for her.

"January."

"Oh." That was too long away to make any plans. Anything could happen before then.

"Sara's is in February."

"Don't even say that."

"Why not?"

"Sara can't have a birthday."

"What?"

"Sara is four. She's the perfect age. We don't want her turning five."

"Why not?"

"You know what happens when kids turn five."

"What? They turn into monsters?"

"No. They go to kindergarten."

"What's wrong with that? She's a smart kid. She'll be ready for kindergarten. She has a great nanny." He smiled.

"But when she goes to kindergarten, she won't need a nanny. Then I'll have to get a real job. I think she should stay four, and I will be her nanny forever."

Mike said, "Kindergarten is a long way off. Besides once she goes to kindergarten, you could always go back to your old school."

"I can't do that."

"Why not? You're a great teacher. They would be happy to have you back."

"How do you know?"

"Because they told me."

"Who told you?"

"Your old boss."

"What? When did you talk to her?"

"Before you became Sara's nanny."

"What?!"

"Come on, I just met you. I couldn't let you be Sara's nanny just because you are pretty, and I needed an excuse to see you again. I had to check you out."

Maggie stared at him, surprised.

"She said you would be a great nanny," continued Mike, "and that if she could, she would hire you back in a minute."

"It's not that simple."

"Why not?"

"Because…" She hesitated. "You know, the last day I worked there, they gave me a wedding shower."

"So? Didn't you give the presents back?" he joked.

"No, I gave them back. But to them—to the other teachers—I'm still the idiot who didn't marry the rich guy."

"They don't think that."

"Yes, they do. That's why I don't hang out with them anymore. That's also why I don't go to the gym anymore."

"You belonged to a gym?"

"I belong to a gym. Paid for a whole year just before Greg proposed."

"You went to a gym? With Greg?"

She laughed. "No. Greg does not go to the gym. I'll bet he doesn't even own a pair of sweats!"

"So why can't you go back there then?"

"I was a little too chatty about the wedding that never was."

"Hey, we should work out together."

"Yeah. That would be fun," she said sarcastically.

"It would be fun."

"For you. You would just make fun of me because I can't lift as much weight as you and I can't run as fast as you."

"I wouldn't make fun of you! And I hope I can lift more weight than you. It would be pretty embarrassing if my girlfriend was stronger than me."

She giggled, glancing at his leg. "Well, I bet I can run faster than you!"

"I was hoping you were done running away from me."

"You never know."

More awkward silence. The silences didn't seem awkward before—you know, when she was sitting next to him with her head on his shoulder. It would be so easy to get up and do that now. Just sit next to him. Would that be so bad?

Mike broke the silence. "I don't think anyone thinks you're an idiot for not marrying Greg."

"On the contrary, everyone thinks that."

"Not if they know the situation. I'm sure Sandy doesn't think so."

"Yes, she does."

"Sandy thinks you should have married Greg?"

"Yep. She thinks I should have married him, divorced him, and then taken half his stuff."

He laughed. That did sound like Sandy.

"I, of course, chose the opposite route. Throw the ring in his face and become dirt poor. Good plan, huh?" she joked.

Mike wondered for the millionth time if she was over Greg.

Maggie said, "I'm not sure that Michelle doesn't think I'm an idiot."

"Michelle does not think you should have married Greg."

"Well, maybe not. But she sure thinks that if you have a rich guy—you don't give him up."

More silence.

Maggie continued, "I used to think he was perfect."

"Greg?"

"Yeah. Before he came along, I thought all guys were stupid." Pause. "Looking back there was a reason for that.

"OK, in high school here is how it would happen. Sandy would come up to me all excited and say, 'I met this cute guy—and he has a friend.' That's how it always started. So we would go on a double date, and I would be sitting there listening to some guy going on and on about whatever stupid thing he was into, thinking, You are so stupid. How do you even get dressed in the morning? I mean, sure, they were always cute, but so dumb. Of course, now I realize it was just Sandy's taste in guys. But back then I decided high school boys were all stupid and that I would have to wait for college.

"In college I met a few smart guys, but let's just say that they were nothing much to look at. So I thought it was one or the other. Either you could have cute and dumb or smart and ugly.

"Then I got attacked, and the only guy I was interested in was Mr. Pepper Spray—whom I slept with every night." She smiled.

"Then I met Greg. He was the dream. Smart and quite good-looking. What more could you want? And he was always perfectly dressed. Always on time. Always a perfect gentleman. He never got mad. I thought he was perfect and we were the perfect couple. We never once had an argument."

"He seemed pretty mad the day I saw him."

"Well, the bubble had popped before then. I don't think he's perfect anymore. Come to think about it, he's a lot like Scott. I have never seen Scott get mad, and some of the things those Trailmen do…it's kind of annoying, really. Sometimes I want to spill a Coke in his lap—just to see what he would do."

She laughed. "Don't tell Michelle I said that. She still thinks he's perfect. Sometimes I wonder if I should warn her. If you think a guy is perfect, he is probably hiding something—or you just don't know him very well."

"Remind me to be careful any time you are drinking a Coke!"

She laughed. "I wouldn't spill a Coke in your lap. I know what makes you angry. You get mad when I leave in the middle of the night. You get mad when I won't call you. You get mad when I won't tell you what's bothering me. Hey, wait a minute. Oh yeah, I saw you get mad once when a guy kicked you during a game. Whew! For a minute I thought I was the only thing that made you mad. That I was the only thorn in your side."

"Not the only one—just the biggest!"

"Thanks!"

"I won't tell Michelle that you think Scott is perfect."

"I don't think he's perfect. She thinks he's perfect. She won't let anyone say anything bad about him. She's worse about him than she is about you. One day Sandy called you a dumb jock. You should have heard Michelle light into her!"

"And what did you say?"

Actually, she and Michelle had said, "He's not dumb" at the same time, but she didn't want to admit it. So she said, "I got out of the way. I didn't want to get into the middle of that fight!"

So I fall into the good-looking and dumb category? thought Mike. Unless, of course, she doesn't think I am much to look at. Let it go, Mallone.

More silence. Then Mike said, "I don't think you're an idiot for not marrying Greg. I think you're strong—and courageous."

She shrugged.

"Come on," continued Mike. "It took courage to call off that big wedding. You stood up to Greg and to your parents. You stood up to all that pressure because it wasn't right for you. Most people would have caved, but you wanted something better, and you deserve to have something better."

Maggie's eyes welled up. She went over to sit next to him. "That may be the nicest thing you have ever said to me." Then she whispered, "That anyone has ever said to me." He put his arm around her. She put her head on his shoulder.

He knew he needed to nip this in the bud, so he said, "I think you promised me some ice."

"Ice! Right," she said.

On her way into the kitchen, she silently prayed, "Please, don't let me do it again. Please, don't let me do it again."

She came back out with the ice and a towel. As she wrapped it around his leg, she asked, "Does it hurt?"

"A little," he responded. "I think I have a strained hamstring. I need to go in for treatment tomorrow."

"Hmm. That almost sounded like you were admitting that you're hurt."

"Nah, you never admit that you're hurt. Then the coach doesn't let you play."

"That explains why you can't admit it to the coach. But maybe you could admit it to your girlfriend."

"I don't know."

"What? Are you afraid that she will call the coach and tattle on you?"

"I don't know. My girlfriend is pretty crazy. It's hard to say what she would do."

Maggie smiled. "Well, rest assured. Your girlfriend doesn't know the coach's number." Pause. "Besides, I don't know if you have noticed, but your girlfriend kind of likes to take care of people. She may, I don't know, bring you ice. Give you a pillow for your back. Maybe get you a Coke or something to drink."

"No Coke," he joked. "But a pillow sounds good and maybe a glass of water."

She got a couch pillow. He leaned forward while she adjusted it behind his back. Their eyes locked.

Maggie pulled her attention away from him. "Where is Sandy with that pizza?"

"Maybe you should call her," he suggested.

"I have a better idea. Where's your phone?"

He pulled it out of his pocket and handed it to her.

She texted, "Where are you? I'm hungry." And pushed send.

"She's more likely to listen to you than me," she explained. "You know, if she hadn't taken Sara, she might never come back."

"If she hadn't taken Sara, she wouldn't need to come back."

Maggie understood what he meant.

Maggie's phone rang. "I'll get you some water," she said as she picked it up and walked into the kitchen.

"Where are you?" asked Maggie into the phone.

"Getting dessert—is it safe to come home yet?" asked Sandy.

"What are you talking about?"

"I saw you two in the bedroom. I was trying to help you out—getting Sara out of the way so you two could get on with your business."

"We weren't doing anything."

"Come on, I know better than that."

"You know, we stopped doing that."

"Yeah, but last night. Didn't you stay at his house?"

"No. And you are definitely not helping."

"Hey, don't get mad at me! I don't even understand this whole not-sleeping-together thing."

"Don't say that in front of Sara!"

"Don't worry—she can't hear me. She's looking at cupcakes."

"Just come home."

"All right, give me ten minutes. But don't expect me to babysit you two."

Maggie brought the glass of water and told Mike they would be home soon. Then she sat in the La-Z-Boy again.

At last, Sandy and Sara came home with the pizza. Mike and Maggie both breathed a sigh of relief.

They ate their pizza at the coffee table. Then they scrolled through the menu on the TV looking for a movie to watch.

"*A Bug's Life*!" said Maggie. "This must be about you, Bug!"

"No, it isn't," laughed Sara.

"Let's watch it and see if there's a Sara Bug in it!"

Maggie started the movie. Sara crawled up into Mike's lap. Maggie sat down next to him, his arm around her shoulders. This is nice, thought Maggie. Now she could relax.

Sara almost made it to the end of the movie before she fell asleep, but not quite. Maggie's phone rang.

She got up to answer it, walking into the hallway so she wouldn't wake Sara up.

"Hi, are you having fun?" asked Maggie brightly.

"Uh, I'm coming to get Sara," said Michelle.

"No, you're not. She's staying here tonight."

"Look, Maggie. She's my daughter, and I get to decide where she spends the night!"

"Michelle, are you mad at me?" asked Maggie, confused.

"I'm just saying—I want to come and get her."

"Is something wrong—aren't you having a good time?"

"Nothing is wrong. I just need to get Sara home."

"You can stay out as long as you want. I'll take care of Sara."

"I'm not going to stay out all night with him. I can't take all this pressure."

"What pressure? There's no pressure. No one expects you to stay out all night."

"Sandy does."

"Oh, come on. Don't listen to Sandy. You go home whenever you want to."

"But I have known him for a year and a half. Don't you think he expects…?"

"No. He doesn't expect anything."

"Are you sure?"

"I am 100 percent absolutely sure that Scott does not expect you to stay out all night with him."

"Well—"

"Come on, Michelle, this is Scott. If you want to go home, just say, 'Scott, I want to go home.' And he will take you home."

"He suggested we get some dessert."

"Do you want some dessert?"

"Dessert might be nice."

"Then go have dessert. It's OK." Pause. "Michelle, I'm sorry if I crossed a line with Sara. You're right. Your daughter. Your decision."

"What's she doing?"

"Sleeping on Uncle Mike's lap."

"I guess there's no need to wake her up." Pause. "Thanks, Maggie. I guess I went a little crazy there."

"It's OK. If you are going to go crazy—well, let's just say you came to the right place."

Mike heard enough of that conversation to be concerned about Michelle. When Maggie sat down, he asked, "Is Michelle all right?"

"Of course, she is. She's with Scott."

Mike ground his teeth together. Of course, Michelle was all right. She was with Scott, who is perfect. You are just here with the dumb jock with no self-control. You know, her attitude about Scott was really starting to bug him.

Chapter 45

The music was so loud! Of course, that was probably because of the seats that the Trailmen chose—right in front of the speakers. Maggie took some Kleenex out of her purse. She wadded pieces to put in her and Sara's ears. That helped some. She looked down the row past Sara. The ten Trailmen were jumping around and waving their arms in the air to the music. Scott was on the other end of the row singing along.

The next morning Maggie woke up with her ears still ringing. Oh, wait that was her phone.

She answered, "Hello?" with a creaky voice. She hadn't checked the caller ID. She wasn't ready to open her eyes.

"Good morning," said Mike. "Did I wake you up?"

Maggie cleared her throat. "Yeah, I guess. What time is it?"

"Well, here it is ten thirty." He was in Chicago.

"What time does that make it here?"

"Eight thirty."

"Oh, well, then you definitely woke me up."

"That's not so early."

"I had a late night last night."

"Why? Couldn't you sleep?"

"No, it was much too loud to sleep! I went to the concert with Scott last night."

"You did? I thought Michelle was going to go and you were going to stay with Sara."

Maggie yawned. "Michelle changed her mind at the last minute. She wanted to stay home and study. She is really freaking out about her finals. She's bringing Sara over here today so she can study all day."

"Michelle likes to get As."

"She already has As. She could probably skip these finals and still pass."

"She wants to graduate at the head of her class so she can get a good job."

"I know. But I think she's going overboard on the studying." Maggie yawned again.

"So how was the concert?" asked Mike.

"Good, but so loud. My ears are still ringing."

"I tried to call you last night."

"Sorry, but there was no way I was going to hear my phone there!"

"When is Sara going to be there?"

"Whenever she wakes up. It was a pretty late night for her too."

"Sara went to the concert?"

"Yeah, I know. I told them it would be too late for her. But they wouldn't listen. She is going to be a crab today."

"How late did the concert go?"

"Well, the concert was over by about ten o'clock, but then we had to take all the Trailmen home." Scott had borrowed the church van so that he could fit all the Trailmen in one vehicle.

"That's late for Sara, but you should have been home before midnight. That's eight hours of sleep." She shouldn't be that tired, even if Scott did bring her home last.

"Yeah, I guess I was home before midnight, but Scott came in for a while."

"Why?"

"To listen to my new CDs."

"What new CDs?"

"Well, you know, this concert was a bunch of bands—I didn't even know exactly who was playing. But one of the bands was my very favorite. When Scott heard them say they had a new CD, he bought it for me.

He also bought their old one, which has two of my favorite songs on it, and a T-shirt!"

"Sounds like an expensive night for Scott," growled Mike.

Maggie shrugged off that comment with, "He has money. He's a doctor."

Her favorite band? thought Mike. He didn't know she had a favorite band. How come Scott knew who it was?

"Who is your favorite band?"

"It's a Christian group. You wouldn't know them."

When Maggie hung out with Scott, they always listened to Christian music. Lately whenever Maggie picked Mike up, the radio in his Jeep would be tuned to the Christian music station. Of course, he always turned it to his favorite station as soon as he got in the car.

"How late did he stay?" asked Mike warily.

"I don't know. We kind of lost track of time. I think I was in bed about two or two thirty."

Mike gritted his teeth. What exactly were they doing for over two hours in the middle of the night?

Maggie knew that didn't sound good. Was he ever going to stop being jealous of Scott? I mean, she could understand him being jealous of other guys, but this was Scott. She decided she'd better explain before he blew it all out of proportion. "We were talking about the Trailmen. See, at intermission during the concert they had big tables set up with pictures of kids that need to be adopted. You could pick a kid and sign up to sponsor him until he gets adopted. You know, send money every month for food and clothes and stuff. The Trailmen helped Scott pick out three kids for him to sponsor; then the Trailmen decided they wanted to sponsor a kid themselves. So we were talking about ways the Trailmen could raise money for their kid. That's all."

Mike didn't respond.

"Wait—I'm getting a text," said Maggie.

Probably from Mr. Perfect Scott, thought Mike sarcastically.

"That was Michelle. She's bringing Sara over. I need to get dressed."

"Are you going to watch the game tonight at Michelle's?" asked Mike.

"Yep. That's the plan," said Maggie, trying to pull her pants on with one hand.

"Will Scott be there?"

"Yeah. He doesn't like soccer that much, but he likes to be with… Ow!" Maggie landed on the floor while she was trying to hold the phone with her shoulder and put her shoe on. "Mike, I can't get dressed and talk to you on the phone."

"OK, how about I call you after lunch?"

"OK. Bye." Maggie hung up before he could even return the goodbye.

Mike stared at his phone. How was Maggie going to end that sentence? He likes to be with us? Michelle? Or me?

He pulled up the picture of Maggie with the curly hair from San Jose. She looked so sweet and innocent. He could trust her, right? If there were two people in this world that he could trust, it would be Maggie and Scott, right? Even alone in the middle of the night. But still why did they have to be alone in the middle of the night?

They spent so much time together. They were always working on some project together either at the church or with the Trailmen. Now Scott was sponsoring orphans—no wonder Maggie thought he was perfect. Sure, Mike went to charity events, but only because he had to. It was good press for the team. Maggie knew that was his attitude about charity.

Scott was Michelle's boyfriend. She spent hours on the phone with him. At least, she did before she started studying so much. And then Scott's schedule had changed. He was working nights at the hospital most of the time now. Which meant his free time was during the day while Michelle was in school. Which meant he spent a lot of time with Maggie and Sara. That didn't mean anything, right? They were just friends.

They were an awful lot alike, though. They always wanted to go to church. They were the only two people he knew who actually listened to the sermon. And discussed it after church! Maggie was always asking Scott questions after church. Scott had grown up in a Christian household. He knew a lot about the Bible. He was always explaining the finer points to Maggie.

Mike knew he could trust Maggie. She was always honest with him—as far as he knew. She surely wouldn't have admitted that Scott was at her house in the middle of the night if she was trying to hide something.

Still, he had to wonder. What if Maggie had met Scott first? What if instead of going to a soccer game on the night of her canceled wedding, she had gone to church and met Scott? Would she be with Scott now? Did she wish she met Scott first before she met Mike and Michelle met Scott? If they could get him and Michelle out of the way, would they be together?

Come to think of it. It was Scott who was encouraging him not to sleep with Maggie. Scott was always checking up on him, telling him to avoid temptation. Scott was the one who got in the way on his birthday when Maggie wanted to stay with him. Was he being a good Christian friend, or did he have another agenda? Deep down did Scott really want Maggie for himself?

Sara was crabby. But that was OK. A crabby Sara was better than no Sara. Maggie was always so bored whenever Mike was out of town.

Maggie tried several things, but nothing made Sara happy. Finally, she made an early lunch. Then both Sara and Miss Maggie were going down for a nice long nap. She decided she better call Mike before that. Otherwise, he might call after they went to sleep.

Mike answered, "Hi, what's going on?"

"We called to tell you something before we took our nap." Maggie handed the phone to Sara. She didn't take it to talk to Uncle Mike. She just yelled, "I don't want to take a nap."

Maggie put the phone back to her ear. "Well, that's not what we called to tell you!"

In the background Mike could hear Sara saying, "I want to go home."

Maggie said, "Just a minute," to Mike, then talked to Sara. "Sara, you know Mommy is studying today. We will go to your house after nap time."

Mike thought Maggie was right. Sara was crabby today!

Maggie continued trying to reason with Sara. "Why don't you go find a book to read?"

Sara cried, "I want the train book. That's my favorite. I want the train book."

Maggie was trying to be patient. "You know that book is at Mommy's house. Go find one in Miss Maggie's room."

"No!" was Sara's only response.

Maggie put the phone to her ear again. "Sorry, I guess I better go deal with this. We were going to tell you nap time was starting early today."

Mike felt bad for Maggie. "Any idea how you are going to get her down?"

"I was thinking about tying her to the bed," Maggie joked.

"Let me talk to her," he said.

Maggie doubted there was anything he could say that would help, but she was willing to give it a try if he was. She handed the phone to Sara and said, "Uncle Mike wants to talk to you."

Mike asked Sara about the concert. She told him about the people playing guitars and that there was fire behind them (a special effect). He promised to take her to the park when he got back. Then he said, "Why don't you and Miss Maggie go lie down now?" Then tonight she could watch him on TV. She said OK and closed the phone.

Maggie and Sara went into Maggie's bedroom and lay down. Maggie sang to Sara and rubbed her back. She was asleep in minutes.

Maggie texted Mike, "Thanks! She's asleep."

"Already?" he texted back.

"I guess Uncle Mike has the magic touch!"

"What can I say? Call you tonight?"

Maggie smiled. "OK. Have a good game."

Maggie stayed in bed next to Sara thinking about Mike. How sweet was he to help her with Sara like that? He was so good with her.

She never really confessed to him how much she missed him when he was gone. She tried to keep busy with Sara and helping Pastor Dave at church and Scott with the Trailmen. And she liked all the volunteer work, but it also helped to fill the time. It always felt like from the minute Mike left all she was doing was waiting for him to come back.

Most of the out-of-town games were on Saturday. Then he would fly home on Sunday. Then came Monday—those were her favorite days. Monday would be his day off. He always spent the whole day with her and Sara. It wasn't an empty promise he made to take Sara to the park. He wasn't distracting her or bribing her to get her to take a nap. He always followed through on those promises.

This Monday was also the day of Michelle's finals. Then she would be finished with school. She had started applying for jobs—had lots of options, but nothing was decided yet. Maggie had no doubt that Michelle would get a job—a great job. She was going to be an excellent nurse. What she didn't know was when she would get that job. And if Michelle wasn't going to school and wasn't working, she didn't need a nanny for Sara. Maggie didn't know what she was going to do for money in the interim. She didn't have any savings to fall back on.

There was another problem. Today was the last away game of the regular season. Next week would be the last home game. Then came the playoffs. Mike's team was at the top of the league. They were expected to go far. Even if they went all the way to the championship, the offseason would come in just over a month. Part of Maggie was thrilled to think about the offseason. No away games—Mike would be home all the time. That would be awesome. But Maggie also knew that when Mike wasn't playing soccer, he was the one who watched Sara. Maggie didn't think Michelle was going to want to pay Maggie if she could have Mike doing it for free. Maggie was going to have to get a job. She dreaded that. Everything was so perfect now. She loved being Sara's nanny, but it also made her available to Mike any time. If he had the day off, he would spend it with her and Sara. Whenever he was done training, he just came and got them. If he wanted to go somewhere, he took them along. If Maggie got a real job, all that would change. Why did things have to change? She didn't want things to change.

Suddenly her Bible verse popped into her head.

"'Trust in the LORD with all your heart,

"'And lean not on your own understanding.

"'In all your ways acknowledge Him,

"'And He shall direct your paths.' Proverbs 3:5–6," she recited.

Then she prayed, "Dear Lord,

"The future is uncertain. I don't know how I am going to pay my rent after Michelle graduates. Please help Michelle get a good job. Please give me a way to pay my rent." Pause. "Also, protect Mike as he plays tonight. Don't let him get hurt." Pause. "I acknowledge You. Amen."

She knew it wasn't an elegant prayer. She really wasn't very good at this. Then she decided she would tell Jesus that too.

"Dear Jesus, I know that I am not good at prayer, but I want to be. I acknowledge that You know everything and You are good. In Jesus' name I pray. Amen."

Then Maggie drifted off to sleep.

Chapter 46

Tomorrow might be uncertain, but Maggie was determined to enjoy today. She was at the park watching Mike chase Sara around. Michelle was taking her finals.

Everything might change tomorrow, but today was good. What was that Bible verse that Scott told her? Something about don't worry about tomorrow because there was enough to worry about today. Good advice.

The next day Maggie slept in. She had nothing to do. Mike was at practice. Michelle was done with school. She was at home with Sara waiting to hear about her grades. Maggie felt for Michelle. She knew that she was worried about getting a good enough job to support her and Sara all on her own. Maggie also knew now where Michelle got the money to pay her to watch Sara—Grandpa Willie's estate. A while ago, Michelle had confessed that before Grandpa Willie died, he had put a provision in his will to ensure that Michelle had enough money to pay for nursing school and her expenses (the lawyers had concluded those expenses included paying a nanny for Sara once GG Rose had her stroke) until she graduated. But now Michelle was on her own—a single mother with the financial burden sitting squarely on her shoulders. No wonder she got so freaked out about her grades. There was plenty of competition for good nursing jobs. The higher her grades, the better her chances.

At her apartment, Michelle clicked on the grades button on the school's website for the hundredth time this morning. This waiting was torture. When would the grades be up? She felt like she had done well on the tests, but these tests were hard. What if she had blown it? What if her grades weren't all that good? How would she get a good job? What if she didn't even pass at all?

Click again. Finally, the little hourglass came up on the screen. The page was opening. There were the grades. She couldn't believe it.

She grabbed her phone to call Mike. No answer. Of course, he was at practice. He couldn't answer his phone. So she called the second person she wanted to tell.

Maggie answered, "Did you get your grades?"

"Yes."

"Well?" demanded Maggie, the suspense was killing her too.

"Get ready to celebrate because I got the best grades in the class!"

"Woo-hoo!" shouted Maggie. "I knew you could do it!"

"We'll be right over to pick you up!"

"I'll be ready!"

In the car, Maggie, Michelle, and Sara were talking and laughing and trying to decide where to go to celebrate. The light at the intersection turned green. Michelle entered the intersection, saying, "I want to go to…"

That was when the truck hit them.

Maggie's hands shook as she took out her phone and lied to Sara again, "Everything is all right." Everything was not all right. She hated to lie to Sara, but what was she supposed to say? She managed to dial Mike's number. No answer. How could she get ahold of him? She needed to get ahold of him. She called Sandy. No answer. She was trying to keep it together for Sara, but she couldn't do this alone.

Finally, she dialed the number for her old school.

Delores, the school secretary, answered with a cheery, "How can I help you?"

Maggie said, "Hi, Delores. This is Maggie Lawson."

"Maggie! So good to hear from you. How are you doing?"

"Not so good. Can I talk to Sandy? It's an emergency."

"Of course, hold on."

Waiting. Waiting. Waiting. Come on, Sandy!

"What's wrong?"

"We were in a car accident."

"Oh no! Are you OK?"

"I'm OK, and Sara is OK. But I don't know about Michelle. A truck hit us," sobbed Maggie, turning away from Sara. "It smashed right into her."

"Where are you?"

"At the hospital."

"I'll be right there."

"Sandy, can you find Mike? He isn't answering his phone."

"I'll find him and bring him with me. Just hold on, OK?"

"Hurry."

Maggie wiped the tears from her eyes and turned toward Sara. A nurse led them to a private waiting room.

Mike was sweating hard as the team ran drill after drill. The coach had given an intense speech this morning about how important it was to stay focused. He needed 100 percent from everyone as they entered the playoffs. Mike was focused until he saw the disturbance on the sidelines. There was Sandy talking to the coaches and waving her arms. What in the world was she doing here?

The coach called Mike over. This was just weird.

Sandy looked frantic. She was talking fast. "You have to come with me. Now! You have to come with me!"

"What happened?" Mike asked, fear rising in his throat.

The coach was calmer than Sandy. He explained, "It seems there has been an accident."

"What accident?"

Sandy cried out, "A car accident."

"Who? Who was in a car accident?"

"Maggie, Michelle, and Sara!"

Owen had jogged over. "Coach, Mike and I carpooled today in my car. Maybe I should take them to the hospital."

The coach agreed. He cared about his players. He didn't want Mike driving now—he seemed to be pretty shaken up. And he sure didn't want him in a car with this frantic girl, whoever she was!

Mike was having trouble figuring out what happened from Sandy. No one was answering Michelle's phone or Maggie's. Maggie had called Sandy, but he knew from Michelle that there were many places in the hospital where there was no cell phone reception.

He asked Sandy to repeat what Maggie had said again. She said, "She said she was OK, and Sara was OK, but Michelle wasn't."

He decided to call Scott. He was a doctor. Maybe he could get some information.

Scott blinked his eyes as he woke up to his cell ringing. He had worked a double shift yesterday. He had only gotten home and asleep a couple of hours ago.

"Hello?"

"Do you know anything about Michelle?" asked Mike forgoing any kind of polite greeting.

"What about Michelle?" asked Scott, wondering why Mike seemed so upset.

"She and Maggie and Sara were in a car accident. Are you at the hospital?"

"I'm at home. Are they all right?"

"I don't know. I'm on my way to the hospital."

"I'll meet you there."

When they got to the hospital, Mike asked for them at the information desk. They said that Michelle was in with the doctors and there was no information on her condition yet, but they directed him to the waiting room where Maggie and Sara were. Sara was coloring. Maggie was explaining to Sara again that they couldn't see Mommy yet. That the doctors were taking care of her.

When Mike walked into the room, Sara jumped up and ran into his arms. She said, "We were in a car accident. It was very scary. But we are all right. The doctors are taking care of Mommy." Mike knew that Sara was repeating exactly what Maggie had told her.

Maggie and Sandy were hugging on the other side of the room. When Maggie looked up at Mike, he could see that she was about to lose it. He put Sara down and said, "Sara, can you stay here with Miss Sandy and Mr. Owen for a minute?"

Sara sat down with Sandy, and they started coloring together.

Mike pulled Maggie out of the room into the hallway. Maggie collapsed into his arms, sobbing uncontrollably.

He held her and stroked her hair, saying, "It's all right. Everything is going to be all right."

"No, it isn't. Michelle is not all right. She kept saying, 'If anything happens to me, promise you will take care of Sara.' She just kept saying that over and over. Something is wrong with her, very, very wrong."

Actually, he was surprised to hear that Michelle was talking. She wasn't even unconscious. That gave him a little hope.

He said, "Scott is checking on Michelle. He will let us know as soon as he finds anything out." Pause. "Maggie, what happened?"

She clung to him even tighter. "A truck hit us."

Mike winced. He decided to concentrate on one person at a time. "We need to get a doctor to check Sara out."

"The paramedics and the ER doctor both checked her out and said she was fine. Not a scratch on her."

Thank goodness, thought Mike. "How about you?'

"I'm OK."

He pushed her back from him to look at her. "Maggie, you are not OK. You are covered in blood."

Maggie teared up again. "It's not my blood," she cried. "It's Michelle's!"

Mike pulled her close again. He decided Maggie's emotional needs at this moment were greater than her physical ones. Where was Scott with a report on Michelle? Maggie needed to know that Michelle was all right. They both needed to hear that.

Finally, Scott found them. Mike immediately asked, "How's Michelle?"

Scott said, "She is stable." Mike thought those were wonderful words. Maggie seemed to think Michelle had some horrible injuries, but he was hoping Maggie was just upset from the accident. If Michelle was stable, she would recover from this. He was sure of it.

Maggie looked up from Mike's shoulder. "Are you sure? Is she really going to be OK?" she asked Scott.

Scott said, "We still don't know the extent of her injuries. But she will be OK. I promise you." He was determined to see to that.

Maggie wasn't convinced. "But there was blood—so much blood."

Scott said, "You are right. She did lose a lot of blood. She will need a transfusion, but it could have been a lot worse. The paramedics told me you did a great job of stopping the blood before they got there. She would have lost a lot more if not for your quick thinking." He meant to make her feel better, but it didn't work. She hid her face in Mike's shoulder as she dissolved into tears again.

Mike held her close as he said, "I'm the same blood type as Michelle. I want to give blood."

Scott replied, "That's a good idea. We are always low on that particular blood type."

Mike tried to comfort Maggie. He said, "It's all right," and kissed her right temple. He tasted blood.

She pulled back and said, "Ow."

Scott asked, "Maggie, have you been checked out by a doctor?"

"No, I'm OK," she replied.

Mike lifted the hair at her temple. He said, "No you aren't. You're bleeding. You must have hit your head."

Maggie lifted her hand to touch the place where her head hurt. They both noticed the bandana wrapped around her hand.

"Come on," said Scott. "I will set you both up."

Maggie grabbed onto Mike. "I want to stay with him."

"I can arrange that," said Scott.

Scott led them to an empty examining room. He left them to get a technician to take blood from Mike. Then he stopped to check on Michelle again. The doctor was still busy working on her. He knew this particular doctor. He was the best in the hospital. But he wanted even better for Michelle, so he stopped to pray. He prayed for her healing and for wisdom and skill for the doctor and nurses. Now he knew Michelle was in good hands.

Scott returned to the examining room. Mike was already lying on the bed, blood streaming into a bag at the bedside. Maggie was standing next to the bed holding his hand as if she were comforting him. Everyone in the room could tell it was the other way around.

Scott stood near Maggie and said, "Let me take a look."

He lifted her hair and gently began cleaning the wound. As he worked, he asked, "Can you tell us what happened?"

Maggie said, "I can, but I don't want to."

"Tell us, Maggie," Mike said gently.

"Michelle got her grades today," Maggie started slowly. "She got the highest grades in the class." The fact that had made them so happy a couple of hours ago now seemed bittersweet.

Maggie continued, "We were going out to celebrate. When the light turned green, Michelle started to go."

Maggie was looking a little pale as she stated, "A big black truck didn't stop for the red light. He crashed right into us."

Mike squeezed Maggie's hand. It felt clammy. Scott finished with her cut. "You don't need stitches. But we should watch you for concussion."

Maggie felt woozy. Scott said, "You need to lie down." He lowered the railing on the hospital bed and helped her into bed next to Mike. Mike put his free arm around her as she lay down. Maggie closed her eyes.

Scott prompted, "Then what happened? Did you lose consciousness when you hit your head?"

"I don't remember hitting my head."

"What is the next thing you remember?"

"There were people standing outside the car on their cell phones. Then I looked at Michelle, and blood was squirting out of her leg." She sniffed.

"How did you think to use a maxi pad to stop the bleeding?"

"I didn't really think of it. The impact of the crash must have opened the glove compartment. Everything in it flew out. The maxi pad was literally in my lap. I just picked it up and put it on Michelle's leg to stop the bleeding."

They all stopped to give thanks for that.

"Let me see your hand," said Scott.

"No. It's all right," she hid her hand under her other arm.

"What happened to it?"

"I cut it a little."

Mike said, "Let Scott look at it."

Maggie grudgingly offered her hand with the bandana to Scott.

"How did you cut it?" asked Mike.

"I was trying to get the glass off of Sara."

Scott remembered, "The paramedics mentioned that there was a glass bottle that shattered during the crash."

"Yeah. Well, Sara was pretty calm until the paramedics came and started taking Michelle out of the car. Then she started yelling, 'Don't take my mommy! Don't take my mommy!' So I went into the backseat to get her out of her car seat. There was glass all over her. I didn't want her to get hurt. I guess I cut my hand brushing the glass off of her."

Scott had gently unwrapped her hand while she told her story. He examined the jagged cut. "Maggie, you have glass in your hand."

"Oh," she said, looking at her hand. She immediately turned away when saw the ugly, bloody cut. "Gross!"

Scott got a bottle of water and a basin.

"Ow! What are you doing?" cried Maggie, trying to pull her hand away.

"We need to clean out the glass."

"That hurts!" complained Maggie.

Mike tried to calm her down. "Maggie, be still. He won't do anything that he doesn't need to do."

It still hurt, but Maggie allowed Scott to do his job. Then she asked, "Where's Sara?"

"She's still with Sandy," answered Scott.

"She needs to come in here. I promised to take care of her."

"Not yet," said Scott. "You need stitches."

Maggie was quiet while Scott worked on her hand and Mike's blood flowed into the bag for Michelle. She reached across her body and held the hand that Mike had on her shoulder.

Finally, Scott finished. She looked at her hand. "That's ugly," she said.

"Let me wrap it up."

"OK, then go get Sara and check on Michelle, OK?"

Sandy and Owen brought Sara into the examining room just as the technician pulled the needle from Mike's arm.

"Come here, Bug," said Maggie. Owen lifted her onto the bed, where she snuggled between Mike and Maggie.

It seemed like a long time before Scott finally came back into the room. He announced that Michelle was going to be fine. The doctor was able to repair the torn artery and set her broken leg. She had a long road ahead of her, but in time she would recover fully, especially now that she had Mike's blood flowing through her veins.

Mike and Scott stepped into the hall to discuss what would happen next. Maggie needed to be watched for concussion. Sara probably should sleep in her own bed tonight to keep things as normal as possible. Mike wanted to stay with both of them, but he also felt like he should be here with Michelle. Scott assured him that Michelle was on painkillers and she wouldn't be waking up tonight, but he volunteered to spend the night at her bedside just to make sure. Mike decided that would work. He would take Maggie and Sara to Michelle's apartment and stay there.

Owen drove all five of them to Michelle's apartment. Sandy wanted to go to the stadium to pick up her car. Maggie didn't like that idea.

"Just leave your car and stay here," begged Maggie. She couldn't stand the possibility of another car accident.

Finally, Owen agreed to drive Sandy to pick up her car and then follow her back and make sure Sandy got back to Michelle's OK. Then Sandy agreed to stay at Michelle's just to ease Maggie's nerves. They could sleep dormitory style. Maggie and Sandy in Michelle's bedroom. Mike on the pull-out couch. Maggie and Mike put Sara in her own bed after tons of hugs and kisses. After Maggie washed all the remaining spots of dried blood off and changed into a pair of Michelle's PJs, Mike hugged her good night. He had already set his cell phone alarm to wake him up in four hours so he could check Maggie for concussion.

He pulled back and gently kissed her uninjured temple, then said, "I'll be right out here if you need me."

"I need you," she replied softly. Then she smiled and went to bed.

Beep, beep. Mike got up and quietly walked into the bedroom. Maggie wasn't there. Mike was confused. Where could she be? He couldn't think of a reason that she would leave in the middle of the night. But this was Maggie, so he checked the front door. The chain was still on it. She couldn't have left. He checked the bathroom. Nobody in there. Maybe Sara's room. There she was sleeping next to Sara. Maybe she was confused. Maybe she did have a concussion.

"Maggie, wake up," he whispered.

Maggie shushed him with a finger to her lips. Then led him into the kitchen so they wouldn't wake anybody else up.

"What were you doing in Sara's bed?" he asked quietly.

"She woke up—had a bad dream."

He hadn't heard her. "Why didn't you wake me up?"

She shrugged. "I was already awake anyway. I had a bad dream too."

He hugged her. She said, "Can we call Scott and check on Michelle?"

"Sure."

He called. Scott reported that Michelle was resting comfortably. He asked how Maggie was. Maggie heard him. She wrapped her arms tighter around Mike's waist, leaning her head on his shoulder, and said, "I'm fine."

Chapter 47

The next morning, Mike called the coach early. They agreed Mike needed to skip training to take care of his family. Sandy needed to go to work, but first she dropped Mike, Maggie, and Sara at Mike's house to pick up his Jeep. Then they went to the hospital.

Michelle was awake by the time they got there. Sara cried, "Mommy!" and ran to Michelle's bed.

Mike warned her to be careful of Mommy's hurt leg.

Sara said, "We were in a car accident. It was very scary. But we are all right. 'Specially you, Mommy. You have Uncle Mike's blood in you!"

Michelle was relieved to see Sara looking so happy and unhurt, but she was confused. "What about Uncle Mike's blood?"

"When your leg got hurt, lots of blood came out. So the doctors took some of Uncle Mike's blood and put it in you. It's OK because Uncle Mike had enough to share. Now you are going to be stronger than ever!"

Michelle didn't know about the transfusion. "I guess it's good to have a twin brother. Thanks, Mike."

"Anytime." He smiled. "How are you doing?" he asked with concern.

"I hear I will be fine. I'm ready to get out of here."

They all looked at Scott. Maggie had never seen him unshaven. He must have spent the whole night by her side. "She should be able to leave today. But she is going to need some help at home," he offered.

He left to make the arrangements.

Mike asked, "Do you need anything, Chel?"

"There is a room down the hall with orange juice. Can you get me some? You guys can have some too."

Mike and Sara went in search of the orange juice.

Maggie stepped up to Michelle's bed. Michelle asked, "Sara's really OK, right?"

"Yep, not a scratch on her."

"Thanks for taking care of her."

"What? Did you think I would leave her on the side of the road?" joked Maggie. Pause. "You know, you had me scared half to death with all that 'if I don't make it' talk." She blinked away her tears.

"What 'if I don't make it' talk?"

"Don't you remember? When the paramedics were working on you, you just kept saying, 'Promise me you will take care of Sara if I don't make it. Promise me you will take care of Sara if I don't make it.' It really freaked me out."

"I don't remember that. I don't remember anything about the car accident."

Maggie huffed. "That's not fair. Every time something bad happens you get to forget all about it, and I have to remember every terrifying minute." Then she smiled. "Next time—next time something bad happens, I get to check out, and you get to be the one who remembers."

"OK," conceded Michelle.

Mike and Sara had walked back into the room, each carrying two cups of juice. Mike said, "I have a better idea. How about there isn't a next time?"

They both agreed to that.

Scott came back into the room. Michelle fussed with her hair.

Mike and Scott went into the hall to discuss what would happen next.

Maggie smiled at Michelle. "Don't worry—you look gorgeous."

Michelle was embarrassed. "I'll bet. Maybe I am dying if you are being that nice to me!"

"He stayed all night at your bedside. He is pretty smitten."

"He's a doctor. That's what doctors do for their patients."

"You're not his patient."

Mike and Scott came back in. Scott said, "Michelle, you will be released this afternoon. I have arranged for a hospital bed to be delivered to your apartment."

"Where will we put that?" asked Michelle.

"In the living room. We will have to put your couch in storage."

Mike turned to Maggie. "Michelle will need to stay in bed for a while. She'll need someone there with her all the time. And someone needs to take care of Sara. We were thinking if you moved in with her, you could take care of Michelle and Sara. I'll be there as much as I can to help out."

"So will I," added Scott.

Maggie looked at Michelle. "Sure, sounds like a plan."

Mike had a meeting scheduled with the coaches and trainers today. They said they wanted to see how everything was going, but he knew this would probably determine whether he played in the game tomorrow.

Mike decided he would be completely honest with them. He wanted to play—he always wanted to play, but the game wasn't that important. They had already clinched a spot in the playoffs. They were pretty far ahead of the other teams. Even if they lost this game, nothing significant would change. But the coaches would want to go into the playoffs strong, and they never wanted to lose a game.

"How are things going with your family?" started the coach.

"Things are good. Michelle, my sister, is healing—getting stronger every day," answered Mike.

"Your niece and your girlfriend were also in the accident, correct? How are they?"

"Sara, my niece, wasn't hurt. Thank goodness," said Mike. Honesty, he thought. "She is still having nightmares—I guess that's to be expected."

"Your girlfriend was hurt, too, right?"

"Yes, Maggie bumped her head and cut her hand. No concussion, but she did get eighteen stitches in her hand. She's doing fine."

"How are you handling things?"

"Great. Maggie has moved in with Michelle, so she is there to take care of her and Sara all the time. She's really taking care of everything."

"And you are living…?"

"At my own house."

"But you probably spend a lot of time with them."

"Yes, sir. I go there straight from training. I go to the grocery store and do errands for them. I help out as much as I can."

"I imagine they need a lot of help. It must be stressful."

Mike thought about the last few days. The first day he got there after practice, they were all three sleeping. They must have been watching a movie because the credits were still rolling on the TV when he came in. Sara was asleep with Michelle in Michelle's hospital bed. Maggie was asleep on the floor.

The next day wasn't nearly as peaceful. He was supposed to pick up milk on the way home, but he forgot. So Maggie was frustrated with him. Michelle wanted to eat chocolate, but Maggie wouldn't let her because Michelle made Maggie promise not to let her get fat while she couldn't get out of bed. So Michelle was frustrated with Maggie. And Sara was frustrated with everybody (including him) because nobody would take her to the park. In the end, he took Sara with him to get the milk. When he got back, Maggie and Michelle were both in her bed eating chocolate. They told him they decided they needed chocolate now, and if they got fat, they would exercise together when Michelle got better.

But for the most part, the fact that they were all three together in one place eased his mind a lot.

He answered the coach, "It has had its ups and downs. But in general, everything is OK."

"Are you taking care of yourself?" asked the trainer.

"Yes, sir."

"Eating well?"

Mike smiled. "Maggie reads your website. She takes all your suggestions and makes healthy food. And she makes it taste good!"

The trainer smiled. "Getting enough sleep?"

This time Mike laughed right out loud. "If Maggie had her way, I would be getting twelve hours of sleep a night! So yeah—plenty of sleep."

The coach was glad to hear it. Usually, players with a family did better than the single ones because they had a better support system. It was often the girlfriends who could be demanding and distracting to the player.

There was one more issue that the coach needed to bring up. "Did you give blood after the accident?"

Mike looked him straight in the eye. "Yes, I did."

"Do you know that's against team rules?"

"Yes, I do." Mike was not going to apologize for giving blood to Michelle when she needed it. If the coach felt he was not fit to play because of it, so be it.

"Thank you for coming in," said the coach. Mike had been dismissed.

As Mike walked out of the locker room, a reporter named Bob caught up with him. Mike liked Bob. He was an ex-soccer player himself, so he knew what it was like to be hounded by the press. Bob wasn't like that. But he also knew that the fans would be very interested in a story about a player's family being in a car accident. Mike got ready for more questions.

"How's it going?" asked Bob.

"Good," responded Mike.

They both knew the next question. "How about an interview?"

The players were instructed to be nice to the reporters. It was important to keep a good team image.

"Sure."

The camera started rolling. Bob began, "Mike, we know that some of your family members were in a car accident at the beginning of the week. Who was in that car accident?"

"My sister, my niece, and my girlfriend."

"That must have been scary news to hear."

"Yeah. Obviously, when you hear that the three people you care most about in this world are hit by a truck, it's pretty scary."

"Now your sister had the most serious injuries. How is she doing?"

"Yeah, she has some damage to her leg. Right now, she is confined to bed, but she will make a full recovery. There is no doubt about that."

"She lost a lot of blood during the accident, correct?"

"Yes, she needed a transfusion."

"And you donated the blood for that transfusion?"

"Of course, I did. She's my twin sister."

"Players are discouraged from donating blood during the season, clearly because soccer is a very demanding sport. You need to be in tip top shape. Will you play in the game tomorrow?"

"That's up to the coach."

"How do you feel about your fitness?"

"I'm ready to play."

"If you are not allowed to play in the game, will you regret donating blood to your sister?"

"Not for a minute."

"Now your niece was not hurt in the car accident and your girlfriend sustained only minor injuries. How are they doing?"

"They are both great." He smiled.

"I hear your girlfriend was quite the hero at the accident. Can you tell us what happened?"

"Yeah, the truck hit the driver's side of the car, so my sister, Michelle, who was driving sustained the most serious injury. The artery in her leg was torn. She was losing a lot of blood. Maggie, my girlfriend, managed to stop the bleeding long before the paramedics got there. It would have been much worse for Michelle if not for Maggie."

"How did she stop the bleeding?"

"With a maxi pad." Mike smiled.

"Quick thinking."

"Yeah, Maggie is pretty amazing!"

That interview was relatively painless, thought Mike. He shook hands with Bob and was ready to get out of there to check on his girls when Bob stopped him to ask one more thing.

"Hey, Mike, your family usually sits in the front row to watch you play, right?"

"Yeah, Maggie, Michelle, Sara, and Maggie's best friend, Sandy, have been to every home game this year. This will be the only one they will miss." They had already discussed this. There was no question that Michelle couldn't go to the game, of course. Maggie, Sara, and Sandy could still go, but it didn't feel right to leave Michelle at home, so they decided they would all stay home and watch it on TV. He was disappointed that his cheering section wouldn't be there, but he would worry less if they were all together safe and sound at home.

Bob asked, "How would they feel about having a camera at their house during the game? The fans would love to see them cheering for you."

He was all for being nice to the press, but this seemed a little intrusive. "I don't know about that."

"Ask them for me."

"OK, I'll get back to you."

Maggie dismissed the idea immediately, saying, "Why in the world would anyone want to see that?"

Michelle simply said no at first. Then Sandy came over. She had heard about it from Owen. Sandy, of course, thought it was a great idea. She wanted to be on TV. She started working on Michelle when Mike and Maggie were busy giving Sara a bath.

"You know, Owen says the coach tells the players to be nice to the reporters."

"This is different. They don't need to come into my apartment."

"We can all go to Mike's. We could do it there."

"Or we could say no."

"Owen thinks it could be good for Mike's career."

Michelle didn't believe that.

"Sure," continued Sandy. "This would put the spotlight on him. He would be a fan favorite. The coaches would like the positive press. It would be good for the team. And what is good for the team is good for Mike."

Michelle didn't believe Sandy thought it was good for Mike. She thought Sandy thought it was good for Sandy. But the spotlight might be good for Mike. He was an important member of the team, but he didn't get as much attention as some of the flashier players, like Brandon. Mike didn't care, but Michelle always thought it was a little unfair. After all he had done for her—especially what he had given up to help her when they found out she was pregnant—this was the least she could do for him.

Michelle told Mike she wanted to do it. Mike was surprised. He looked at Maggie. "Whatever Michelle wants." She shrugged.

The coaches put Mike in the starting lineup despite the emotions of the car accident and the blood donation. They felt he was fit—which was good considering it would be weird if the cameras were at Mike's house watching his fan club watch him sit on the bench.

They played the interview Mike had given yesterday during half time. Maggie sputtered when the reporter called her a hero. She would have described herself as a basket case, especially after Mike showed up.

Michelle said, "A maxi pad?"

Maggie blushed.

"I guess I should thank you for keeping me from bleeding to death," said Michelle only half kidding.

"What can I say? I had to do something. You were getting blood all over the car."

"You mean the car that was completely totaled?" asked Sandy.

Scott said, "I think you are a good person to have around in an emergency."

Maggie rolled her eyes. "Yeah, I'm a rock."

Maggie didn't know why there was a cameraman there. As far as she could tell, the only time the camera was on was after Mike scored a goal. They all (except Michelle, of course) jumped up and celebrated. Even GG Rose got out of her wheelchair to do a little dance, yelling, "That's my boy!"

After the game, Bob interviewed Mike. "Well, we know it has been a tough week for you, but you played well out there. Take us through the goal."

Mike described the buildup to the goal and his part in it.

Bob continued, "Because of the car accident, your family is watching from home. Do you want to say hi?"

He smiled into the camera and said, "Hi, guys!"

"The three people who were in the car accident are listening in—do you have anything you want to say to them?"

"Sure. Hi, Sara Rose. Uncle Mike loves you."

"And your sister?"

"Hey, Chel, get better soon."

"How about your girlfriend? What do you want to say to your girlfriend?"

Mike paused for a moment, thinking about what he wanted to say to Maggie. Finally, he threw caution to the wind and said, "Maggie, I love you. Will you marry me?"

Maggie stared at the TV screen with her mouth wide open. She looked at Michelle. "Is this for real?"

Michelle nodded her head yes.

Maggie stared at Mike on the screen until Sandy whispered loudly, "Say yes."

Maggie said, "Yes, yes, yes, yes, yes" crescendoing louder and louder to a peak. Then her yeses decrescendoed "yes, yes, yes, yes" until the last one which was a quiet, happy "yeah."

Bob said, "Well, that was a surprise." Then the cameras cut back to the studio.

Back in the locker room, Bob found Mike to tell him there was quite an uproar going on at his house.

Mike said, "Well, she said, yes, right?"

"About a dozen times," Bob replied. "You want to see the tape?"

He showed Mike what the viewers at home saw after he made his proposal. Maggie was staring at the TV like a deer caught in the headlights at first. But after Sandy prodded her, she looked pretty happy and excited and so beautiful.

Then Bob switched the monitor to a live shot of his house. The camera man asked the group what they wanted to say to Mike.

GG Rose said, "Congratulations! I am so happy for you!"

Michelle said, "Good choice, big brother!"

Sandy said, "It's about time!"

Sara said, "Uncle Mike, now Miss Maggie is gonna be my Aunt Maggie."

Last, the cameraman turned the camera to Maggie. She asked, "Can he hear me?"

The cameraman nodded yes. She looked into the camera and said, "Come home."

Mike never got dressed so fast in his life.

On the drive home, Mike thought that was wild. He hadn't planned on asking her to marry him. Well, actually he had been thinking about asking her for a long time. He remembered the first time he thought about marrying Maggie. Way back at the end of March, after the three-game road trip. That night that he came home to her. Of course, it had been way too early to ask her then. He'd had to wait until she was over Greg. Then several weeks ago, they had actually run into Greg at the movies.

Mike remembered watching Maggie closely during the interaction. They had just seen a movie that was a combination of science fiction and Western. Maggie had laughed through the entire movie as though it were a comedy.

As they exited the theater, Maggie was talking about how preposterous the whole premise of the movie was when Mike spotted Greg. He decided to try and shield her vision and get her out of there before she saw him. But it didn't work. Greg saw Maggie and called out, "Margaret!"

Maggie looked around Mike to see Greg.

Greg said, "Hi, Margaret."

Maggie looked at Greg warily and responded coolly, "Greg."

"Did you already see the movie?"

"Yeah."

"How was it?"

Maggie answered, "Hilarious," with a small laugh. "You're gonna hate it."

Greg said, "I'd like to introduce Stephi." He gestured to the girl standing next to him.

Maggie said, "Hi."

Stephi returned, "Hello," in a voice dripping with superiority and boredom.

There was a pause in the conversation as Greg looked at Mike. Maggie pointed her thumb back at Mike and simply said, "Mike" in the way of introduction.

"Listen," said Greg. "Maybe we could all go get a cup of coffee—you know, catch up."

Maggie didn't seem to want to do that. "I thought you were going to see the movie."

"You said I wouldn't like it."

Maggie shrugged. "I've been wrong before."

"So how about that cup of coffee?"

"No, thanks," said Maggie. "Bye, Greg." She turned around to leave, tugging on Mike's arm. Then she started talking about the movie again. "Surely you didn't buy it when…"

All the way home from the movie Mike had wondered what Maggie really thought about that encounter—until they got home. Maggie immediately told Sandy, "We saw Greg at the movie!"

Sandy said, "You are kidding! What happened?"

"He was with a girl named Stephi!" There was definite mocking in her voice as she pronounced the girl's name.

"What did she look like?"

"Snooty and bored." She shrugged. "Actually, she looked perfect for him. They will probably be very happy together," she said with a smile and not a trace of sarcasm.

That convinced Mike that Maggie was over Greg, but he still wasn't sure about asking her to marry him until the car accident. As bad as the car accident was, the fact that she had called him first was encouraging. She hadn't even thought to call Scott. At the hospital it had been his shoulder she cried on; he was the one she clung to. And that night before she went to bed, she admitted she needed him. That was the deciding factor. That night he decided he was going to propose. But he hadn't planned on doing it on national TV.

He hoped she really meant it when she said yes. He hoped she hadn't agreed just because she was on TV and Sandy told her to. He hoped she wasn't having second thoughts. He better get home and quick.

Maggie was waiting on the porch swing with a smile on her face when Mike got to his house.

He said, "Maggie, I didn't mean…"

Her face fell.

He tried again, "I mean, this is what I wish I had said."

He got down on one knee and held her hand. He said, "Maggie, I have loved you since the moment I met you. You are sweet and kind and smart and funny. And, oh, so beautiful. I know we haven't known each other for very long, but I can't imagine my life without you. Will you please marry me?"

She smiled. "OK."

As he smiled back at her, she said, "There's something I wish I had said too."

"What?" he asked.

"I love you too."

"Yeah?"

"So much," she exclaimed with feeling.

Mike lifted Maggie off the ground and spun her around as he kissed her. Then he took her into the house to share their joy with their friends and family.

Chapter 48

Inside the house, there were handshakes and hugs and congratulations all around.

"That was pretty sly how you set all this up," said Sandy.

"Yeah," said Michelle. "You acted like you didn't even want the cameras here and all along you were planning to propose."

Mike held up his hands in innocence. "I didn't plan anything."

"What?" they all exclaimed.

"I wasn't planning to propose. Bob just asked what I wanted to say to Maggie." He smiled at Maggie. "That's what I wanted to say."

"Just like my Willie," said GG Rose.

They all turned to her and listened to her story.

"I met my Willie just a couple of months before he was drafted into the army. I wrote to him every day while he was away fighting in the war. I never got any letters back, but I just couldn't stop thinking about him. I couldn't stop writing.

"Then one day almost a year after he left, I opened my door. There he was looking all handsome in his dress uniform. He had a stack of letters in one hand and a dozen roses in the other. For a moment we both just stood there, staring at each other. Then he got down on one knee and said, 'Rose, I love you. Will you marry me?'

"It wasn't until years later that he confessed that he hadn't planned on proposing that day. It was much too soon. But he said when he saw me, he just couldn't help it."

She drew her mind back from the past and looked at Mike. "You are just like him. You are just like my Willie."

Mike thought that was the best compliment he had ever gotten.

Soon it was time for everyone to leave. Scott loaded Sara, Michelle, and GG Rose into his car. Sandy was off to see Owen. Mike drew Scott off to the side. He said, "Can you stay with Michelle for a while?"

Mike knew what Scott was thinking. He reassured him, "It's OK. I don't have to have her tonight. I get to have her for a lifetime. I just want to be with her—talk to her. I will bring her to Michelle's in a little while."

Maggie and Mike sat on the porch swing, rocking slowly back and forth.

"Since the moment you met me, huh?" Maggie teased gently.

"Come on, I got the feeling you kinda liked me too that night."

"Ha, I was so messed up then, I didn't know which way was up."

"So this love thing is a relatively new development?"

"Nah, it's been a while. Actually, I can tell you exactly when it happened. I can tell you the moment I fell in love with you."

"Well, tell me!"

"Remember when we thought you had a concussion after that game."

"Bits and pieces."

"Remember we went back to my house, and you went into my bedroom to lie down."

"Yeah."

"And I found you, and I was rubbing your back."

"That I remember."

"For once you were still. And I got to take care of you a little bit. And my heart just kind of melted." She sighed. "Yep, my heart completely melted and dripped down my arm and into you. And you've had it ever since." They locked eyes. "You know, you should be careful with it. It's kind of fragile."

He brushed the hair out of her eyes. "I will."

Then he smiled. "So all I had to do to get you to fall in love with me is get kicked in the head?"

She laughed, "Yeah, I guess."

"Totally worth it."

They rested back against the swing, content just to be together.

Mike asked, "So when do you think you want to get married?"

"Well, you have the day off tomorrow, right?"

He laughed, "You want to get married tomorrow?"

She leaned forward. "Yeah, all we have to do is call Pastor Dave. We could do it tomorrow afternoon at his church."

"Come on, we need to have a real wedding. I want to watch you walk down the aisle toward me in a beautiful white wedding dress."

"I have a wedding dress. Never been used. I'll walk anywhere you want me to!"

He smiled. "Be serious."

"I am. Just give me fifteen minutes. I'll get the dress. You get everyone back here—we'll do it right now!"

"You're crazy!"

"Well, you already knew that! Come on, it would be great!"

"I think you need a marriage license."

"Oh, right." Pause. "How long would it take to get to Vegas?"

"Maggie!" Pause. "To think I was afraid you were going to say no!"

"Like I have ever said no to you! I don't see any reason to wait."

"How about so our friends and family can be there?"

"Oh, all right," she conceded.

They sat together snuggling a while longer.

Suddenly Maggie sat up. "Wait—you do want to have kids, right?"

"Yeah." He smiled.

"Whew!" She leaned back again.

"How many are you thinking?"

"I don't know. What do you think?"

"I think you can have as many as you want."

"Well, I definitely want more than one. It's awful to be an only child. But Sandy has four brothers and that seemed like a lot. So five is too many."

"So two to four kids?"

"Yes, two to four kids."

More snuggling. Finally, Mike said reluctantly, "I better get you back to Michelle's."

The next morning, Scott volunteered to stay with Michelle so Mike could take Maggie to church. She wanted to tell Pastor Dave they were engaged and discuss the possibility of getting married at his church with him.

Pastor Dave saw Maggie sitting with Mike absolutely beaming. She looked like she was bursting with good news! He hadn't seen her since the car accident, but he had the whole church praying for her and Michelle. He was surprised to see her so happy.

After the service, Maggie hung around up front with the band until Pastor Dave was finished shaking hands with the congregants.

The drummer asked Maggie, "Did you like the songs today?"

"Yeah, it's like you picked all my favorites."

"We did," claimed the guitar player.

Maggie thought back. The week before the car accident she had been at the church while the band had been rehearsing. She had clapped for them after they sang a song with a beautiful halleluiah chorus. She told them it was her favorite song. Then they talked about a few other songs she liked. Apparently, they played them all today for her. That was nice.

She pointed her thumb back at Mike and said, "This is Mike."

The guitar player shook hands with him.

The drummer said, "This is Mike? I thought he didn't exist."

"What?" said Maggie. Then she laughed, "Oh, you thought he was too good to be true?" She smiled at Mike.

"No," said the drummer, "I thought you made him up."

"Why would I do that?"

"To keep all the guys away! You know, like, 'Stay away from me. I have a boyfriend. He's never here, but I still have a boyfriend.'"

Maggie laughed, then conceded, "That does sound like something I would do! But I didn't. He's here. He's real."

Pastor Dave walked up and gave Maggie a big hug. He said, "You are looking happy today."

Maggie said, "I am. Guess what?"

"What?" he asked.

"We're engaged!" She put her arm around Mike's waist. He already had his arm around her shoulders.

Pastor Dave beamed. "Congratulations!"

The guitar player added his congratulations. The drummer looked momentarily disappointed but then added his as well.

Mike thought, I need to get a ring on her finger.

They went back to Pastor Dave's office. Maggie said, "I was hoping we could get married here. What do you think?"

"I'd love that."

"And you would marry us?"

"I would be honored."

Maggie flung her arms open and said, "Yay!"

"I usually have people come in for a premarital counseling session."

Maggie pretended exasperation. "More counseling! You know everything about me. What could we possibly have to talk about!?"

He smiled. "Marriage is a big step. Humor me."

"OK." She smiled.

They set up an appointment. Then chatted about how everyone was doing since the car accident.

In the car, Mike asked, "How come whenever you introduce me—you just point at me and say, 'This is Mike'?"

"What do you want me to call you?"

"I want you to say, 'This is my boyfriend, Mike.'"

"The guys in the band already know that."

"Greg doesn't."

"What?"

"When we saw him at the movie that day, you didn't tell him I was your boyfriend."

Maggie thought back. "Oh, I'm sorry. You're right." Then she teased, "You want me to call him right now and tell him?" She picked up her phone, smiling.

"No, don't do that. Just remember next time."

"No, can't do that. I can't introduce you as my boyfriend 'cuz you are not. You are my fiancé!"

At Michelle's, Mike was excited to call his mom and tell her the good news. Maggie didn't think his mom was going to be as excited to hear the good news.

Maggie had only met Mike's mom once. One day Mike announced that he was taking Maggie and Sara to his mom's house on his day off. Maggie remembered looking forward to meeting her. She thought the rest of his family was so nice, she couldn't wait to meet his mom. It didn't go well.

Everything was OK as long as Mike was around. But then he went outside to take care of some chores. That left Maggie and Sara alone with The Mother.

The first thing she said to Maggie was, "Is Michelle paying for your services today?"

Maggie answered, "Yeah."

"That must be nice," shot back The Mother.

Maggie was taken aback. She wasn't sure what she meant. So she said, "Well, it is true that taking care of Sara is so easy, it doesn't seem like a job."

"Then maybe you shouldn't be taking my daughter's money. Especially when Uncle Mike is here to take care of Sara."

That hurt. Maggie didn't know how to respond.

All afternoon Maggie tried, but she just couldn't seem to win. If she told Sara what to do, The Mother would say, "I think I can take care of my own granddaughter."

If she hung back, she'd say, "How much does Michelle pay you for this?" sarcastically.

When she went outside to hang out with Mike during Sara's nap, she said, "Do you always ignore my granddaughter like this?"

When Maggie answered, "No, Mrs. Mallone," she said, "Mrs. Mallone is my mother-in-law."

So Maggie said, "No, ma'am."

She said, "Ma'am is just a code word for old."

Maggie sure wasn't going to try to call her by her first name. So she mumbled, "No, sir." That just got her a look of derision.

That's why Maggie and Sandy secretly called her The Mother now.

There was talk of Mike's mom coming to help with Michelle after the car accident, but she never did. She had visited Michelle in the hospital, but not while Maggie was around. Maggie didn't think that was a coincidence.

Now Mike was happily saying, "Hey, Mom, guess what?" into the phone.

"Maggie and I are getting married. Isn't that great?"

"Yeah, I know—it all happened so quickly!"

"Well, we don't know when yet. We'll let you know."

"Oh. OK. I'll let you go, then. Bye."

The next day, Maggie decided if Mike could call his mom, she could call hers. It took her all morning to work up the courage, but at nap time, Maggie announced to Mike and Michelle that she was going to call her mom. Sandy was there too. Maggie hadn't talked to her mom at all since the painful phone call when her mom had announced that she wished Maggie had never been born. Her mom didn't have this number, so she couldn't call her. But she had stopped calling Sandy too.

Now things had changed. She had good news to tell her. This was going to be OK, right?

Maggie's hands shook a little as she dialed the number. "Hi, Mom."

"Margaret." It wasn't a question. It was a statement. But it wasn't a statement that held any hint of happiness.

Maggie continued with trepidation. "I have good news," she stated nervously. "I am getting married."

"You are!" Now there was happiness in her mom's voice. "That's great!"

Maggie smiled, relieved. "I always knew you would call him!" her mom continued.

Maggie was confused. "Call who?"

"Greg, of course. I knew if you called him, he would forgive you of all this nonsense."

Maggie rubbed her forehead—not this again. "Not Greg. I'm not marrying Greg!"

"Then who?"

"Mike."

"That soccer player?"

"Yeah." Maggie smiled at Mike. He was standing at the sink hand washing a few dishes from lunch.

"Why would you want to marry a soccer player? Margaret! Are you pregnant?"

Maggie ran her fingers through her hair. "No, Mom."

"How much money does he make?"

"I have no idea how much money he makes."

"Well, we are not paying for another one of your weddings. You still owe us for the last one."

Maggie was tempted to say, "Not even if I married Greg?" But she didn't. She didn't respond at all. What was there to say?

Finally, Maggie's mom continued, "Margaret, you need to promise me that you will call Greg. Before you make this mistake, you need to make one more attempt to fix things with Greg."

Maggie was done with this. "Bye, Mom."

She closed the phone and said to the three of them, "The next time I tell you I'm calling my mom, stop me."

The phone in her hand rang. She looked at the caller ID. It was her mom. She just stared at the phone. Mike tried to take it from her, saying, "Let me try."

Maggie cried, "No," and threw the phone into the soapy water.

Mike yelled, "Maggie!"

Sandy intervened. "You stay with Michelle. I got this," she said to Mike. She pushed Maggie out the door.

Nobody knew the pain Maggie endured in the relationship with her parents like Sandy did. Nobody knew how hurt Maggie was when they ignored her or how lonely she was when they left her alone in that big house. Only Sandy understood.

So she took her to their house and let Maggie vent and cry and then vent and cry some more. Finally, Maggie was spent. She collapsed on the couch and then noticed an envelope addressed to her on the coffee table.

"What's this?"

"Oh, that came for you last week. Between the car accident and the big proposal, I forgot to give it to you. Looks like a bill."

It did look like a bill—from the bank. Maggie was confused. She didn't have a savings account or even a checking account. She didn't have any money to put in the bank. She opened the bill and smiled. She had forgotten all about this. This was great! So her mom didn't want to pay for the wedding? That was fine!

Sandy asked, "What is it?"

"This is how I am going to pay for my wedding! Let's go!"

Sandy drove Maggie to the bank. The teller led them back into the vault to a safety deposit box. Maggie carefully pulled out a beautiful and very expensive looking necklace.

Sandy asked, "Where did you get that?"

"Greg gave it to me last year for Christmas. It looked so expensive, I was afraid to wear it. So I put it in this safety deposit box, and then I forgot all about it. Let's go to the jewelry store and see how much it's worth."

It was almost supper time before Sandy brought Maggie back to Michelle's. She looked sheepishly at Mike as he gave her her phone. "I dried it out with a hair dryer. I think it still works."

"Thanks," said Maggie. "Sorry about that."

"So are you OK now?"

"Oh yeah, Sandy calmed me down."

"How did she do that?"

"She reminded me that my mom has always been a horrible person and I still get to marry the hottest guy on the soccer team," she said as she wrapped her arms around his waist.

"Sandy said that."

"Those were her exact words, 'The hottest guy on the soccer team.'"

He smiled. "So where were you all afternoon?"

Miss Lori

She smiled back at him. "Planning a wedding."

"Oh, do you need any help with that?"

"Oh no, we got this—unless you want to help."

"Not really. But I'll do whatever you need me to do."

"All you need to do is show up—in a tux!"

"I can do that."

Michelle piped up, "I want to help."

"Great," said Maggie. "I have all sorts of things I want to show you." She produced a bag with a dozen bridal magazines in it.

"Looks like you guys have this covered. I think I'll go home and pack."

Maggie walked him to the door. He was leaving early tomorrow morning. The end of the season tournament began with a home and home series. That meant that Mike was going to play in Dallas. Then Dallas would come to LA to play. They would combine the scores of the two games to determine the winner. If they lost, they were done for the season, but if they won, they would go on to the conference championship that would be played in LA. If they won that, they would play in the national championship, which would also be played in LA. All this meant to Maggie was that this was the last away game. This was the last time she had to say goodbye to him.

They stood at the door hugging and kissing and exchanging "I love yous."

Finally, Michelle said, "You know the worst thing about this car accident? I can't get up and leave the room when you guys get all kissy-faced."

Maggie giggled. Mike said, "Close your eyes, Chel." He gave Maggie one last goodbye kiss, leaning her backward in classic movie style. Then he called goodbye to everyone in the room and left.

Chapter 49

They narrowly won the away game. Tomorrow they would play the home game against Dallas.

Maggie was making fried rice for supper. She tried to open the soy sauce. The lid was on so tight that it pulled at the skin of her injured hand.

"Ouch!" she yelled. "I keep doing that!"

She grabbed the injured hand with the other hand and pressed it to her chest to soothe the pain.

Mike asked, "You OK?"

"No, it hurts," Maggie whimpered.

"Let me see it."

"I don't want to."

"Maggie."

She reluctantly offered him her hand. He gently unwrapped it.

He said, "You know, it would heal better if you left it unwrapped. Open to the air."

"I know. I have a doctor and a nurse telling me that every day."

"Then why don't you do it?"

"Because it hurts. Do you know how many things you do with your right hand every day? I do because it hurts every time I touch anything."

Scott had taken the stitches out yesterday. Maggie had had to lie down with Michelle so that she didn't pass out.

"Don't touch it. It hurts!"

Mike rolled his eyes at her.

"I guess I'm kind of a wimp. We can't all be as tough as you."

Mike looked at her hand. "Maggie, when we get married, are you going to take my last name?"

She smiled, thinking he was just trying to distract her. "Yeah."

"Then I think you are monogramed."

He traced the natural creases in her hand that formed an M and said, "Maggie."

Then he traced her scar, which started near the middle of her palm and ran across her hand toward her thumb, then down, up, and down again—forming another M. "Mallone."

Maggie stared at her hand. She didn't like to look at it. It was an ugly reminder of a horrifying experience. But now she saw what he saw and said, "Or I have been branded." She imitated him tracing each M and said, "Mike…Mallone."

He took her hand back and kissed her palm.

Michelle called out, "You better wash that hand. You're getting germs all over it."

Maggie smiled. "She is such a grump lately."

Michelle retorted, "Yeah, yeah, yeah. Hey, Mike, can you get me my power cord? My computer battery is dying again."

Mike opened the soy sauce and handed it to Maggie before he went to help Michelle.

Maggie returned to cooking, but she didn't wash the kiss off her hand.

They won the home game. They were moving on in the tournament.

Sunday morning, Mike picked Maggie up to take to her church and then counseling with Pastor Dave. It had been raining for the past two days, so it was chilly out. Maggie was wearing a soft pink sweater and baby blue pants. Like always she smelled like vanilla. He kissed her hello and tasted her vanilla lip gloss. He commented, "You taste like cotton candy. Come to think of it, you smell like cotton candy too." He stepped back and looked her up and down. "You even look like cotton candy. Maggie, are you made of cotton candy?"

Maggie giggled, "Yep, cut me open, and that's what you get. You know, sugar and spice and everything nice," she joked.

"Well, you look beautiful."

She walked past him to leave. He grabbed her hand and pulled her back. "I said, 'You look beautiful.'"

"I heard you." She smiled and tried to walk away.

He pulled her back again. She looked at him, considering, and then said, "Oh, you look good too." And waited for him to let go. He didn't. She bit her lip, trying to figure out what he was waiting for.

He looked deep into her eyes and said, "You look beautiful," with feeling.

She could feel his gaze to the pit of her stomach. Finally, she looked down and softly said, "Thank you."

The counseling session with Pastor Dave was short. He had to admit Maggie was right. When it came to Maggie and even Mike, he already knew the answers to most of the stuff he discussed with engaged couples.

There was just one question he needed them to answer.

"What do you want out of this marriage?"

Maggie looked at Mike and said, "I want to be his most loyal fan. I want to celebrate with him when he wins and commiserate with him when he loses. I want to bring him ice when he's hurt and rub his muscles when he's sore. But mostly I just want to be wherever he is."

Mike smiled at her while he made his own declaration. "I want to take care of her and protect her. I want to laugh with her when she's silly, hold her when she's sad, and calm her down when she goes crazy. I want to come home to her after a road trip. But, most of all, I want to spend the rest of my life telling her how beautiful she is."

Pastor Dave was fully satisfied with their answers. Most people, when asked that question, answered what they wanted their mate to do for them. He was absolutely sure that Maggie wanted Mike to do exactly what he had described for her and vice versa. But the fact that they had both responded with what they wanted to do for the other one set a good tone for their marriage.

They won the conference championship. Only one more game to go. There was no stopping this team!

Mike took Maggie out to lunch after church. Then back to Michelle's apartment to relieve Sandy of Michelle duty.

Maggie commented, "There sure are a lot of cars in the parking lot."

Mike walked her to the apartment door and said, "I'll see you later."

Maggie said, "Where are you going?"

Mike smiled. "I was told to have you here at two o'clock and then make myself scarce."

"Why?"

Mike just smiled bigger, opened the door to the apartment, and walked away.

"Surprise!" sang out a chorus of voices. And Maggie was! Surprised, a little scared, and totally confused.

Sandy pulled Maggie into the apartment and said, "Happy wedding shower!" because she knew Maggie hadn't figured it out yet.

Maggie looked around the room at a dozen faces she hadn't seen since the Greg Debacle. Faces she had been avoiding since the Greg Debacle. Most of them were the teachers and Delores from the preschool.

They all started talking at once. "Maggie, congratulations!" "So good to see you!" "Seems like it has been forever." "So who is the guy?" "Where is your fiancé?"

Sandy organized everyone to play some silly shower games. She made Maggie wear a toilet paper bridal veil. They drank punch and ate finger sandwiches. Maggie had to admit this was kind of fun. It was good to see all her old friends from school.

Then Michelle announced it was time for the slide show. Michelle had the computer hooked up to the TV. Up popped a picture of Maggie and Sandy in kindergarten.

"What is this?" laughed Maggie.

"The lives of Mike and Maggie." Michelle smiled.

"So this is what you have been so busy working on that your computer battery kept dying?"

The first section of the slide show was about Maggie's life. Pictures of Maggie and Sandy in the band, Maggie and Sandy in their Halloween costumes, Maggie and Sandy all dressed up going to a dance. There weren't any pictures of just Maggie when she was growing up because no one had taken any. All these pictures were from Sandy's parents' camera. Then Sandy had gotten a camera in college. Then there were plenty of pictures of Maggie—all embarrassing.

Then it was time for Mike's life. Maggie sat down on Michelle's bed next to her. There were baby pictures of Mike. Maggie exclaimed, "He looked just like Sara!"

Then pictures of Mike in every type of sports uniform—baseball, football, basketball, and, of course, soccer. He was a cute kid! Maggie was fascinated as Michelle told her about each picture. The other ladies were getting a little bored and starting to chat among themselves until a present-day picture of Mike filled the screen. That caught everyone's attention. They all exclaimed, "Wow, he is gorgeous!" "Does he have a brother?" "Or a friend that looks just like him?"

Maggie smiled. The slide show ended with pictures of Mike and Maggie together—mostly kissing. (Michelle had dozens of them!)

The ladies left one by one, wishing Maggie well and inviting her to visit the preschool again.

When Mike got back, Maggie and Michelle were sitting on Michelle's bed again still looking at pictures of Mike while Sandy cleaned up.

Mike asked, "How did the shower go?"

Maggie smiled. "It was fun." She pointed to the TV. "Look how cute you were!"

He thought, Well, at least she thought I used to be cute. He still wondered what she thought of him now.

Later that evening, Maggie was in the bathroom preparing for bed. She took a Tylenol because her head hurt. She had depended on Tylenol for the first several days after the car accident. But gradually she needed it less and less. Now her headaches were only occasional. But this headache wasn't from the bump on her head.

The shower had been fun. Sandy knew how to throw a party. At times the party had gotten kind of loud with all those ladies talking at the same time. But that hadn't caused her headache either.

It was the stress causing this headache. The wedding planning was going well—amazingly well. When Mike had suggested they go ring shopping, Maggie had convinced him to go to the jewelry store where Greg had bought the necklace. Of course, she didn't tell him about the necklace.

Maggie confessed to Mike that she had never liked the engagement ring that Greg had given her. It was big and ostentatious. It was constantly getting snagged on her clothes, but she was too afraid to take it off because it was so expensive. So now when she had the opportunity to pick her own ring, she picked something smaller with a simple, elegant design. A ring she loved. They picked out a simple gold band for Mike. They left the rings with the jeweler to be sized. Later Maggie went back to have the inside of his ring engraved. "You will always have my heart." She couldn't wait to give it to him. She paid for his ring with store credit from the necklace. His ring wasn't nearly as expensive as the necklace. She took the additional money to pay for other things for the wedding.

She didn't need to pay for much. Pastor Dave was letting her use the church for free. They would have the wedding outside in front of the waterfall and the reception right there. He insisted that he wanted to perform the ceremony for free. After all the volunteer work she had done at the church, he felt that was only fair. The church band had offered to play the music for free, too, as a wedding gift to Maggie.

For the rest of wedding, she used the nonrefundable deposits that her parents had paid for the wedding that never was. She had canceled that wedding in time, so they hadn't paid for most of the arrangements, but every place had had a nonrefundable deposit. That was the money she "owed" her parents. Turns out the deposit on a huge wedding for 400 was just about right to pay for a reasonable wedding of about fifty.

When she had been planning her wedding to Greg, she and Sandy had poured over magazines and had all kinds of ideas for the wedding. Then Maggie would go wedding shopping with her mom and future mother-in-law and somehow those ideas didn't seem to matter. For example, Maggie wanted her colors to be pink and baby blue. Somehow the colors ended up being red and ivory. Sandy's maid of honor dress was red and Maggie's wedding gown was ivory.

The flowers ended up being red and ivory roses. Maggie wanted pink roses with blue baby's breath. Greg was going to wear some hideous ivory tux with tails. In short, that wedding was nothing like Maggie wanted. This wedding was going to be different.

She and Sandy had used the deposit at the florist for the pink and blue flowers. They used the deposit at the reception hall to rent chairs, tables, and a tent in case of rain that would be delivered to the church. They used the deposit at the caterers for nuts, mints, and punch—this one wouldn't serve a meal. They changed the cake from chocolate (who has a chocolate wedding cake?) to vanilla with butter cream frosting decorated with pink and blue flowers. The invitations were a little trickier because, of course, they had sent out the invitations for the wedding that never was. But Maggie had canceled the matching thank you notes. The credit for those covered the invitations. The best part, though, was the dress. She was able to trade in that huge, puffy, ivory wedding dress with the annoyingly long train for a simple, white, lacey one. With the leftover store credit, they had a flower girl's dress made for Sara.

This wedding would be the wedding of her dreams—if it happened. That was what was causing this headache.

All the people at the shower had been good. No one mentioned the wedding that never was. No one even hinted that she was an idiot for not marrying Greg. But now they knew about it. They weren't invited to this wedding. Maggie hadn't invited anyone but Sandy and her parents. She hadn't told anyone except Sandy, her mom (which hadn't gone well), and Pastor Dave because she needed the church. Mike told everyone he met! But Maggie always hesitated, not because she didn't want to marry Mike but because she was deathly afraid that this wedding wouldn't happen either. She couldn't face another wedding that never was.

She knew Mike thought she had been kidding about getting married right away. But she hadn't. If she had her way, they would call Pastor

Dave right now and get married in Michelle's living room. That way she wouldn't have to worry.

She wouldn't admit it to anyone—not even Sandy. But every night she had nightmares about what might happen. She dreamt that his plane crashed on the way back from Dallas. She dreamt that he had some terrible secret that everybody knew but her. She dreamt about fires and earthquakes. She was afraid to go to sleep at night. She kept it together pretty well during the day. She was pretty sure he didn't have a secret that was bad enough to keep her from marrying him. But she still couldn't shake the feeling that something would happen to prevent this wedding. She couldn't figure out what. But she hadn't seen it coming last time either.

She looked in the mirror and thought she ought to pray. But she didn't want to. She knew she should acknowledge God. She should put it in His hands. But she was too afraid. God took Greg away from her. What if He took Mike away too?

Chapter 50

There were two weeks between the conference championship game and the national championship game. Mike was fidgety. He was having trouble sitting still—even more trouble than usual. He asked Maggie to take a walk with him after supper when Scott could stay with Michelle.

Maggie watched Mike as they walked along. He looked tense. She thought this waiting should be classified as cruel and unusual punishment.

Mike needed a topic that would take his mind off the upcoming game.

"How's the wedding planning going?" he asked.

"Great—it's all arranged." The wedding was scheduled for the day after the championship game. Maggie had said that way they would have the whole off season to honeymoon. But she really just wanted to do it as soon as possible.

"Really? Isn't it hard to plan a wedding in just a month?"

"It's a lot easier if you have already done it before."

"Oh, so you are just doing everything exactly the same?" He sounded disappointed.

"Absolutely not! That wedding was ostentatious and gaudy. This one will be simple and classy!"

"Why would you plan a gaudy wedding?"

"I had two mothers breathing down my neck telling me what I *really* wanted. It's a lot easier now that it's just me and Sandy."

"So…how are you paying for all of this?"

"I have my ways." She shrugged. She didn't know how he would feel about her using the necklace she got from Greg to pay for his ring and extras for the wedding.

"What ways?"

"Don't talk about money—it's gosh."

"Gosh?" He thought about how she had told her mom that she didn't know how much money he made. "I'll make you a deal. I'll tell you how much money I make if you tell me how you are paying for the wedding."

"No deal."

"Why not?"

"I don't want to know how much money you make."

He repeated, "Why not?" clearly annoyed.

"Because I don't care."

"Because you will just be disappointed because I am not rich like Greg?"

They had been holding hands. She pulled her hand out of his and said, "That may be the meanest thing you have ever said to me. I wasn't marrying Greg for his money!"

"I know—he was perfect. He was the dream—good-looking and smart."

"I didn't say he was perfect. I said I thought he was perfect. And I was wrong—totally wrong!"

"He was still good-looking and smart. Now you have to settle for the poor, dumb jock."

Where was this coming from? He had never said such hurtful things before. Was this it? Was this how it was going to end? Her eyes teared up. She sniffed.

Finally, she said, "You're not dumb."

"Look, I'm sorry, Maggie, but it's hard to listen to you tell me that Greg is perfect and Scott is perfect. Sometimes I just wonder…"

What? she thought. What did he wonder? What she thought of him?

She walked around in front to face him. "Greg was only the dream because I hadn't met you yet. I never would have agreed to marry Greg if I had any idea there was a guy like you out there."

"But he is good-looking and smart."

She put her arms around his waist. "You are way better-looking than Greg!"

He still wasn't satisfied. "So I'm good-looking and dumb."

"You are not dumb. I have never said you were dumb."

"But not as smart as Greg."

"I don't know. I'd have to compare your SATs," she joked.

"I didn't take the SAT. I didn't go to college," he retorted. He pulled away. She decided this wasn't the time to joke.

"I was kidding. I know you're smart. You're very smart."

"I could have gone to college, you know," he said defensively.

"I know. I'm sure you had all kinds of scholarship offers."

"No. I mean I could have graduated from college. I could have gotten a degree."

"I have no doubt about that." Pause. "Mike, you have to know Greg is not the dream."

"How about Scott? Is he the dream?"

"Scott? I don't know—maybe he's Michelle's dream."

"You spend an awful lot of time with him."

"That's only because you leave me alone too much!" She wished she hadn't said that.

"Only because I have to! You two seem to have an awful lot in common. You are a lot alike."

"Hmm. I wonder how that happened—your fiancé and Michelle's boyfriend are a lot alike."

"Come on, he is smart and rich."

That made her mad. She pointed her finger at him and said, "I'd like to point out that you are the only one bringing up this rich thing!"

He tried to calm himself. "Maggie, I need to ask you something."

"What?" she was still mad.

"What would have happened if you met Scott first?"

Maggie was flummoxed. "What?"

"What would have happened if you met Scott first?"

"I have no idea what you are asking me."

"What would have happened if you met Scott before me? Would you have gone out with him?"

She still didn't understand what he was getting at. "Before I met you, I was engaged to Greg, so I am gonna have to say no."

"That's not what I mean. Pretend there is no Greg."

"I often pretend there is no Greg," she joked.

"There is no Greg, and Scott asks you to go to a concert. Would you go?"

"Probably. Wait—where are you in this scenario?"

"You haven't met me yet."

Finally, she understood what he was asking. "Ohhh. So, in this hypothetical situation, I am dating Scott, and then I meet you. And you are asking what I would do?"

"Yeah, what would you do?"

"That's easy. I'd dump him."

"Yeah?"

"In a heartbeat. I'd dump Scott. I'd dump Greg. Are you kidding? I'd throw them both under a bus for you!"

"Maggie, be serious."

"I am! They are not the dream. You are the dream. No, you are better than I ever dreamed. You are good-looking and smart and strong and nice. So nice. You are nicer to me than anyone has ever been. I love you and only you." She snuggled into his arms.

Finally, he was at ease. "I love you too."

A couple of days later—another walk.

Mike had been thinking about how she was paying for the wedding. He thought maybe her parents were paying. Maybe she had talked to her mom again and smoothed things out. Maybe he should let it go. She was still so weird about money.

"Maggie," he said. "We're getting married in a week and a half."

"I know." She smiled.

"It's probably OK if you know how much money I make."

"No. Don't tell me!"

"Why not? I know you're not marrying me for my money. But you should know I'm not exactly poor." He made a better-than-average salary, he would say. Certainly enough to easily support a family.

"It's not about that. I just don't want to know yet."

"Why not?"

"So, if my mom asks, I can truthfully say I don't know. It's not important to me. But it's way too important to her."

"Have you talked to her again?"

"No. But I sent her an invitation."

"Don't you think you should call her? They need to come to the rehearsal dinner. Your dad is going to walk you down the aisle, right?"

Well, she hadn't exactly asked him. She hadn't talked to him, since… hmm, when had she last talked to him? She knew she hadn't talked to him since the Debacle. He was there at Thanksgiving last year—the night Greg proposed. But she had spent Christmas at Greg's house. Had she talked to him since Thanksgiving? She really couldn't remember.

She looked at Mike. "I know you're right. I need to call them."

On the way home, Maggie tried to work up the courage to call her mom. Surely, her mom was over this Greg thing by now, right? She should have received the invitation. Surely by now she had accepted the fact that Maggie was marrying Mike. She would call and invite them to the rehearsal dinner. Everything would be fine.

As they walked in the door, Sara ran up to Maggie, "Miss Maggie, remember you promised to play Candyland with me today."

"That's right. I did." They had tried to play Candyland all afternoon. But things kept getting in the way—a phone call from Sandy, Michelle needing to get up to go to the bathroom (she still needed Maggie's help), then Uncle Mike got there, and Maggie needed to make supper. "OK, I need to make a quick phone call. You get the game all set up. I will be right out."

Maggie went into Michelle's room to call her mom.

"Hi, Mom."

"Margaret." Her mom's voice was as cool as always.

"Did you get the invitation?" Maggie said brightly, hoping to set the right mood.

"Oh, yes, we got the announcement that you are marrying that soccer player."

He has a name, Mom, thought Maggie. It was on the invitation. "Great," Maggie's voice was losing its brightness.

"Margaret, I am busy packing right now."

"Where are you going?"

"Aruba."

"But you will be back in time, right?"

"In time for what?"

"My wedding. You know, the day I become Mrs. That Soccer Player." There was no brightness left in her voice. No one could push Maggie's buttons like her mom.

"No, Margaret. We will not be back. Your father and I are not going to watch you make the biggest mistake of your life."

"Mistake! I'm not making a mistake!" Maggie was flat out yelling at her mom now. She had never yelled at her mom before.

"Margaret! You will not use that tone with me!"

"Or what? You'll leave me penniless when my life falls apart—oh yeah, you already did that! You'll try to force me to marry a man I don't want to marry—you did that too. Oh, I know, you'll threaten not to come when I marry the man I actually want to marry!"

"Margaret! I will not be yelled at! You can talk to me when you can keep a civil tongue in your mouth."

"I got a better idea. How about I don't talk to you at all! Ever!" Maggie hung up.

So her parents weren't even planning on coming to the wedding. Were they going to tell her that? Guess her dad wouldn't be walking her down the aisle seeing as he would be in Aruba. Now what was she supposed to do? Walk down the aisle all by herself?

Pastor Dave had explained that the father walking the bride down the aisle was meant to be symbolic. The father walking the daughter to her waiting husband-to-be symbolized the daughter moving from the father's protection to the husband's. That didn't apply in Maggie's case. When had her father ever protected her?

She remembered a specific incident when she had been in high school. Sandy had wanted to go shopping at a store across town. It was supposed to have new, edgy clothes. Her parents told her in no uncertain terms that she was not allowed to go. This just made her want to go all the more. Sandy never told Maggie why they didn't want her to go. Just that they were being overly overprotective because she was the only girl in the family. So, one afternoon after school, Maggie and Sandy went to check it out.

As they drove around the unfamiliar part of town searching for the store, Maggie began to realize why Sandy's parents didn't want her there. This was a scary part of town. They never found the store. They just kept driving around—until they ran out of gas.

Some shady-looking guys stopped to offer to help them, but even Sandy wasn't crazy enough to get out of the car with those guys around. Sandy called home. She didn't want her mom to know where they were, so she asked for her older brother. He wasn't home. Sandy decided Maggie should call her dad. They were in real trouble here. They needed someone to come and get them. Maggie had never called her dad at work before. But this time she was scared enough to do it.

Her dad's secretary answered the phone. She said her dad was in a meeting and couldn't be disturbed. Maggie said it was an emergency. The secretary wasn't convinced. She wanted to know what kind of emergency. Maggie answered, "Car trouble." The secretary still seemed reluctant but finally agreed to interrupt the meeting.

After what seemed like a very long time to Maggie, the secretary came back on the phone. She said your father says to call AAA. Then she hung up.

That would have worked if they had been in Maggie's car, but they weren't. They were in Sandy's mom's car.

Finally, Sandy called her dad. Sandy's dad wasn't the head of a company like Maggie's. He couldn't just leave whenever he wanted to. His boss was angry at him for asking to leave work in the middle of the day. But he finally let him go. He brought the gas, filled the tank, and then followed them to make sure they got home safely. Then, of course, he grounded Sandy for a month.

Maggie's dad? He didn't even ask about the car trouble. He must have forgotten all about it.

Maggie decided she was fine walking down the aisle all by herself. She had never had her father's protection. Maybe he didn't even have the right to walk her down the aisle.

Maggie walked out into the living room. There was Mike sitting on the floor with Sara—playing Candyland! That brought a huge smile to Maggie's face. She knew how much he hated Candyland. It was almost as if he was taking a bullet for her! Her mom thought he was the biggest mistake of her life. Maggie knew the truth. He was the best thing that ever happened to her.

After Sara was in bed, Maggie walked Mike to the door. He said, "Maggie, I was thinking—maybe we should go to see your parents this weekend."

She answered, "They're going out of town."

"I know. I heard. Let's go talk to them together."

"I'm not going."

"Maybe I should go talk to them, then."

"Don't you dare!"

"Come on, I'm not such a bad guy. Maybe if they met me, they would like me."

"Oh, I'm sure they would like you! It's me they don't like!"

Chapter 51

Maggie was lying in bed, talking to Sara after reading her a bedtime story. Sara wanted to sing the Sara Bug song. In the living room, Mike muted the TV so he could hear them sing. Maggie was going to be an amazing mother!

After the song, Sara asked, "When you get married, you will be my Aunt Maggie, right?"

"That's right!" Maggie smiled.

"Then what will Uncle Mike be?"

"Oh, Bug, he will still be your Uncle Mike. He will always be your Uncle Mike. And he will always love you."

Pause. "Mommy says you and Uncle Mike will have lots of kids!"

Maggie laughed, "I hope so."

"I hope so too. I want a baby sister."

"Well, if Uncle Mike and I have a baby girl, she wouldn't be your sister. She would be your cousin."

"Oh, but I want a sister."

"Well, your mommy would have to have a baby girl for you to have a sister."

"Oh, well, then Mommy can have a baby!" Sara beamed like she just had the most brilliant of ideas.

"It takes a mommy and a daddy to have a baby," said Maggie.

"Oh, we don't have a daddy." Sara was so sad that it broke Maggie's heart. "I wish I had a daddy. Why don't I have a daddy?"

Maggie said, "Well, some men aren't very good at being daddies. You know what I think happened?"

"What?"

"I think even before you were born, God looked down here and saw you. And He said, 'That Sara, she is so cute and smart and sweet. She needs to have a really good daddy.' Then He looked at your daddy and decided he just wasn't good enough. Not for someone as special as you. So God is still looking for just the right daddy for you. A really, really good daddy. In the meantime, He sent Uncle Mike to take care of you. Uncle Mike does all the things that a daddy would do for you, like take you to the park, play soccer with you, and teach you to ride your bike."

"When will God find me a good daddy?"

"I don't know; it might take a while. He has to be a very good daddy."

"How about Dr. Scott? He could be my daddy."

"I don't know. Mommies and daddies need to be married."

"Dr. Scott could marry Mommy."

Maggie thought, Oops. I opened a can of worms now. "Maybe, but marriage is a very important decision. You have to be very, very sure you want to get married."

"Why?"

"Because then you have to stay together for the rest of your life."

"You are marrying Uncle Mike."

"That's right."

"Are you very, very sure?"

"I am very, very sure I want to marry Uncle Mike."

"Why?"

"Because I love him."

"Oh, do you want to stay together with him?"

"Forever and ever."

"I love Uncle Mike too."

"I know you do."

"Dr. Scott takes me to Chuck E. Cheese. That's kind of like a daddy, right?"

"Kind of."

Sara thought a moment. "You take care of me too. Did God send you to take care of me?"

Maggie smiled thinking back. "I think it was the other way around. I think God sent you to me."

"Why?"

"Because He knew I needed a little girl to take care of to make me happy."

"Were you sad?"

"Yes, before I met you, I was very sad. But then I met you and Uncle Mike, and now I am happy. Very, very happy!"

"I am happy too!"

Mike had heard the whole conversation and thought, That makes three of us!

Mike and Maggie were taking another walk. Only three more days until the big game, thought Mike. He was so tired of waiting for it. He wanted to play it now. He wanted to win it, of course. But he was looking forward to playing it. Then maybe he could relax.

Maggie thought, Only four more days until the wedding. She was tired of waiting for it. She was still scared something was going to happen to prevent it. She was looking forward to having it. But she was also looking forward to it being over. Then maybe she could relax.

Mike was desperately looking for a topic of conversion to distract him.

"Hey, Maggie, is driving a Corvette as cool as it looks?"

"I don't know. I've never driven a Corvette."

"You haven't? I though Greg had one."

"He did. I never drove it, though." This topic annoyed her. "Why do we always have to talk about Greg?"

"Sorry. I was just curious. Don't you ever get curious?"

"Nope."

"You know, you can ask me about Bianca if you want."

"No, I can't."

"Why not?"

"Because in Maggieland she doesn't exist." Why did he want to talk about her? He never talked about her.

He laughed, "Really."

"Yep, you were a complete choir boy before you met me."

"Is that a fact?"

They walked in silence for a while.

Then he said, "Still, don't you think it is good to talk about the past?"

Oh no, thought Maggie. He wanted to talk about her. What did this mean? Was he having second thoughts? There probably wasn't any avoiding this. Maybe she could ease into it slowly.

"How did you meet her?"

His mind had wandered. "Uh, she had a flat tire. I fixed it for her."

"Oh, the old damsel-in-distress routine. Works every time."

"Huh? No, her tire was really flat."

Maggie thought about what she had heard about Bianca. Nobody talked about her much. Sara said she was mean. Michelle called her demanding. Even GG Rose had nothing good to say about her.

She said, "She must have been awful pretty."

Mike smiled. "Not as pretty as you."

"I wasn't fishing for a compliment. I was taking a shot at your ex. Nobody in your family seems to have liked her. I figure she must have been pretty to make up for being such an awful person."

Hmm, thought Mike. Maggie has some claws. This was kind of fun. "She wasn't an awful person."

Maggie was joking on the outside and dying on the inside. She wished he wouldn't defend her. Why was he thinking about her? Did he call her to tell her they were getting married? What did the manipulative loser say to that? Maybe she should remind him of the bad times.

"Who broke up with who?"

"She broke up with me."

But now you called her. She has changed her mind and wants you back. And you are thinking that may not be such a bad idea. "So she's stupid."

And you are jealous. I like it! "Actually, she gave me an ultimatum."

Oh, no. She wanted to get married, and he said no. She is going to try to get him back. What if she shows up at the wedding? What if she stands up and says, "I object"? What if he thinks he never should have let her go? This was going to be bad. This was going to be worse than the first time.

"…Sara's birthday," finished Mike.

"What? What about Sara's birthday?"

"I said Bianca didn't want to go to Sara's birthday."

"No wonder Sara says she is mean."

"Well, it wasn't quite that simple. Michelle had planned a birthday party for Sara, and we were going to go. But then Sara got sick. So Michelle had to postpone it to the next weekend. Bianca had already bought tickets for us to go to this play she wanted to see. We had a huge fight. She said I had to choose—Sara or her."

"You chose Sara."

"I didn't want to miss Sara's birthday. But Bianca said I always chose Sara over her. That she felt like she was in third place behind my family and soccer. I guess maybe she was." Pause. He turned to Maggie. "But I don't want you to feel that way."

She shrugged. "I would have gone to Sara's birthday party."

He was serious. "My family is important to me. They will always be important to me."

"I know that. I love that about you. I love that you love your family. I love how you take care of GG Rose. I love how you are always there for Sara. And I know how much you have done for Michelle."

"I feel like it is my job—they're my responsibility."

"I thought that families like yours only existed on TV. You know, all those families on Nick at Nite who actually talk to each other and care about each other and are involved in each other's lives. I wish I had a family like that."

"You do."

"My family is not like that!"

"My family is your family."

MISS LORI 349

She smiled. "In four more days!"

"No, now. Maggie, when Grandpa Willie died, it was so overwhelming. I was trying to take care of GG Rose, Michelle, and Sara, all without his help. It was so much responsibility. Then you came along. You helped me. You took care of Sara and visited GG Rose. And Michelle—Michelle has never had a friend like you!"

"I guess I just horned my way in."

"No. You just fit in. You belong in my family. You help me take care of them."

"Maybe my job is to help you."

"But I don't want you to feel like they are more important to me than you are."

"Mike, Bianca is stupid. You don't have to choose. It's not like we are in a sinking boat and you just get to save one of us. Although if that happens, save Sara."

He smiled. "I'd find a way to save you all!"

Maggie felt better. So she said so, "Well, I'm glad we had this talk. Now I know that Bianca is stupid, mean, and ugly, and I hope has fallen off the face of the earth."

"I have no idea where she is." Pause. "I'm glad too. I heard you talking to Sara last night. That was an amazing way to explain the daddy situation to Sara. The way you told her the truth but still made her feel special. I hope you understand that I have to be there for them."

"I understand."

"Maybe God sent you to help me."

"No way. He sent you to save me."

Chapter 52

Michelle was determined to go to this game. There was no way she was going to miss her brother winning the national championship. Maggie, Sandy, and Sara had gone to the last two games while she stayed home with Scott. She had felt left out and angry, but she had pretended she was fine with it. She knew how much Mike wanted Maggie at the games.

Scott had taken her to the doctor a while ago. The doctor had replaced her original cast with a lighter one. She could now get around her apartment on crutches without too much trouble. It was just exhausting.

The walk from the car to the stadium was going to be long. The walk down the stairs to the front row was even more daunting. But she was determined to do it.

She made it! They were settled in in their regular seats. Sandy went to get the hot dogs.

The game was intense. Still 0–0 at the half. Michelle was sweating in her seat, feeling the thrill of the competition, willing her brother to give it all he had.

Then in the seventy-second minute, Michelle could feel it—the moment had come. Mike was in the box. He latched on to a perfectly hit cross. It was in the goal! He scored! The crowd went wild! Mike and his teammates all ran to the corner flag hugging and jumping and celebrating the goal.

Maggie watched as Mike ran back toward the middle of the field. As he approached their seats, he kissed the palm of his hand and raised it in the air. The crowd cheered, thinking he was blowing them a kiss. But Maggie knew what he was doing. He had kissed the exact place on his hand that corresponded with the scar on her hand. The red M on her hand that he kissed every day. She knew he couldn't see her, but she kissed the M on her hand in return.

After the trophy presentation, Mike went to the locker room to celebrate with his teammates. Maggie took Sara and Michelle home and helped them to bed. Michelle was extremely excited for Mike and chatted and rehashed the goal all the way home. Her brother was the hero! He was a national champion!

Once they got home, though, the exhaustion hit her, and she was asleep in minutes.

Sara didn't even make it all the way home. She was asleep in her car seat.

Mike called as Maggie was getting ready for bed. He was still pumped up and excited. He was going out with the team to celebrate their victory. He wanted Maggie to come. She said she better stay there with Michelle and Sara. But that he should have fun.

Maggie looked in the mirror as she brushed her teeth. She was happy for Mike. He'd worked hard. He deserved to celebrate.

It felt like a moment to pray.

"Dear Lord, thank You for letting Mike win the tournament. Thank You that he didn't get hurt." She paused. She knew she should pray about the wedding. But she was still scared. She thought maybe if she didn't bring it up, God might not notice. Maybe she could quickly get married, and then later, God would notice and say, "All right, as long as you are already married, I'll let it go."

What she was really afraid of was that God was still mad at her for sleeping with Mike the day they met. She hoped it counted that they weren't sleeping together now, but she just wasn't sure. She wanted to beg God not to take him away because of that, but she just couldn't talk to Him about it. She just couldn't take the chance.

She went to bed. Not to sleep but to bed. She laid in bed all night thinking of all the things that might happen to prevent this wedding.

Only one more hour to go. If she could just make it one more hour, she and Mike would be married. Then everything would be all right. She, Sandy, Sara, and Michelle were in the library of the church getting dressed. Sara looked adorable in her flower girl dress. Sandy looked stunning in the maid of honor dress she had traded the red one for. Maggie thought no one would be looking at her walking down the aisle when she followed those two. But that was fine with her. Those two could have all the attention. She didn't care about anybody there except Mike. As long as he was there, it would be fine.

He had texted Michelle. He and Brandon (his best man) were on the way to the church. They would get dressed in Pastor Dave's office. Wasn't it early for him to be coming to church? It only takes him like five minutes to get dressed. Maybe he wanted to talk to her. Maybe he waited until now to tell her some big secret. Maybe it was something awful, like he was an ax murderer or something. This is why the groom isn't supposed to see the bride before the wedding. So he can't make some awful revelation that would change everything.

Still, if he was an ax murderer, wouldn't she want to know before she married him? No, she didn't. She didn't want to know. After all, he had had plenty of opportunities to kill her. If he was an ax murderer, he would just kill other people. That was bad, but not a reason not to marry him, right?

Sandy said, "What are you doing just sitting there? We need to do your makeup. You need blush—you are white as a ghost!"

Sara walked down the aisle throwing pink rose petals and smiling at Uncle Mike. Sandy walked down the aisle, smiling for the camera. Happy for her friend. Maggie took a deep breath, then stepped into view. She looked down the aisle and saw Mike looking absolutely yummy in his tux. She felt her shoulders relax. Finally, she thought, I am actually getting married today!

They exchanged vows and rings and a long kiss, and they were married—just like that!

The wedding reception passed quickly while they fed each other cake and drank to the toast given by Brandon.

They mingled with the wedding guests, mostly Mike's teammates and their families, and received congratulations. They stayed together holding hands, Maggie standing just behind Mike's shoulder. One of the last people to greet them was the owner of the bar where they had met. The rehearsal dinner had been scheduled to be held at the bar, but last week there had been a small fire in the kitchen. The bar had had to be closed to fix the damage. They were ready to open again, but they had to wait until tomorrow for a final inspection. The owner knew Mike and knew the story of how Mike and Maggie had met at his bar. He couldn't sell food and drinks, but there was nothing to prevent him from throwing a private party there. He asked Mike if they wanted to move the party to the bar.

Mike took Maggie aside to discuss it.

She responded, "We could do that if you want."

He said, "I don't know. If we go there, it probably will turn into a victory celebration for the team. This is your day. I don't want you to feel overshadowed."

She shrugged. "The wedding is over. I have the ring! I wouldn't mind dancing…with my husband," she ended shyly.

"Sounds good to me!"

The whole wedding party moved to the bar. There was a buffet with chicken wings, pizza, and an open bar.

When all the guests had assembled, Mike pulled Maggie to the stage with him, holding her hand with one hand and a glass of champagne with the other.

He said, "I want to thank all of you for coming. As most of you know, I met Maggie right here in this bar after the very first game of the season. And what a season it has been!" All his teammates cheered in agreement.

"It was a season of ups and downs. Sometimes everything was clicking—going unbelievably well. Other times were frustrating—and we were full of doubts. There were a variety of challenges to handle, including miscommunications and injuries. But we persevered. We stuck together, and in the end, it was all worth it. And the best possible outcome happened." He paused as he looked around the room. "I got to marry my sweet Maggie Mallone!"

Every female in the place said, "Awwww!" as he raised his glass and smiled at Maggie.

Then he looked back to the crowd to his teammates and added, "Oh yeah, and we won the championship!" His teammates cheered loudly.

Maggie smiled at him as he led her to the dance floor. She said, "Have I mentioned how yummy you look in that tux?"

"Yummy?"

"Absolutely! And that little speech—you are quite the charmer. Every girl in the place is wishing she were me right now."

"Girls, what girls?" he asked.

She laughed. He continued, "All I know is that I married the most beautiful girl in the world. And all the guys in the room are wishing they were me right now."

"Guys, what guys?" Pause. "Hmm, isn't it amazing that we ended up at our wedding reception in a room all by ourselves?"

"As it should be."

They ate and drank and danced and celebrated.

Finally, Mike put a special song on the jukebox and led Maggie back to the dance floor. He pulled her close as the lyrics floated toward them.

"Do you remember this song?" he asked.

"Sure, we have danced to it several times here at the bar," she replied.

He said, "We danced to it the first time we were here at the bar."

"The very first time?"

"Yep."

She didn't remember. He remembered. He remembered everything about that first dance.

He whispered the lyrics into her ear.

She said, "Yes."

"What?"

"Didn't you just ask me to dance?"

He smiled. "Yes, for the rest of my life," he confirmed.

"Love to." She smiled.

He kissed her until the song ended, then whispered in her ear, "Are you ready to get out of here?"

"Whenever you are."

"I am."

He hooked his arm under her knees and carried her out the door while Sandy and the other guests threw popcorn at them instead of rice, shouting congratulations.

Mike put Maggie in the Jeep and folded her wedding dress in around her.

As they drove off, Maggie said, "Whew. I can't believe that it's over. I can't believe it really happened!"

"What? Did you think it wasn't going to?"

"I was positive it wasn't going to. I was positive that something would prevent it from happening."

"What did you think would happen?"

"All kinds of things—plane crashes, car accidents, earthquake, fire. Yesterday I was completely convinced that they would take you off the field on a stretcher, and then today—" she stopped.

"What? What did you think was going to happen today?"

She looked at his profile as he drove and played with the ring on her finger. Finally, she decided it was all right. She could tell him. After all, they were already married. "I thought you were going to tell me you were an ax murderer."

He laughed right out loud.

She smiled. "I bet you thought this crazy thing was just a phase you had to get through. Now you are wondering just what did you marry!"

"I know what I married," he said. "I married the love of my life."

Maggie put her hand to her heart, then pointed at him. "And that is how you could get away with being an ax murderer because you say things like that."

"You know, if I were an ax murderer, it's not like I would tell you," he joked.

"Well, you will be happy to know that I decided I would still marry you, even if you were an ax murderer."

"Really?"

"Sure, I figure you wouldn't murder me, just other people." She was laughing right along with him now.

"OK, so I would go out, do my little murdering gig, come home, hand you the ax, and say, 'Honey, I got blood on my clothes. Do you think you could get it out?'"

"Yeah, that sounds right."

He laughed again, then said, "I didn't think it was going to happen either."

"Why? Did you think I was an ax murderer?"

He said, "No. But I'm not surprised to hear that you're crazy enough to think that I am!"

"What did you think was going to happen?"

"I thought that you would disappear—that you would find some crazy reason to run away."

"That's ridiculous!"

He looked at her. She said, "OK, maybe it's not that ridiculous."

"But I had a plan," he said.

"Yeah, do tell."

"I was going to find you. Throw you in the Jeep and then drive away until I convinced you to marry me."

"Oh yeah. Now I remember you're not a murderer—you're a kidnapper! So where would you take me?"

"Probably Las Vegas. That way, as soon as you said yes, I'd marry you before you could change your mind."

"Ooo, crossing the state line. That makes it a federal offense."

"I even researched wedding chapels on the internet."

"You're kidding!"

"Nope."

She laughed. "It's a good thing you didn't tell me that. I would have run away for sure."

"If I told you, you would have run away?"

"Yeah! That sounds like fun—we definitely should have done that!"

Finally, she realized how long they had been in the car.

"Are you lost?" she asked. The bar wasn't far at all from his house.

"No. I know exactly where I'm going."

"I thought we were going to your house." The team was playing an exhibition game in Australia in about a week. She had been told that that was going to be their honeymoon.

"Nope. We're going on a honeymoon."

"Really?"

"Yep."

"Cool."

"Aren't you going to ask where we're going?"

She considered, "Nope. You can take me anywhere you want to."

He drove. She fell asleep.

Finally, he stopped the car. She woke up. "I'm sorry," she said. "I didn't mean to fall asleep."

"That's OK. I've missed watching you sleep."

"Really? I haven't slept in weeks—maybe months. I can't remember the last time I had a good night's sleep."

"Well, maybe you can sleep now."

"Really? That's what we are going to do tonight? Sleep?"

"Well, sooner or later. Wait here."

She looked out the window. She couldn't see much in the dark, but she could see a cabin in the snow.

Mike went around to the back of the Jeep and took out two suitcases and brought them inside the cabin. Then he came back for Maggie. He carried her into the cabin.

She exclaimed, "This is adorable. How long are we staying?"

"Until Thanksgiving."

"Well, then I am going to have to wear a wedding dress for four days, or I'm going to be very cold."

"What makes you think you're getting out of bed?"

"Oh, OK."

"I'm kidding. Sandy packed you a bag."

"Oh, then you should be very happy for the next couple of days!"

"I'm already very happy. Shall we find the bedroom?"

"I'm all yours. Have been for a long time," she said with feeling.

"No, I wanted you to be mine. I acted like you were mine. But until today, you weren't. But now—now you are mine!"

"Forever and ever."

He carried her to the bedroom to begin their honeymoon.

Chapter 53

Maggie woke up. She looked at her husband sleeping next to her and smiled.

She went downstairs, made herself some hot chocolate, and sat down in front of the big picture window overlooking the lake.

Her heart was overflowing with thanksgiving. She wanted to—no, had to—thank God for all that had happened.

Dear Lord, thank You for letting me marry Mike. Thank You for forgiving us our sins and showing us the right way to do things. Your way is the best way. And most of all thank You, thank You, thank You for not letting me marry Greg! Amen.

It was interesting to think about it. Less than a year ago, she was devastated because she wasn't going to marry Greg. Now she was thankful for it! She had thought she wanted to marry Greg, but that was only because she didn't know there was someone like Mike out there. Maybe that was how God worked. He gives you what you think you want. Then He takes it away. That hurts, but He lets it happen so that He can give you what He knew all along you really needed. How much more did she appreciate Mike knowing how it could have been with Greg?

Thank You, God, for watching over me.

She and Mike had made a lot of mistakes along the way, but in the end, God answered her prayer. She had always prayed, "Help me to do what is right." And He did.

"Maggie?" called Mike.

She smiled. Maggie loved Mike with all her heart. And now, with no shame, guilt, or regrets, she could go upstairs and show him.

About the Author

For most of her life, Miss Lori was a preschool teacher. But at one point she found herself without a job. Her prayer was, "I only want the job You want me to have." She had no job for years. Then, one day, things changed. She always had stories swirling around in her head. So she made God a promise. She said, "I'll write down whatever You tell me too."

The result was this book—and much more.